WHAT LIES WITHIN

Also by Annabelle Thorpe

The People We Were Before

WHAT LIES WITHIN

In an unfamiliar city, how will she recognise the truth?

annabelle thorpe

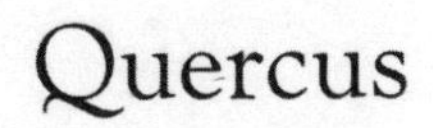

First published in Great Britain in 2018 by

Quercus Editions Ltd
Carmelite House
50 Victoria Embankment
London EC4Y 0DZ

An Hachette UK company

A CIP catalogue record for this book is available from the British Library

TPB ISBN 978 1 78429 945 3

10 9 8 7 6 5 4 3 2 1

Typeset by CC Book Production

Printed and bound in Great Britain by Clays Ltd, St Ives plc

For Mark

GLOSSARY

Jemaa el Fna	Marrakech's main square
Salaam Alaikum	Peace be upon you (greeting)
Alaikum Salaam	And upon you, peace (response)
Shukran	Thank you
Jaddah	Grandmother
Ummi	Mother
Baba	Father
Sayyid	Respectful form of address (like Sir)
Habibi	Term of endearment (my love)
Insallah	God willing
Masallah	Thanks to God
Babouche	Leather slippers
Djellaba	Hooded cloak
Kufi	Brimless cap
Ghutra	Traditional Arab head-dress
Thobe	Full-length white robe
Shalwar Kameez	Indian-style trousers and tunic
Ghayta	Reed instrument
Darija	Moroccan Arabic language
Sahridj	Fountain
Tadelakt	Lime-plaster wall covering
Chebakia	Crispy honey and sesame pastries

PROLOGUE

Taroudant, Morocco

'Are you ready, monsieur?'

Hamad glanced down at the book; the signature was unrecognisable. His fingers had locked around the pen; the final *i* was turning into an elongated *r* as the weight of his hand dragged the nib across the page. 'I need a moment.'

'*Bien sûr.*'

His phone vibrated; the screen glowed brightly in the dim light. *Freya.* He didn't have the words. Not yet.

'OK.' What was he waiting for? To feel better?

'Shall we proceed?'

Hamad nodded. His gums were coated with a thin, sour liquid; his palms slid greasily against the weave of his jeans. The man gestured towards the strip-lit corridor, following closely behind. His shoes clicked on the grubby linoleum.

'*Ici.*' He slipped a key into a metal door, heaved it open with a grunt. Thin, refrigerated air rushed at them. Hamad shivered. 'Through here.'

The room smelt of cleaning fluid and something odd, like stale tea. An older man was leaning against a desk; sallow-skinned with thinning hair. The gendarme muttered something in Darija, pointed to the large steel cabinet that took up most of the far wall. Hamad had seen enough films to know what it was. Six compartments. Six bodies. Even in his state of shock he could feel the grotesqueness of the situation. He had always been unusually squeamish.

The balding man pulled down the handle on one of the panels, slotting his fingertips underneath to lever out the drawer. The runners squealed. Lying on the shelf was something wrapped in what looked like white plastic.

'Are you ready?'

'I am.' He smoothed his thumb and forefinger over his beard. The plastic sheet crackled as it was peeled away. He glanced down. The body was discoloured, mustard and purple bruises spreading like faded ink beneath the skin. Her hair was smoothed back from her forehead, lashes long against her cheeks. The room swung gently. He reached out his hand to steady himself on the corner of the gurney.

'Monsieur. Is this . . . ?'

Hamad closed his eyes for a moment; he felt disorientated, unable to process what he was seeing. A word rose in his throat; he swallowed hard.

'I understand this is difficult.' The man's voice was surprisingly gentle. 'But can you . . . ?'

'Yes.'

'Monsieur Al-Bouskri? My apologies, but I must be clear. You are saying this is . . . ?'

'Yes.' His fingernails bit into the skin on his palms. He looked into the man's blank face. 'This is the body of Racine Delacroix.'

CHAPTER 1

Cambridge: June 1999

The beaches on Ko Phi Phi Don were the most beautiful Freya had ever seen. Arcs of white sand fringed with lush, green jungle, clusters of bungalows just visible through the palm trees. She could almost feel the heat on her skin, the turquoise water pooling around her legs. There would be full-moon parties, shopping on the Kho San Road, elephants in Chiang Mai. *Promise me you'll have adventures.* Her throat tightened. She closed the book and passed it mutely to the shop assistant. It didn't seem possible it would be a year ago, next week.

Outside, the heat was cloying; summer was suddenly everywhere. She walked past the Antica Bella, trying not to see the notice in the window: *Waiting Staff Required.* Her head still ached from her leaving party – sludgy spoonfuls of tiramisu and countless glasses of spumante. In a day or two, a different girl would be weaving between the tables, flirting with Marco, slipping off her shoes at the end of the night. It felt as if she were disappearing out of her own life.

She could feel the weight of the guidebooks on her shoulder – a reminder to look forward, to keep focused on the adventure that was coming, rather than everything she was leaving behind. The city rose up around her, tour groups spilling out between the columns of the Fitzwilliam, families picnicking in the shade of the plane trees, kids smeared with suncream, clutching ice creams and fizzy drinks.

Past the chequerboard turret of Queens', the river barrelled along beneath dozens of punts, some zigzagging wildly from bank to bank, others barely moving.

The backs of her eyes began to sting; what would she do without all this? The lectures and the term papers and the three-minute walk from her flat to the house on Davison Road. Student life was what had sustained her, somehow held her together through the darkest months of her grief. She had built it; they had built it, the three of them, her and Hamad and Paul. Thailand was something to look forward to; then Australia, California. Three months before they were back in London, before reality really struck home. But it hung there, in the distance: a great, unknowable void.

'*Frey.*' On the other side of the square a man was waving; beside him a taller, dark-haired figure was talking to a waitress. She quickened her pace. It soothed her to see them together.

'Scones?'

She caught the word as she sank into the seat between them.

'Hey, sweetheart. You OK?' She nodded as Paul kissed her. He turned to look at Hamad. 'I say again . . . *Scones*?'

'Scones. Absolutely.'

'I see you two are having your usual intellectually challenging conversation.'

'I just asked him what he was going to miss most about England,' said Paul, his features knitted together in mock surprise. 'He's lived in one of the most beautiful cities in the country for three years. We've taken him to London, to Brighton . . . I've introduced him to *Star Trek* marathons and late-night kebabs, and what's he going to miss most?' He picked up a half-eaten scone from his plate and waved it in front of Hamad's face.

'What can I say? I'm a man of simple tastes.'

'Of course you are. Private jet ready to take you home tomorrow, is it?'

'BA, as you well know,' said Hamad, raising his eyebrows at Freya. 'I'm so sorry to leave you on your own with this idiot, Frey. You're sure you won't come to Doha with me? I can take you away from all this, you know. Just say the word.'

'Excuse me, but we've got travel plans of our own.' Paul nodded at the carrier bag. 'Did you get the guidebooks?'

'Just two. I didn't get one for California. Dad will be able to show us around when we're there.'

'Things better between you?' Hamad raised his eyebrows.

'Kind of. Hard to stay angry with someone when they buy you a round-the-world trip. We both know it's guilt-funded. As long as I don't have to meet *her*.'

Paul took her hand. 'We'll just stay a night or two, and then we'll go off exploring. No one's going to make you do anything you don't want to. Your dad will understand.'

Freya sat back and sipped her tea. The anxiety was beginning to dissipate, although she sensed it had simply stepped back, rather than disappeared. It had started to build before she'd seen the notice in the window at Antica Bella: someone had pulled at her arm in the bookshop, asking for directions to Newnham College. She'd answered without having to think; the streets and alleyways were mapped out in her head, set down in that first glorious year when she'd swum in the Cam and landed the job at Antica Bella and thought that being at university was the most extraordinary thing in the world.

Hamad had been integral to those first carefree months, and then, when she returned after the summer, Paul had come into her world. By then, it had become clear what her role in Hamad's life was to be, and when Paul had appeared outside the Antica Bella, stumbling through an obviously-rehearsed speech, she had found him irresistible. No one had ever called her extraordinary before. They had quickly become inseparable, the three of them, her happiness complete, until the damp March morning when her father rang, and she had had to ask him to repeat his words, because what he was telling her simply couldn't be.

She glanced across at the two of them: Hamad's neat, dark features made Paul look even messier than he actually was. Unshaven, thick sandy hair flopping into his eyes, jeans that were ripped from an unplanned encounter with a bike rather than any concession to style. A memory popped into her head: her twenty-first birthday, the previous October. She'd woken early and Paul had taken her to King's College Chapel, where she'd lit a candle and sat among the empty pews and cried, because her birthday card said only *Love, Dad*. Afterwards the river had carried them away from the city, until Ham had appeared on the bank near Grantchester and helped pull the punt from the water. They'd sat for hours in the Orchard Tea Garden beneath the low October sun, eating scones and drinking hot chocolate, the trees outside ablaze with hundreds of fairy lights.

'I'm really sorry, guys, but I'm not going to come tonight.'

'Go on, Frey.' Hamad pushed out his lower lip. 'It's our last night.'

'I know. I'm sorry. I just . . . I just don't feel like there's anything to celebrate. I want it to be the end of term, or the end of a year. Not . . .'

'I know.' Paul covered Freya's hand with his. 'I can't believe it either. Three years. Where did that go? But there's loads to look forward to . . .'

'For you two,' said Hamad. 'Whizzing round the world for three months – with a job to come back to, Frey, and Paul sorted with his course. What's waiting for me in Doha? *Ummi* will start introducing me to a procession of dull cousins, none of whom I've any intention of marrying, and *Baba* will just keep on about when I'm going to come and work for him.'

'Well at least that will wind Mourad up.' Freya knew there was little affection between Hamad and his older brother.

'There is that.' He smiled. 'I'll have to take my pleasures where I can, I guess.'

'You can always sit and count your money.' Paul shoved his shoulder into Hamad's. The table jolted; teacups clattered on their saucers.

'If you don't want to work with your father, start your own business. You've got your own income, haven't you?'

'Yes, but . . .'

'Ham, you're rich and well-connected,' said Paul. 'From what you say, the possibilities in Doha are endless: buildings shooting up, foreign companies wanting to invest. I may not be Richard Branson, but even I can see it's got to be a good place to start a business.'

'In what, though?'

'I don't know . . . You could open a hotel? You always say there's nowhere that feels really Middle Eastern in Doha, just big international chains or basic *pensions*? You could open somewhere different, really authentic.' Freya thought of Hamad's eccentric grandmother, famous for her solo travels and extraordinary, anecdote-filled books. 'Why don't you talk to Dame Edith? She must have stayed in pretty much every hotel on the planet. She could be your consultant – how cool would that be?'

'Oh, she would love that. Can you imagine?' Hamad arched his left eyebrow. 'Well, darling, there I was, sipping a mojito in the Long Bar, when in walked Noël Coward . . .'

Freya burst out laughing. 'You do her perfectly. Does she know?'

Hamad shook his head. 'She might find it funny, but on the other hand . . .'

'The Stare of Disdain?'

'Exactly.'

'Terrifying.' Freya pulled a face. 'I've only ever witnessed that once, but it's been imprinted on my memory. Have you said your goodbyes?'

'We're having lunch tomorrow. She's off herself in a couple of weeks. Sailing down the Amazon, some tribe or other that's caught her eye.'

'And she's how old?' Paul signalled for the bill.

'Seventy-four. I'm hoping I've inherited her genes.'

'Don't we all.'

'Say goodbye from me too,' said Freya. It was Dame Edith who had brought Ham into her life, striding into Antica Bella in a black, fur-fringed cardigan that swept to her knees, strings of beads piled over her chest, wisps of white hair escaping from a wide grey fedora. She'd settled in opposite Hamad and peered at Freya's name-badge, firing off questions about whether she was a student, at which college, on which course. It was the first time Freya had witnessed the pace at which the older woman made things happen; within seconds a third chair was brought, the maître d' had been smoothed over, and the cost of Freya's shift added to Edith's bill.

She had already been aware of Hamad, much like the rest of her year. The son of a Qatari millionaire, she'd watched him stride mutely across the court, face hidden behind gold-rimmed sunglasses, funnel-necked jacket buttoned up against the unaccustomed cold. Unlike almost everyone else, however, she'd suspected a large part of what lay behind the carefully contrived hauteur was loneliness. He'd walked her home from Antica Bella; the next day he'd turned up outside her room, and the day after that. At first she found it almost overwhelming: the constant questions, the way he'd take her hand and keep hold of it, his body oddly close to hers.

'You won't disappear, will you?' She was used to him now, didn't hear the accent, or find his presence claustrophobic. The concept of personal space was alien to him; it amused her to watch other people stepping back as Hamad moved closer, an awkward, cross-cultural two-step they would giggle about afterwards. 'We'll stay friends, won't we? We'll still see each other?'

'Only if you come to the party. Please? You can't miss the chance to see Paul in a dinner jacket. He might even look smart.'

'I just don't feel like it. I'm sorry.'

Paul smiled at her. 'Don't worry. No point in coming if you won't enjoy it. But stay at ours tonight. Everything is in boxes at your house and we've barely started. I'll drive so we won't be back late. If Hamad's got lunch with Dame Edith tomorrow, he's going to need his sleep.'

She thought how much she loved him, then, that he didn't try to persuade her she would be better among people, distracted by noise and chatter. She'd tried that in the early days – to readopt the pace her life had moved at before she had noticed how often her mum had headaches, before her speech had begun to falter. She'd spiralled, drinking more, sleeping less, skipping lectures, trying to blot out the grief and the furious regret that the term paper had needed submitting on the very day her mother slipped away. One morning, months after the funeral, she had woken up and been unable to stop crying. It was then that Paul had suggested the counsellor.

The waitress appeared with the bill. She blushed when Hamad smiled up at her and passed a note, shaking his head at her suggestion of change.

'Just as well you're leaving,' said Paul as they stood up, 'You must have dated all the women in this city by now.'

'You're just jealous.'

'Why would I be?' said Paul, slipping an arm around Freya's shoulders. 'I've got the only one that really counts.'

'True,' said Hamad. 'Sure I can't persuade you to come with me?'

'And leave this one to his own devices?' She kissed Paul on the cheek and stretched out her arm to take Hamad's hand. 'But you'll come and see us, right? We'll all stay friends?'

'Stop worrying, Mrs Gloom.' Hamad pulled her out of Paul's grasp and hugged her. 'You two are the only real friends I have. You've got me for life.'

*

Long before the call came, Paul knew he shouldn't have come to the party. He couldn't shake the thought of Freya, sitting alone in their messy lounge, surrounded by piles of music magazines and videos and the wonky tower of Diet Coke cans that Ham had carefully assembled over the past months. He'd recognised the anxiety in her face earlier; it still made him angry that she should have had to bear such a crippling loss. These last few months it felt as if she were coming back to him: the funny, feisty girl he had first met in the long queue for Rhodri's chocolate-coated cappuccinos. She'd had such an energy, an internal freedom that brought a touch of recklessness into his life, a loosening of his stiff, slightly awkward, shoulders. As the weeks passed he had tried increasingly not to mind that she clearly already had a boyfriend, said to be Saudi, or Yemeni, or from somewhere in that part of the world, and whose father, it was rumoured, was funding the new Middle Eastern Studies building.

'Is there a Paul Hepworth here?' A waiter had appeared at the head of the table.

He'd known instantly it would be her. He pushed past the chairs, shrugging slightly as Hamad raised his eyebrows.

'Freya?'

'I'm sorry. I tried your mobile . . .'

'There's no signal up here. Are you OK?'

'Not really. I'm really sorry . . .' She was crying; little gasps of breath broke up her words.

'Don't be. I'll come home. I shouldn't have come.'

'I wanted you to. I just . . . I'm all panicky. I thought I'd got past it.'

'You have. Things are just weird right now, everything's changing, and I know . . . well, it's a difficult time.' It would be a year next week. Five days after that, the anniversary of the funeral. 'Put the TV on. I'll be home before you know it.'

'You don't mind?'

The odd thing was, he genuinely didn't. Helping Freya, supporting her; it made him feel older, of some use. The youngest of four, a boy after three girls, he'd been cooed over and mothered throughout his childhood. At times during the first year he'd felt horribly young alongside some of the other boys, worried he'd gone out into the world soft and unformed. And then Freya had come along and provoked a side of himself he hadn't known existed. She made him feel like a man.

He placed the receiver back in the cradle; stood for a minute, wondering how long it would take to get a taxi.

'Is she OK?' He turned to see Hamad, his face etched with concern.

'A bit upset. Worried about having a panic attack. I'm going to head back.'

'Mind if I come with you? This isn't really my kind of thing. You can drop me at Edith's if you two would like a bit of space.'

'She won't mind you turning up this late?'

Hamad grinned. 'She'll be sloshing back the whisky with the great and the good. There's always someone famous sitting in an armchair, trying to keep up with her. I think she measures the calibre of her guests by how much liquor they can put away.'

'You must be a great disappointment, then.'

'Quite possibly. But we should go – I'll tell Jed we're leaving. Get the coats.'

Paul watched him move towards the dining room, envying the easy confidence that hung from his lean frame. It was a gentle jealousy – he was resigned to it – balanced by the knowledge that Hamad was quite different to the way he was perceived; a seam of vulnerability hidden beneath the cool, slightly arrogant, exterior. He was the other gift Freya had bestowed on Paul; their friendship had easily flexed to include him. At times he found their closeness unusual, even a little exclusive. It would have worried him more if he hadn't known Hamad's post-university life would be thousands of miles away, in Doha.

Outside, the sky was darkening in preparation for a storm, the white scoop of the moon sailing in and out of ominous walls of cloud. Until now he hadn't really considered what leaving Cambridge would mean. Everything had been about Freya, how she would manage, what they would do. His parents had helped with the deposit on the small flat in Battersea, she'd got her internship at the publishers, Parker & Lyle, the transition was going to be as smooth as he could make it. From now on it would be just the two of them. He realised, with a twinge of guilt, that part of him was pleased at the thought.

'It's going to pour.' He turned to see Hamad on the other side of the car. 'Do you want me to drive?' Hamad asked.

'You're not insured.'

'No, but at least I'm sober.'

'So am I. I've had a couple of beers and maybe a glass of wine, two at most. And there'll be nothing on the roads at this time.'

'I really think . . .'

'Look, by the time we've debated it we could be halfway home. I'm absolutely fine. Get in, it's starting to rain.'

Hamad slid into the passenger seat and pulled the door shut. 'Now that is something I'm really going to miss.'

'Rain and scones. You're such a freak.'

'And you and Freya. Really. I will miss you both.'

Paul felt a twinge of embarrassment. He wanted to say something similar, but the words felt too sentimental. 'You're not going all . . . exotic on me, are you? Remember that whole stiff upper lip thing we talked about?'

Hamad rolled his eyes. 'Of course. Sorry. What was I thinking?'

An easy silence settled between them as Paul swung out of the car park. The sharp turns of the lane frustrated him; it was a relief to get back onto the main road, to be able to push the ball of his foot against the accelerator and feel the car gain pace beneath him.

'I will . . .' He took a breath. 'I'll miss you too, you know.' He glanced at Hamad. 'You—'

'*PAUL!*' He saw the dog too late, snatched at the steering wheel; the car lurched across the empty road. The brake flexed beneath his foot but there was nothing, no bite. Lights flooded the windscreen, a colossal weight smacked into the left-hand side of the car. For a moment it was if they were floating across the road, his body pushed forward, knees locked, air thick with shouting.

And then, quite suddenly, it was over. The car tipped into a ditch at the side of the road, the engine died; his body smacked hard against the seat. On the windscreen, the rain made translucent veins on the glass.

'Paul? You OK?'

'Think so. You?'

'Yes.' Relief swept through him. He looked across. Hamad's eyes were wide, his breathing noisy in the silence.

'Christ. I didn't see it . . .' He put his hand to his head. 'You're sure you're OK?'

'I need to get out of the car.' The rain grew louder as Hamad opened the door and slowly levered himself into the darkness. 'Oh, shit.'

'What?' Paul pushed at the handle, but his fingers wouldn't grip. 'What is it?'

'The other car,' said Hamad. 'We need to call an ambulance.'

CHAPTER 2

Doha, Qatar: December 2009

It was cool, out on the terrace. Hamad stood to let his eyes adjust after the darkness of the empty restaurant below. Across the water, the sculpted towers on West Bay rose up to the thickening skyline, shrouding the morning sunshine in a web of cloud. Something wet fell against his cheek; spots of damp were beginning to freckle the white sleeve of his *thobe.* He could smell the moisture rising above the diesel fumes and the construction noise echoing off the skeletal building frames that sprouted up from every street in the city. A memory surfaced: piling into the car with his brother and sisters, the cold waters of the *wadi* rushing around his feet. As a boy, rain had seemed a miraculous occurrence; even as an adult it still brought him a small sense of joy. But not today. Today it could spoil everything.

'Where's Karim?' He raised his eyebrows at the two Pakistani boys unravelling a canopy on the other side of the terrace. They froze, eyes wide, mouths pursed with uncertainty. The squeal of a drill broke the silence; on the far wall a third man was screwing a hook into the freshly made hole. His head throbbed; the headache that had begun during the argument with Racine was worsening. He'd been aware it was a risk, inviting Paul and Freya for New Year without telling her, but he hadn't anticipated the anger it would provoke. The day had not begun well.

'Coffee, *sayyid*?' He turned to see Karim place a swan-necked coffee pot and two lacquered cups onto a table. 'Do you need an umbrella?'

Hamad shook his head. 'Strange weather, isn't it? You're still arranging everything to be outside this evening?'

'I am. The rains will have passed by late afternoon. The canopy is just a precaution.'

He took the cup Karim offered. 'I never knew it rain this late in December. An odd end to an odd year.'

'Perhaps a fitting one.' Karim gestured to the sky. 'My *jaddah* always used to say clouds promise, rain delivers. Is that not what you're hoping to do tonight? Fulfil a promise?'

'In a way, I suppose. I just hope it's what they need, that they can see the possibilities. Paul and Freya have always been such good friends to me and when I saw them in October . . . it was such an awkward evening. I thought it would be a celebration. Freya's sister getting the all-clear was such wonderful news. But it was obvious something was wrong. And then Paul was so offended . . .' He winced at the memory: the stilted welcome on the doorstep, Freya's tear-stained face. She and Paul had tried, unconvincingly, to brush things off; reminisced about Cambridge, listened to his stories about the new hotel he was building in the mountains outside Marrakech. He hadn't mentioned Racine's unexpected move to Morocco, or Edith's equally shocking revelation. It was only later, when Paul had gone to bed, still bristling from their unfortunate exchange, that he and Freya had begun to tell each other the truth.

'You had your own problems to deal with at that time,' said Karim. 'Racine moving to Morocco, it was a big adjustment.'

'It was a joint decision,' said Hamad unconvincingly. 'Doha's not an ideal city for someone with a career in the wine industry. A year as Chief Sommelier at the Nanda was a great opportunity for her. But this hotel in Marrakech – it's selling itself as the most luxurious in the whole country. It's a big step forward in her career.'

'I don't understand why she works at all. Her father owns half of Bordeaux . . .'

'You do know, because I've explained it in the past. She works because she wants to, because she doesn't just want to live off her father's money – or mine. You of all people know how different that is to most of the women I've been with.'

'Of course.'

Hamad wished he hadn't spoken. It happened sometimes, a reminder that Karim was an employee, not a friend, however many years they went back. He glanced at him; the first strands of grey were appearing at his temples, poking out from beneath the neat *ghutra*. He didn't want Karim to age; wanted him to stay the gap-toothed son of the chauffeur, who screamed with delight when the two of them spun through the jets of water from his father's hosepipe, and who adored him with a devotion that went some way to making up for Mourad's lack of brotherly affection.

'It is a shame your grandmother couldn't have been here.'

'Edith?' He sighed. 'She's just not well enough.'

'Does she know of your plans?'

'Some of it. You know how persistent she can be. I've told her we'll be in Marrakech the day after tomorrow, and that I have a proposition for her. I suspect she thinks I'm going to try and persuade her to move to Doha again.'

'This would not be welcome?'

'Last time I suggested it, she said if she wanted to live in a shopping mall she'd pitch a tent in Galeries Lafayette.'

Karim smiled. 'I expect people would pay money to see that.'

'I might suggest it to her as a business venture.' He shook his head. 'But I understand her not wanting to move, she's much loved in Morocco. The turn-out for her eighty-fifth proved that. Mustapha Chenouf called her "the grande dame of Marrakech" in his speech. He's looking frailer these days.'

'Not everyone can have your grandmother's verve.'

'Indeed.' Hamad thought back to the party: he'd personally oversee all the arrangements, designed a menu that represented each epoch of her life, booked out an entire wing of La Mamounia for guests from overseas. He'd known that neither his sisters nor Mourad would come; an air of mutual distrust existed between Edith and the rest of his family. He'd rather liked the feeling of being the only person at the party who had a real claim to her, among the motley mix of expats and *djellaba*-clad Moroccans who made up his grandmother's circle. Which was why the revelation that she had *another* grandson, casually announced on the morning of the party, had come as such a shock.

'You don't think she'll be . . . offended that you didn't ask her advice about buying the Farzi houses? If the family are as well-known in Marrakech as you say, she probably would have known them.'

Hamad watched as the boys began to unpack three large cardboard boxes, unravelling strings of fairy lights and thick pillar candles. 'It was a complicated enough process without involving Edith,' he said, moving towards the wide mosaic table, covered with three flat packages encased in bubble-wrap. 'Between you and me, if it was any other deal I'd have walked away weeks ago. The Moroccan way of doing business is not ours. But . . . I don't know. They were the right houses, Karim. It may not be the tidiest deal I have ever done, but I felt them to be mine – or rather Racine's – from the moment I first walked into the courtyard. Omar Farzi knew that. He told me Allah had brought me to their door.'

Karim snorted. 'You know what my *jaddah* would have said? A wise man trusts in Allah, but he will always tie his camel first.'

'Your grandmother is a wise woman. Perhaps I should bring her in on my next deal. She and Edith would make a fierce negotiating team.' He pulled a framed photograph from the wrap and looked at it: a crumbling door in a Moroccan archway, studded with diamond-shaped bolts. 'Hang this one on the left. Then the yellow one in the middle. Then the blue.'

'Of course.' Karim glanced at his phone. 'The car is ready whenever you are. If you want to see Racine before we go to the airport . . .'

'I think it would be . . . advisable.' Hamad smiled ruefully. 'She was more than a little unimpressed earlier. Perhaps I should have told her sooner that Paul and Freya were coming.' He thought of the last time he had seen Freya: mascara-smudged eyes, dark shadows beneath them. 'I hope things are better between them.'

Karim raised his eyebrows. 'But then perhaps they won't need what you're offering? Won't want it?'

Hamad placed the print back in its wrapping and moved towards the stairs. 'She said they needed a change, Karim. Isn't that exactly what I'm offering? It's an amazing possibility for both of them – for all of us. There's no way they'll be able to say no.'

It felt good to be getting away. Freya tipped her face to the window; a cornflower sky yawned back at her. Far below, the dirt-yellow wastes of the Saudi Arabian desert rippled across the surface of the earth. How long was it since they had last been in Doha? Eighteen months? She smiled, remembering the trip to the camel farm, her and Paul clinging on as the animal swayed and bobbed beneath them, Hamad and Karim laughing as if they had never seen anything quite so hilarious. It was just before Racine had moved to the city; Freya had been guiltily delighted that the weekend had just been the three of them. She'd known, even then, that Racine was going to be different to all the women who had come before.

'You would like breakfast, madame?'

'Thank you.' She glanced at Paul, his face half hidden by an eye mask. 'Dead to the world.'

'Just press the call button if he'd like something when he wakes up.'

Freya nodded, stretched out her legs and began to rotate her ankles. She hoped he'd sleep a little longer. The sense of solitude was pleasing; a chance to try to soothe the anxiety that had been flickering ever since they'd got home from spending Christmas at her sister's. It should have been the happiest in years – Ali glowing with health, the kids fizzing with energy, Simon looking ten years younger, released from relentless anxiety about what the future might hold. Even though it had been over two months since Ali had been given the all-clear, it still felt new, as if none of them could quite believe the cancer could genuinely be consigned to the past. It was a long time since she'd been around such easy contentment. She'd been ashamed at how envious she had felt.

Somehow, that day in October had changed everything. She hadn't expected the elation to evaporate so quickly, driven home from the oncology clinic light with happiness, planning the evening's reunion with Hamad. When Paul had come through the door she'd almost bounced with relief as she told him the news, expecting his delight to match her own. Instead, his low-key reaction had left her infuriated: *Does this mean I get you back?* He'd realised immediately that she'd taken it as accusatory, insisting that he had simply missed her. But it was the spark she needed to unleash all the agitation that had been building for weeks. She called him selfish, heartless, accused him of not caring about her sister. She knew the words weren't really fair. They were still hanging in the air when Hamad had arrived on the doorstep.

She rather suspected that his invitation to spend New Year in Doha was a result of what she had told him that night. The memory of it was slightly blurred, but she remembered talking about the miscarriage and the pressure of caring for Ali, about the merger of Paul's firm and how he'd struggled with the changes. She wasn't sure Hamad had quite understood what she was trying to say, didn't know if she could define it herself. It wasn't as if they rowed constantly, more that they had simply disengaged from each other, too caught up in their own lives to offer the support the other needed. Christmas with Ali's family had been a distraction, but she suspected New Year's Eve would have seen them asleep on the sofa before midnight, a half-drunk bottle of prosecco warming on the coffee table, fireworks exploding on an unwatched TV.

'Did I miss breakfast?' She turned to see Paul's face, bleary with sleep. He peered at her tray. 'Ooh, smoked salmon and scrambled egg. Nice.' He stretched out an arm to press the call button. 'I might have some champagne.'

'It's only ten o clock.'

'Come on, Frey. We're on holiday. I've been looking forward to this for weeks.' He smiled at the stewardess. 'Good morning. We'd like a couple of glasses of champagne please. Starting as we mean to go on.'

'Quite right too.' The woman disappeared back behind the curtain.

He planted a kiss on her cheek and grinned. 'Let's get squiffs. Remember when we went to Berlin? We'd spent so long in the bar at Stansted we couldn't remember the name of the hotel. What was it in the end?'

'The Hotel Berlin.' She laughed at the memory; it was good to be reminded of those days. Sometimes, recently, it felt as if everything he did irritated her, even when he was doing nothing at all. He'd been so odd the last few weeks; distracted, almost monosyllabic, and then suddenly there would be a gesture – a meal out, a night away – when he would make her laugh and compliment her and they would drink too much wine and have unexpectedly intense sex. She felt unbalanced, as if she were trying to reconnect with the couple they had been before Ali got sick, before the miscarriage, only to find that those people no longer quite existed.

*

'I can't stop thinking about this business proposition, or whatever it is,' she said, sipping the champagne. 'Do you think he's going to offer you a job? You could design his next hotel.'

'Don't think I haven't fantasised about that.' Paul shook his head. 'But projects on that scale need an army of architects. And I'm not sure he'd be the easiest man to work for.'

'That's a bit mean.'

'Not at all. I just mean that you don't get to be as successful as Hamad without being a bit of a control freak. He's built Nanda Hotels up from nothing in ten years, and that's because he's involved in every single detail. I know he has Karim, and probably hundreds of lackeys to do all the legwork. But whenever we talk about business, I'm always amazed at how intricately he knows every property and every deal. He lives and breathes Nanda. I wish I had half his focus.'

Freya laid a hand on his arm. 'Don't start thinking about work. There's no point in worrying about things until you're back in the office. And you said things were going well with the project in Lyon . . .'

'Let's not talk about that right now.'

'And you and Hamad? Things are OK with you two?'

'Of course. It was months ago, Frey, and like I said at the time, it was something and nothing. You know Hamad, he doesn't have that English sensibility, just weighs in with whatever he's thinking. No subtlety. But it's all forgotten now.'

'And of course you're such a master of diplomacy yourself.' She smiled to show she was joking.

He grinned. 'Most of the time. And the rest of it I have you to stop me from being a complete pompous arse. You love me, right?'

'Of course I do, you idiot.'

She looked at him. The skin around his eyes had begun to crinkle when he smiled; tiny, jagged crevices that she could see sometimes late at night, or first thing in the morning. They were recent; life slowly pencilling its presence on his features. 'I wonder if Racine will be there too. Did Hamad mention her in his emails?'

'What, apart from the fact she's moved to Marrakech?' He shook his head. 'I suspect she's gone the way of all the Al-Bouskri women. Apart from you, of course.'

'I'm hardly one of his women.'

'Not even just a little?' He leant his chin on his palm and batted his eyelashes at her. 'Oh, Ham. You're so wise. So thoughtful.'

'Shut up.' She laughed in spite of herself. 'Well, I won't be sorry if she's no longer on the scene. I still feel guilty about that time you ended up having dinner with her.'

'Rightly so, longest night of my life.' He poked her. 'I still owe you for that, ducking out at the last minute . . .'

'I didn't duck out.' She hadn't meant to snap. 'I told you, Ali got an infection . . .'

'All right, all right.' He settled back in his chair. 'I was just joking. Blimey.'

Before she could reply, a bright English voice burst over the PA system. A wave of energy rippled through the cabin: seatbelts clicking together, feet wriggled into newly tight shoes, papers gathered up. Freya peered out of the window. The outskirts of the city were beginning to mushroom up from beneath the desert landscape, ribbons of road snaking towards the gleaming towers and squat, cavernous malls. She closed her eyes and tried to ignore the irritation, praying instead that whatever Hamad had in store would be enough to jolt them out of their current difficulties and set them on a road to something new.

She saw Karim first, waiting in front of a black Mercedes, deep in conversation with a woman in a neat grey suit, hair swept up, lips a bold gash of scarlet. As they drew closer, the rear door of the Mercedes opened and Hamad sprang from the car, grinning like an overexcited child.

'Surprise!' Before Freya could speak, he had pulled her towards him, his beard bristly against her cheek. 'Welcome back to Doha. It's wonderful to see you.' He shook Paul's hand and turned towards Karim. 'Take their bags, would you? This is Rhea, she'll escort you to the hotel. How was your flight? Did you get any sleep?'

'When I could stop this one chattering about your mystery business proposition.' Paul slipped his arm around Freya. She rolled her eyes at Hamad, trying to adjust to the sight of him cloaked in the white *thobe*, face shaded by the red and white cloth of the *ghutra*.

'I just want to know what you've got up your sleeve. Won't you tell us, now you're here?'

'In the middle of a car park?' He winked at Paul. 'I see patience is still not one of her strong suits.'

'I am here, you know.' She pushed him gently. A look of horror passed across Rhea's face.

'You see, Rhea, how disrespectfully they treat me?' Hamad raised his eyebrows at Freya. 'I'm tremendously important and powerful out here, you know. Do try and remember that.'

'Right, yes.' She pulled a face. 'Of course, your worshipful highness.'

'Rhea, forget the suites. I'm sure there's some box room you can find for them both. Don't waste any of the good rooms on such ungrateful friends.' He gestured towards the limousine. 'Seriously, I have to go. I have a meeting at three. But Racine and I will meet you in the lobby at seven.'

Paul raised his eyebrows. 'Racine's here?'

'I know.' Hamad grinned. 'Had to pull quite a few strings to get the Palais to give her a few days off . . . They seemed to think tonight was going to be busy, for some reason or other. But I wanted you all to be here, for us to see in 2010 together. I think it's going to be an extraordinary year for all of us.' He glanced at Freya. 'And no, I'm not saying any more than that.'

Paul nodded and moved to the other side of the car. Hamad pulled Freya towards him. 'How are things?'

'They're OK. It's good to get away, though. I think we both need a break. You? Things OK with Racine?'

'Good. Very good. All will be revealed tonight.' He clicked open the passenger door; she slipped in beside Paul. 'Get some sleep, both of you. I'll see you later.'

Freya let her body fall back against the soft leather seat. The road stretched ahead, jammed with gleaming 4x4s, a discordant chorus of horns muffled by the tinted windows. As the towers of West Bay came into view, the traffic parted unexpectedly to reveal a flock of wooden *dhows*, clustered in the harbour, the stark white lines of the Museum of Islamic Art carved into the horizon, flanked by palm trees. She became aware that there were men everywhere, hundreds of them, sitting in tight huddles on the grass verges, thin, wiry bodies crammed into the wooden seats, some picnicking on the roundabout.

'Friday.' Rhea's voice was dismissive. 'The Nepalese, the Filipinos – it's their day off. They bring food, sit on their haunches and just talk, talk, talk – all day. Like rabbits.'

Paul raised his eyebrows at Freya; she shook her head, glad they shared the same sense of discomfort. 'Everyone's allowed time off,' he said mildly.

Rhea tutted. 'But they make the city look such a mess, don't you think?'

Freya placed a hand on Paul's knee. 'Let it go,' she mouthed. He pulled a face, squeezing his lips together and wrinkling his nose; he looked so ridiculous that she burst out laughing. Rhea's back stiffened.

When the car finally drew up at the hotel, Freya barely noticed the towering octagonal lobby, shimmering with gold leaf, or the wide marble corridor that led to their suites. She was aware Rhea was talking, but her mind was increasingly fogged by sleep; she wanted to slip under the duvet, feel Paul's body beside her, try to find some unspoken connection that would ground them both. Finally the door clicked shut and she sank gratefully onto the bed.

'Two suites?'

'You know why. If Hamad wants to come and hang out, it's more appropriate that it's my suite rather than ours.'

She nodded sleepily. 'Your place or mine, then?'

'Look, we're both so tired, why don't we take advantage of the space and get some shut-eye in our own suites?' He bent down to kiss her. 'They've already put my suitcase in the other room, so I may as well go in there. I'll set an alarm for five. Sleep tight.'

He was gone before she had a chance to reply. As the door clicked shut, she glanced around the room; dove-grey armchairs filled with cream silk cushions, a bottle of Krug in an ice-bucket, copies of *Vogue* and *Tatler* fanned out beneath a vase of stargazer lilies. A pair of silk pyjamas were folded on the pillow; she pulled off her dress and slipped them on, the material like gossamer against her skin.

Sleep failed to materialise. She felt unsettled; by the unexpected presence of Racine, by Hamad's impending proposition, by Paul's desire to sleep alone. After half an hour she switched on the light and pulled a book from her suitcase, her eyelids drooping as the words fused together. She was too tired to concentrate. Perhaps Paul was awake too. She could slip in next to him, feel the warm of his body against hers; they could have slow, semi-conscious sex.

She slipped out of bed and padded across the room. The door handle was cold to the touch, the room beyond it swathed in darkness. She was halfway towards the bed before the silence became meaningful; as her eyes adjusted, she realised the cushions were still arranged neatly against the pillows, the duvet as smooth as when they had walked in. On the opposite side of the room, Paul's suitcase stood unopened by the wardrobe. Nothing had been touched, nothing disturbed. It was as if he had simply vanished.

CHAPTER 3

'It's quite a sight, *non*?'

Freya followed Racine's gaze along the jetty. At the very end, beyond where Paul and Hamad stood talking, a curved building twisted up out of the water, each floor wrapping around the next, occasional pools of light heightening the structure's elegant sweep. It contrasted perfectly with the skyline behind – square-shouldered peaks that rose and fell along the horizon, winking and glittering above the inky waters of the Arabian Sea.

'It's extraordinary. I'm sure it wasn't there last time we were here. But then every time I come the city looks different, new buildings seem to appear at an astonishing rate.'

'You like Doha? You and your husband?'

'We just come to see Ham, really.' Freya glanced ahead to where the two men were silhouetted against the night sky; Paul, all limbs and angles, Hamad cloaked in white. 'You don't like it?'

Racine shook her head. 'Doha thinks it's the future, but to me it always feels like a city without a past. I find it soulless. For a place to feel, for a place to really *be*, it must value its history, the place from which it came. Don't you think?'

'I do.' She glanced at the Frenchwoman, her long legs cloaked in wide black trousers, her upper body draped in burnt-orange silk. There was something extraordinary about her; a combination of height and the carelessly elegant way she moved. Freya was painfully aware that much of her ambivalence about Racine stemmed from the feelings of inadequacy she provoked. 'Is that why you moved to Marrakech? To be somewhere more *real*?'

She slipped her arm through Freya's. It felt oddly conspiratorial. 'Perhaps. When I first came to Doha I thought it would be so exotic, such an adventure. I imagined being surrounded by fascinating people, who would open up new possibilities, introduce me to new ideas. But all that really matters here is money. Making it, spending it. Who has the most. Don't be misled by the lights and the spectacle. It's just a small town, in many ways as predictable as provincial France.'

'So Marrakech suits you better?'

'For now. It's not somewhere I'd ever thought to live, but sometimes . . . things just happen, don't you find?' She glanced out towards the twinkling skyline. 'It was sheer chance that Maxim, the general manager of the Palais du Jardin, stayed at the Nanda. We were discussing wine, and when I told him my father was Michel Delacroix, that in time I'm going to make Château Delacroix the most prestigious wine house in France, he just laughed and asked me what I was doing in Doha. And I had no answer.'

'Apart from Hamad.'

'Of course.' The words came a little too fast. 'But he was right, you know? I can't make the right contacts or build the kind of relationships in the industry that I need to from here. Marrakech is different, it's awash with French expats, of exactly the right kind.'

'What kind is that?'

'Moneyed, obviously. But fashionable, you know? Early adopters, style arbiters – people who want to know what the next big thing is going to be, and get involved ahead of the curve. My father's wine is good, it sells well and we've won some small prizes. But I want to make it so much more. So a year, maybe two, in Marrakech, and then home to Lyon. We'll work together, he and I. Make Château Delacroix one of the most famous brands in France.'

'We had a great weekend in Marrakech, years ago,' said Freya, as Hamad and Paul walked towards them. 'Stayed in a – what do they call them? – riad? An old town house, they'd done it up really beautifully, it was right in the middle of the medina.' She reached for Paul's hand. 'What was it called?'

'Riad Noga,' he said, smiling. 'It had a fabulous roof terrace. We smuggled a bottle of fizz up there on our last night, remember?'

'You cut the bottom off two water bottles to make champagne saucers. I thought you were a genius.'

'I didn't know you were such a romantic,' said Racine, glancing at Paul.

'Resourceful, perhaps, rather than romantic,' said Hamad.

Paul laughed. 'Damned with faint praise.'

'Not at all.' Freya leant across to plant a kiss on his cheek. 'He can be very romantic when he wants to be.'

Hamad winked at her. 'I'm glad to hear it.'

Freya noticed a flicker of irritation pass across Paul's face. There was an edge to the evening. It had been there from the moment they had met; the first awkward moments of small-talk undercut by something less easy to define. Racine's lukewarm greeting had left Freya in little doubt that she was unimpressed by their appearance in Doha, but she had sensed something more: a general jitteriness that seemed to make every comment feel more pointed than it might otherwise have been. She thought of Paul's empty room, the unasked question still sharp in her mind.

'Shall we go in?' Hamad stepped forward and extended his hand to Racine.

'*Bien sûr.*'

Freya watched them disappear through the double-height doors. 'She's quite the girl.'

'You two looked thick as thieves. What was she saying to you?'

'Nothing much. How dull Doha was. How dull France was. I think we'd have got on to how dull Ham was if I hadn't changed the subject.'

Paul said nothing.

An image of the undisturbed duvet rose in her mind. 'You look tired. I thought you said you slept well?'

'I did.'

She glanced at him; it was too late to ask now. She should have said it back in the suite, when he'd made her leap with surprise by appearing on the other side of the shower door. But he'd spoken before she even had time to frame the question, yawning and stretching and saying he felt refreshed. The question was hot on her tongue, but she had sensed a risk, the possibility of a disagreement. It wasn't fair to do it to Hamad again.

'Mr and Mrs Hepworth, good evening.' She hadn't noticed Karim, standing mutely on the other side of the door. 'Would you like to come this way?'

She felt Paul move beside her, followed him into the unlit restaurant. Inside, a dozen round tables were laid for dinner; cutlery glinting in the half-light. On the far side of the room, two flares threw spirals of light up a wide, curving staircase.

'Are we the only ones here?'

Karim nodded. 'The restaurant isn't actually open yet, but the owner is a friend . . . If you'll just follow me up to the terrace . . .'

'More theatrics,' Paul muttered. 'Do you think there's any chance of him actually telling us what all this is about?'

'He'll tell us when he's ready.' She couldn't dislodge the image of the undisturbed bed. 'People like to have secrets, don't they?'

Freya had to admit Paul wasn't wrong about the theatrics. The whole terrace sparkled with hundreds of tiny lights, running along the walls, tumbling from the edges of the canopy, trickling through potted palms and miniature olive trees. In the centre, a table was set for dinner; beyond it, Hamad was standing beside a square of wall covered by a black curtain, twitching slightly in the breeze.

'So, what do you think?' He nodded at Karim to hand out glasses of champagne and beamed at Freya. 'An acceptable spot to see in the new year?'

'I don't know, Ham, you could have made a bit of an effort.' Paul took a glass and slipped his arm around Freya's shoulders. 'We came all this way . . .'

'Ignore him, it's beautiful.' She watched Hamad pull Racine towards him and drop a kiss on her cheek. 'Does this mean . . . ?'

'It does. Finally, I can reveal my proposal.' Hamad nodded at Karim, who unhooked the curtain and flicked a switch. A row of spotlights snapped on, illuminating three wide canvases. 'Come and look at these photos. Tell me what you see.'

Freya stepped forward. The first photograph was a carved wooden door, studded with rusty bronze diamonds, and with a small, round keyhole. The second was barely a door at all, just a slab of rotted wood that seemed to have bled into the pinkish-grey walls that flanked it. The last was more of a gate, blue paint flaking off to reveal the wood below, the top half framed by a rounded arch that looked vaguely Moroccan.

'Is that Marrakech?' She realised Racine was next to her, her scent, a sharp, clean citrus, perfuming the air. 'Have you become patron to some struggling Moroccan photo-artist?'

'I've not become a patron to anyone.' He glanced at Paul. 'I'm interested in what you see.'

'That it's a miracle any of the buildings are still standing?' Paul moved past Freya and peered at the photos. 'That . . . all the doors belong to the same house?'

'That's uncanny. Although they're not one house, not yet. At the moment they're separate but interconnected riads – just like the one you stayed at – in the oldest part of Marrakech medina. They've been owned by the same family, the Farzis, for at least a century. But not any more.' He paused. 'Now they belong to me.'

'*Quoi?*'

Hamad winked at Freya. 'I've done the impossible. Shocked the unshockable Mademoiselle Delacroix.'

'You've bought three houses in Marrakech? What for?'

'For you.' He took Racine's hands and pulled her towards him. 'Because it's where you live, for now. And so I have bought us a home there. A real home, somewhere that you can design and create to be exactly as you want it to be. And who better to design it with –' he turned – 'than my very good friend and renowned architect, Mr Paul Hepworth?'

Freya spun round to see Paul's face, wide with astonishment. 'I'm sorry?'

'My very good friend –' Hamad moved towards him, clapped an arm around his shoulders – 'and renowned architect, Mr Paul Hepworth. I'm offering you a job. In Marrakech. On what will be, what has the potential to become, the most beautiful houses that the city has ever seen. I've got to be honest, they're in a bit of a state now – well, two of them are. Back in the day they were the most ornate, the richest in the whole medina. They can be that again. There's no budget for this project, no limits on what can you do. They come with a few . . . conditions, but nothing major. Basically, they can be whatever you and Racine want them to be.'

'Oh my God. You're serious?' Paul shook his head slowly. 'Of all the things I thought you were going to say . . . I'm speechless.'

'In a good way?' Hamad winked at Freya.

'Of course. I mean, what an amazing opportunity, Ham. Just incredible. I just . . . I don't think, if I'm honest, I can take you up on it. But that doesn't mean I'm not . . . I don't know . . . flattered. Honoured. I just don't really do freelance projects. Work's so busy with this new project in Lyon . . .'

'But isn't that an office complex?' Hamad frowned. 'I'm talking about the chance to do something really extraordinary, truly creative. That's what you've always wanted, isn't it? I know you haven't been happy there since the merger, that you don't feel they value you.'

'Who said I don't feel valued?' Paul glared at Freya.

'Well, whether you do or you don't, they'll never offer you an opportunity like this. It will catapult your name into another league. If you don't want to leave, I'm sure they'd give you a sabbatical. It's the kind of project any firm would want to be associated with. There'll be nothing in Marrakech – in the whole of Morocco – to match it.'

'I still can't believe you bought me three houses.' There was a palpable disbelief in Racine's voice that Freya found oddly touching. 'It's the most incredible thing anyone's ever done for me.'

'But what about Freya?' Hamad slipped an arm around her shoulders. 'I know what you're thinking. What will I do while Paul is in Marrakech? Is Hamad crazy?' She smiled awkwardly. 'On the contrary. While Paul is working his magic on the houses, I thought you might like to do something similar with my grandmother's life story. I talked to Edith about it after her birthday. She wants to write her autobiography. Or rather, she wants someone else to. And I thought of you.'

'Me?'

'You.'

'But I'm not a writer, I'm an editor. And anyway, didn't you tell me she's always said autobiographies were only for . . . What was it?'

'Egomaniacs and megalomaniacs.' He grinned. 'She did indeed say that. But things change. Her health is starting to fail and I think she's realising that if she doesn't set things down, a lot of her achievements will simply be forgotten. It's not like fiction, Frey, there are her diaries and she's agreed that you could interview her over a period of months.'

'You've suggested me already?'

'I have. She loved the idea. And since she lives at La Mamounia – in Marrakech – it's perfect.'

'She lives at La Mamounia?' Freya raised her eyebrows. 'Isn't that a hotel?'

'It is. The most beautiful in Morocco.'

Racine tapped her ring against her glass. 'Until the Palais du Jardin opened its doors.'

Hamad laughed. 'We disagree on this. But I have to remain loyal to Mamounia – Edith wouldn't let me say anything else.'

'I've never known anyone live in a hotel,' said Paul. 'How gloriously old-days-of-the-Raj.'

'It works for both parties,' said Hamad. 'It gives her a kind of eccentrically regal status, which she loves, and when she's well enough, the hotel wheels her out for dinners and talks. They call her "the last of the great women travellers".'

'Which is exactly what she is,' said Freya, beaming at Hamad. 'You know I've always been a huge fan of hers. Read all her books. What an amazing opportunity. I can't believe you're serious.'

'I've never been more serious about anything,' said Hamad. 'The more I thought about it, the more perfect it all seemed. So what do you think? Come on, Paul, at least say you'll consider it?'

'Of course I will.' He drained his champagne glass. 'It's just so . . . unexpected. We wondered if you were going to suggest something in Doha, but I never dreamt of Marrakech. We'll definitely think about it.'

Freya raised her eyebrows. 'I'm not sure there's anything to think about.'

'There's a huge amount to consider. Not just our jobs, but . . .'

'Look, let's not spoil tonight with practicalities.' Hamad nodded at Karim, who pulled out a chair for Freya and lifted the napkin to place in her lap. 'And you need more information, too, before you can make such a big decision. Which is why I've arranged for the jet to take us all to Marrakech tomorrow evening. Racine has to head back anyway, so I thought we'd all go, take a look at the houses, drop in on Edith.' He settled in at the head of the table and raised his eyebrows at Paul. 'Does that sound like a plan? Good, I'm starving. Let's eat.'

CHAPTER 4

Marrakech

Paul looked out over the rooftops, the angular Doha skyline replaced by a jagged-edged sea of crumbling walls, strings of washing, satellite dishes sprouting from blackened chimney stacks. It was unsettling; as if they had flown not just between continents but also worlds, the first to the third, air-conditioned Land Cruisers and sprawling shopping malls replaced by battered trucks and dented taxis and the maze-like souks that knitted together the medina walls.

He should never have allowed things to get this far; but it had been impossible to find the right moment. Hamad had dominated the dinner, describing the houses, telling anecdotes about Dame Edith, prompting Racine to share a little of her life in Marrakech. By the end of the evening, his head fuzzy with champagne and red wine, he'd found himself agreeing with Freya that it was an amazing opportunity and that they would be fools not to accept. All of which had made the conversation the following morning even harder.

'Coffee?' He looked up to see the dark-haired woman who had checked them in earlier, settling a tray onto the table. The call to prayer rang out before he could reply – louder than in Doha, more insistent. 'I think your wife is in the shower. You have time.'

'Thank you, Jacqueline.' She couldn't be anything but French: slim and chic in white linen trousers and a black sleeveless top. 'You'll join me?'

'For a moment.' As she took off her sunglasses, Paul realised she was older than he had thought; early fifties, perhaps, beneath the flawless make-up and carefully tousled hair. 'So you're the one?'

His stomach flipped. 'I'm sorry?'

'The architect. The friend of Hamad's. The very old, very good friend, *n'est-ce pas*?'

'That's right. Since university. He's asked me to take a look at the houses he's bought, see what the possibilities are.'

'The Farzi riads.' Jacqueline poured the coffee. 'Quite a coup. Those houses have been in that family for generations. They've had offers before – the Swiss ambassador, when he retired, a fashion designer from France. The old man would never sell. Hamad must have been . . . persuasive.'

'I guess so.' Paul thought back to the conversation on the plane. He'd tried to speak then, while Racine and Freya slept and the engines kept up a low roar, but somehow the moment never came. Instead he'd listened while Hamad talked of the first chance meeting with Omar Farzi, the subsequent conversations and lengthy negotiations. It had become clear that the whole process had become deeply convoluted, that the Marrakchi had proved an unpredictable, somewhat chaotic man to do business with. Paul rather sensed that Hamad had found himself outmanoeuvred, forced to accept a deal that was not of his making. 'He says two of the houses are barely habitable. Maybe they just realised it was time to move.'

'Perhaps. But I get the feeling there was more to it than timing. I do not like to think how much money changed hands.'

'I often feel that way about Hamad's business deals,' said Paul, smiling. 'It all starts to feel a bit like Monopoly money to me.'

'So are you going to work on them? The houses?'

'I'm not sure.' Suddenly, sitting on the roof terrace in front of the

Frenchwoman, he longed to say yes. For a moment he played out a scenario of strolling into the boardroom in London, telling the newly anointed CEO exactly what he could do with the office complex in Lyon. The fantasy faded, replaced by a quite different image. A shiver of guilt ran up his spine. 'I don't think we can, really. I might take a small advisory role. Something peripheral. But Freya and I both have jobs in London, our lives are there. We can't just drop everything and move.'

'I think you're very wise,' said Jacqueline unexpectedly. 'Marrakech is not an easy city. Sometimes I have guests, they stay two, three days, and then announce they would like to move here, that they are envious of the life I have. A glimpse of something, a taste . . . it can be very alluring. But it is not real. Change should not be built on a fantasy.'

'Indeed.' He found himself unable to meet Jacqueline's gaze. 'But you're obviously happy here?'

'I am. It's a world away from Paris, but it suits me at this time in my life. Business is good, although we have just six rooms. And then we have the smaller riad next door too.'

'We?'

'My husband Alain. *Un professeur*. In term-time he is in Paris. And I am here. A good arrangement, don't you think? But not one that works for everyone. Not one for you and your wife.'

Before Paul could reply, footsteps broke across the conversation; he looked up to see Freya weaving between the cluster of tables, draped in a sleeveless, sky-blue wrap dress that fastened at the side with a wide silver hoop. She'd put her hair up, the odd loose strand falling to her neck; it made her look younger, reminded him of the ponytail she'd often worn as a student. Guilt spiked again.

'You look nice.' The word seemed inadequate; she was sparkling, her face lit up. He had forgotten she could be like this, the memory overlaid by months of brittle weariness, the constant shadow of Ali's chemo looming over their lives.

'I'm so excited. Jacqueline, I'm so jealous that you live here. I'd forgotten what an amazing city it is.' He knew what she was doing; it was a familiar pattern – from anger to resentment and then complete denial. She always reverted to it if they disagreed, if he ever tried to say no to something she really wanted. It usually worked; she would simply pretend that whatever she wanted to happen *was* going to happen, and became the brightest, most charming version of herself until Paul found it impossible to resist and gave in. She was like a force of nature. It occurred to him suddenly that it was something she had in common with Hamad. Both of them usually got what they wanted in the end.

'Are you ready?' She beamed down at Paul. The row by the pool, the stilted atmosphere on the plane, the monosyllabic conversation when they had arrived at Riad des Arts – it was as if none of it had happened. 'Hamad's just texted. They're outside.'

'OK.' Paul stood; he could feel Jacqueline watching them. 'Thanks for the coffee.'

'*De rien.*' She smiled at Freya. 'You're off to meet Dame Edith Simpson?'

'After we've seen the houses. I can't wait to see her again; I met her a couple of times in Cambridge, but that was years ago.'

'From what Racine tells me, age hasn't mellowed her. *Bonne chance, chérie.* I rather suspect you are going to need it.'

Outside, the air was thick and sweet. It felt odd to see Racine and Hamad standing in the alley, their joint elegance at odds with the crumbling walls and rutted paving stones that led away towards the light. Freya's voice broke the silence; he let her walk ahead, watching how lightly she moved, the blue of her dress contrasting with the faded pink hues that framed her. Regret twisted through him; a familiar nag, like a muscular ache that never quite seemed to fade.

He glanced at Racine, walking mutely beside him. Before he could speak, the alley opened into a street lined with fast-food kiosks and dirty-windowed shops selling mobile phones and car stereos. On the pavement, women swept along in brightly coloured *djellabas*: electric-blue, deep mauve, warm, chocolate-browns. Others moved more quietly, their bodies cloaked in black, faces dipped towards the ground, while men huddled together on street corners, the pointed hoods of their *djellabas* tipping together.

'There's Karim.' Among the chaos, the black Mercedes gleamed like a beacon. He slid in next to Freya, the door clicked shut, the world outside evaporated as suddenly as it had materialised.

'It's going to be amazing,' she whispered. 'What an opportunity.' Her fingers were tight around his hand, her body pressed into his. They'd have sex later, if he said yes; she'd be at her most passionate, fired up by a sense of victory he knew she would never admit to.

'We haven't agreed to anything yet.'

She kissed him. 'But we're going to. Aren't we?'

He didn't answer. Beyond the glass, the city spun around them, mopeds buzzing angrily between dustcarts and delivery vans, the medina walls rising up behind, fringed with clusters of olive trees and strips of tired-looking grass. Karim nosed the car beneath the curve of an ornate brick archway. The street grew busier, lined with vegetable stalls and hunched-over women clutching faded shopping bags.

'We walk from here,' said Hamad, as the engine slowed. Paul sighed; he would have liked to have stayed in the car, to remain at one remove from the chaos outside. He wasn't like Freya; she could arrive somewhere new and simply wander the streets, let the difference wash over her, absorb it until the city's pace became her own. She'd tease him for his awkwardness, telling him to relax, to go with the flow, but it was a concept he found messy and ill-defined. He didn't want to have to adjust to someone else's pace; he was quite comfortable with his own.

As he stepped out of the car, noise barrelled towards him. A wide square, hung with faded carpets, funnelled them under a second, smaller, archway into a covered street filled with wrought-iron lamps and window grates. The blackened workshops echoed to the whirr of blowtorches, the discordant clang of metal on metal. They followed Hamad into a side alley; immediately the din subsided. It was as if the souk had vanished, the noise of the metalworkers obliterated by thick, heat-stained walls.

'Here we are,' he said, pulling Racine towards him and handing her a key. 'Welcome to your new home. Want to do the honours?'

Paul recognised the door from the photograph. He followed Freya into a dark lobby that smelt of dust and thick, mildewed air that had been left to stagnate behind unopened shutters.

'We'll start in the garden,' said Hamad, leading them towards a wide shaft of light. 'Just don't expect the other two houses to look like this.'

Beyond the entrance, the crimson-walled courtyard was soaked in sunshine, the light picking out tangles of jasmine blossom and the cerise bougainvillea that hung off the cracked, whitewashed balconies. Four squares of garden spilled leafy tendrils onto the mosaic floor; in one section a creeper-clad tree twisted up to the balcony above, studded with crinkled pink flowers.

'This place is *so* beautiful.' Paul glanced over to where Freya was standing, her fingers tracing the looping curves in a panel of carved Arabic script. 'Racine, this is *yours*. Can you believe it?'

'Not really.' She laughed. 'Hamad, this really is an astonishing thing to have done. This house alone would be amazing, but three . . .'

'They kind of came as a set.' He gestured around the courtyard. 'Why don't you explore? Everything's open. It's all yours.'

'It's quite a place,' said Paul, as Racine pulled open a door and Freya followed her into the darkness. 'No wonder you bought it.'

'There's a feeling to it, don't you think? Real history. That's what drew me. In Doha everything is so new – the old ways my grandfather talked of . . . all gone. But here it feels . . . worthwhile to own something with such history, something that we can maintain.' He ran his fingers around the stone bowl. 'This *sahridj* is hundreds of years old.'

'*Sahridj*?'

'Fountain. In an Islamic garden there should always be running water.' He pointed to a slim channel that bisected the mosaic tiling. 'See? Water from the *sahridj* would flow through there.'

'You think Racine will want to keep it like this?'

'She doesn't really have a choice. I told you Omar Farzi imposed some conditions on the deal. One is that this house has to be a public space. A museum.'

'I'm not sure she'll like that.'

'She still has two houses to play with. And it was a deal-breaker for the old man – well, one of them. He told me that when he was a child, these houses were the most beautiful in the whole city. The Farzis were rich. They were merchants, some sort of dealers. But their business turned bad and the houses slowly crumbled. For decades, he hung on in the hope that he or one of his sons would make enough money to restore them. I've offered to re-create this house exactly as it once was, and to open it to the public. That's why this is such a great project for you, Paul. You get to carry out Racine's designs – art deco or minimalist or whatever she wants, and then with this house you'll get to really re-create history.'

'Hamad, I haven't said yes.'

'But you will, won't you? I know it's a big change, but where else will you get a similar opportunity? And Frey . . . now her sister's well again, isn't it the perfect time to take off and do something like this?'

'Maybe.' He hated being told what was best for Freya. It had always been there: a slightly disappointed sense that he wasn't taking care of her quite as he should. Things had come to a head in October; Hamad's suggestion that he could have been more supportive while Ali was going through chemo finally provoked the response he'd been biting back for years. There'd been a moment, in the strained silence when he'd finished speaking, when he genuinely thought Hamad was going to stand up and leave. Instead there'd been an unexpected apology, heartfelt and genuine, but it did little to assuage his indignation.

'Come and see the rest of the house,' said Hamad, pushing him back towards the lobby.

'I know you mean well,' Paul said, following him up a damp-smelling stairwell. 'But you can't just clap your hands and gift some-one a new life, you know.'

'Is that what you think I'm trying to do? You and Freya are like family to me. In my culture, families help each other out.'

'Why do you think we need help?'

Hamad raised his eyebrows. 'Look, don't get all defensive. I know you and Freya can manage your lives just fine, of course you can. But I also know it's been a really tough time. Not just with Ali, but before that . . . I know how . . . disappointing that was. But a few months out here, maybe a year, could be a fresh start for both of you. It would be a positive thing for all of us – building something solid from all our years of friendship.' He pushed open a door. 'This would be the master bedroom. Think what you could do with it.'

Paul followed mutely, taking in the carved wooden screens, the smooth *tadelakt* walls, the plump, curved archways leading to the bathroom and dressing room. The upstairs needed work; floors dipped underfoot, walls dissipated into clouds of papery dust when he brushed his fingers against them. But the potential was breath-taking. With every door Hamad opened, he could feel an idea begin to germinate: an ornate palace that fused nineteenth-century design with cutting-edge lighting and heating systems, built to sustainable principles, unlike anything the city had seen before.

'Want to see the second one?'

'You bet.' It couldn't do any harm to look, even if it was just a theoretical exercise. A plan was beginning to crystallise; he wanted to sketch ideas out, note things down, get an idea of the potential across all three houses. He followed Hamad back out into the courtyard and raised his eyebrows at Freya as they headed out into the street.

'Isn't it amazing?' She squeezed his hand. 'You could do so much.'

'I know.'

'This one's more of a wreck.' Hamad heaved open the battered wooden door. A cloud of dust whirled up as they stepped inside, fragments of broken tile and clusters of rubble crunching beneath their feet. A rhythmic sound of sweeping broke the silence.

'Hamad?' Paul squinted towards the balcony. 'There's someone up there.'

'That'll be Yusuf. He . . . kind of comes with this house.'

Racine frowned. 'What does that mean, exactly?'

'It means this is where he lives. Where he's always lived. He was born here, Omar told me. Son of the Farzis' cook, back in the time when they had staff. It's a good thing, actually. A lot of houses in the medina have live-in guardians; to have one that really cares about the place is a blessing.'

'Can we meet him?' Paul was intrigued.

'Yusuf?' Hamad called up something unintelligible in Arabic. 'He speaks Darija, but we can understand each other.' Within seconds a diminutive figure had appeared on the balcony, broom in hand, his face almost entirely shaded by the pointed hood of his *djellaba*.

'Yusuf, *salaam alaikum*. My friends, Racine, Freya and Paul.' When Hamad had finished speaking, the old man raised his right arm and flapped his fingers downwards a few times, mumbling a string of words that sounded almost like a chant. The skin on the back of Paul's hands prickled slightly. He looked down and rubbed them together. When he glanced back up, Yusuf had disappeared.

'He looks a bit of a character,' said Freya. 'It's quite the set-up you've got here. Strikes me you've bought a lot more than just houses.'

'You're not wrong there.' Hamad slipped an arm around her shoulder. 'I've also bought a rather spectacular view. Want to come and see it? This house has the best roof terrace.'

She nodded. Paul watched them walk to a door in the corner of the courtyard and disappear through it. Racine didn't move.

'You're not going up?'

'In a minute.'

'This is quite a thing, isn't it?'

'You could say that.'

Paul lifted his chin. 'I didn't ask him to do this.'

'I know. But he's done it anyway.' She moved closer; he could smell her scent in the air. 'Only Hamad could do something so . . . overblown.'

'You're not pleased?'

'It's an incredible gesture. I don't question his generosity. But if I am to live in his house in Marrakech, why did I not just stay in Doha?'

'They're your houses. You can make them however you want.'

'With you?'

'*Hey.*'

Paul looked up to see Freya's face above the top-floor balcony.

'Are you coming? The view's incredible.'

'On our way.' He looked at Racine and shrugged. 'We'd better go up.'

She didn't move. 'What are you going to say?'

'I don't know. Freya wants this . . . and it is an incredible opportunity. It's going to be very hard to find a reason to say no.'

'Really?'

Paul squeezed his fingernails into his palms. 'Not one I can share.'

'Well, I suggest you come up with something. Say you've been given a promotion. That your father is ill. You don't like Morocco. Any reason, Paul. Anything but the truth.'

CHAPTER 5

It was Freya who saw him first. A tall, bearded man in a grubby beige *djellaba*, striding past the concierge desk, out of time with the muted flow of La Mamounia's grand lobby. She knew, before the first shout, that he was coming for them. His eyes locked on to Hamad, deep in conversation with Gerard, the silver-haired hotel manager.

'Bouskri.'

The lobby fell silent. Heads turned. Before Hamad had time to react, the man was in front of him, shoving him backwards with thick, hairy fists. 'Bouskri*, va te faire foutre, enculé!*'

'Hey.' Paul lurched forward, but Karim was quicker, twisting the man's arm up behind his back.

'*Tu partiras*,' he snapped, pushing him forward.

'*Je vais te faire souffrir*,' yelled the man as Karim marched him back towards the doors. Freya glanced at Hamad; he looked shocked. She had the sense he had no idea who the man was.

'Monsieur Al-Bouskri, I am so sorry.' Gerard's face was puce.

Hamad smoothed down his shirt. 'Your doormen need to show better judgement in future. This was unacceptable. My grandmother is in Bar Menzeh I presume?'

'She is. I do apologise . . .'

But Hamad was moving already, his shoulders rigid, face set.

'What was that about?' Freya whispered to Paul as they fell into step behind him. 'Do you think they knew each other?'

'Well, the other guy clearly thought he knew Hamad. Did you hear what he said? *I'll make you suffer.* I don't think they're friends, put it that way.'

Freya slipped her arm through Paul's and squeezed him to her. She wanted to forget what had just happened, didn't want anything to slow the momentum she had created. It still didn't feel real. She knew there was a chance Paul would go back on what they had agreed on the roof terrace. Between Hamad's promises and her pleading, they had made it almost impossible for him to say no, although she was aware his agreement had lacked enthusiasm. She was at a complete loss as to why.

She realised Hamad was holding a door open for them. 'You OK?'

'Of course. Just some crazy person. Forget about it, Frey. I have.'

A low whistle broke across their conversation. 'This is quite some place,' Paul said as they moved into the sunshine. 'What an extraordinary garden.'

Freya shaded her eyes and looked out across the lawns, shaded by palm trees that towered above the rose beds and the neat, stepped terraces, dotted with cacti. To the right, a square pool glittered in the sunlight; ahead of them a wide gravel path led to a small pavilion, half screened by olive and citrus trees.

'Beloved of everyone from Kipling to Churchill to our very own Edith,' said Hamad. 'Not a bad place to call home, eh?'

'You're not kidding. I still can't believe she lives here. I hope . . .'

'There she is.' He quickened his pace towards a cluster of white parasols that blossomed above rattan seats and low glass tables. Freya felt the muscles in Paul's arm tense slightly.

'*Salaam alaikum, jaddah.* How are you? Look who I brought to see you. You remember Paul and Freya?'

For a moment, Freya wondered if she should curtsy; the woman in the chair exuded a kind of regal eccentricity that had clearly been amped up in the intervening years. She sat, stiffly erect, her thin body swaddled in a sequin-studded pashmina, face half hidden beneath a wide-brimmed panama. Beneath the scarf a cream kaftan fell to her knees, matching linen trousers running down to beaded sandals. A tangle of heavy silver chains and a huge pendant, engraved with Arabic calligraphy, hung around her neck.

'Of course I remember Freya.' The voice was slightly fractured. 'I introduced the two of you, didn't I? In that grubby little Italian . . . what was it called?'

'Antica Bella.' Freya met the older woman's eyes; blue and clear.

'Well, I certainly picked well.' The eyes warmed. 'You've seen them all off, haven't you? Ten years on, still keeping an eye on my grandson.'

'I'm not sure I keep an eye on him.'

'I suspect that's exactly what you do.' She leant forward and peered at Paul. 'And Paul too? Well, you haven't changed.'

'Dame Edith.' He moved towards her, stretched out to take her hand. Their fingers touched briefly. 'It's a pleasure to see you again.'

'Indeed.' She turned to Hamad. 'I was expecting just you and Freya.'

'That's not true. I said I'd be bringing Freya *and* Paul. Perhaps you just forgot?'

'I'm quite happy to make myself scarce,' said Paul quickly. 'Ham, I'd love to go and take another look at the houses. I quite understand that it's Freya you want to talk to, Dame Edith, and I don't want to tire you out.'

'I'm not dead *yet*,' she snapped.

'No, of course.' He turned to Hamad. 'Is that OK? I'd like to see them again while it's still light, and we've an early flight in the morning.'

'Well, I can't fault your enthusiasm.' He gestured towards the hotel. 'Karim's with the car. He'll take you.'

'If he's finished sorting out that loony . . .' Freya tailed off as Hamad shook his head, eyebrows knitted together.

'What loony?' Edith's voice was sharp.

'Nothing, *jaddah*.'

'I'll see you back at Riad des Arts, shall I?' Paul was already moving away. 'Dame Edith, wonderful to see you again.'

'Still master of the disappearing act I see,' said Edith. 'All right, Hamad. Stop glowering at me. Why don't you go and rustle us up some tea, and get them to bring something sweet. *Macarons.* Something like that. If I'm to share all my secrets, Freya and I are going to need to know each other a little better.'

Hamad crouched by her chair. 'I suspect that if you tell Freya all your secrets, your book will never see the light of day. Just promise me you don't have any more shocks up your sleeve.'

Edith tutted and raised her eyebrows at Freya. 'He's talking about Timothy. My other grandson. Can't see why it makes any damned difference to him, but he's been in quite the huff ever since I told him. Always could sulk, even when he was little. Refused to speak for a whole day once, when Mourad got some present he wanted. Little horror.'

Freya stifled a smile. 'Well, I'm just really honoured, Dame Edith. This is such an amazing opportunity. I've read everything you've ever written.'

The bangles clattered dismissively, as if to signify flattery was unnecessary. 'Hamad. Tea.'

'Of course.'

'It does him good to be told now and then.' She watched him affectionately as he moved across the grass. 'He's too much like his grandfather in that respect, too set on going his own way without listening to anyone's counsel. Apart from yours, perhaps.'

'I don't think he needs my counsel.'

'That's where you're wrong. I'm not sure he's ever needed it more.

What do you make of his latest extravagance – buying the Farzi houses for Racine? It is the grand gesture, no?'

'It's certainly that. But she obviously makes him very happy.'

Edith let out a sharp, humourless bark. 'You don't make a man happy by moving thousands of miles from where he lives. These houses . . . It's classic Hamad, I'm afraid, trying to buy control of the situation. He thinks he's met his match in Racine, but she's cut from very different cloth to him. She's wilful. Reckless.'

'I don't really know her that well.'

'You don't need to know someone very long to see who they are,' said Edith. 'There is much in Racine that I recognise. I knew her the first time we met. As I did with you. I knew you were what my grandson needed: steady, sensible. He was never going to jump into bed with you.'

The words were said carelessly but Freya felt stung. In the early days of their friendship she had been more than a little infatuated with the exotic-looking Arab who had dropped so unexpectedly into her life. It had taken some time to accept they would only ever be friends, but gradually she had come to realise that friendship offered a more lasting relationship than any kind of romantic entanglement. Women came and went from his life without ever enjoying the closeness they shared. She had always assumed that when he finally picked a wife she would be Qatari; a little-seen figure whose world would barely impinge on theirs. But now there was Racine. She changed everything.

'I've upset you.' To her surprise, Edith looked concerned. 'One of the curses of old age is a tendency to speak carelessly. It's an irony, no? We look so vulnerable – in our wheelchairs, with our walking sticks – and yet we have become so toughened by the long years of life that there is little anyone can say to hurt us. We have become immune. You, of course, have not.'

'It's fine.'

'Don't.' The voice was sharp again. 'I detest that phrase. If we are to work together, I need honesty at all times. I can't stand dissembling or posturing. You have mistaken my words as criticism. In fact they are born of a deep gratitude. I know Hamad believes his future lies with this woman. But that will not come to pass, I guarantee you. And when he realises that, he is going to need you, Freya. More than ever.'

'And Paul. They're going to be working side by side on the project . . .'

'Ah, yes. Paul.'

'It's such an incredible opportunity for him, too. He's so grateful to Hamad . . .'

'I should think he is. I . . .' She looked at Freya for a moment, then glanced down at her hands. 'But it is not a project without challenges. Everyone knew the Farzis had fallen on hard times, but still, the idea of the houses being sold, of the family leaving the medina . . . There is already much unhappiness about how many riads are being bought by expats, but when houses like this go to outsiders, questions are asked. Do you know what Hamad offered Omar Farzi?'

'Money, I guess. Hamad would have paid whatever was necessary.'

Edith waved her hand. 'Money wouldn't be enough. Marrakech is an old city, there are scores to settle that go back decades, centuries even. I fear whatever deal Hamad has done, it will not be without ramifications.'

Freya thought of the bearded man in the lobby. 'Paul said Hamad told him one of the houses was going to be a museum, that they were going to restore it to how it was when the Farzis were wealthy.'

'A museum?' Edith shook her head, her eyebrows disappearing under the brim of her hat. 'I'd take that with a large pinch of salt. It's a good story, but if I know Omar Farzi, there'll be more to it than doing up a few rooms with some pretty mosaic tiling. Hamad's become quite the power-player in the last couple of years. The Gulf

States are pumping money into Morocco, and Qatar more than most. It gives him leverage. Power.'

'I don't know . . .'

'Shh.' Dame Edith shook her head and glanced at the waiter approaching across the lawn. 'Not in front of the staff.' She glanced up as the dark-haired boy placed two jewel-coloured glasses on the table and a tray of candy-coloured *macarons*. 'Watch how Claude pours. He lifts the pot so high that the mint will bruise when the water hits the glass, and make the tea more fragrant. Isn't that so, Claude?'

He nodded, his eyes focused on the thin stream of liquid. He filled the second glass, wiped an invisible drop of water from the table and moved silently away. The older woman leant forward, fingers extended to clasp a pale pink *macaron*.

'Dame Edith? You were talking about Hamad?'

She stared at her glassily. 'Was I?'

Freya remembered suddenly what Hamad had told them in the car: the shock of Edith's diagnosis, the long weeks of recuperation after the stroke. She'd found it impossible to think of the elderly woman as confused, or reduced in any way. It was disconcerting to see.

'But we should talk of you,' Edith said suddenly, as if the previous topic had been closed and dealt with. 'If I am to tell you my whole life story over the next few months, it seems only fair I hear a little of yours.' She popped the *macaron* into her mouth, chewing noisily. 'What have you been doing with yourself since Cambridge?'

'Working, mostly,' said Freya, thinking of their flat in Battersea, the crowded commute to work, the piles of books and manuscripts stacked up around her desk. 'We did some travelling in our twenties, had a wonderful round-the-world trip just after uni. I'd love to have done more, but Paul was studying, and then he got taken on straight away by a really top architectural firm. And Hamad told you

I'm an editor, I think? I used to love it, but publishing's changing and I've been thinking for a while it might be time to do something different. Change isn't easy, is it? And then stuff happens, life gets in the way . . .'

'Your sister's been ill, I believe?'

'Yes.' She thought of Ali suddenly; wondered how she would take the news. 'Breast cancer. But last year she was given the all-clear. It's partly why this has come at such a good time. It's been . . . tough.'

'I'm sure.' Edith sipped her tea. 'No children?'

Freya felt the cool slick of gel on her stomach, saw the frown on the nurse's face as she stared at the monitor. 'No. Not yet.'

'Well, how old are you? Thirty-two? Thirty-three? Still plenty of time. If you want to, of course. That's what feminism was all about, wasn't it? Have them, don't have them, work, don't work. Such freedoms. But, anyway, none of my business.' She sat back in the chair. 'And you've been married how long?'

'Eight years. But we've been together for nearly twelve.'

'Not bad by today's standards. And you're happy?'

'Happy?'

'In your marriage?'

'Oh, yes.' Freya didn't blink. 'Very happy indeed.'

Paul let the door swing shut behind him. His skin felt clammy beneath his T-shirt; he'd been unprepared for how Edith's reaction would make him feel. Just the sound of her voice brought back their last conversation, ten years before; standing by the roadside in the sodden darkness, his fingers clenched around the phone. *There's been an accident. Hamad says, can you come?* She hadn't responded straight away; he'd gabbled at her, adrenalin speeding up his words. He could still hear the scorn in her words: '*You stupid little boy.*'

She clearly hadn't forgiven him. And now they were going to be living in the same city; another reason why he should have pushed back against Freya and Hamad. Somehow, in spite of everything, saying no had still felt like an impossibility. He knew Freya would have had a response to anything he could have come up with, that the argument would have spiralled, inevitably reaching an impasse that would have been almost impossible to overcome.

He stepped out into the courtyard; wanted to let the house slowly enfold him – the damp, sweet smell that rose from the piles of mildewed leaves, the snippets of birdsong twisting into the air. These first moments, when it was just him and the house he would come to know . . . He'd never told anyone, apart from Freya, but there was almost something spiritual about it. In spite of everything, he could feel the anticipation of a beginning, a rebirth that could absolve him, move focus from the chaos of the present to a new, neater time.

The brittle creak of the door broke the silence. '*Âllo?*'

'Racine?' She'd changed into pencil-thin black trousers and a sleeveless, jade-coloured top that rose up her throat in a sheer scarf. The shock was almost as visceral as it had been in Doha; incontrovertible proof that what he had tried to box away as nothing more than fantasy had actually taken place. It still didn't quite seem possible; a moment of dysfunction that was entirely incompatible with the man he believed himself to be.

'I don't appreciate being summoned,' she said coldly. 'I told you that in Doha.'

'I know. But we have to talk, don't we? This . . . situation. It needs managing.'

'Managing?' She brought her hand down on the edge of the *sahridj*. 'There shouldn't be any situation to manage. What on earth possessed you to say yes? How do you think this is going to work?'

'I said yes because it's an incredible opportunity.' He found himself staring at her bare shoulders; tracing the line of her arm down to her fingers, angled neatly across her hip. 'That's the irony – what

Hamad's done, it's just perfect. Freya's always wanted to write a book, and those houses – a blank cheque, complete creative control? Opportunities like that are once in a lifetime. There's no reason I could have given him.'

'Apart from the fact you slept with his girlfriend?'

'Just once, Racine. We agreed it was a mistake. A one-off that should never have happened.'

'You didn't think you'd ever see me again, did you?' She leant back against the *sahridj* and crossed her arms. 'That's why you never contacted me after what happened in Lyon. You thought Hamad and I would separate. I would go and live in Marrakech and you and Freya and Hamad could resume your . . . *ménage* without ever having to acknowledge what you did.'

'What *we* did. And it was you who left. When I woke up in the morning and you'd gone, I just assumed . . .'

'We went through all this in Doha. What was there to say? We drank too much wine, Paul, listened to each other's sad stories. It was an escape, perhaps, from our own difficulties. But in the morning, what would we have been left with? Guilt? Regret? The humiliating sense of having become the worst kind of cliché.'

'I would have liked to have said goodbye. I told you that in Doha. I've never . . . It meant something, Racine. Even if only for that night.'

She glanced at him; gave a small, rueful smile. 'Yes. It was . . . memorable. To not hear from you – even just an acknowledgement that it had happened – that's why I was so angry in Doha. Did you really think it was necessary to tell me to pretend it never happened, that your wife must never find out? You think I want Hamad to know?'

'Of course not. I just panicked. I didn't expect you to be there.'

'And now I am here all the time. How do you think this is going to work? You say what happened in Lyon was a one-off, but do I need to remind you about that dinner in London, all those months ago? If I had invited you back to my hotel then, you would have come.'

'That's not true.' The memory of that kiss, his body hard up against hers in an unlit street, shamed him almost more than what had happened in Lyon. He'd tried to dismiss it as an unexpected venting of his frustration with work, with Freya's unexpected no-show, with the sense that his life was atrophying with each day that passed. Better that than admit he had longed to touch her from the first moment she had walked into the restaurant.

She moved closer. 'You think I can't tell when a man wants me? You think I didn't know that's what you were hinting at when you sent that email? *Oh, Racine, I'm going to be in Lyon next month. Any recommendations?*'

Paul closed his eyes; he remembered typing the email the day after Hamad had visited back in October, still smarting from the uninvited judgement on his relationship with Freya. 'I wasn't trying to start anything – I didn't even say when I was going to be in Lyon. It was just, I don't know, fate that you were there at the same time I was. It was you who suggested I take the tour of your father's vineyard.'

'And you who chose to go.'

'I couldn't have known you'd be there.' He hadn't even seen her at first; standing at the back of the group, reading the pamphlet on *terroirs* and grape varieties. It was only when she spoke that he looked up; caught the expression of surprise on her face, the vaguest hint of pleasure. 'Look, we were just both having a difficult time. But things are different now. You're obviously happy here in Marrakech, and Freya and I – this is a chance of a fresh start for us . . .'

'You really believe that? Meetings, dinners? You, me, Hamad and your wife around a table? Wasn't it uncomfortable enough in Doha?'

'I know it won't be easy.' He laid a hand on her arm; something static, some kind of shockwave, jumped across his skin. 'I can't pretend there's not something between us. But we have to put it away. I don't want this to destroy my marriage. I love Freya.'

'And I love Hamad.'

He felt something twist slightly, in spite of himself. 'Well, good. We can make this work, I promise you. No one will ever know.'

CHAPTER 6

Marrakech: February 2010

Hamad watched the gold-inlaid doors close in front of him, and sensed the ground rise beneath his feet. It was ridiculous to feel this way, like a small boy summoned for a ticking-off. But he had never quite outgrown his childhood relationship with the eccentric, exotically dressed woman who swept into his life every few months, brightening it, scooping him up from beneath the weight of Mourad and his sisters. They never welcomed her; made clear their resentment of the mongrel genes she had given them, diluting their quintessential Arabness. He didn't understand their resentment; he loved the feeling of otherness it gave him, the possibility of experiencing two diverse worlds.

It was obvious what the breakfast invitation was about. Outside the door to Edith's suite, he straightened his shoulders and ran his fingers across his scalp. He wasn't going to take a scolding. The flat tone of the bell rang somewhere inside. Almost immediately the door swung back and a thin-faced waiter gestured to him to enter the room. 'Monsieur Al-Bouskri. Dame Edith is expecting you. She is on the balcony.'

'Is that my errant grandson?' She stood as he came towards her, swathed in a scarlet-and-blue paisley kaftan, a thick pink scarf wound around her neck. 'Thank you, Jean-Paul. That will be all.'

Hamad felt her palm against his face as he kissed her. 'Good morning, *jaddah*. What are you doing out here? It's freezing.'

'Don't exaggerate.' Edith adjusted the position of her scarf and looked across to the distant rooftops of the medina, hazy in the early morning sunshine. 'I know "outside" is an alien concept in Doha – that you just drive from one ghastly air-conditioned mall to the next. Here we have such a thing as scenery. Fresh air. It's good for you – opens the pores, gets the blood pumping. Although it sounds as if you don't need any help with that at the moment.'

'What does that mean?'

She raised an eyebrow. 'You think I didn't hear about the fracas that happened last time you were here? Getting into a fight in the lobby? Honestly, Hamad. I was mortified.'

'I didn't get into a fight. I don't even know who he was.'

'Don't insult me. A man accosts you in public and you don't bother to find out his name?' Hamad shifted awkwardly in his seat. 'Of all the riads in the city, why did you have to buy the Farzi houses? And why didn't you talk to me first? I could have told you Omar Farzi was a bastard.'

'I can handle him.'

'Can you?' She shook her head. 'Then why won't you tell me what the deal was? And don't start wittering on about some museum. That's just window-dressing.'

Hamad picked a cherry from the pile in the fruit bowl and slipped it into his mouth. He knew she wouldn't stop asking. 'There was some land . . . a farm or something. In the Ourika valley. Omar said it used to belong to his family, that it was bought unfairly, they were pressurised into selling. He said he'd offered countless times to buy it back for a fair price, but that the family who owned the land refused to sell. If I could . . . I don't know, persuade them to change their mind, then he would agree to sell me the houses.'

Edith's cup clattered on its saucer. 'Persuade *who* to change their mind? Which family, Hamad? He must have told you.'

'If he did, I don't remember. In the end, I didn't really get involved with that part of the deal. You know what the Moroccan legal system is like. I flew in Mahmoud – he heads up my legal team in Doha – and left it to him.'

'What do you mean, you left it to him? What have I always said? Check everything yourself. See every document.'

'I know.' Hamad picked up the coffee pot and poured slowly, trying to buy time. He wasn't sure if he could explain why he'd distanced himself from the deal; part of him suspected that if he had looked too closely, he wouldn't have liked what he found. But he hadn't wanted to find a reason to walk away from the Farzi houses. It had become a battle of wills, almost an obsession. 'It was just a very busy time. I was in and out of Rabat, meeting the government as part of the Emir's delegation. It just seemed easier to hand the process over to someone else.'

'Just as long as the Azoulays weren't involved,' she said. Hamad felt his eyebrows lift. '*Hamad*? God almighty,' she went on. 'Please tell me you haven't sold the Azoulay land to Omar Farzi?'

'That might have been the name.'

'You *stupid* boy.' He glanced across at her, taken aback at the ferocity of her voice. 'Don't you know those families have been feuding for generations? Lives have been lost over that land. How the hell did Mahmoud get them to sell?'

'All I can tell you is that he asked if I had any contacts at the Ministry of Agriculture. Since we'd just had all these meetings in Rabat, I did know a couple of people. I assumed he wanted to check the deeds or the history of the land ownership. You know how complicated those things are in this country.'

'I know the Azoulays would never have sold that land from choice.' Edith fell silent, staring out across the rooftops. 'But an enforced purchase . . . It's happened before. The Ministry announces it needs to buy a particular parcel of land, and the owners have to sell. Then it magically gets sold on to someone else. Check the records, Hamad. I suggest you will find that Omar Farzi bought the land from the Ministry of Agriculture, rather than Hassan Azoulay.'

'Oh.' Hamad thought of the man in the lobby, the anger on his face. 'Well, if that's what Mahmoud's done . . . that seems . . .'

'It's fraud.'

'It's not fraud, but it's not how I do business. I'll get Karim to do some digging. Maybe I can persuade Farzi to sell it back?'

'Don't be so ridiculous. If Omar Farzi's got his hands on that land, he'd die before selling it. It must have been Hassan Azoulay who caused the scene last time you were here. Do you know where the family moved to?'

'They could have gone anywhere, the amount of money they got for the land.'

Edith's hand slapped heavily against the table, her rings clanking on the marble. 'It's not *always* about money. When will you learn?'

'Let's change the subject, shall we? I have to go in a minute, and I don't want an argument. Freya flew in last night and Paul's been here since Thursday. I said I'd meet them at the houses at ten.'

'So you're definitely going ahead with this?'

'Don't you want to write your autobiography?'

'I'm not talking about the book,' she snapped. 'I like Freya. I'm happy to work with her. But Paul? As if you haven't got enough problems.'

'You have to let it go,' said Hamad. 'Twelve years of friendship is more important than the events of one night. And yes, it's absolutely all going ahead. They've both handed in their notice, some relative or other is going to rent their flat. They're out here this weekend to look at Jacqueline's riad and for Paul to take some more details about the houses, and then they move over properly at the beginning of

March. I don't expect you'll see them, but if you do . . . it's all a long time ago, *jaddah*. Let it go. Otherwise Freya is going to start asking questions.'

'I'm just looking out for you, Hamad. You are a good boy.'

'I've not been a boy for a long time.'

She leant forward to touch her palm to his cheek. 'You're right, of course. Just be more careful in future, that's all I'm saying. You're not in Doha now. This is a city that plays by very different rules.'

It wasn't until they stepped into the alley that Freya felt as if she had actually arrived in Marrakech. The whitewashed rooms at Riad des Arts, sparsely furnished with modern art prints and stark, minimalist furniture, felt more like Paris than Morocco; the French radio that chattered quietly in the background and Jacqueline's Gallic elegance adding to the sense of dislocation. Only the call to prayer had reminded her, rising above the roof terrace where they had eaten breakfast: warm bread and crispy *msemen* accompanied by glazed saucers of home-made jam, and glasses of thick, sweet orange juice.

'Did you bring the map?' She swerved to avoid a pair of small boys, kicking a wizened football against the wall. 'Paul? We'll only get lost.'

'We don't need a map.' He lowered his sunglasses and grinned. 'I've become quite the local, found my way there and back yesterday. It's quite straightforward: left out of here, up to the main square, and then it's just a matter of finding the metalwork souk, and taking a right turn at the end.'

'Get you.' Freya slipped her hand into his. 'Making the town your own already.'

'Well, it's our town now, isn't it?' He stopped walking. 'Look, Frey, I know I didn't take to the idea quite as enthusiastically as you, but you were right – as always. It's an amazing opportunity, a real adventure. I know how much that means to you. I want us to . . .'

'*Attention. ATTENTION!*'

She pulled him towards her as a moped roared past, so close Freya felt the handlebar graze her hip. Paul stepped back, his foot knocking over a pile of walnuts spread out on a dirty white sheet. An old man, sitting cross-legged beside them, waved his arms and shouted something in Darija. Behind them, the sound of hooting rose above the chatter. A battered three-wheel truck was reversing out of an alley, a shopkeeper was shouting and gesticulating at the driver.

'This is one crazy city.'

'I know.' She laughed. 'Isn't it fabulous?' They walked on, more carefully, picking their way between wobbling cyclists and nervous-looking tourists poring over maps. 'At least I feel like we're properly here now. At Jacqueline's, we could be in Paris.'

Paul nodded. 'You'll like Dar Simone, it's much more traditional.'

'You've seen it?' Freya frowned at him. 'When? I thought we'd look at it together.'

'Oh. Sorry, it just sort of happened.' He rolled his eyes. 'Jacqueline had me trapped up on the roof terrace yesterday, telling me her life story. We got on to the subject of kids. She asked if we had any. I said no and then it all came out . . . They don't have children, she always wanted them, IVF – you can imagine. I didn't really know what to say, so I asked if I could see the house.'

Freya said nothing. Somehow, the subject of children always rendered her mute: an odd, dull panic that left her mind entirely empty. It wasn't even really about the miscarriage now, more about what had come after – the months of sleeping in the same bed like strangers, any sexual impulse neutered by the long hours on the oncology ward with Ali, the constant fear of what the next consultation would bring. They'd both agreed her going back on the pill was the most sensible thing while her sister was sick; she thought of the six fresh boxes, still in the paper bag from the pharmacy. It just seemed easier to keep on taking them.

'So we're going to meet Laila this morning?' She hoped he wouldn't register the change in subject.

'I think so.' He shook his head at a boy holding out strips of postcards. 'I've decided not to mind that Hamad appointed her without talking to me. She's worked on a couple of similar projects, apparently, and I need someone on the team who knows how things work out here. And I could do with a bit of background on the Farzis, and whatever deal Hamad did. I'm getting an increasing sense that there's more to it than a museum and a few million dirhams.'

'Edith said much the same thing,' said Freya, ducking underneath a row of kaftans. 'And after that scene at Mamounia . . .'

'I'm going to have to ask him.' He steered her gently into the metalwork souk. 'I need to know what I'm getting—'

'Morning, architect.'

She spun round to find Hamad behind them, his neatly tailored appearance at odds with the grubby piles of wrought iron and half-soldered lamps. 'Of all the cities in all the world . . .' She leant towards him for a kiss. 'How are you?'

'I'm good.' A high-pitched whirring roared out of one of the workshops; he cupped his mouth to shout above the din. 'You remember? *The Towering Inferno*? Sunday evenings at Davison Road, something film night – what was it you called it?'

Paul laughed. 'Cheesy.'

'That's right. Cheesy Film Night. Every Sunday evening, chicken chow mein and another terrible seventies movie.' Hamad pulled a set of keys from his pocket and slotted one into the rotting door. 'Ironic, really, that one of your favourite films is a disaster movie where the architect is, well, the cause of the disaster.'

'It wasn't Paul Newman's fault. That's the whole point. It was the pressure put on him by the developers, the money men.'

Freya followed them into the house. To her surprise there were voices coming from the courtyard; in the sunlight she could see the hooded figure of Yusuf, broom leant against the *sahridj*, talking to a young woman with a mass of dark curly hair.

'Yusuf.' Hamad strode up to them. '*Salaam alaikum*. You know Laila?'

'My uncle and Yusuf have known each other for many years,' said the woman. 'And of course we all know Dame Edith.' She said something to Yusuf in Darija, who nodded and let out an odd, rasping noise. It took a moment for Freya to realise he was laughing. 'I was reminding him of your grandmother's birthday party,' she said, smiling at Hamad. 'It was quite a night.'

'It was indeed. Now, can I introduce Paul, who you'll be working with, and Freya, his wife?'

'It's so lovely to meet you both.' She sounded young, Freya thought, but genuine. 'Hamad's told me so much about you. How amazing to have been friends for so many years.'

'Well, he does pay us handsomely.' Paul stepped forward to take her hand. Freya caught Hamad's eye. It had been a joke between them, in the early years: Paul's tendency to flirt with any attractive woman that crossed his path. Occasionally they'd tease him about it, mimicking the way he spoke and moved, chorusing the phrase he always came out with. *I wouldn't do it in front of you if it* meant *anything.* She'd accepted that for years, understood that it was born more from a sense of insecurity than any kind of ego trip. She'd always assumed one day he would grow out of it.

She felt a hand on her arm and looked up to see Yusuf peering at her from beneath the hood of his *djellaba*. '*Salaam alaikum*,' she said softly.

For a moment he didn't speak. Then, slowly, he raised his hand and wrapped his fingers around the peak of his hood, slipping it back onto his shoulders. '*Alaikum salaam*.' Freya felt the coarse skin of his palm on her arm; looked up to see a stubble-blurred face, jagged with wrinkles and sagging, sun-bleached skin. Unexpectedly, his face twitched into a smile, dark eyes cloaked by the crinkled folds of skin beneath his eyebrows. He began to speak, low and fast, the unrecognisable syllables fusing together.

'Laila?' Freya raised her eyebrows. 'Can you tell me what Yusuf is saying?'

'He says that you are welcome in these houses,' she said, smiling. 'He hopes you will find happiness here.'

'But they're not my houses.' She turned towards Yusuf, shook her head. 'Does he think I'm Racine? You must tell him they belong to her.'

She watched the old man as Laila spoke. His face fell; he snatched the hood back across his head, barking out words, his hand slicing through the air.

'He didn't like that much,' said Laila as Yusuf reached for his broom and shuffled away. 'He's convinced the houses belong to Freya. I told him you bought them for Racine, but it made him quite agitated. He's concerned about the jinns.'

'Jinns?' Paul frowned at Hamad. 'Who are the Jinns?'

'Don't worry about that now.' Hamad gestured towards a door in the far corner. 'Let the old man think what he wants, I don't want him upset. Come and see the office.'

'Why don't I make some coffee,' said Laila. 'Freya, will you have one?'

'I won't, thank you.' The incident with Yusuf had intrigued her; an odd, inexplicable connection. She wanted to be out in the city, to let the unfamiliar streets swallow her up. 'I'll leave you guys to it. I'm off to explore.'

Two hours later, Freya was buzzing with an unexpected sense of triumph. She had done it: found her way through the labyrinthine medina alone, batting away comments and bartering with vendors to buy a new leather satchel for Ali and a pair of chocolate-brown *babouches* for Simon. There had been moments; a shoe vendor had noticed her examining the sandals that hung from the walls of his cubbyhole and followed her along the alley calling *Hey, London, buy my shoes!* There'd been the odd whistle, too, a teenage boy who'd murmured compliments in such an intimate tone it felt like a moment between lovers rather than the words of a stranger. But none of it had been hostile, or threatening.

Now, sitting in a café sipping mint tea rich with sugar, she knew, without question, the decision to move to Marrakech was the right one. There'd been moments, back in London, when anxiety had begun to creep in: the surprise on the faces of some of her colleagues, the thought of leaving Ali for so long. She'd said nothing to Paul, aware that even the smallest show of ambivalence might provoke him into suggesting they forget the whole thing. She remained perplexed as to quite what he felt; at times his enthusiasm almost overwhelmed hers, at others she got the sense that the only reason he had agreed was because she wanted it so badly.

She glanced out over the square. Travelling was something she was good at; unfamiliar places stimulated rather than daunted her; she knew how to stay still, to let the newness wash over her. *Promise me you'll have adventures.* Paul knew why this meant so much, but it was still an amazing thing he'd done for her, upending his life, changing everything. Freya looked across at the craggy-faced Berber women, sitting on low stools beside piles of crocheted hats and thickly knitted scarves. She'd buy a hat for Paul; it would make him laugh.

In the wide open space of the Jemaa el Fna, the heat was blistering. A young woman waving a *Henna* sign tried to catch her arm; the orange-sellers shouted as she walked past. Out of the corner of her eye she could see the snake-charmers unrolling their mats; beyond them, a white-haired man sat behind a desk, a row of implements glinting in the sunshine. One of the water-sellers sprawled on a chair opposite; both had their heads tipped back, smoke twisting from their mouths. It reminded her of two off-duty actors sharing a break before their time on stage. She stopped to absorb the moment; to take a mental snapshot of the extraordinary city she was going to call home.

And then the Café Limonia exploded.

CHAPTER 7

'Are you OK? *Êtes-vous blessée? Madame?*'

Freya couldn't move. Acrid smoke was streaming from the upper windows of the café, the air was thick with shouting and the clattering of chairs and tables shoved aside as people ran from the building. Someone was speaking, but she couldn't think how to reply. Her mind was blank, wiped by the sense that she was caught up in something alien and unforeseen.

'You're bleeding.' A man was crouching beside her, peering at her knees. 'I think they're just surface scratches but you should get cleaned up, check there's no glass in there.'

Freya looked down. Her left kneecap was flecked with blood; a thin red line ran across the bottom of her right shin.

'It's nothing. We should help.' She raised her eyes as he stood up. *Tall*, she thought, and then wondered how she could notice something so trivial in the midst of such chaos.

'Oh, God.' She swallowed. 'I think I'm going to be sick.'

'Breathe. Take some deep, slow breaths.'

'Was it a bomb?'

'I don't think so. Different sound. More likely some sort of gas explosion. These cafés run on a wing and half a roll of gaffer tape. Any better?' Freya swayed slightly. 'You need to sit down. Are you

OK to walk?' She nodded; his arm locked around her shoulders. 'I'm Tim, by the way. Tim Matheson. You're going to be fine.'

She knew the name, but in the cloud of panic and adrenalin she couldn't think why. Her feet dragged a little as they walked. His body felt strange beside hers, his ribcage pressed into her side. Something in his physicality soothed her, a sense that he was unalarmed by what had occurred, knew how to navigate the situation. It was reassuring but unsettling; it made her feel something else, something she couldn't define.

'Here.' She realised they had reached the Café Aziz on the other side of the square. A sea of anxious faces looked beyond her towards the Limonia.

'Don't expect to get served.' A corpulent American at the next table rolled his eyes and tutted. 'They've all gone charging over there to see what's going on. Another lunatic extremist, I suppose. Probably gone to help celebrate.'

Tim pulled out a chair for Freya and turned to the man. 'Celebrate what, exactly?'

'Well, you know. More of us infidel hurt or maimed.'

'We don't know what's happened yet. And I suspect Mohammed and Ahmed have gone to try and help. Is this your bill?' He picked up the white slip of paper tucked under the ashtray.

'Hey.' The American looked concerned. 'Yes. Why?' His eyes widened as Tim tore at it, letting the shredded strips flutter across the table like confetti. 'What the hell are you doing?'

'Believe me, they won't want your money.'

'You're a nut.'

'Better that than an ignorant, prejudiced . . .' But the man was already out of earshot, his bulk wobbling through the chairs, shoulders hunched in indignation.

'Wow. You don't pull any punches, do you?'

'I just get sick of that kind of crap. Look, I have to go and see what's happening, but I'll be back in a few minutes. Just sit. Sit and breathe.'

She watched him walk across the square, his body merging into the figures outside the Limonia, muddied with smoke and the sound of sirens. Tim Matheson. *That* was why he was familiar: they had met before. Hamad's cousin. Edith's recently revealed second grandson.

'*Madame? Voulez-vous boire quelque chose?*'

'*Oui. Un café. Noir, s'il vous plaît.*'

The waiter nodded and disappeared. The nausea began to recede. She pulled out her phone; Paul's voice was flattened slightly by the recorded message. Her words got tangled as she spoke. A coffee appeared on the table, the scent warm and bitter in the air. She found Hamad's number on her phone. Another voicemail.

'Feeling better?'

He had appeared without a sound. She remembered him clearly now: the dark, slightly too long hair that fell into his eyes, the square-framed glasses that balanced up the angular chin.

'Yes. I'm fine. Thank you.' She sat up straighter. 'Don't feel you have to look after me. I'm staying a few minutes' walk away, I'll just drink this and head back. I'm sure the people over there need your help more than me.'

He raised his arm and signalled to the boy who had brought her coffee. 'Miraculously, they don't, really. It was a gas leak, but up on the top floor, and they only use that space for storage. There were a couple of people with some quite nasty burns, and a few with cuts and bruises, but no one seriously injured. The worst affected will be the owners. Their livelihood's gone for several weeks.' He pushed his glasses up his nose and peered at her. 'I know this sounds like a line, but have we met before?'

'We have, actually. In Cambridge. It was a dinner for Dame Edith's birthday. Years ago.'

'You're Hamad's friend.'

'Freya. Freya Hepworth. And you're the new grandson.' She put her hand to her mouth. 'I'm sorry. I don't know why I said that.'

'Because it's true?' He grinned. 'Don't worry, I've had some time to get used to the idea. I think Hamad's going to need a while longer, though.'

'He hasn't really talked about it.'

Tim took his coffee from the waiter and laughed. 'Never kid a kidder, Mrs Hepworth. I'm sure my esteemed cousin has had plenty to say.' He sat back in his chair, long limbs stretched out beneath the table. 'So you're the one writing Edith's autobiography? Which means it must be your husband who's getting his hands on the Farzi houses? That's quite a project.'

'It is. He's very excited about it, says the possibilities are incredible.'

'I'll bet they are. Sky's the limit in terms of budget, I'd imagine. Whatever else you say about Hamad, he's not afraid to spend his money.'

'You don't like him?'

'Let's just say he and I have history. I may have only recently found out I'm officially Edith's grandson, but I always felt like she was the grandmother I never had. We used to stay with her sometimes in the holidays. She was always living in exotic places – Sharjah one year, Amman the next. Often Hamad and his siblings would be there too.'

'I didn't think she was close with anyone else in his family?'

'She's not, really. I suspect Hamad's father saw it as a kind of duty visit. Once he died, I think his wife was quite happy to draw a veil over that part of the family's history. To not be one hundred per cent Qatari – that kind of thing still matters out there.'

'It doesn't matter to Hamad.'

'I know. It's one of the things I do respect about him. So, where are you staying?' Freya sensed the change of subject was deliberate.

'At the moment we're in the Riad des Arts.'

'Jacqueline's place?'

'God, everyone really does know everyone in this city, don't they? Once we're out here permanently we'll be renting her place next door, Dar Simone.' She became aware, suddenly, that he was asking all the questions. 'And you? You live out here?'

'Some of the time. I'm a foreign correspondent – well, a kind of hack of all trades these days. I should be based in Rabat, but it's hardly a city to love. Marrakech . . . It has something, you know? It's changed massively, of course, far too many expats and tourists for my liking. But they bring in money, so who am I to complain? Can't be one of those ghastly people who secretly wants the locals to remain the picturesque poor.' He said the last two words in a broad American accent, mimicking the tone of the man whose receipt he had ripped up. 'You won't let this put you off, will you? Marrakech is safe – I mean, I know it's crazy and hassley, but there's nothing to be afraid of.'

'I know.' Freya felt vaguely patronised. 'I was having a great time in the souks before that happened. It's a fascinating city. Kind of mystical.'

'I'm glad. Some people just can't handle it. They dismiss the medina as dirty or dangerous or downright medieval.' The accent again. 'Or worst of all, they don't really engage with it at all, and just live in some elite, expat bubble.'

'Well, that's not my plan. What's the point of moving abroad if you're just going to live as you do at home?'

'Quite.' Tim sipped his coffee. 'And how is she going to live, our French heiress? Shacked up with old Yusuf and a couple of hundred jinns.'

'What? Someone mentioned the jinns this morning. I thought they were another family.'

'Not quite. Jinns are . . . well, I suppose we would call them spirits. Not ghosts, though, jinns are something quite different. Moroccans believe – particularly older generations – that they live alongside us, in some sort of parallel dimension.'

'That sounds a bit sci-fi.' She smiled. 'And people really believe this?'

He raised an eyebrow. 'Very much so. It's not something that's easy to understand. Moroccans rarely talk about jinns – they take the supernatural very seriously. But you should be aware of it, particularly when it comes to the Farzi houses.'

'Why?' Freya felt vaguely alarmed. 'What's special about the Farzi houses?'

'Don't look so worried. It's just a myth that's grown up around them, a story Omar Farzi used to tell. He's always had quite an overblown sense of his own importance. In the last few years, in that area of the medina, there's been quite a lot of problems – subsidence, walls collapsing, sewage pipes rupturing. Locals believe it's the jinns, unhappy at the number of foreigners moving into the area. But nothing ever happened to any of the Farzi houses, even when the riad next door almost caved in entirely. The way Omar Farzi tells it, his grandfather made a deal with the jinns: as long as the houses stayed in the family, the spirits would leave them in peace. But if they ever sold the houses –' Tim shrugged – 'if they were sold to someone the jinns didn't approve of, well . . .'

'Well what?'

'It would incur their fury, I guess.'

'Which means . . . what, exactly?'

'Come on, Mrs Hepworth. You said you thought Marrakech was a mystical city – well, here's an example, right in your own life. Don't worry, you're not going to wake up one morning and find the houses have burned down. But beliefs like this should be respected, and if Yusuf says he can manage the jinns, your husband would do well to listen. Tell him not to be fooled by that doddery-old-man routine. He's sharp as a tack – and very Old Marrakech. Make friends with him, he's a man to have on your side.'

She felt exhausted suddenly, overwhelmed by the drama at the Limonia and the stream of information she was having to absorb.

Her phone vibrated. She looked down, disappointed not to see Paul's name. She gestured an apology to Tim.

'Hi. Yes, I'm fine . . . No, really. I'm at the Café Aziz with . . . No, I don't know, he's not answering his phone. There's no need . . . it'll be quicker to walk. Oh, OK then. See you in a minute.'

'Your husband?'

Freya shifted a little in her chair. 'Hamad. He's coming to pick me up.'

'Well, if His Highness is on his way, I might head back to the Limonia, see if I can get a quick chat with the owners.' She couldn't miss the sarcasm. 'Will you be OK, Mrs Hepworth?'

'I'll be fine. And you can call me Freya, you know.'

To her surprise, he blushed. 'I'm sorry. I've no idea why I'm doing that. Maybe I don't feel like I know you well enough. Yet.'

'Well, goodbye then, Mr Matheson.' She realised she was flirting. 'And thank you for rescuing me.'

'I don't think you needed much rescuing,' he said, smiling. 'Do say hello to Hamad for me. He'll be delighted to know we've met.'

CHAPTER 8

March 2010, Marrakech

They had done it. Freya set down her coffee cup and tipped her face towards the warmth of the early morning sun. Everything was different: the chorus of car doors and revving engines now replaced by the rattle of the luggage porters' trolleys in the alley below, and the dark-haired woman on the opposite rooftop hanging out washing while a small boy spun between her legs. Paul would be up in a minute; she warmed at the intimacy of how he had woken her. Something had changed since the explosion at the Limonia, as if the shock of what had happened had somehow dissipated the mist between them. When they got back to London he'd taken her for dinner high above the city, spinning tales of how their life in Marrakech would be. She had gazed out into the twinkling darkness, the curve of the river far below them, and realised how long it was since she had truly felt happy.

He'd taken charge of the moving process – arranged the shipping, the overseas bank accounts, even a surprise leaving party two nights before they left. And now, a week after the move, his enthusiasm remained unwavering, even with the unpacked boxes and the infinite and complex paperwork that seemed to accompany everything from utility bills to residency permits. In the evenings, Jacqueline took them to soirées at friends' riads where they were introduced to artists and interior designers, all of whom seemed fascinated by their friendship with Hamad, and the gossip surrounding his purchase of the Farzi houses.

Tonight, they had agreed to avoid Jacqueline's latest invitation. Freya decided to make their excuses now; she pushed open the gate that led to the neighbouring terrace and peered over the balcony. The house was silent. Just as she was about to move, a door opened on the floor below. The young night porter stepped into the light, paused for a moment and turned to pull a woman into a lingering embrace. Freya gaped. Two nights ago she and Paul had eaten dinner with Jacqueline and her erudite, quietly spoken husband. She had thought how fond of each other they had seemed, noting the good-humoured way Alain let his wife tease him about his dry life as an academic.

A squawk shattered the silence; she moved quickly back through the gate. Above her, a stork flapped down to land on the crumbling ramparts of the Badii Palace.

'I bet you see everything, don't you?' A second bird glided in, landing effortlessly beside the first.

'Who are you talking to?' She turned to see Paul, his hair a little mussed up from the shower.

'The storks, of course.'

'You're bonkers.' He kissed her and glanced at the empty table. 'Weren't you making breakfast?'

'Sorry. I got distracted. I went to tell Jacqueline we wouldn't be going tonight and . . .' She pulled him closer. 'She's only sleeping with the night porter.'

'Really?' He raised his eyebrows. 'How do you know?'

'I saw them. He was coming out of her room. Let's just say I don't think they'd been discussing room reservations.' She frowned. 'And after that long speech she gave me about – what did she call it? *Un arrangement agréable*, Alain being in Paris in term-time – I genuinely thought they were happy.'

'Perhaps they are.' Paul reached for her coffee cup. 'Who knows what it takes to make a marriage work after thirty years, or however long they've been together? If getting a frisk on with the night porter gives her something that's missing from their relationship, who's to say it's a bad thing?'

'Is that really what you think? That affairs are OK? Inevitable?'

'Don't be daft, of course that's not what I'm saying. But you know what the French are like, infidelity's practically a national sport. And if Alain doesn't know . . .'

'What, that would make it OK?' She nudged him affectionately. 'Are you trying to tell me something?'

'About what – me having an affair?' He rolled his eyes 'Bloody hell, we've just moved countries, how would that work? Who do I know in this city apart from you? And where would I find the time?'

'All right, all right.' Things felt fragile suddenly; it shocked her to realise how quickly the warmth could dissipate. 'I was only joking.'

'Glad to hear it. Look, I don't have time for breakfast now . . .' He paused; Freya could almost see the effort it took to soften his tone. 'I'll cook tonight, shall I? Treat us to something that isn't tagine?'

He brushed his face against hers and disappeared off the rooftop. Moments later the front door banged shut. She swept her hair back from her face and pulled it slightly so her scalp tingled. It was just a minor flare-up – the first since they had been back in Marrakech, but that didn't mean anything. She scooped up the coffee cup and glanced over to the other terrace, where the first couples had surfaced for breakfast. It really didn't mean anything at all.

'Freya. Good Lord, you look like a grease spot on linen. Don't tell me you walked here?'

'I did,' said Freya, sinking gratefully into a wide armchair. 'It seemed like a good idea at the time.'

'My dear,' said Dame Edith, wagging a finger so that the bangles on her wrist rang like cowbells. 'Only mad dogs and Englishmen go out in the midday sun. Not Englishwomen. They don't make up these sayings for nothing, you know. I applaud your . . . *courage*, but really. *C'est fou.*'

Freya couldn't help feeling that if anyone looked a little *fou*, it was Dame Edith. Her silver hair was wound into two long plaits, twisting down onto a linen poncho covered in scarlet and cream swirls. It gave her the appearance of a Native American squaw.

'I won't do it again.' She decided not to mention the two wrong turns, the bemused gendarme. 'But that's what this is all about, isn't it? Learning all the time.'

'Indeed,' said Edith. 'I applaud that kind of attitude. So much so that I've asked a dear friend to join us for lunch. I thought about what you were saying last time we met, that you're only meeting French people, other expats. Frankly, if you rely on Jacqueline you may not meet anyone Moroccan for your entire stay. You need – want – someone to show you something more authentic, I think? And there is no one better than Mustapha Chenouf.'

'That sounds wonderful,' said Freya, relieved to find she was finally cooling down.

Edith held up a hand to show no acknowledgement was necessary. 'Few people know Marrakech like he does. He's been a tour guide for over thirty years, walked the streets with everyone from . . .' She frowned suddenly, looked out across the empty bar. 'Well, I'll leave him to tell you actual names. These days his son, Madani, does most of the guiding. Mustapha has a beautiful hotel, the Riad Jasmina. Doubtless he'll invite you to visit his roof terrace. Do say yes. The gin and tonics are the best in the city, and he does love an audience for his stories.'

A buzzing cut through the fragranced air. Dame Edith peered at her phone. 'Ah. A shame.' She glanced at Freya. 'I had asked my grandson, Timothy, to join us, but he's off on some story or other. You met him, I believe? When there was all that nonsense at the Limonia?'

'I did.'

'But you didn't mention it last time we met? I felt quite the fool, telling him all about you, only to learn that he'd already made your acquaintance.'

'I'm sorry. I didn't feel . . .' Freya tailed off, frustrated with herself. Something about the whole incident felt awkward, and there was clearly a backstory with Tim's family and Edith she didn't fully understand. She had feared that mentioning him in the wrong way, or at the wrong moment, might be unhelpful in the relationship she was trying to build with the older woman. It was tricky enough.

'Didn't feel what?' Edith tutted. 'This is Hamad, isn't it, making you feel it's some grubby little secret. Honestly, I would have hoped he'd have got over it by now. That boy needs to realise the world doesn't revolve around him. Well, there's nothing to feel awkward about. The facts are simple. Timothy's mother – Anne – is my daughter. She was adopted at birth by Timothy's grandfather and his wife. Nothing more complicated than that.'

'But you stayed in touch with the family?'

'Of course. I was the child's godmother. I insisted on that, and Robert . . .'

There was a pause. After a moment, Freya realised the older woman was struggling to hold back tears. 'Dame Edith? Are you all right?'

'Of course.' She pulled a tissue from the sleeve of her poncho and pressed it briefly to eyes. 'He was the love of my life, you see. Robert Jenner. Timothy's grandfather.'

'So the child, Anne . . .'

'Was his and mine, yes. I was nineteen, living in Cairo, with my parents. My father was an Arabist, an academic. He'd been part of Lawrence's gang for a brief time – in a scholarly way of course. He didn't go around blowing up trains. He was a captain in the British Army.'

'Your father?'

'Don't be so ridiculous. *Robert Jenner*.' She frowned. 'You are listening?'

'Very much so, Dame Edith.'

The older woman ran her fingers down her plaits and let her head fall back against the cushions. 'I knew he was married, but I didn't care. The war was raging, no one knew what the next day would bring, let alone the next month, or year. There was something liberating about it. War makes you reckless, even a little nihilistic. Both of us were looking for an escape – him from the discipline of army life, from a distant, unhappy marriage, me from a stultifying colonial existence. And he . . . he was a lion of a man. I adored him.'

'You were very young.'

Edith nodded. 'But hardly your average nineteen-year-old. We were one of the first white families to settle in Bahrain – a childhood like that prepares you for anything. All the well-spoken, wishy-washy boys I was introduced to . . .' She shook her head. 'I wanted an all-consuming, overwhelming love. And I found it. With Robert. But of course, before long the inevitable happened. I fell pregnant.'

Freya listened while Edith talked without emotion of the decisions made on her behalf: the long journey to Switzerland, the last, lonely weeks of pregnancy, the moment the warm, wet body was taken from her arms. 'It was what happened in that era. Robert's wife appeared with her sister and took the baby three days after she was born. She was such a . . . small woman. She thought she'd won, but when I got back to Cairo I insisted to Robert that he made me godmother.'

'And he agreed? Didn't his wife mind?'

'It was a fair request,' said Edith quietly. 'And he was a fair man. I promised the truth would never come out, and I kept to that even after his wife died, even after we became close, again. But when he passed away certain papers came to light, certain letters, that told a different story to the one Tim had always believed to be the truth. He came to me and I saw no reason to keep the secret any longer.'

Freya shifted awkwardly in her chair. 'That must have been very difficult for him.'

'Yes. Although he did say he'd always thought that his grandfather and I were very close. He wasn't wrong in that.'

'And your daughter? Anne? Have you seen her? Does she know?'

Edith shook her head. 'She's not well. Some sort of cancer, I think. She and I are both old women now, why rewrite the histories we have carried throughout our lives? Timothy tells me that Anne adored her mother and finding this out would cause her considerable distress. Truth is overrated, Freya. I would have taken it to my grave if those letters had never been found.'

'You don't want her to know?'

'It's an odd thing,' said Edith slowly. 'Almost as if my genes skipped a generation – I recognise myself more in Timothy than I ever did in Anne. Being his grandmother is who I am. But being Anne's mother? I'm not sure I was ever really that.'

'Dame Edith?' Freya jumped; the waiter had appeared without a sound. 'Monsieur Chenouf is in reception.'

'Excellent. Freya, perhaps you could go ahead and meet him on the terrace? I just need a moment. Too much nostalgia on an empty stomach is never a good thing.'

She knew, before the introduction was made, that the old man sitting alone would be Mustapha Chenouf. He turned at the sound of their footsteps; a scattering of silver hair beneath an embroidered *kufi*, a short, stout body cloaked in a cream *djellaba,* striped with faint blue lines.

'Freya? *Enchanté.*' His lined, weathered face broke into a smile; she felt the scratch of his beard against her cheek. 'It's wonderful to meet you.' He peered behind her. 'But where is Edie? Not unwell, I hope?'

'She just needed a moment.' There was something soothing in the elderly man's presence. 'We'd been talking . . . I think perhaps she was a little upset.'

'Robert Jenner?'

'Yes.'

'Ah.' Mustapha nodded at the waiter to pour water and tightened his fingers together in his lap. 'This is difficult for Edith. And all this with Tim . . .' He shook his head. 'The past is a different country. Once left, it is rarely wise to return.'

'You think the book is a bad idea?'

'I'm afraid I do.' He smiled at her. 'I'm sorry, Freya. I know it is your project. And Edith has had a very long, very unusual life. But the truth is that not all of it will benefit from being exhumed.'

'The last thing I'd want to do is cause her any distress. But Hamad thought . . .'

'Ah, Hamad. The one person she can never refuse. She has spent her life indulging that boy.'

'I think he thought she wanted to do it. I know he feels it's important that her achievements are not forgotten. He adores her.'

Mustapha stroked his beard with his thumb and forefinger. 'Yes. And he may genuinely believe that he is helping her achieve something she wants. The problem is that Edith doesn't always know what she wants, not any more. And she certainly doesn't know what's best for her.' He lifted the *kufi* from his head and tucked it on his lap; without it he looked older, a little more worn. Unexpectedly he leant forward and laid a hand on Freya's arm. 'Forgive me.'

'For what?'

'Perhaps we should start again. When it comes to Edith I get a little . . . strong sometimes. And I have been so looking forward to meeting you. I know she enjoys your conversations. It's so good to see something stimulate her. Such a mind, to see it start to fade . . . She has been better since you've been here, Freya. I'm grateful for that.'

'She's a fascinating woman. I read all her books at university. This is just the most amazing opportunity for me, but I'd hate to think . . .'

Mustapha raised his hand and twisted it back and forth in the sunlight. 'Ignore the musings of an old man. We move on. I want to hear about you. How is it that you find yourself here? Such a big change. For your husband too, I think?'

'Yes.' She remembered suddenly the rush of irritation on the balcony. 'He's working on the Farzi houses, as I'm sure you know. It's an amazing project, although I'm not sure Paul quite knew what he was taking on when he said yes.'

'They need a lot of work?'

'Yes. But that's not the problem. It's more . . . I don't know, it feels like there's so much gossip about how Hamad came to buy the Farzi houses. Sometimes I'm not quite sure what we've walked into.'

'A feeling you will become accustomed to if you live in this city,' he said, smiling. 'But you mustn't listen to gossip, Freya. I'm sure Edith has already warned you that this is a city that runs on stories – both true and false.'

'Do you know what went on?'

Mustapha stroked his beard with his thumb and forefinger. 'I know a little. And it's true that some of Hamad's decisions—'

'What about Hamad's decisions?' Edith unlinked her arm from the waiter at her side and sank gratefully into a chair. Mustapha leant across to kiss her; there was a gentleness to it, an intimacy that left Freya feeling almost embarrassed. 'I hope you're not gossiping, Mustie. It's a terribly unattractive habit.'

'Freya and I have just been getting to know each other, *habibi*.'

'How long have you two been friends?' asked Freya.

'Oh, centuries,' said Edith.

'We met in Algiers, almost fifty years ago,' said Mustapha, winking at Freya. 'I was the concierge in a hotel there. I had become friendly with Farouk – Edith's husband. He introduced us.'

'And Farouk was . . .' Freya tried to work it out. 'Hamad's grandfather?'

Edith nodded. 'He was a great friend to me, during the Cairo days. And we stayed friends after our divorce. It wasn't a long marriage, but it came at the right time in my life.'

'Come now, Edie.' There was a note of caution in Mustapha's voice. 'Freya tells me you've already taken one long promenade into your memories this morning. Let us not start another.'

'He's like an old mother hen,' Edith said to Freya, shaking her head. 'Worried I might say the wrong thing, or get confused. He thinks I'm going doolally, don't you, *mon vieil ami*?' An expression passed across her face; a dark, brief anger. 'And of course he's right. This bloody fog. But that's why I have you, isn't it? So everything will be written down, so that I don't have to rely on a mind that's slowly packing up.'

To Freya's relief a cluster of waiters appeared and a dozen small bowls were laid on the table, purple beetroot, cubes of liver, slices of carrot thick with honey and sesame seeds. She watched as Mustapha spooned a little of each onto Edith's plate and then did the same with hers. For a moment she felt like a small child, eating grown-up lunch with her parents. It wasn't an unpleasant feeling.

'Farouk was a wonderful man,' said Edith, apropos of nothing. 'He . . . well, he saved me, you see.'

Mustapha raised his eyebrows at Freya. 'Why don't you tell us of the plans for the Farzi houses?'

'Because *I* am talking,' said Edith sharply. 'Have you ever felt real heartbreak, Freya? I was devastated. Lost the love of my life, lost my child. And Farouk had long made plain his feelings for me. It helped, to be with someone, and of course it gave my parents and their crowd something new to talk about. Such a ghastly, small-minded group of people. In a way it was a relief to leave all that, to escape to Farouk's village.'

'I really think you've talked enough,' Mustapha's voice was firm. 'Freya, I'm sure you understand that Edith tires easily.'

'Just *stop*. That's what she's here for, isn't it? To hear it? All of it? Stop being such an old woman, Mustie. It's ancient history now. No one cares.'

'There are people who will care. Who will care very much.'

'I really did love Farouk,' said Edith, closing her eyes. 'It was different to Robert, but it *was* love. Cairo was . . . difficult, for both of us, so we went back to Arabia, to his family. We had to, after what happened. And Farouk had been away so long, it was quite feasible the child was ours.'

'Child?'

'*Habibi* . . .'

Edith's eyes snapped open. 'Our son. Abdullah. Hamad's father.'

Freya frowned. 'But why would anyone think he wasn't yours?'

'What?'

'You just said *it was quite feasible the child was ours*. As if people might have thought he wasn't?'

'Of course Abdullah was ours. What are you suggesting?' She stared at Freya, her face set and angry.

'She's not suggesting anything.' Mustapha leant back and gestured to the waiter loitering in a nearby pool of shade. 'Edie, I'm going to insist we bring this to a close. You need a rest and Freya and I will be very happy to lunch *à deux*. I'll have an omelette sent up. No.' He raised his palm; to Freya's surprise, Edith allowed the waiter to slip a hand under her elbow and gently lever her to her feet. 'You always do this. You push yourself and then you wonder why you're shattered.'

'Will you excuse an old woman?' Edith smiled ruefully at Freya. 'He may be a terrible fusspot, but I'm afraid he is right.'

'Of course.' Freya stood. 'I'm sorry if—'

'Tshh.' Edith waved her hand dismissively. 'Can't bear apologies. Just doing your job.'

Freya watched her hobble across the restaurant. 'I'm so sorry, Mustapha. I didn't mean to upset her. It's just hard to know . . .'

'It's not your fault,' he said kindly. 'But you have to understand, if this book is published, people are going to get hurt. And no one more than Edith.'

CHAPTER 9

Paul locked the door behind him and stood for a moment in the dusk. It was the time of day he liked best, when the sun finally slipped below the horizon and the pace of the city dipped. It was only a brief hiatus; a few quiet minutes when the street vendors sank back on their stools to drink *thé marocain* and retreat behind the pages of *Assabah*, while tourists were cocooned in their riads, showering off the grime of the city. In half an hour the tidal darkness would sweep through the medina's archways, bringing clutches of workers to queue at snack stalls and loiter around strip-lit cafés, watching the night's football game. It felt like an alien world then; chaotic and oddly threatening.

He wouldn't have admitted it, but the weeks since they had arrived in Marrakech had been the most challenging of his life. The scale of the work on the Farzi houses was daunting and Hamad's tendency to try to micro-manage, even from Doha, only added to the pressure. Freya, happier than she had been for a long time, seemed to be building a life in the city that had little in common with his, filled with people he barely knew – Mustapha, his son Madani, the woman across the street from them, whose small son clattered about on the roof terrace early in the mornings. Apparently she had started teaching her English. Paul didn't even know her name.

But all of that would be manageable if it wasn't for Racine. He had barely seen her since they had moved to the city, yet she invaded his thoughts whenever his mind fell quiet. It still shamed him to remember where he had been when the Limonia exploded; sitting in the Frenchwoman's villa, drinking wine, plans unrolled on the table behind the sofa. Even though there had been nothing inappropriate about the meeting – Laila sat in the armchair opposite Racine, taking notes as she spoke – his thoughts told a different story.

Later, when Freya was asleep, he had gone up to the roof terrace, made a promise to himself. He had never considered himself a weak man, but Racine exuded something unfamiliar and intangible that he found almost impossible to resist. The answer was simple; they must never be alone together. He would see her only when absolutely necessary, and always with someone else present. Slowly he would reinvent her as nothing more than a client. The memory of that one wild sexual interlude would eventually fade.

He glanced down at his phone: *We need to talk. Tonight? Half seven, Mogador Palace? R x.* It had arrived in the middle of a meeting with Massoud, the foreman; he'd lost the thread of what Laila was translating, typed a response before he could think what it meant. And now, when he should be walking home, he was threading his way through the crowds on the Jemaa el Fna, wilfully breaking the resolve he'd sworn to keep. As he reached the hotel, he stopped for a moment to gather his thoughts. On the road behind a limousine slowed unexpectedly; a cacophony of horns rose into the dusk. He didn't turn; didn't see the elderly woman raise her hand from behind the window. Instead he stepped into the lobby, telling himself he would stay for just one drink. Then he would go home. Home to Freya.

'Am I late?'

Racine stood, her slim body encased in a sharply tailored cream dress that tapered into her waist, accentuating the curve of her hips. He shivered as her lips dusted his cheek.

'I was early.' She gestured to the seat opposite; he sat, clumsily.

'Didn't trust you to choose the wine. Went for a Chablis.' She lifted the bottle from the cooler. 'It's rather good, actually.'

He lifted the glass; the liquid was cool on his tongue. 'You're right, it is good.' The blood was pulsing in his wrists. 'I was surprised to get your text.'

'Perhaps it was my turn to summon you.'

'Fair enough.'

'I wanted to talk.' There was a pause. 'I had an idea. About the houses.'

'Of course.'

She leant towards him; he could see a sliver of black lace beneath the neckline of her dress. 'I've had an idea. If Hamad can open this museum, then I'm going to open a . . .' She paused, sat back for a moment. 'A wine bar. Well, not so much a bar, more of a *maison du vin*. We'll hold masterclasses, tastings, have the best cellar in town. There's nothing like it in the city.'

He tried to focus on what she was saying. 'A wine bar? In the medina? You do like a challenge, don't you? Are you sure it mightn't be better somewhere in the Ville Nouvelle?'

'But my houses aren't in the Ville Nouvelle. Anyway, Hamad will sort out the . . . What's the English expression? Red tape? He and his coterie are practically bankrolling this country at the moment. If that doesn't buy you the right to bend a few rules . . .'

'I didn't think that was Hamad's style.'

She smiled. 'This is Morocco, Paul. When in Morocco . . .'

'Do as the Romans do?'

'Something like that.'

He tried to think what to say. She wrong-footed him like no other woman he had ever known; he found it impossible to predict what she would do or say next.

'Paul, do you ever wonder why I slept with you in Lyon?'

'Constantly.' He felt ludicrously pleased to see her laugh.

'I'm serious. To betray one's lover is bad enough, but with his best friend?'

'I'm not proud of it either.'

'When we last talked, I told you that I knew you thought Hamad and I were going to separate, that you'd never see me again. The truth is I thought the same thing. I knew how hurt he was by my decision to move to Morocco – although of course, being Hamad, he never said anything. But life in Doha was not what I had hoped. I found it claustrophobic. Behind all that exoticism, Hamad is a very proper man. I suppose I imagined that once I was living in Marrakech, the relationship would gently start to fade – the time between visits getting longer, life taking over.'

'You underestimated him.'

'Yes. When he announced his plan for New Year, I was so *angry* – how dare he talk to my employer behind my back? Make decisions for me? I was going to tell him in Doha, but then suddenly you and Freya were there, and then the whole thing with the houses . . . it just became impossible.'

'So you're with him out of what? Guilt?'

She shook her head. 'It's not that simple. He surprised me. I mean *really* surprised me. I thought I knew Hamad, but I then find he's capable of generosity, of thoughtfulness on a scale I've never known. To buy those houses for me it was the most incredible gesture. I thought perhaps I had judged him wrongly, that there could be a future for us. But a long-distance relationship . . .' She ran her finger around the rim of her glass. 'It is not an easy choice. All of the downsides of being with someone, with few of the benefits.'

'Look, Racine, if you're . . . if you've brought me here to . . . I mean, I'm incredibly flattered but . . . Freya's here. I love my wife.'

To his surprise she burst out laughing. 'Oh, Paul. The arrogance of men. You think I brought you here to seduce you?'

He blushed. 'Clearly not.'

'It isn't possible that I genuinely just wanted to talk about the houses? I want them to be beautiful, Paul, really unique. We need to get over what happened, to be able to meet and discuss things, to really keep a dialogue going.'

'Architect and client?' Paul raised his eyebrows. She laughed.

'Exactly.'

'You're right, of course. It's important that I understand what you want.' She held his gaze unexpectedly; he felt his stomach flip, poured more wine into both glasses. 'So tell me about this *maison du vin* idea. It sounds interesting.'

He tried to concentrate on what she was saying, but instead he found himself watching her lips, tracing the long, slim contour of her neck, the curve of her hip against the bar stool. A memory surfaced; the intense, dizzying pleasure of feeling himself inside her, the candlelit room in Lyon, a sense of having stepped outside himself, just for a few lost hours.

'Another bottle?'

He looked up at the waiter, his mind blurred by the intensity of his thoughts. 'I don't think . . .'

'Perhaps just a glass?' Racine smiled; laid a hand on his knee.

'A glass, then.'

By the time they rose to go, Paul couldn't remember why the meeting had ever seemed a bad idea. Racine wobbled slightly as she stood; it seemed natural to slip an arm around her shoulders, to feel her fingers on his waist. Some indefinable chemistry was knitting them together; there was an inevitability, a known end point. They walked mutely into the medina, turned into a silent alleyway, dark save for one pool of light, thrown down onto the street from a room above.

'You make me feel alive.'

He pushed her towards the wall; her lips were soft and warm, his hands under her shirt, her body pressed against his. The sense of release was dizzying; he felt as if he were soaring, lifted up out of the minutiae of his life, that nothing else mattered; there was no one else in the world, just her.

'Are you sure you won't come with us?'

Paul tried to focus on what Freya was saying. It was four days since he had stumbled away from Racine, his mouth wet with the taste of her. It had taken everything he possessed to pull away; the alley had echoed to the sound of her voice, but he hadn't turned around. He'd expected – wanted – to feel relief at having stopped things from escalating; instead he found himself constantly imagining what might have been, reliving the sensation of her hands on his skin. It was like battling an addiction; a constant, relentless fight.

'I'm sorry, Frey, I'm just really knackered.'

'But I'd like you to meet Madani. He's such a nice man and he knows Marrakech like the back of his hand. It's amazing to see it through his eyes – it's a totally different city to Jacqueline's expat world. Come on, it'll do you good.'

Paul flexed his fingers until the veins stood out above the tendons; it wasn't *fair* to find Freya irritating, just because she wasn't Racine. 'I'm sure he's charming, and I will meet him another time. I'm not sure why you're being so sniffy about Jacqueline's expat world, as you call it. I happen to think they're mostly nice people. And why is her version of Marrakech any less valid?'

'Because it just is. You know what I mean.' She rolled her eyes. 'When we're with them we might as well be in Paris or Marseilles. When I'm with Madani it's so different. Yesterday afternoon we sat in this tiny square up in the north of the medina. There was a food stall, a real hole-in-the-wall place; just one ancient guy bent over a rusty deep-fat fryer. When I asked Madani what he was cooking he told me: sheep's feet. So I drank mint tea while he ate sheep's feet and there were old men playing *felli* and backgammon, and then the muezzin called and there was no one English there, no other women. I felt like I'd stepped into a different world. Don't you want to see that, experience it? Isn't that we came for?'

'Of course it is, and it's brilliant that you're having all these experiences, Frey. It's just that my days are quite different; when you've spent three hours stuck in a sweltering planning office, the last thing you feel like doing is—'

A phone buzzed; Freya snatched it up. 'Oh. Jacqueline's coming too, apparently. With Racine.'

'Really?' Paul swallowed back what he had been about to say. 'All right then, I'll come.'

'Great.' Her phone buzzed again. 'They're downstairs. I'll go and let them in.'

'Fine.' He felt a stab of irritation as she crossed the room; there was a bruise on her leg, the back of her dress was creased. It struck him that she moved inelegantly, almost like a man.

He stood for a moment, looking through the clothes in his wardrobe. He'd moved to a different city, left behind his friends, his job, all the routines he had built up over the years. How could she accuse him of not wanting to experience anything new? He pulled a linen shirt from the hanger and imagined Racine's long, varnished nails slowly undoing each button. There was no harm in having dinner with her. They'd probably barely speak, but at least he could see her; watch the way she moved, maybe brush against her skin. It would be something. The memory of the kiss filled his mind. It had to be enough.

Freya looked across at Paul and felt her face colour with embarrassment. The food on his plate lay barely touched; the tip of one sausage sliced away, a small chunk of fish missing from the silver-skinned flesh. From the moment he had set foot outside the door he'd been odd, his conversation with Madani stiffly polite. Thank God the others had come; he had spent most of the evening talking to Jacqueline, allowing her to be submerged in the cacophony that rose up from the square; the pulse of the drumming and the shouts of the storytellers, the sudden rip of flames from the grills.

'You're not eating, Paul?' She looked across as Racine leant in to take a piece of fish; she looked out of place among the backpackers and the middle-aged tourists, like an emissary from the glitziest quarter of the Ville Nouvelle. 'Too adventurous for you? You would always rather eat at home? Stay with what you know?'

'Not at all.' He held her gaze. 'I'm just not hungry.'

'Perhaps.' Racine smiled. 'Or perhaps you don't have the stomach for something different, something with a little . . . risk?'

'I just think the risk has to be worth it.' He put his arm around Freya's shoulders and pulled her towards him, kissing her cheek. 'God, I'd love a beer.'

'We'll go for a proper drink afterwards,' said Jacqueline. 'I'll take you to La Scandale. You haven't been there yet, *non*? It's fun. Nothing else like it in the city. And it will definitely take your mind off your stomach, eh, Racine?'

Before Freya could decipher the meaning behind Jacqueline's words, she noticed a slim, tall man settle onto a seat at the counter, lean forward to shake hands with the man in the stained apron. The muscles around her spine contracted; a spasm of recognition, even though it was weeks since they had sat together at the Café Aziz. She watched him light a cigarette, laughing at something the cook was saying. Almost without realising what she was doing, she shrugged off Paul's arm, pushed her chair back and wove through the tables towards him.

'Hello, Tim.'

He turned; plates clattered on the counter, the stool creaked beneath his weight. 'Mrs Hepworth. We meet again. How are you?'

'I'm really good. I thought it was you and, well, it is you.' She took a breath, tried to slow her words. 'I was only talking about you the other day.'

'So I've heard.' He grinned. 'Edith is a terrible gossip, I know all about your meetings. She's very pleased with you, though.'

'I'm glad. She's quite a woman.'

'Indeed she is.' She remembered the intensity of his gaze, the way it made her feel slightly awkward, almost gawky. 'So, how long have you been here now?'

'Almost a month. I can't believe it's been that long already.'

'Marrakech clearly agrees with you.'

'It does. I feel like I'm really getting to know it. Edith's introduced me to Mustapha and Madani – he's teaching me about the city. He's over there actually –' she pointed – 'with my husband and . . .'

'That's Jacqueline, isn't it?'

'And Racine.'

'Of course. The divine Ms Delacroix. I met her briefly at Edith's party. I'd love to say hello. Can I join you?'

'Of course.' Something began to unroll in Freya's stomach as she watched Tim pick up his glass and walk towards the table. Madani rose to clap an arm around his shoulders, nodding at Freya in mute thanks for finding him an ally.

'You two know each other?' She smiled at Tim.

'A journalist knows everyone, *vraiment*?' Madani grinned and gestured around the table. 'Jacqueline, of course. And this is Paul, Freya's husband. And Racine Delacroix.'

'We've met before.' Tim raised his hand. 'Although not since you've become mistress of the Farzi houses. How does it feel to be the most talked about woman in Marrakech?'

Racine laughed. 'Am I really that?' Freya got the sense she didn't find it an unpleasant thought. 'Wait till they know what we're planning to do with the houses – eh, Paul? That will really give them something to talk about.'

'Indeed it will.' Paul leant forward to shake Tim's hand. 'I need to thank you for being so kind to Freya when the Limonia went up. I'm very grateful.'

'It was nothing.' Tim winked at Freya. 'I'm just glad I was there. So you're the architect? What a coincidence, bumping into all of you – I was only talking about those houses this afternoon.'

'Really?' Racine tipped her head to one side and considered him. 'What were you saying?'

'I was more doing the listening,' said Tim, spearing a sausage. 'How are you finding it, Paul? Quite different to England, I'd imagine. A lot less planning regs, but then I don't expect you have to deal with evil spirits lurking in the bathroom when you're doing a conversion in Penge.'

Freya giggled. 'You were right about the jinns. Paul says Yusuf's always going on about them, leaving food out, saying how dissatisfied they are with the plans for the houses.'

'I'd think a few disgruntled jinns would be the least of your problems.' said Tim.

Paul raised his eyebrows. 'What do you mean?'

'I heard about what happened at La Mamounia. Hassan Azoulay trying to start a fight with Hamad? Not that I'm surprised. For a foreigner to get involved, to take sides between the Farzis and the Azoulays? I can only think Hamad didn't understand what he was doing.'

'Hang on.' Paul raised his hand. 'Who are the Azoulays?'

'You don't know?'

'Clearly.'

'I'm sorry . . . You're the lead architect on this project and you don't know how Hamad came by those houses?'

'He did not *come by them*.' Racine glared at Tim. 'He paid for them. As one usually buys houses.'

'He said he'd had to agree to some conditions,' said Paul, 'but I presumed he meant the museum. He never said anything about any other . . .'

'Then you need to ask him. Ask him about the Azoulays, about their land in the Ourika valley. About how Omar Farzi has finally managed to get his hands on that land, about how it's broken the old man's heart. Talk to Yusuf. He knows.'

'Hamad wouldn't do anything illegal. I know you and he have issues, but we've been friends a long time. I trust him.'

'But this is business, not friendship,' said Tim. 'And Marrakech is a very different city to London. Whether something is legal or not – that's not always the most important factor. Ask Hamad about the Azoulays. It's something he should have told you.'

'Then why don't you tell us?'

'Because they're not my houses, and it's not my story. I shouldn't have said anything, I just assumed . . .' He glanced at his watch and stood up. 'I have to meet a friend, I'm sorry.' He smiled. 'Mrs Hepworth, it's been delightful to see you again. Madani, give my best to your father. Jacqueline, Racine.' He paused. 'Paul.'

'Jean-Charles and Sabine are having a house party next week,' said Racine suddenly. 'He said I should invite anyone who might be *sympathique*. We should all go.'

'Not my scene,' said Tim, picking up his cigarettes. 'I don't think I qualify as *sympathique*.' He gestured towards Paul and Freya. 'Just make sure they know what they're in for.'

Freya watched him weave his way through the tables and out into the square. 'What does he mean by that?'

'Oh, nothing,' said Racine airily. 'Absolutely nothing at all.'

CHAPTER 10

Even several days later, Freya still couldn't quite work out how the argument in the taxi had begun. The bar Jacqueline had insisted on taking them to after the dinner in the square had turned out to be a crimson-walled den in the Ville Nouvelle, where burlesque dancers shimmied on stage and the entire audience appeared to be either French or German. She and Paul had left after one drink, her disappointment with the evening sparking a row that was the worst since they'd come to Marrakech. Each accused the other of flirting, he with Jacqueline, her with Tim. Things had been uncomfortably formal between them ever since; it was one of the reasons she had agreed to the invitation to Villa Merteuil, hoping it would prove a distraction, something to change their mood.

The car jolted suddenly; she glanced across at Jacqueline. 'How do you know Jean-Charles and Sabine?'

'I knew them in Paris. Jean-Charles was in banking and Sabine is an artist. Performance, mainly. Avant-garde in style, quite risqué. I remember one performance.' She smiled, shook her head. 'She'd chained herself to a lamp post on stage and spent an hour alternately shouting suffragette slogans and barking like a dog. Something about the perceptions of women in society. It was always that sort of thing with Sabine.' She leant forward and tapped Paul on the shoulder. 'I think you'll find their place interesting. It's the remains of an old kasbah. It was falling apart when they bought it, but they've created something quite special.'

'Sounds fascinating.' He turned to look at Freya; moved his lips silently. 'Why are we going?'

She giggled at the expression on his face; mouthed back, 'It'll be fun.'

Something about the interaction warmed her; soothed the unease that had recently become a low, constant hum. As the weeks passed, instead of getting to know the city better, she found herself feeling increasingly disorientated. The day after the row in the taxi she had accepted Mustapha's invitation to Riad Jasmina; the story he told of the Farzis and the Azoulays – the decades of bad feeling, the underhand deals – did nothing to allay her fears. And it was becoming clear that to Edith, truth – either deliberately or because of her illness – was something of a vague concept. Her tales of life in Cairo during the war and Algiers during the 1950s had been a welcome distraction from the anxieties about the houses and the jinns and the unseen families whose lives they had stumbled into. It was only when she got back to Dar Simone and thumbed through an old biography of Freya Stark that she realised why some of her anecdotes sounded so familiar.

'Stunning, isn't it?'

She looked out of the window; the evening sun was flooding the orchards and plantations with a luminous glow that lit up the stone cottages and picked out the silver spindles of the almond trees, flecked with spring blossom. A truck rumbled out of a side road, the open back filled with a dozen labourers clad in filthy green overalls, faces upturned to the sun. Freya envied their sense of peace. Marrakech wasn't doing what she had hoped; instead of bringing her and Paul closer together, she could feel them diverging from each other, experiencing the city in ways the other didn't understand, or even respect.

'*Nous somme arrivés*,' said Jacqueline, as the car swerved onto a dusty track. 'I hope you're both feeling adventurous. Nights at Villa Merteuil are always something to remember.'

By the time Freya was seated at the long, flower-decked dining table, all her anxieties had been forgotten. From the moment she had stepped through the double-height doors, she felt as if she were walking towards something quite extraordinary. The kasbah was spectacular – room unfolding into room, some with exposed brick walls and roaring fires, each with one statement piece: a vast woven rug, studded with diamanté flecks and geometric patterns in scarlet and black, an abstract painting that stretched from floor to ceiling, a button-back chesterfield in bright blue velvet. In the courtyard, dozens of lanterns flickered around the pool; rope-held swings hung from tree branches, fires burned in small braziers. And beyond it were parts of the kasbah that had not been restored; roofless chambers draped in leafy trails of clematis and ivy. At one end, a crumbling wall reared up in the darkness; at its centre, an arched window space framed the night sky.

She smiled as the waiter refilled her glass. She was aware she had already drunk too much champagne while they stood among the flickering lanterns and Jean-Charles and Sabine – two of the most stylish people she had ever met – introduced them to the other guests. They had been a diverse mix: a journalist from *Le Monde*, two women who did something indecipherable on the Paris stock exchange, a French-Japanese artist called Peng and then the house guests, as Sabine called them. Freya was a little mystified at where they fitted in: three English and two French couples who all seemed perfectly, unremarkably nice.

'Hello.' She turned to the man sitting on her left; his dark hair was expensively cut, his angular face blemish-free. 'I'm George. Good to meet you. Quite a place, isn't it?'

Freya nodded. 'It's stunning. Odd, but stunning.'

'A bit like our gracious hosts.' Freya listened while he talked, watching him fork up slivers of foie gras. It felt like a rehearsed monologue; he was a model-turned-actor, he lived in Stoke Newington, his girlfriend Eva was also a model. Freya looked at the woman opposite George. She had the most extraordinary face: oval eyes and a long fluted nose that made her look almost feline. Her hair, jet-black and cut into a heavy, angular bob, swooped in towards a scarlet pout.

'Your girlfriend's very beautiful,' she said, laying her knife and fork together.

'Isn't she?' He leant towards her. She felt oddly examined. 'And you . . . Freya, isn't it? How is it that you find yourself in this . . . den of iniquity?'

Before she could ask what he meant, the chink of metal against glass made her glance towards the head of the table, where Sabine was standing, her peroxide-white hair glinting in the candlelight. '*Mesdames et messieurs. Bonsoir, tout le monde.* I hope that you have enjoyed your *entrées* and begun to discover a little about those who sit beside you. We take time now so that these new *encounters* –' she paused, a soft murmur of laughter rippling up the table – 'may be explored further, within this place, this kasbah, this relic of hundreds of lives. Love, passion, betrayal, death – they have all taken place between these walls. Now you may add your stories. Enjoy.'

Freya looked across at Paul, but his face was turned to Jacqueline; she was talking, apparently unmoved – or uninterested – in Sabine's speech. She could feel George beside her, waiting for a chance to speak. She didn't turn, mesmerised by the changing configurations as people began to melt away; one of the English husbands taking the hand of the Parisian stockbroker, Peng, the artist, rising slowly to her feet, the journalist from *Le Monde* following behind her. As she walked towards the gardens, Freya saw him run a finger down the ripple of her spine, exposed in a low, backless dress. There was no mistaking the intention.

She glanced at George. 'Is this what I think it is?'

He grinned. 'That depends.'

'Is this . . .' She smoothed the napkin in her lap. 'Is this some kind of swingers' party?'

'Oh, don't call it that, darling, our hosts definitely wouldn't like it.' George flipped open a cigarette case and shook two out. 'Have one. You look like you need it. Sabine calls it *maison ouverte* – open house.'

'You've been before?'

'I'm here a lot for photo shoots. It's hardly the raciest city in the world, there's not a lot of choice if you fancy something . . . diverting. Not that I'm thinking I'll get much action judging by this group; not my types at all, far too up themselves. Unless you . . . ?'

Freya shook her head gently. The nicotine had hit her wine-infused system and she was slightly concerned she might throw up. George seemed unfazed by her rejection. 'I'm thinking Eva's got lucky, though,' he said, scanning the room.

'Don't you mind? If she's . . .'

'Getting it on with the gorgeous Jean-Charles? Of course not. It's not like he's any kind of threat. Why should it matter?'

Freya didn't have an answer. She looked across for Paul; felt herself sway. He and Jacqueline had disappeared. 'I don't know,' she said slowly. 'I just . . .'

'Look, this kind of thing isn't for everyone,' he said, flicking his cigarette into the ashtray. 'In fact it makes me quite cross on your behalf. No one should come to something like this unprepared. It's essential everyone understands how to behave and what the rules are. Not that you have to have sex, of course – if you end up sitting next to people you don't fancy, you just go home and sleep with your girlfriend, like normal.'

His tone was kind but slightly condescending. She felt caught out suddenly, as if the city had tricked her again; revealed a situation she thought she understood to be something quite different.

'I just . . .well . . . I'm here with my husband. We don't really . . .' She tailed off, wondering, suddenly, whether Paul had known what the party might entail. 'I need to get some air.'

George nodded politely. Outside the darkness was warm and thick. Heat swirled up out of the braziers, creating patches of thinned air that shimmered against the crumbling walls and blurred the outlines of the archways. Freya felt lost; what had seemed so romantic, so mysterious, now felt like a theatrical contrivance, the whole flower-draped kasbah just a backdrop for the wealthy and bored to feel *outré* and bohemian. On the other side of the pool, a couple were writhing on a day-bed, their moans of pleasure mingling with the squawks of a trio of parakeets in the tree above. She looked away, embarrassed.

At the far end of the garden, a swing hung from the branches of a willow tree; she moved towards it, feet silent in the grass. The rope was rough against her palms; she slipped off her shoes and pushed back. It felt wrong, somehow, to be doing something so childish.

'*Madame? Voulez-vous quelque chose?*' She looked up to see a waiter standing on the path, his skin so dark she could barely make him out. She thought of Madani, listening to him explain the different Berber tribes as they sat outside a café on the Place des Ferblantiers. That was what she wanted, not this. She wrapped her fingers tightly around the rope of the swing; she needed to *feel* something, an anchor point to grip onto.

'*Un verre de vin blanc, s'il vous plaît?*'

He turned away; she heard the soft sludge of dew-heavy grass underfoot. Perhaps she would just stay on the swing, drinking glasses of white wine brought by the Tuareg waiter until it was time to go home. She felt inadequate suddenly; *vanilla* – wasn't that what people like Jean-Charles and Sabine called people like her? She wondered why she couldn't be anything else; why the idea of slipping away into the darkness with a handsome stranger was such anathema to her. The sound of muffled voices broke across her thoughts, slowly growing louder, seeping through the cracks in the wall.

'. . . isn't Freya's sort of thing.' Relief rippled through her at the sound of Paul's voice. 'I don't understand why she told you it would be mine.'

She slipped off the swing and moved noiselessly across the grass.

'Oh, come on.' Jacqueline's voice was low, slightly amused. 'Don't play the innocent with me. We have no secrets, *n'est-ce pas*?'

'Don't. Freya could be anywhere.'

She felt a touch on her arm. The waiter was behind her; the wine glass glinted in the darkness.

'But that is nothing new, *chéri*. And it hasn't stopped you before.'

Her eyes flicked wider, something cold shot across her skin.

'It's over, Jacqueline, you know that.'

'If you say so, *mon ami*. If you say so.'

Freya couldn't move. The wine glass lay beneath the swing. The fingers of both hands were knitted so tightly around the rope, the skin on her palms was beginning to burn. She stared at the wall; tiny purple flowers were bursting out of the stonework, long-leaved weeds spilling out of every hair's-breadth crevasse. She'd read something once about the resilience of weeds; their ability to weave infinitesimal roots into the most minute space. She began to count the flowers, to focus on something besides the insistent thought that kept pushing forward in her mind. It wasn't the fact of Paul's infidelity. It was the *who*. She had always suspected he was capable of being unfaithful, that one day, his need to charm – to be found charming – would solicit a reaction he would find impossible to resist.

A gong sounded, barrelling through the darkness. Paul and bloody Jacqueline? She stood unsteadily; stupid Freya, ignorant Freya, *vanilla*

Freya. How dare he put her in the position of gullible wife, the kind of woman who made her husband breakfast and ironed his shirts and shooed him out of the door into another woman's bed? And how bloody ironic that she had found out here, in a place designed for exactly the kind of careless betrayal he was apparently capable of. She strode across the garden, an unfamiliar sense of recklessness pulsing into her veins.

'Good evening.' She slipped back into her seat and found herself looking into the gracefully weathered face of Jean-Charles. 'You were expecting the gorgeous George I expect? But we change places between courses – the men at least. We are such dull creatures. We cannot expect to entertain a woman for a whole evening.'

Freya held his gaze; she was not going to be intimidated. Beyond him, Paul was already in conversation with Sabine. Her fingers tightened around the stem of the glass; she wanted to hurl it at him, humiliate him in front of everyone, cause a scene they would all talk about for weeks to come. She took a breath and smiled at Jean-Charles.

'Some men are dull creatures.' Her voice sounded odd, the words coming fast and tight. 'But you seem . . . intriguing.' She allowed her eyes to sweep over him: wide shoulders beneath a navy shirt, charcoal-and-silver hair swept back from his face, dark eyes that sagged a little into the wrinkles beneath.

'I'll take that as a compliment.' He lifted the neatly folded napkin from her plate, flicked it theatrically and laid it on her lap. 'But I suggest the same word could be applied to you.'

'Perhaps.' She lifted her wine glass, sipped once, then again. 'Tell me about the house. It's such an amazing place.'

'I'm glad you like it.' She tried to focus on his words; stories about rebuilding the kasbah, anecdotes that made her laugh, a high, false sound that came from somewhere new inside her, somewhere she hadn't even known existed. A plate of food was placed in front of her; mouthfuls of something spicy rolled back towards her throat; wine again, honeyed and soothing. And then a slight pressure on her leg, a soft, tickling sensation against the hem of her dress.

'Would you like to see the rest of the house?'

'I would.' She raised her napkin to her lips. 'Very much.'

She stood, aware of the weight of Jean-Charles's hand in the small of her back. She didn't look at Paul as they walked from the room; this was what the house was for, wasn't it? Sex with strangers, meaningless, transient sex. You could use that kind of sex for whatever reason you liked; it didn't have to be about love or intimacy or forging bonds. It could be about anger or revenge or self-bloody-worth. As Jean-Charles led the way out of the dining room and up the stairs, she allowed her fingers to drift across the surfaces: mahogany banisters, shot-silk curtains, a marble bust on a slim, teak plinth. He was talking of the art works he had commissioned, painters he knew, but she was too impatient to listen properly; this had to happen now, while the wine was still thick in her veins and the fury rendered her numb enough to feel nothing.

'You recognise the name of the house, of course?'

'Of course.' She followed him through a doorway and onto a long, candlelit balcony, half covered by linked, Moorish arches. To her left, a large rattan daybed was scattered with cushions. 'Laclos. *Les Liaisons Dangereuses.*' He smiled approvingly. 'But I'm interested; why Merteuil? Why not Villa Valmont?'

'Because it is always about the women. Laclos knew that. He created a woman with more power, more sexuality, more brilliance than any man could ever hope to match. To call this place Valmont would have been to insult Sabine. We men are mere ciphers compared to you . . .' He moved closer and ran a finger down her neck and along her collarbone. 'You vicious, delicious creatures.'

Freya locked her fingers around the balcony railing; he was so close; all around her, the air was thick with the scent of him: red wine, anise, tobacco. Her heart was thudding, pulse popping against her wrist. He had done this, Paul had *done this*, lived these moments, the before, the anticipation of each teetering step before the final leap, the irreversible move away from everything that had always mattered.

'How do you find Marrakech?' he murmured, his hand gliding down her arm. 'You like it here?'

'I do. It's very un-English.'

'And you?' His hand moved upwards, lifted her chin; she could see thousands of hairs in his neat beard, some charcoal-grey, the colour of metal filings, others white, others almost blue-black. 'Are you un-English too?'

She held his gaze for long enough to be an answer; the adrenalin pulsed into her body as his fingers slid across her collarbone. Something warm touched her neck; she jerked away so that he lifted his face to hers and suddenly they were kissing, his tongue inside her mouth, wet and hard, *different*. She felt him slide the straps of her dress from her shoulders. The night air was cold against her breasts. Suddenly her hands were tearing at his shirt, running her fingernails up his smooth, warm back. Desire shot through her; his lips were soft and wet; she tipped her head back and a shout of laugher rippled up from the garden below. Reality snapped back in. Was someone watching them? Some total stranger, looking on while she allowed – no, enjoyed – being undressed by a man she barely knew?

She pushed Jean-Charles away, pulling the straps back over her shoulders. 'I can't do this.' She felt nauseated; violated, in spite of her complicity. 'I'm sorry. This isn't me, this isn't who I am.'

For a moment he said nothing and then a smile spread across his features. 'How very English you are.' The amusement in his voice, the hint of Gallic condescension, made her want to scream. 'And how very disappointing.'

'Because I don't want to cheat on my husband?'

He kissed her lightly on the cheek. 'No, *ma petite*. You do want to cheat on your husband. You just don't want to do it with me.'

CHAPTER 11

Freya was living another woman's life. It had been . . . how long? Thirty-six hours? She'd barely slept the first night, but listened to the dawn call to prayer mingle with the rasp of Paul's breathing, his body curved away from her, arm stretched out above his head. It was the same as every other morning and yet nothing was familiar. She'd always loved those first quiet moments of wakefulness; a simple, unassuming intimacy, shared before the day began. They were supposed to be exclusively hers; she cleaved to them as unspoken proof of what bound them together. And now it had all been exposed as a lie.

'What a dreadful evening that was,' Paul had muttered as he'd pulled himself out of bed, face stained from lack of sleep. 'Promise me we never have to go there again.'

And she hadn't said, *You had a dreadful evening?* There'd been no sign of her anger or disbelief; the truth was she had no idea what to say, her mind blurred by stale wine and the obscene memory of Jean-Charles' hands on her skin. She'd pleaded a headache to avoid breakfast; once the front door had closed behind him she'd run a bath and lain in it until the water was cool against her skin.

'Freya?' Edith's voice cut across her thoughts. 'Have you heard anything I've said? I realise you've got that app thing on your phone recording me, but I would consider it polite if you could at least pretend you're listening.'

'Sorry, Dame Edith.' This morning had been even more unsettling; waking in the spare room, the bed empty beside her. She knew he hadn't believed her excuse of a migraine. 'I don't mean to be rude. I've just got a few things on my mind.'

'I can see that. You look dreadful. Jumpy. That husband of yours giving you the run-around?'

'What makes you say that?'

'When a woman looks like you do, it's usually something to do with her husband. You don't get to be my age without recognising the signs. Do you want to talk about it?'

'He's having an affair.' The words felt like a spasm.

'Oh.' Edith sighed. 'I'm sorry to hear that. Men are such fools. Do you know with whom?'

Freya was nonplussed. She'd expected reassurance, even dismissal, wanted Edith to chide her for being paranoid. 'You don't sound very surprised.'

'At a man cheating on his wife? Are you?'

'I don't know. I always thought . . .' She looked across at the elderly woman, draped in a bright blue pashmina, eyes sharp beneath a straw panama. What was she doing, telling Edith? 'It's not just . . . It's who he's having the affair with.' She found herself launching into a description of the evening at Villa Merteuil, the conversation she had overheard. When she finished, Edith's face was dark, two deep lines scored between her eyebrows.

'Those bloody awful people, Jean-Charles and Sabine. Playing with people's lives. Villa Merteuil indeed! Have you ever heard anything so pretentious? Honestly, you'd think those two had invented sex, the way they go about it. It's just a cheap little knocking-shop, with a good wine cellar and some clever lighting.' Freya smiled in spite of herself. 'But Jacqueline? I don't think so.'

'I heard them. I heard him say it was over. I couldn't have misunderstood.'

Edith placed both hands on the arms of the chair and slowly rose to her feet. 'Walk with me a little,' she said, swaying slightly. 'Once round the gardens – does my circulation wonders.' Freya let the older woman tuck her hand through her arm; her skin felt like tree bark, thick and parched.

'The fact is, dear girl –' Edith's words were short, punctuated with laboured breaths – 'it is always possible to misunderstand. This is a city that runs on gossip and rumour, usually put about by those who have too much time, or who are guilty of something themselves and wish to create a distraction. But the only currency that matters is fact. For something to be true, you must be able to prove it. Do you have proof of this affair? You do not. You need to learn that the only way to keep a clear head is to ignore everything but what you know to be true.'

'Are you saying you don't think he's having an affair?'

Edith stopped to lean on the back of a chair. 'No. You may well be right. I just don't believe it's with Jacqueline.' Freya went to speak, but she shook her head. 'You want to know why I think that? Because Jacqueline is a whore. She thinks she's being bohemian, but the fact is she's just a lonely, middle-aged woman who sleeps with young boys to try and make herself feel better about her husband's countless affairs with his students.'

'Alain?'

'Don't be taken in by that unassuming, academic air. He's had more wide-eyed teenagers than I've had *macarons*. From what I know of Paul, however, I would say he has an ego. A large one. He won't want to be just another notch on some sexually voracious fifty-something's bedpost. He'll need it to mean something, he'll want to feel special to the woman he's involved with.'

Freya listened to the rhythmic crunch of the gravel beneath her feet; it reminded her of the coarse rope of the swing against her skin. She found these small, physical confirmations of her presence oddly comforting; something to combat the rising sense that she was losing herself. 'You don't like Paul very much, do you?'

'What makes you say that?'

'It's obvious. That first day we came . . . he said . . . he said that you'd always thought he was a bad influence on Hamad. But you've always said to me how good you thought we were for him, providing some sort of normality, being his friends.'

Edith said nothing, leant a little more heavily on Freya as they made their way back to the terrace. 'Things happen,' she said absently. 'In times of crisis we don't always make the best decisions. I suppose I, of all people, shouldn't blame him for that.'

'Crisis?' Freya eased Edith into the chair and knelt down next to it. 'Is Paul in some sort of trouble?'

'What? No, no.' She patted Freya's arm; there was something almost maternal in the gesture. 'Ignore me. I don't know any reason why he would do this, I'm afraid. Why do any of them?'

'I've got to talk to him, I suppose.' She tried to imagine the conversation; awful, clichéd accusations, the trading of blame and guilt.

'And what if he lies?'

'How will I know? He can be very persuasive.'

'Exactly. Talking to him before you have the facts is pointless.' She leant forward. 'I tell you what we'll do. Hamad is flying in tonight. I'll arrange a dinner at Larousse on Sunday. We'll invite Paul and Jacqueline, and put them in a group – people are never on their guard in the same way when they're in a crowd. We'll come together – Racine and Hamad, perhaps Mustapha and his son, Tim if he is in town – and then you and I will watch.'

Freya shook her head. 'I don't know. It's all a bit theatrical, isn't it? Maybe I should talk to Jacqueline?'

'And give all the power to her? No, no, no. At the moment you have the advantage. Paul doesn't know you are aware of his secret . . . whatever – or whoever – it is. Keep it that way. Allow those who are guilty to expose themselves, without even realising they are on trial. Now, is there anyone else we should invite?'

'Perhaps Laila. The architect my husband works with. They spend a lot of time together.'

'Of course. So you'll leave me to make the arrangements? You can keep your counsel until Sunday?'

Freya nodded; since she had no idea what to do, it seemed easier to allow Edith to take control.

'Good. Then it's decided. We shall have a dinner of truth, you and I. Find out what is really happening in your marriage.'

The office was a mess. Paul looked at Laila, kneeling on the floor and pulling together the reams of paper that were scattered across the tiles. Behind her the desk was upended, his drafting table on its back, covered in fragments of pottery and a coating of earth. The ficus had been almost snapped in two; it lay like a broken limb in the corner of the room, leaves already thirsty.

'What the hell happened?'

Laila stood up, pushed her hair out of her eyes. 'I don't know. It was like this when I got here. It must have happened last night.'

'Have they taken anything?'

'Have you got your laptop?'

'Yes.'

'Me too. So no, I don't think so. They even left the money in the petty-cash box.'

Paul picked up a cushion and tucked it back onto the sofa. He sat heavily. 'Where was Yusuf? Isn't he supposed to be the guardian of this place?'

'You're not going to like it. He says . . . he says it was the jinns.'

'What?' Paul ran his fingers through his hair. 'For God's sake. Has he seen the state of the front door? Jinns with spray cans, I suppose? Do you know what it says?'

'*Thief. Thief* and *devil.*'

'Great. Just great. And where are the builders? Why is no one working?'

'They've gone home. The foreman said . . . they won't work somewhere that the jinns are . . . unhappy.'

'It's not the bloody jinns. It's the Azoulays, isn't it? Or someone doing it on their behalf. Christ, what has Hamad got us into? He's got no idea of the work these houses need – I've been reading the surveyor's report this morning, we might as well pull them down and start again. What with that and . . .' He glanced at her; she looked pale, a little shaken. 'Sorry. It must have been a horrible shock coming in and finding the place like this. Why don't you take the rest of the day off, I can straighten things up.'

'Are you sure?'

'Of course. Just make sure you leave me Massoud's number. If that bloody workshy crew aren't back here first thing tomorrow morning, I'll fire the lot of them. Including him.'

'*Âllo?*'

Paul glanced out of the window and felt his stomach turn over. 'Racine?'

She appeared in the doorway, sleek in cropped grey trousers and a cream shirt, her hair pulled back into a ponytail. The pull was immediate, almost overwhelming. 'I heard about the break-in – one of the busboys at the Palais lives in the next street. Why didn't you call me?'

'I've only just got here myself.' He glanced at Laila. 'Go home. Seriously. I'll call you if there's a problem with the crew, otherwise just come in tomorrow as normal.'

'Thank you.' She smiled at Racine and disappeared through the doorway. The air seemed to thicken with her departure.

'I would have rung you.' He busied himself, straightening papers and slotting pencils back into the pot. 'But it's nothing serious. They haven't taken anything, it's just a point being made.'

'Do you think it's the Azoulays?' She walked into the office and sat on the arm of the sofa, crossing her legs so that one sandal swung from her foot. Her toenails gleamed a pale shade of blue.

'It's the jinns, apparently. So Yusuf says.'

Racine laughed. 'Spirit burglars?'

'I'm starting to think anything's possible in this town.' He shrugged. 'I might just leave things in this state. Feels like a metaphor for the whole bloody project. This house is OK, but the other two are literally coming apart at the seams.'

'And you?'

He didn't expect the question, or the gentleness in her tone. 'Feel a bit that way myself. And it doesn't help, to be honest, being sent to some bloody awful swingers' night. Why on earth did you suggest it? Particularly as you didn't even come.'

'I don't know.' She smiled, a touch sheepishly. 'I was angry, I guess. That night we had dinner in the Jemaa el Fna, I found it . . . humiliating.' She stood up unexpectedly, walked towards the window. He could feel her proximity to him; if he stretched out his arm he could touch the waistband of her trousers. 'I don't like being treated like some sort of toy to be picked up and put down, to be played with when you want to. And so I thought, if that's how he wants to be, then I will send him to a game. That's all it is to Jean-Charles and Sabine. A game.'

'Well, it's a bloody sleazy game. And if you really believe that's how I think of you then you couldn't be more wrong.'

'Really? What am I supposed to think, Paul? You kiss me, then suddenly you walk away, leaving me in the middle of the medina on my own. The next thing, I'm having dinner with you and your wife. How do you think it felt, seeing your jealousy around her and Tim?'

'I wasn't jealous. I couldn't take my eyes off you. But I'm married. And you're . . .'

'With Hamad. I do know that, believe me.'

'You don't exactly sound happy about it.'

She shook her head slowly. 'We talked about this before, didn't we? I'm trying, but . . . I don't know. Perhaps he's just too good for me.'

'That's a silly thing to say.'

'Is it? Think of what we did.'

'I spend all my time trying not to think about it.'

'Really?' She moved towards him; he could smell her scent, see the curve of her breasts beneath the shirt. 'Isn't that . . .'

'It's a nightmare.' His hand was moving, he was powerless to stop it; his fingers were in her hair; twisting against his skin like silk. 'I thought I could just . . . put it away, you know? It was just once, an aberration. I love . . . I love Freya. But you . . .'

'What about me?'

For a moment, he couldn't speak. He knew what should come next; his hand falling back to his side, a stuttered apology, the slightly contemptuous expression on her face as she moved away towards the door. A moment crystallised, a tipping point and then suddenly, unexpectedly, it shattered, and he was kissing her, slipping the shirt from her body, the desk hard beneath them, both oblivious to the rhythmic sound of sweeping, echoing across the courtyard outside.

CHAPTER 12

'Jacqueline?'

'I heard them.' Freya reached for her wine glass. 'I don't mean . . . I heard them talking. At a party.'

Hamad frowned. 'Are you sure?'

'Yes. She said something about them having no secrets, and he told her to be quiet, as I might be anywhere. She said, *Well, it hasn't stopped you before.* And then he said . . . he said that it wasn't going to happen again.'

'Well, that could mean anything.'

'Don't.' Freya pressed her lips together, she could feel the tears burning at the back of her throat. 'I need you to believe me. I've got no one else. I don't want to worry Ali and—'

'Have you talked to Paul about it?'

'What do I say?'

'Well, I guess, *Are you sleeping with Jacqueline?*' She felt the warmth of his hand on hers. 'He won't be, Frey. I don't know why he said that, but there'll be a reason. Paul adores you, he always has.'

'The thing is, Ham, you just don't how it's been. It's not like that any more. I told you in October things have been difficult for a long time. I thought coming here would help, you know, give us a fresh start, but it's just been one thing after another. All this stuff with the Azoulays, I think it's really worrying Paul. Ever since the break-in he's been really preoccupied. I think we both underestimated how different things would be here.'

'We all did.' Hamad ran his fingers across his beard. 'I feel a lot of this is my fault. I don't know what happened with buying those houses, I broke every rule of how I work – didn't oversee it, let someone else make the deal. It just felt as if they were the answer, as if they would bring us all closer, but instead the opposite seems to be happening. Maybe Yusuf is right. Maybe the jinns did curse it.'

'You don't believe all that stuff.'

'Don't I?' Hamad raised an eyebrow. 'Remember who my grandmother is, Frey. She always told me that if travel had taught her one thing, it is to respect the beliefs of the old. They've seen it all, she used to say. They hold their beliefs for a reason.'

'I told her. About Paul. I don't know why.'

'She does that. I always end up telling her things I don't mean to. Maybe it's because she has that air of having seen everything. Being unshockable.'

'Well, she certainly wasn't shocked. Didn't even seem surprised, although she did say if Paul is having an affair, she's sure it isn't with Jacqueline. That's what this dinner tonight is about. She said we should get everyone together to see how they behave. Something about how people give themselves away when they don't think anyone's watching. She told me not to accuse him of anything until I have some proof.'

'Well, she's right about that, but I don't see how a dinner party is going to prove anything. You should have called me. Told me. That's what I'm here for.'

'But you're not here, are you? You're in Doha. And I needed, I don't know, an ally. A plan. I feel so weak. Paul's cheating on me and I haven't done anything or said anything, but I just don't know what to do. If we were at home I'd see Ali, talk to friends, sit on the beach. Here, I've no . . . structure, no traditions to fall back on. I feel like I'm floating sometimes, like I'm not anchored to anything. It's difficult.'

Hamad stood up and moved to sit next to her on the banquette. 'It's a huge adjustment being out here, Frey. It's bound to take time to get used to things.' She felt his arm around her shoulders, drew into the warmth of his body. 'Don't take this the wrong way, but you know your imagination can get a little . . . inventive at times. Remember that girl at Cambridge, what was her name . . . Sophie Clarke? You were convinced she'd slept with Paul.'

She pulled back. 'Bloody hell, you're like an elephant.'

'Oh.' Hamad smoothed down his T-shirt in mock offence. 'I like to think more of an oryx.'

'No, I mean your memory. That's why people ditch old friends, isn't it? Yes, I was wrong about her, but that was ten years ago and I . . .' Her mother's face appeared in her mind. 'I was a bit all over the place. And just because I was wrong then doesn't mean I am now.'

He signalled for the bill. 'Freya, you're gorgeous. Funny. Clever. Paul's lucky to have you – why would he risk all that for some middle-aged Frenchwoman? There'll be an explanation, I guarantee you. Would you like me to talk to him?'

'No. God, absolutely not. Please don't tell anyone, not Racine or Karim, not until I know what's really happening, and what I want to do.'

'OK.' He glanced at his watch. 'Shall we go and face the music then? I guess we'd better head downstairs and get Edith's little charade underway.'

Freya stepped onto the terrace and stood for a minute, looking across to the long, candlelit table, set slightly apart on a raised section of patio. They made a striking group: Laila's dark head of curls bent towards Hamad, Edith – resplendent in a fuchsia *shalwar kameez* and sequinned, midnight-blue wrap – looking wildly exotic next to the plain lines of Mustapha's *djellaba*. Her stomach tightened as she looked towards the end of the table: Jacqueline, sleek in black T-shirt and cropped jeans, laughing at something Paul was saying. He'd been odd since the moment he arrived, bursting into the bar full of a story about one of the bedroom floors almost collapsing. She'd recognised the overconfidence as nerves, a jittery energy that only served to reaffirm her suspicions.

'I've had a text from Racine,' said Hamad, as she slipped back into the chair next to him. 'Some crisis at the hotel; she's had to stay on a bit. Sorry, *jaddah*.'

'I wonder what constitutes a sommelier crisis,' said Edith crisply. 'A misplaced corkscrew perhaps?' The bangles on her arm jangled irritably. 'I'd have expected better of Timothy, however. I do abhor lateness.'

'Young people have lives, Edie,' said Mustapha, laying a hand on her arm. 'Look, here comes the *pastilla*. You must try it, Freya, it's the best in the city – the flakiest pastry, spiced pigeon and almonds.'

'And how is Yusuf?' Edith nodded at Paul. 'You should take the time to get to know him. He knows the city inside out.'

'He doesn't talk much,' said Paul, sipping his wine. 'Too busy with the jinns. I'm still not quite clear why he didn't move out when the Farzis did. Doesn't he have any family of his own?'

'I don't know,' said Hamad. 'Omar Farzi just said he was the guardian of the houses and had always lived there. I didn't ask any more questions.'

'Perhaps that might have been a good idea.'

Hamad raised his eyebrows. 'Well I can think of one or two I'd like to ask right now.'

'This *pastilla* is delicious,' said Freya loudly. 'Pass your plate, Ham. You have to try it.' She caught his eye, gave a minute shake of her head. 'Yusuf's not a problem – is he, Paul? He's just very traditional, that's all.'

'He's certainly that,' said Paul. 'I'm not sure how he's going to cope with one of the houses being a wine bar.'

'A wine bar?' Edith's voice thundered from the top of the table. 'In the medina?'

'More of a wine school,' Hamad said quickly. 'A place to taste and learn about wine. But it won't be all three houses. As you know, one—'

'But this is a Muslim country.' The whole table fell silent at Edith's appalled tones. 'Hamad, you don't even drink, for God's sake. What are you thinking? Leaving aside the rights and wrongs, you'll never get permission.'

'Permission for what?' Freya glanced up to see Tim, looking unexpectedly smart in a black linen suit. 'You sound scandalised, *grandmère.* Clearly I've arrived just in time.'

'Timothy.' Edith tilted her face forwards for a kiss. 'You've decided to grace us with your presence.'

'I apologise for my lateness. You're looking spectacular, as always.'

'You won't get round me with compliments. Sit.' She gestured to the chair opposite Hamad. 'Flanked by my two handsome grandsons. Such a treat to get you together.'

'Such a treat,' Hamad muttered to Freya.

'You know everyone, I think,' said Edith, glaring at Hamad. 'Just perhaps not Laila.' She gestured to the far end of the table. 'She works with Paul on the Farzi houses.'

'Ah, yes.' Tim helped himself to wine. 'And how's that going? Made any progress on who was behind the break-in?'

'Just kids, I'm sure,' said Paul. 'The door's so old anyone could open it with a bit of a shove.'

'Strange Yusuf didn't hear them, don't you think?' He glanced at Hamad, who shrugged and shook his head. 'No comment, is that it? Well, how about the theory that Hassan Azoulay was behind it – or one of his sons? Any comment on that?'

'What would be the point?' Hamad's voice was cold. 'I suspect you've written the story already. What could I possibly have to add?'

'Well, that depends. Do you know all the facts?'

'Timothy, for goodness' sake.' Edith slapped her hand against the table. 'You arrive late, then turn dinner into an interrogation . . .'

'*Bonsoir tout le monde.*' Eight faces turned to look at Racine, her silver dress gleaming in the candlelight. She strolled around the table towards Hamad, heels clicking like snapping fingers, then slid her hands onto his shoulders. 'Well, this looks like quite the party. I'm sorry I'm late. What have I missed?'

Edith felt the evening change with the appearance of Racine. There was a power shift, away from her end of the table, to the young Frenchwoman at the other. She felt a stab of irritation as Hamad fussed around her, pouring wine and water, calling for fresh *pastilla*, laughing at something she was saying. His obvious infatuation always made her impatient; tonight, unusually, the level of attentiveness seemed to be reciprocated. Racine appeared to be hanging on his every word.

'A pleasure to meet you, Mademoiselle Delacroix,' she heard Mustapha say, his blue eyes twinkling across the table. 'Forgive me, but the name is familiar. You're not anything to do with—'

'Château Delacroix?' Her face broke into a smile. 'I am indeed. Michel Delacroix is my father. Do you know our wines?'

Mustapha nodded. 'We stock them at Riad Jasmina. They're very popular.'

'Well, I'm glad at least one riad in the city has a decent cellar.'

'I hear you're about to make that two,' said Edith thinly. 'A wine bar in the medina? This is a Muslim country, Racine. I presume you are aware of that?'

'Of course.' She smiled tightly. 'But times change. There's a huge expat population here and that's a massive, untapped market for wine sales. We'll hold tastings and masterclasses . . . have exclusive previews of Delacroix wines. There's a new Viognier I tasted when I was home in the autumn, I think it's our best white yet.' She turned to Mustapha. 'It's not officially on sale until the summer, but I'll have them send you a case. My father hopes it will win him the Grand Prix.'

'It's delicious,' said Paul.

'You've tasted it?' Edith's bangles clattered against the table top.

'Oh.' She caught a momentary exchange of looks between Racine and Paul. 'Yes. I have a project in Lyon, an office complex. Last time I was there my meeting was cancelled so I took a tour of the vineyard. Did some tastings.'

'How interesting.' A thought presented itself; Edith pushed it away. 'And do you have designs in mind for this . . . wine bar?'

Paul nodded. 'I'm going to Fez next weekend to see some *maalems* . . .'

'*Maalems*?' Edith's eyebrows were raised in amusement.

'It means . . . master craftsmen, I suppose.'

'Dear boy, I know what it means. I'm just surprised you do.' She leant across the table towards Freya. 'Your husband is becoming quite the local, my dear. Are you joining him on this jaunt to Fez?'

Freya frowned. 'What jaunt to Fez?'

'I did tell you,' said Paul irritably. 'Laila and I are going to Fez for a couple of days. We need to get some design ideas.'

'You didn't tell me. When did you decide that?'

'I *did*—'

'I'm going to Imlil next weekend,' said Tim unexpectedly. 'It's a small Berber village up in the foothills of the Atlas mountains, totally different from Marrakech. Going to be home to another of Hamad's little projects, or so I hear?'

'You mean the Nanda?' Hamad smiled. 'You can dig all you like on that one, my friend. There's no story for you there.'

'Well, that's what I'm going to find out.' He glanced at Freya. 'You should come with me. If your husband is off in Fez, it seems only fair you should see a bit of the country too.'

'You should go,' said Edith. 'Imlil is wonderful – a complete contrast to Marrakech.'

'We bought some beautiful rugs there, when we went to visit the hotel,' said Racine. 'I'd like to sell them at the Farzi houses. They do something similar at the Mogador Palace – bring local people in, let them have a small space in the foyer to sell what they make.'

Edith felt something cool run down her spine. 'Now that's a hotel you should see, Paul. Have you been there? Stunning mosaics and carving, really traditional Marrakchi design.'

He shook his head. 'I don't think so.'

Yet it had been him, standing outside the ornate frontage of the Mogador Palace. She remembered the annoyance; the way he'd strode into the foyer just as the limousine had slowed to a halt. She couldn't remember now what it was she'd wanted to ask him; whatever it was hadn't been pressing enough for her to get out of the car and follow him into the hotel.

'*Habibi*? Are you all right?' For a moment she lost all sense of where she was, and what she was trying to disentangle. 'Edie? Do you need something?'

She turned towards Mustapha, her mind slowly clearing. She knew better than to believe in coincidences. If it had been just one thing – the visit to the vineyard, or the lie about the Mogador Palace, or Racine's odd over-attentiveness – she would simply have put it down to the inexplicableness of life. But together, they told a story.

'Don't make a drama,' she muttered. 'But I need to go. Now.'

He peered at her. 'Is everything all right?'

'No, it most definitely is not. There's nothing for you to worry about, but I must leave. Can you ask Hamad, quietly, if Karim can drive me home? I don't want any fuss.'

She watched as Mustapha bent his head towards Hamad's, caught the worried expression on his face as he glanced across the table. Something pulled in her heart; a mixture of sadness and fury. How could they *do* this to him? She raised a finger to her lips, forced herself to smile. He nodded, mouthed the words 'Shall I come?' She shook her head, watched Mustapha rise to his feet and slowly began to lever herself out of the chair.

'Dame Edith? Are you leaving?' She glanced across at Freya; another stab of anger. Her heart was beginning to flutter.

'I am. Please don't worry. A simple case of too much rich food and –' she glanced at Racine, and then Paul – 'stimulating company. I am just an old woman who needs her bed. Goodnight to you all.'

She turned before anyone could speak, grateful for the feel of Mustapha's arm beneath her palm. The stairs tilted towards her, for a moment she thought she might fall. It was a relief to settle into the car, Karim at the wheel, to feel herself cocooned from everything, even her old friend.

'Good evening, Dame Edith.' Karim smiled at her in the mirror. 'How are you?'

'There are no words,' she said limply. 'Believe me, Karim. There simply are no words.'

CHAPTER 13

Freya glanced around the table. With Dame Edith's departure, the dinner felt oddly fragmented, the underlying tensions that had been muted by her presence slowly rising to the surface. Through the candlelight, she could see Racine holding court to Laila and Jacqueline. Across from her, Hamad was watching Tim's conversation with Mustapha with an expression of intense annoyance, as if he suspected confidences were being shared about Edith that he was not party to. Only Paul sat apart, turning the stem of his wine glass slowly between his fingers.

'You all right?'

He raised his eyebrows; she thought how tired he looked, devoid of the slightly manic energy that had characterised him earlier in the evening.

'Just a bit weary. I did tell you about Fez, you know.'

'OK.' She knew he hadn't. Was it Laila that she should be worried about? She looked down to where the three women were deep in conversation; perhaps Jacqueline had been talking about someone other than herself. 'I might go to Imlil. Sounds like somewhere to see. It would be good to get out of the city.'

'Oh.' He looked surprised. 'Well, yes. If you want to.'

She felt beaten suddenly. This was what she'd wanted, wasn't it? To be somewhere new and unfamiliar, sitting on a candlelit roof terrace above a strange, exotic city with a group of people she hadn't even known existed just a few months before. She'd longed for adventure, and when Hamad had gifted it to her, to both of them, she had never stopped to consider whether it would be anything but positive.

'What do you see?' She turned to see Tim smiling at her. 'You look as if you're scrutinising everyone very closely.'

Freya sat back. 'You know that old saying, "Be careful what you wish for"? Well, something along those lines.'

He raised his eyebrows. 'That doesn't sound good. Are things not working out as you'd hoped? Edith seems very happy with you.'

'She's fabulous. I want to *be* her when I'm eighty-five. I hope she's OK.' Something about Edith's early departure had unsettled her: the sudden display of frailty at odds with how she had dominated the earlier part of the evening. 'I think something had upset her.'

A burst of laughter broke across her words; she looked over to see Jacqueline with her hand on Paul's arm, clearly sharing a joke. Hamad caught her eye; she felt a spark of humiliation, leant forward to reach for the wine just as Paul swung out his arm to illustrate the story he was telling. His hand fell against hers, tipping the bottle across the table, splashing liquid as it fell. She stood up to see a rash of red spreading across the dress.

'Oh, Paul.'

'Sorry. Did I get you?'

'Yes. I'm going to have to go and sponge it off.'

'Sorry, Frey.' The words hung in the air as she weaved through the tables, fighting back tears of frustration. As she squeezed down the staircase, she caught sight of a couple in one of the booths: a bare-shouldered girl in a coral sundress wrapped around a dark-haired man. He was whispering something to her, their faces turned towards each other, entirely oblivious to those who sat around them. She felt a stab of longing, of sorrow for things past.

Inside the cubicle she took a deep breath, and steadied herself against the door. The damage to the dress was clear; there seemed little point in trying to rub away the stains. The whole evening had been a disaster. Hamad was right; she should never have let Edith inveigle her into such a ludicrous charade. She pulled out her phone and texted Paul: *Dress ruined, have headache, getting taxi home. Didn't want to break up the party. Make my apologies to Mustapha and everyone. x.* She rifled in her purse to make sure she had dirhams for the cab and stepped out into the hall. To her surprise, Tim was leaning against one of the archways, smoking a cigarette.

'Mrs Hepworth. Are you OK?'

'It's *Freya*. And no. Not really. I'm going home.'

'Why?' He moved towards her; his proximity made her feel slightly light-headed. 'Your dress doesn't look that bad.'

'I'm not going because my dress is spoilt. I'm going home because . . . because . . .'

'You look like you need a drink. Come back upstairs. Not to the restaurant. We'll sneak past and go on up to the bar. And you can tell me all your problems. Or none of them.'

Freya knew she should go home. Whatever Paul was doing, whoever he was doing it with, going for a drink with a man she hardly knew wasn't going to help the situation. She thought of the taxi ride home; the quiet rooms of Dar Simone, the empty roof terrace above the silent kasbah.

'OK then. Just one drink.'

It was quiet on the upper terrace. The barman who had served her and Hamad led her to a low, cream sofa that overlooked the open space of the Place des Ferblantiers. Freya glanced over the rail; how long was it since she had been there with Madani? They had peered into the workshops, she'd haggled for a pair of wrought-iron lanterns, sipping *thé marocain* and waiting for him to nod when the price became reasonable. It was the same day they had gone to Villa Merteuil.

'Penny for them.' She felt the sofa pull as Tim sat down beside her.

'Just thinking how quiet it is down there,' she said, pointing to the square.

'It's a different city at night. For somewhere so crazy by day, it's very much an early-to-bed kind of place.'

'Was that your excuse? An early night?'

'I didn't really need one,' he said, nodding as the waiter laid two glasses of wine on the table. 'Mustapha was just leaving, and I don't get the feeling either your husband or Hamad were particularly sorry to see me go.'

'You really don't like Hamad, do you?'

Tim sipped his wine. 'It's more that I don't like his attitude. It makes me angry . . . He thinks he can buy whatever he likes, whoever he likes. That might be fine in Doha, it's probably how it works. But things are different here.'

'People can never see past the money with Hamad. But when you get to know him, it's the least important thing about him.'

'To you, perhaps. But I think you have an unusual perspective. You've known him how long?'

'Twelve, thirteen years. But he's not changed.' Tim raised his eyebrows. 'He *hasn't*. He just sees the world differently to us, that's all. But that's cultural as much as anything.'

'And how do you see the world, Mrs Hepworth?' He propped his head on the palm of his hand. His face was so different to Paul's; sharply angular, a wide, easy smile.

'I don't think I know any more. Sometimes I think there's nothing about being here that I recognise.'

'Well then, you should allow me to familiarise you with some of it.' She took a sip of wine. 'Seriously, come to Imlil with me.'

'I don't think I can.' She kept her eyes on the sofa. 'I'd love to but . . .'

'I'm not suggesting anything illicit. Separate rooms, all above board. I just think you'd love it. And . . . well, to be honest, you look like you could do with getting away for a couple of days.'

'Maybe.'

'So you'll think about it?' His voice was low; she had to lean in to catch the words.

'Why?' She lifted her chin; her stomach curled as she met his gaze. 'Why do you want me to come?'

She didn't expect the kiss. It took a second before she realised what was happening; a sudden warmth against her face, a shocking sense of something new and unforeseen. For a moment it was as if her entire body were illuminated, every nerve ending and synapse firing together, before reality snapped back in and she pulled away. 'What are you doing?'

He didn't move. 'I'm sorry. God, I just . . . I didn't even know I was going to do that. You just . . . bewitch me.'

She raised her fingers to her lips. 'I'm married. You can't just—' Suddenly, unexpectedly, something heavy smacked against her knee; cold liquid splashed onto her thigh.

'Sorry. Sorry, God, I'm so sorry.' She looked up to see a tall, silver-haired man in a pink shirt hovering apologetically. 'Did I get your dress?'

'Yes.' She tried to focus; a young Moroccan man was standing next to him, clutching an empty champagne glass and trying not to laugh.

'Khaled, look what you did.' The man waggled his finger. It was obvious he was drunk.

'Do you think this is funny?' Tim stood up; the older man pulled out his wallet and produced a card.

'No. I really am sorry. Such a beautiful dress.' He let his eyes drift over her body; Freya felt distinctly uncomfortable. 'Please get it dry-cleaned and send me the bill.'

She looked at the card. *Wilhelm Björnsson*. 'You're Swedish?' She didn't know what else to say.

'I am. Swedish and mortified. Please. Send me the bill. Apologies again.' He smiled; there were too many teeth in his mouth. As they walked away, Wilhelm slipped an arm around the Moroccan boy's waist. Her skin prickled.

'That dress is doomed.' She turned to see Tim smiling at her.

'I have to go.'

'Please . . . I shouldn't have done that. I'm sorry.'

'I wish you hadn't. Everything is such a mess, I just can't make sense of anything. I need a friend right now, Tim, that's all. If you can be that, then great. But—' His phone buzzed suddenly. He glanced down at the screen.

'Sorry. Really sorry. I do have to take this.'

She sat limply while he moved to the balcony; looked at her untouched wine glass on the table, a bowl of nuts beside it. Had she known what was going to happen when she'd agreed to lie to her husband, to come for a drink just one floor above where he was sitting? There'd been something irresistibly enticing about it; an act of rebellion that felt far more dangerous than the encounter with Jean-Charles. She watched him walk towards her, tried to ignore the frisson of excitement in her stomach.

'Everything OK?'

He flung himself onto the sofa and lifted his wine glass. 'No. Not really.'

'Oh.'

'It was a friend of mine, he's a gendarme. He rings me sometimes, with a tip-off, gives me the stories first. But this one . . . I kind of wish I didn't know it.'

'Why?'

'It's Hassan Azoulay.' He ran his fingers across his forehead. 'I don't really know how to say this. They found him this evening, on the land he used to own, the land that was sold to the Farzis. He'd hanged himself from a tree, Freya. He's dead.'

CHAPTER 14

Hamad nodded at the doorman, swept down the steps of the Palais du Jardin and raised a hand at the waiting Mercedes. He was beginning to loathe Marrakech. What had seemed diverting on earlier visits – the chaotic streets, the old city walls, the sense of a place with history, so different from his life in Doha – was becoming horribly frustrating. Once the novelty of the houses had worn off, Racine had reverted to being cool and distant, Freya and Paul's marriage appeared to be falling apart rather than growing stronger, and Edith seemed to be more diminished each time he came.

'Good morning, Karim.' At least there was one person he could rely on. 'Are you OK?'

'Good morning, *sayyid*. I am well. But I do have some rather upsetting news.'

'Oh?'

'Hassan Azoulay is dead.'

'What?'

'He killed himself. They found him yesterday evening, in an orchard in the Ourika valley. On what used to be his land.'

'You know this how?'

'It's in the morning paper.'

Hamad leant against the car. He thought of the man in the lobby at La Mamounia, the rage in his face, the way Karim had stepped in, as always, and swept him away. 'Very well. Thank you for informing me.' He slipped into the back seat of the car. 'The Farzi houses, please. I presume we're checked in for the flight?'

'Of course.'

The door clicked shut. He felt claustrophobic suddenly. It happened rarely these days but occasionally the memory surfaced: the car spinning beneath him, Paul shouting as he fought for control. He'd never regretted the decision he'd taken, although Edith had been horrified. Those who wondered how he could live with himself never understood that the guilt belonged to someone else. And now the sin he was thought to have committed had finally caught up with him. A death on his hands. Whatever he felt about suicide, there was no other way to think about it.

'The streets are quiet this morning.' Karim eased the car onto Avenue el Mouahidine; clusters of tourists had already begun to gather outside the Koutoubia. 'We'll soon be there.'

Hamad didn't reply. He had little desire to visit the houses; it was becoming increasingly difficult to avoid the feeling that buying them had been an error of judgement. He had mismanaged things from the start, allowing Omar Farzi to see how much he wanted them, accepting his demands without properly looking into the ramifications. Even now he wasn't sure why they had become such an obsession. Control, Edith had said. Perhaps she was right; he couldn't seem to get a grip on anything else.

'How was my grandmother last night? Did she say anything to you on the way home?'

'Not really. But I thought she seemed tired. A little upset, perhaps.'

'Yes.' He thought of Edith's face when she had left the dinner; lips pursed, eyes over-bright. It had been an unexpected turn in an evening that had been unsettling from the start, everything undercut by Freya's suspicions, the anguish he had seen on her face. He remained convinced that she had misunderstood – or misheard – the conversation at Villa Merteuil. Racine had shared enough about Jacqueline's liaisons for him to know her taste was for younger men, preferably Moroccan. But he had kept an eye on Paul during the dinner, and sensed an air of tension behind the banter.

Karim pulled up next to Bab Agnaou. 'Be back at midday.'

'Yes, *sayyid*.'

He strode across the square, ducking into an alley. The sour tang of the souks swept in; he thought of Souk Waqif, rebuilt, sanitised maybe, but at least clean. He missed Doha. People said it was chaotic, that laws were made up according to whatever mood the Emir was in on a particular day, but he understood it, knew how relationships worked. He told himself it wasn't surprising that Morocco's labyrinthine bureaucracy had defeated him, that he'd employed others to seal the deal on the Farzi houses. But a sick feeling of guilt was knotting his stomach. A man was dead because of him. He thought of Paul and Freya, the secret he had kept from them for ten years. It had been the right thing to do, whatever Edith had said.

To his annoyance, the graffiti still hadn't been removed from the door. He walked into the damp lobby. The place looked like a bomb had gone off: walls half gone, grubby cement bags lying in piles, tangles of wires dangling from ripped-out plasterwork. Heaps of rubble and piles of broken bricks were scattered around the *sahridj*. A rhythmic scratching was coming from above; he looked up to see the peak of Yusuf's hood moving slowly along the balcony.

'Yusuf. *Salaam alaikum*.'

The sweeping stopped. A moment later a figure appeared above him. '*Alaikum salaam*.'

'You are well?' He struggled to follow the stream of Darija. 'You must tell the jinns there is no need to be unhappy. They must know that I want the best for these houses.' He looked around at the destruction. 'That which has been destroyed will be rebuilt. I ask you to trust me, Yusuf.'

Before the old man could reply, the door to the houses swung open and Paul stepped into the courtyard. Yusuf swung his right hand dismissively and moved out of sight.

'Ham. You're early.' He smiled, slightly nervously. 'I'd hoped to get here first. Straighten things up a bit.'

'It could do with it.' Hamad had no intention of masking his annoyance. 'It looks like you've gone at the place with a wrecking ball. I presume there are some designs I can see?'

'Of course. Are you all right?'

'You haven't heard?'

'What?'

'Hassan Azoulay killed himself yesterday.'

Paul turned, his eyes wide. 'Oh my God. Shit.' He looked blankly around the courtyard. 'Come into the office, I'll make some coffee.'

'I'm to blame.' Hamad walked behind the desk and sank into the chair. 'His death is my fault. My responsibility.'

'You can't feel like that. You weren't to know what had gone on between those two men.'

'I should have known. I always do full background checks, on everyone I plan to do business with. Reputation is everything in my world.'

Paul placed a mug of coffee in front of him and sat, awkwardly, in the chair opposite. 'Hamad, sometimes things just happen. You and I know that better than anyone. And you said that the family had plenty of money, that they could resettle anywhere.'

'It's not always about money.' He thought of Edith; she would know by now.

'No, it isn't. And I can see that this is an awful shock. I do understand, Ham. I know it was years ago, but I can still remember the awful guilt I felt about . . . you know, the accident and everything. I used to have dreams about that woman in the other car, about how much worse it could have been. But that was no one's fault but mine.

This man committed suicide. You didn't cause that. You've got no idea what else was going on in his life.'

Hamad balled his fingers into fists. Until now, he'd never felt any resentment towards Paul for the decision they'd made on the night of the accident, both numb with shock, half blinded by headlights and driving rain. It had been the only way to save Freya from more distress, to avoid a court case, newspaper headlines – *Students in Drunk-Driving Horror*. He couldn't have foreseen what would happen, the ramifications that would stretch across the years; that a decade later he would be sitting opposite Paul longing to absolve himself from one tragedy in order to be able to process another. Freya's face, pale with suspicion, appeared in his mind. He couldn't do it to her now, just as he couldn't then.

'I saw Freya yesterday. Before the dinner. She seemed upset. Is everything OK between you two?'

'Yes. Of course. Why, what did she say?'

'Oh, nothing specific. I just . . .' Hamad tailed off; he found conversations like this desperately uncomfortable. 'Paul, we've been friends a long time. If there was anything . . . you'd tell me, wouldn't you?'

'Tell you what?'

'I don't know. Just . . . Freya doesn't seem herself. There must be a reason.'

'She might be a bit homesick, I suppose. Or maybe she's upset that I'm going to Fez with Laila.' He glanced at Hamad. 'It's just a business trip, Ham. You know that, right? All above board.'

'Of course.' He attempted a smile. 'Well, if you say everything is good between you then at least that's something. I'd just hate to think that you two coming here has caused problems.'

'We're fine, really.' Paul leant down and pulled his laptop from his bag, flipping open the lid. 'Do you want to see the latest plans?'

'I do.' He watched his fingers jerk across the keyboard; there was something agitated about how he moved, a sense of tension, carefully controlled. 'Racine's really excited about all this, you know. I'd thought of suggesting that we came to Fez with you – but she says she's off on some wine course in Paris. News to me, I didn't think there was anything left for her to study.'

'Right.' Paul didn't look up from the laptop. 'Yes, I think she mentioned something about that.'

'She thinks Tim's got a bit of a thing for Freya.'

'What?'

'Oh, she was just joking. Just said he'd been a bit flirtatious over dinner.' Hamad sipped his coffee. 'It was nice, actually. We sat up for hours when we got back from Larousse, talking about the houses, the future. It's a while since we've had the chance to . . .'

'Here are the latest designs.' Paul pushed the laptop towards Hamad and stood awkwardly. 'Look, I'm really sorry, but my email calendar just flashed up a reminder. I'm due to meet with the surveyors at eleven. I have to go. Everything you need to see is there, but email if anything's not clear.'

'You're going?' Hamad raised his eyebrows.

'Sorry. Completely forgot. Have a good flight. Let me know what you think.'

Before he could answer, Paul disappeared through the door and out into the courtyard. Hamad sat back in the chair and pressed the tips of his fingers together, trying to decipher what had provoked the sudden change in mood. He was in no doubt the meeting was a fabrication; knew Paul well enough to recognise it as his way of bringing to a close a conversation that was making him uncomfortable. For once in his life, Hamad felt utterly bewildered: by Freya's suspicions, Paul's behaviour, by Edith's sudden departure from the previous night's dinner. On the screen in front of him, the floorplans blurred into a maze of black lines. Hamad tilted his head back and closed his eyes. There was nothing but the sound of sweeping.

*

'That bloody boy.' Edith crashed her phone onto the table with such force that the *macaron* bounced off the saucer. 'I suppose he's in that ridiculous jet of his already.'

'Dame Edith?' She glanced up to find a dark-haired waitress looking down at her. 'Is everything all right?'

'Yes, yes.' The last thing she needed after the events of last night was to be fussed. The girl didn't move. 'Was there something?'

The waitress bent down and picked up the *macaron*. 'Monsieur Chenouf is in reception. He asked if you were available.'

Edith stroked her fingers up and down the plaited silver chain that hung to her waist. Her hands shook a little. She had been awake most of the night, going over the conversations in her head: Paul's visit to the Delacroix vineyard in Lyon, his lie about never having been to the Mogador Palace. Moments from the dinner had crystallised in her mind like photographs: the brief exchange of looks between Paul and Racine when he had mentioned tasting the Viognier, the hint of a smile on Racine's face when the trip to Fez had been mentioned. Once the first wave of shock had faded, she was in no doubt that she had stumbled across the truth.

The problem lay in what to do with the knowledge. She pictured Mustapha's face if she told him what she had discovered; he would be horrified, of course, but she feared he would attempt to lessen her fury. She couldn't allow that. But to see him would be . . . comforting. Irritation flickered; she loathed feeling vulnerable.

'Please ask him to join me,' she said. 'And bring *thé marocain*.'

The girl moved away; Edith envied the fluidity with which she walked. She could remember moving like that, careless of her limbs, her body supple and free-flowing. Now simply rising from a chair felt like starting up an unwieldy machine. Her phone buzzed; she picked up her glasses, hoping the text was from Hamad. *Sorry you are unwell. Tomorrow is fine. Look forward to seeing you then. F.*

'Edith, *habibi*. How are you? No Freya?' He bent slowly to kiss her, and she felt the very maleness of him, beard rough against her cheek, the scent of mint and cologne. She let her fingers rest on the arm of his *djellaba* for a moment; his eyes lingered on her face. She remembered, wistfully, how it had been.

'I put her off. Not in the mood for it today.'

'It's not going well?'

'It's . . . tiring.' The girl reappeared with a tray of tea things; once she had placed it on the table, Edith waved her away.

'I feared it might be.'

'I know.' Edith hated being wrong. She'd never been one for looking back, had learnt early on that if one was to remain undaunted by the unfairness of life, there was only one direction of travel. Move fast enough and you could carve your own stories, create versions of events that eventually became fact. Now, with her brain permanently clouded, it was these versions she was finding difficult, her mind no longer sharp enough to distinguish between what she had created as truth, and what was actually real. 'But why shouldn't I tell my stories? Women like me get forgotten while the men, they're heroes. They get museums named after them, films made about their lives.'

'Of course you should tell your stories,' said Mustapha gently. 'Just not all of them. The past is never truly buried, Edith. Look what happened with Tim.'

'He would have had to find out anyway. I'm just sorry Hamad took it so badly. They're still barely on speaking terms. Look at that kerfuffle last night.'

'Yes.' Mustapha stroked his beard. 'But I'm afraid I agree with Tim. What Hamad did, getting involved between the Farzis and the Azoulays . . . It was very foolish.'

'You've heard, then. About Hassan.'

'I have. I wasn't sure that you—'

'Of course I've heard. I'm not entirely out of it, whatever you may think.'

'Edie—'

'It's that bloody woman. She's the root of all of this.'

'You mean Racine? She's very beautiful, isn't she? And quite the heiress. It's an amazing success story, Château Delacroix wine. I read an interview with her father in *Le Monde* a few months ago – he only started the label in his thirties, he was a banker or something before that. Obviously has the gift.'

'Well of course, it's in the genes,' said Edith briskly. 'They've been a wine-making family for generations – his parents and grandparents produced Beauvarin wines. I looked her up when she first got involved with Hamad. Remember Château Beauvarin? It was all we ever drank in Cairo. I can't imagine why he didn't keep the name, it had such a reputation.'

'Beauvarin?'

'Yes. Why, you don't have a bottle in the cellars at Jasmina do you? It'd probably be worth a fortune by now.'

'No. It's not that. It's just . . .' He tailed off, thumb and forefinger tracing the outline of his beard.

'*Mustapha*.' Edith's irritability crackled in the air.

'Sorry. It just reminds me of something someone told me once. I'm sure it's nothing.' He peered at her. 'Are you sure you're all right? You seem, I don't know, a little fractious. I was quite concerned when you left last night. Is something going on?'

'What do you mean?'

'Come along, *habibi*, I know you too well. No one's birthday, no anniversary, nothing particularly special to celebrate. And yet you go to the trouble of getting everyone together.'

'Hardly everyone. My grandsons, my oldest friend, my biographer.' She let out a short, humourless laugh.

'And then you leave your own party early. Before dessert, even.'

He chuckled. 'This is when I knew it was time to worry. Can't you tell me what upset you so? And don't tell me you were just tired. There's more to it than that.'

'I don't know what you mean.'

'Edith, I have known you for fifty years.' He laid his hand over hers. 'We are old, aren't we? Our deeds are done. All that's left to us is to watch the young live the lives we once inhabited. But last night, in the early part of the evening, you were at the heart of it all, the dinner belonged almost entirely to you. And then, suddenly, you leave. Perhaps you were tired. But I think you were shocked, too. Angry, even.'

Edith looked down at his hand, warm against hers. 'Do you believe in giving people second chances?'

Mustapha raised his eyebrows. 'An unexpected question.'

'But not a difficult one. If someone does something, if they commit an act of weakness, of . . . cowardice . . . do you forgive them? Even if the impact on someone you love is terrible?'

'Everyone is capable of making mistakes. I suppose it depends on how bad the impact is. But forgiveness is always the best way, both of ourselves and of others.'

'So you have always said. And that has given me great comfort over the years. But now I find that someone I once forgave has committed another sin. One that I cannot allow to go unpunished.'

'Edie, I don't like to hear you talk like this. Who has upset you? Will you tell me?'

She shook her head. 'I can't. Not yet.'

'Because?'

'Because I'm not sure what I'm going to do. This person, these *persons* . . .What I found out about them last night will change everything, for everyone who was at that dinner. And so I must make sure I get it right.'

'Get what right?'

Edith straightened up in her chair, pulled her hand away and locked her fingers together in her lap. 'Vengeance, Mustapha.' Her face was mask-like, skin taut across her skull. 'I need to find the right revenge.'

CHAPTER 15

We have to talk. Freya turned the words over in her mind: such a simple, short sentence, yet it had the power to shatter the increasingly stultifying status quo. She glanced across the terrace; Jacqueline was moving between tables, pouring coffee for the handful of couples who had already risen for breakfast. Was she *really* sleeping with her husband? Hamad and Edith – and even her sister, via Skype – had dismissed her suspicions out of hand, but how else could she interpret what she had heard in the garden at Villa Merteuil? It was all very well for Edith to talk about establishing proof, but the dinner party had done nothing but complicate her suspicions. Something about the trip to Fez with Laila felt odd, too. She couldn't put the conversation off any longer.

Her phone buzzed unexpectedly. *Still mortified by general mark-overstepping at Larousse. In your neighbourhood this morning; allow me to buy you breakfast for full apology and grovelling? Tim.* She reread the message twice, smiling in spite of herself. *Thanks but I'm seeing Dame Edith this morning. Have a good day. F.* Her situation was complicated enough without a further entanglement. What was needed now was honesty – from both her and Paul. She would tell him about the kiss with Tim, he could explain about the conversation at Villa Merteuil, and then they would move on, start again, engage with Marrakech together rather than continuing to drift apart.

She moved downstairs, wondering if Paul was up. The bed was empty; she could hear the muffled whirr of the shower, the pipes rattling out in the hall. On the chair beside her bed, a brown package lay unopened; she untied the string and pulled the teal-blue *djellaba* from the paper, slipping it over her head. The cotton was smooth against her skin; she felt cocooned, somehow, oddly protected.

'Wow. That's quite a look.' He had appeared in the doorway, damp-skinned, a towel around his waist.

'Fatma gave it to me yesterday.'

'Who's Fatma?' He crossed the room, pulled on jeans and an old Blur T-shirt she had bought him years ago. She saw them, suddenly, queuing at the merchandise stand at Wembley, hot and crumpled after bouncing around in a mass of other bodies, bellowing out the words to 'Girls and Boys'. Sadness swept over her. They had been happy. Really, properly happy.

'She lives in the house opposite. I'm helping with her English – I have told you about her. She had her uncle make this.' She picked up a pair of earrings and turned towards the mirror. She wasn't used to it yet, this new version of her; cloaked and unfamiliar.

'You're amazing.' Paul came to stand beside her. 'The way you make friends. The only Moroccan person I know, apart from Laila, is Yusuf, and he drives me crazy. I'm going to have to hide his broom if he doesn't stop with the endless sweeping.'

'He's an old man,' said Freya, staring at their reflection. Was that really them? They looked so disconnected; Paul's long, tawny-skinned limbs cuffed by the T-shirt and navy shorts, her body hidden away beneath the unfamiliar folds of the *djellaba*. 'It will have been a shock, what happened with Hassan Azoulay. He's old and everything he knows has changed. Give him time.'

'I know. Azoulay was a shock for all of us. It feels like . . . I don't know, like there's some kind of shadow over the houses. Yusuf would probably say it was the jinns.' He slipped an arm around her shoulder and kissed her cheek; she fought down an urge to push him away, smack his hand from her skin. 'God knows how he's going to react when he finds out about the plans for the wine bar.'

'I can't see that happening, however much money Hamad throws at it.'

'It'll happen. If a *maison du vin* is what Racine wants, a *maison du vin* is what she'll get. I get the impression that Ms Delacroix has never not got anything she wanted.'

'Your grammar's appalling.' She squeezed his arm and then remembered. How could they be like this? As if everything were normal? 'Paul, we need to talk.'

'OK. Shoot.'

'I don't mean a quick chat. I mean a proper talk. Things have been weird recently. We need to sort it out.'

'Oh.' He bent down to lace his trainers. 'Right. Have they?'

'You know they have.'

She waited for him to speak. 'Paul.'

'Well, yes, I guess things have been a bit . . . odd. But they're bound to be, aren't they? This is all a huge adjustment.'

'That's what Hamad said.'

'You've been talking to Hamad about us?'

'Not . . . us, exactly. About me, I guess.' She could sense his annoyance. 'I'd rather talk to you, though. Look, why don't I come to the houses later – you could show me how it's all coming on. I feel like I don't know anything about how you spend your days.'

'I see.' He looked at her for a moment, then smiled unexpectedly. 'OK. Why don't you come after five? It'll be quieter, the workmen should have gone by then.'

'I'll bring a bottle of wine.'

'Lovely.' He kissed her.

'And we'll talk?'

'Yes, Freya. We'll talk.'

*

Freya pulled the door to Dar Simone shut behind her and glanced up the alley. She knew every inch of it now: the potted palms outside the door to La Culinaria, the lascivious concierge who loitered in the doorway of Riad Zoukia, the names of the dusty-kneed boys who kicked the wizened football between them in the hours after school. Sometimes, an image of their street in Battersea rose in her mind: the row of terraced houses, neatly planted front gardens, parked cars nose to tail on the street. It seemed almost two-dimensional in comparison; an orderly landscape for orderly lives.

'*Salaam alaikum.*' Fatma waved from the neighbouring rooftop; Freya stopped and did a slow twirl.

'*Alaikum salaam.* What do you think?'

'You are Moroccan girl now. Perfect. You are perfect.' A small face appeared beside her; tousle-haired, grinning. '*Marhaba*, Freya.'

She waved and walked on, squeezing past a grey-haired luggage porter tucked into a pool of shade, sucking gratefully on a cigarette. The main alley was already busy, tourists ducking beneath racks of leather satchels, women queuing for the scrawny-necked chickens that drooped from grubby hooks on the butcher's stall. A bicycle bell rang out behind her; she stepped back to let the cyclist pass, the back of the bike piled up with a dozen open cartons of eggs. In the tailor's cubbyhole, a bespectacled figure was bent over a machine, dwarfed by bolts of material stacked up against the wall.

It struck her, as she walked, that no one was paying her the slightest attention. Cloaked in the *djellaba*, she was absorbed into the same world as the hawkers and the vendors and the trios of snap-thin boys who wound their way through the souks, dodging the three-wheeled carts and the scooters and the creaking bikes. Somehow, in spite of all her concerns, when she was out in the medina she felt elated, as if she were inhabiting a newer, braver version of herself. It was only as she approached the rose-draped walls of La Mamounia that a thought struck her: she felt this way around Edith, around

Hamad, even around Tim. But, somehow, she never quite felt it with Paul.

'*Bonjour*, Madame Hepworth.' The man in the gatehouse waved her through, the doorman ushered her into the lobby. As she passed the reception desk, she remembered Hassan Azoulay roaring towards them, the fury on his face. It didn't seem possible he was dead. The guilt nagged at her. It was easy to blame Hamad, to accuse him of throwing his money around, buying his way into situations he didn't understand. But they'd all benefited from the Azoulays losing their land, however indirectly.

'Good Lord, what are you wearing?' Edith peered over the sheaf of papers she was holding and looked the *djellaba* up and down. Freya couldn't help feeling sartorial criticism was a little rich, taking in the older woman's cherry-red kaftan, turquoise pashmina and long strings of purple beads. 'Actually, it's nicely put together.' She slid the papers back into a large brown envelope, stretched out a gnarled arm and twitched the fabric between her thumb and forefinger. 'Good quality. You didn't get that in the souk.'

Freya shook her head. 'My neighbour, Fatma. Her uncle's a tailor.'

'How much did you pay?'

'I didn't. I'm teaching her English in return.'

'Good girl. You're learning how it works here.' She peered at her more closely. 'How are you? You look tired.'

'I am tired.' The words shot out. 'Sorry. I don't mean to snap.'

'Things no better with that husband of yours?'

'I don't . . . No. Not really. I just . . . I don't know what to do. What did you think on Sunday night? It felt to me like he spent pretty much the whole night talking to Jacqueline . . . but then that makes me think if something *was* going on, surely they'd have been more careful?'

'I'm afraid Sunday night showed very little, apart from what a dreadful woman my grandson has got himself involved with. I was so distracted by her rudeness, her *arrogance* . . .' Edith took off her glasses and laid them on the table. 'Forgive me. I am still not quite myself. But if life has taught me anything, it's that so often we fear the wrong things. We try to protect ourselves from something that was never going to hurt us anyway and instead something totally unexpected wreaks the damage. The greatest shocks are those we never saw coming.'

Freya frowned. At times she had difficulty distinguishing between Edith's tendency to be elliptical, and days when her Parkinson's was simply getting the better of her. 'I'm not really sure what you mean.'

'Then let me give you an example.' She tapped her glasses on the brown envelope. 'Mustapha came to see me last night. He brought me these papers. They belonged to a very old friend of ours, a man named Jacques Richaud. He and I and Mustapha knew each other in Algiers in the fifties. They were lovers for a while. Jacques died fighting in the civil war. He left all his notebooks and papers to Mustie.' She sat back and closed her eyes. 'I cannot remember the last time I thought about that period of my life, and yet last night we were back there, strolling the whitewashed streets of Bab el Oud, drinking *anise* in the Café de la Poste.' She shook her head. 'Don't get old, Freya. It comes to something when reminiscing is one of your greatest pleasures. But we conjured up the past, he and I, for a quiet hour or two, and then . . .' She wriggled her hand upwards. 'The shock. *La grande surprise*. It turns out Jacques Richaud is to have a role in my present, as well as my past.'

'I'm not sure I know what you mean.'

'I mean that we all are a product of our own histories, I suppose. And that they can ensnare us, at any time, even decades later. More than that I can't say.' Her face softened. 'I am sorry that you must bear all this . . . upset. Too often in life, trouble is visited upon those who deserve it least.'

'I just wish I knew what to do.'

'In my experience, when one does not know what to do, it's often best to do nothing. Who knows, events may overtake you. Take this.' She picked up the envelope, held it to her chest. 'Jacques Richaud, a man I had forgotten I ever knew, has come back from the dead to offer me the solution to a problem I had no idea how to solve. This is what I mean, do you see? Life has a way of resolving things, and rarely in way we could ever have predicted. Now –' her eyes were clear and sharp on Freya's face – 'shall we move on? I don't have much time this morning; the car is coming to collect me at midday.'

'Oh.' Freya felt more than a little adrift. 'Are you doing something nice?'

'Not really.' A shadow passed over the older woman's face. 'I'm going to see the Azoulay widow. Pay my respects. And then I thought I'd drop by the Farzi houses. See what that husband of yours is up to.'

Paul picked up his phone and felt the breath whistle into his lungs. Any relief that the text wasn't from Freya was instantly superseded by the realisation that Dame Edith was on her way to the Farzi houses, and clearly expected to find him there. He tilted his head on the pillow; Racine was sleeping, her lips slightly parted, the skin around her mouth still raised. Guilt flooded his system. Even after what had gone before, it was still a shock to see her face in the bed beside him.

Life had become a series of stages, first set in motion by the frenzied sex in the office at the Farzi houses. In the immediate aftermath, he had been horrified by his own weakness, resolved afresh that it must never happen again. Within days, the fantasies had begun, then the first exchange of texts, the suggestion of a meeting, a mounting anticipation that seeped into his dreams and dominated his thoughts. He had never understood how all-encompassing desire could be. The exquisite relief at the moment of giving in obliterated the memory of everything else in his life. Until this, the final stage, the guilt-laden comedown when he thought of Freya and Hamad and tried to understand what sort of man he had become.

Things were out of control. They were taking risks; lost hours locked in the office at the Farzi houses, snatched moments at her villa when he had to have her before they had even reached the bedroom. It hadn't stopped when Hamad was here; if anything, the longing had been even worse. In the stolen hour before the dinner at Larousse, he had said things that seemed shocking when he remembered them later. He could never leave Freya. And yet he had meant it at the time, her body hard against his, desperate to say something that would make her understand the depth of his infatuation.

'Who are you texting?' He glanced over to see Racine staring at him sleepily, her hair messy against the pillow.

'Edith. I didn't know she even had my number. She's coming to the houses. Wants to see how "things are progressing". Apparently Freya told her I'd be there all afternoon.'

'Lucky you.' She sat up and smiled. 'Won't that be fun. Sitting around making conversation with the mad old bag, while I –' she turned onto her back and stretched an arm behind her head – 'just have a lazy afternoon. Might have a bath.'

'Don't torture me.' He tried to sound flirtatious, but the moment had gone. 'There's never enough time, is there? I hate this – squeezing in a half-hour here and there. I want more of you. I want *all* of you.'

'I don't think there's anything left of me you haven't had,' she said, raising an eyebrow. 'And we're going to have time, aren't we? Lots of time. In Taroudant.'

'But that's days away . . .'

'It'll be worth the wait, I promise. Just think. To everyone else, you're on a working trip to Fez, I am on a wine course in Paris. It will be as if we have disappeared from the face of the earth.' She pouted and wriggled her shoulders. 'There is something sexy in that, *n'est-ce pas*?'

'There is something sexy in everything, when it's with you.' His phone vibrated again. He glanced irritably at the screen. 'Bloody hell, she's texted Laila too. Look, I'm going to have to go. God knows what it's about, but it's not worth putting her back up. She's not got the highest opinion of me anyway.'

'Yes, I've noticed that. I like it . . . Takes a little of her *désapprobation* from me.' She watched him pull on his clothes. 'Be careful, though. Edith may be many things, but she's not stupid. The last thing we want is her getting suspicious.'

Paul stopped outside the door to the Farzi houses and smoothed down his shirt. He still found it hard to believe that the extraordinary interludes with Racine left no evidence; that it wasn't obvious to everyone he was embroiled in something that apparently had the power to change who he was as a person. It was becoming increasingly difficult to know how to behave around people; he found himself questioning every facet of his behaviour, unable to reconcile this new version of himself with the man he had always believed himself to be. At times it felt as if he were going mad, his mind dominated by a maelstrom of elation, self-loathing and fear, all bleeding into each other, contaminating his thoughts.

He stepped into the courtyard to be met by the familiar sound of sweeping, overlaid by faint strains of tinny music, coming from the workers' radio in the second house. The door to the office was open and he could see Edith, sitting behind the desk, peering at an open laptop.

'Paul.' She glanced up as he walked in, her face hidden by a pair of thick-rimmed glasses. She took them off and laid them on the desk; he noticed her fingers twitch against the laptop keys. 'How delightful to see you.'

'Dame Edith. My apologies for not being here when you arrived. I hope Laila has been looking after you?' He glanced around. 'Er, where is she?'

'I had to send her out.' She snapped the laptop lid closed and sat back in the chair. 'Wasn't feeling quite the thing. I suffer with low blood sugar, you know. Asked her to pop out and get me some chocolate.'

'I'm sorry you're feeling unwell. Can I get you anything? Water? Tea?'

'That's kind.' She didn't smile. 'You're a hard man to track down, aren't you? Never quite where one expects you to be.'

'If I'd known you were coming . . .'

'Ah, but where would the fun be in that?' She smoothed down the folds of a purple silk kaftan, bangles jangling as she moved. 'Hamad asked me to keep an eye on how things were progressing. It was so fortunate that you left your laptop in the office. I've been able to see all of the plans. I'm surprised, though, that you don't need them for a meeting with the planning department.' Her eyes narrowed. 'Laila said that's where you were.'

'That's right. But naturally the plans are on their system, too. I hope you liked what you saw? These houses are going to be magnificent once the project is finished. There'll be nothing like them in the city.'

'Of that –' Edith slid her stick off the arm of the chair and slowly pulled herself up – 'I am quite sure.' Paul stood to let her pass. She paused unexpectedly, her face directly opposite his. 'I must say, I've always found the process of restoring old buildings fascinating. Stripping something right back, leaving nothing but the bare bones. It can make a house feel so exposed, don't you think? All its secrets suddenly revealed.'

'You'll have to ask Yusuf about those,' said Paul, trying to keep his tone light. 'He's the keeper of secrets in this place.'

'He is, isn't he? Just imagine what he must have been witness to over the years.' She let her eyes rest on his face for a moment. 'Well, I must be going. Don't want to stand in the way of progress.' The sound of the front door slamming cut across her words.

'Dame Edith.' A look of surprise passed across Laila's face. 'You're feeling better? I brought you—'

'Keep it,' said Edith, glancing at the bar of chocolate. 'You look as if you need it more than I do. When was the last time you had a proper meal?' She raised her eyebrows at Paul. 'Why are all young women these days so thin?'

He shrugged, keen to avoid beginning another conversation. 'Can I arrange a taxi for you?'

'No need. I asked Jean-Paul, my driver, to be here at four.'

'Then Laila will walk you to the door. Thank you for dropping in.'

'My pleasure entirely.'

Paul waited until she was safely out into the courtyard, pulled his laptop towards him and scanned the open tabs. Edith didn't strike him as particularly technologically adept, but he needed to reassure himself there was nothing incriminating to discover. He communicated with Racine by text, each one deleted as soon as it had been sent or received. The success of his duplicity just made the guilt even worse.

'Did you say she could look at the plans?'

Laila stopped in the doorway. 'How could I say no? It didn't seem unreasonable. I was going through them with her and then she suddenly went all limp and peculiar, asked if I could get her some chocolate. I could hardly take the laptop with me.'

'No, I suppose not.'

'I do have a bit of good news, though.' She reached into her bag and pulled out a sheaf of papers. 'The *maison du vin* has been officially . . . What is it they say in films? Green-lit.'

'Really? No conditions?'

'Only small ones. The museum must open first, the *maison du vin* mustn't occupy a larger space, the entrances must be on separate streets. But they loved the plans for the Farzi House Museum. I thought—'

A yell from the neighbouring house cut across her words, then another; the sound of tools clattering to the floor.

'That doesn't sound good.' As he followed Laila across the courtyard, Paul realised that he had almost been waiting for an accident to happen. The builders soldered without goggles and plunged pickaxes into the ground barely a whisker from their workmates' feet. He'd tried to give them ropes and safety equipment, but they'd just laughed at the high-viz jackets and thrown the safety glasses back into the bag.

'What happened?' The foreman gabbled at Laila in Darija, pointing to a wide trough, with bits of discarded pipe piled up behind it. Paul could see the handle of a spade sticking out above the ground.

'Massoud says they started digging here this morning.' Laila nodded at the foreman. 'They needed to lay pipes. They broke through tiles and concrete and then . . .'

Paul crouched down, peering nervously into the hole. 'Jesus.'

'What is it?'

'Look for yourself.' She came to stand next to him; he heard a sharp intake of breath.

'Oh my God.'

Paul said nothing. The skin on his arms had puckered, every hair spiking upwards. The foreman spoke, but neither of them answered. The muezzin crackled into life. He didn't move. He just carried on staring, down into the trench, where the outlines of a human ribcage and two neat splays of finger bones gleamed white among the dark, disturbed earth.

CHAPTER 16

Freya woke. She lay in the darkness for a moment, her head thick with the fog of sleep and the sour remnants of wine. Something was different; her body felt unfamiliar, limbs a little longer, shoulders less knotted and tight. Snippets of the evening began to float into her mind; omelette and salad eaten on the roof terrace, a sense of urgency, or anxiety, along with an unexpected closeness. She remembered the feeling of a woollen wrap placed around her shoulders, warm hands gentle on her feet.

She turned over; the bed was empty. Memories flooded back: the phone call, Paul's voice thin with shock; the conversation she had been planning. Her visit to the Farzi houses had been forgotten; instead she'd put the wine back in the fridge, beaten eggs and chopped salad, trying not to think of what the discovery of the bones could mean. They'd eaten dinner without noticing the food, both focused on her laptop, flicking through websites, trying to translate the pages that gave any clue as to how such a discovery could be managed under Moroccan law.

'This could close us down for weeks,' he'd said, his face creased with worry. 'We'll have gendarmes crawling all over us, people from the department for heritage, or whatever it's called . . .' He'd looked so crestfallen that she'd leant across the table and kissed him, more to comfort than arouse. When she'd gone to move away, his hand had slipped around her waist, pulling her onto his lap.

It had been unexpectedly intense. He'd led her off the roof terrace without speaking; somehow she had been able to give herself over to the physicality of what was happening. It was only now, cocooned in the early morning darkness, that she understood why. In the heat of her passion, she had pinned his arms against the pillow, slid on top of him and all the fear and insecurity and shock fused into a strange, overwhelming energy, a desire to obliterate any memory of the hideous Jean-Charles, and Jacqueline, or Laila, or whoever it was that had replaced her, however temporarily. He'd looked up at her; she'd held his gaze. In that moment there had been no one else; they had been entirely, exclusively, each other's. Afterwards, there had been comfort; the hazy familiarity of the tangled bed sheets, the repetitive thud of his heartbeat when she lay against his chest.

The door clicked open and a shaft of light shot across the bed. 'Morning, gorgeous.' Paul appeared, holding two mugs. 'I've brought you tea. You awake?'

'Just about.' She pressed her fingers to her eyes and sat up, drawing the sheet across her upper body. 'Draw the blinds a bit, will you?'

She watched him move across the room; remembered the feel of his body against hers. How long was it since they had been like that? The bed groaned as he sat beside her; she could smell the tang of coffee twisting up from the mug. Something cold rippled across her skin. She'd managed to shut off her mind last night, muffled the suspicions with wine and lust. Now, in the low-lit beginnings of the day, she could feel the questions – the uncertainty – start to rise.

'That was quite an evening.' He smiled, touched his palm against her cheek. 'And you're quite a woman.'

'Really?'

'Of course. You really helped last night, you know? Not just –' he gestured to the rumpled sheets – 'the fun bit, but also just talking everything through. You always help me see things more clearly, get my thoughts in order.'

'Well, glad to be of service.'

He peered at her. 'You OK this morning? I feel like—'

'I'm fine.' She pulled the sheet more tightly around her body. She needed him to go, didn't know what to feel or how to be. 'Are you going to tell Hamad what's happened?'

'We talked about this last night. I don't want to tell him until I know what we're dealing with. He'll be on the first plane from Doha . . .'

'They are his houses.'

'They're Racine's, actually. And while I'm managing the project, they're mine.'

'All right, don't snap. You should at least tell her. She's bound to be at this gallery thing tonight. You don't want to have to tell her in the middle of a crowded bar.'

'God, is that tonight? Do we really have to go?'

'I've promised Dame Edith.'

'Couldn't we just meet back here and –' he kissed her – 'have a rematch?'

'You've got a one-track mind.'

'Who can blame me, when I've got such a sexy wife?' She stared at him for a moment; it was as if they had stepped back in time: a glimpse of how things had been before the miscarriage, before Ali. Part of her wanted to say something flirtatious back, to pull him towards her, feel his hands on her body. The face of the Tuareg waiter floated into her mind.

'Well. I guess I'd better go and face the music.' He leant in to kiss her and disappeared into the bathroom. After a moment, she picked up her phone and read through the text she had sent the previous afternoon. She wondered if it was too late to cancel.

*

'I thought you said coffee?' Freya raised an eyebrow at Tim, holding the taxi door open.

'I did. I just didn't say where.' He gestured to the pockmarked back seat. 'Come on, hop in. I thought you wanted to have adventures?'

She looked at him for a moment, then ducked her head and slid into the hot, stale air. She should have cancelled, should have sent the text she had written while Paul was in the shower. Distancing herself from a situation that could only further complicate things was the only sensible option. But she felt out of control, lost in a situation she didn't understand. Doing something reckless, almost self-destructive, felt oddly fitting.

The car lurched suddenly across a roundabout, narrowly avoiding a scooter that swung out from behind a slow-moving garbage truck. 'I'm not sure I'd class this as an adventure,' she said, wrapping her fingers around the leather door handle. 'More a near-death experience. Can't you ask him to slow down?'

'Tends to have the reverse effect. I promise you, it'll be worth it when we get there.'

Freya smiled uncertainly as the driver picked up speed. Everything began to rattle; prayer beads jangled against the rear-view mirror, a CD case vibrated against the dashboard, the passenger door next to her seemed loose in its frame. She glanced out of the back window; the walls of the medina were shimmering slightly in the afternoon heat, growing smaller and more distant as the taxi pulled away.

'So this discovery at the Farzi houses . . . What's Paul planning to do? Off the record, obviously.'

'I don't know – I don't think he knows. He'll have to talk to Hamad, of course, and I suspect he'll want to shut the whole project down until there's been a proper investigation.' She wondered if they'd spoken yet, tried to imagine the conversation – Paul growing frustrated, Hamad's irritation rising off the laptop screen like smoke.

'It's a tricky one. I don't think they're exactly seeing eye to eye on everything to do with those houses.'

The taxi veered across a junction; Freya fell across the back seat. 'Bloody hell . . .' She realised her hand was on his leg, felt herself blush. 'Sorry.'

'Don't apologise.' She moved back to the other side of the car. 'Come on, Mrs Hepworth. I'm just kidding.'

'Don't you think we should go to the police?'

'I think you'll have to, in the end. But I understand Paul's concern. If you get unlucky and they call some busybody down from the Ministry of Culture, the project could be shut down for weeks. Not that that would bother Hamad – I'm sure he could cover those builders' wages until they retire without even noticing.'

Freya said nothing as the taxi pulled up outside two iron gates. Tim passed a handful of dirhams to the driver, who barely acknowledged the transaction. A tall man in a coffee-coloured *djellaba* came forward to help her from the car; his long face broke into a smile.

'*Alors, Monsieur Matheson. Comment allez-vous?*'

'Claude. It's been too long. How are you? Allow me to introduce my friend, Freya Hepworth.'

'*Enchanté, madame. Bienvenue à La Vie en Rose.*'

'*Merci beaucoup.*' She stepped away for a moment to let the conversation run its course and watched as the gates slowly creaked open. Beyond them, dozens of rose beds rippled out towards a low, crenellated building; swathes of pink, scarlet and yellow blooms, neat squares of foliage framed by sprinkler-fresh lawns.

'What a gorgeous place.'

Tim appeared beside her. 'It used to be a rose farm, got converted into a hotel about ten years ago. Not what you expect from Morocco, is it?'

'Hardly. I feel like I'm in the South of France.'

'That's why I wanted you to see it – show you there's more to

Marrakech than the medina. Do you ever go up to the Ville Nouvelle? Do your shopping at Carrefour, have a coffee at Starbucks?'

'God, no.'

'Well, you should.' He linked her arm through his and they began to walk. 'You say you want to live here, live like a local? This city is a mix of the old and the new, and people move between them all the time. The medina isn't really authentic any more. So many of the houses are owned by expats. The irony is, you'd probably get a better sense of how local Marrakchi live in a backstreet in Gueliz.'

'You do like to lecture, don't you?' Freya bit back the irritation. 'I'm bloody trying my best to build a life here, but it's not easy. First there was that explosion at the Limonia – that was before we even moved here. Then there was the break-in, Hassan Azoulay's suicide, now they've found a body at the Farzi houses. Added to that, half of Edith's anecdotes seem to have been borrowed from other people, Hamad seems to be turning into the Aga Khan, and Paul . . .' She tailed off.

'Stop, *stop*,' said Tim, holding up his hands. 'You win. It's a disaster. The houses are probably cursed. Hamad's a megalomaniac. And Edith, God love her, is entirely bonkers. That's why sometimes you have to stop and –' he waved his arms around, sniffing dramatically – 'smell the roses.'

Freya stared at him for a moment, and began to laugh. 'Wow. This is quite a routine you've got going on here, isn't it? Does that line usually work?'

'I swear I just thought of it.'

'Really? I'll just pop back and ask Claude how many others you've brought here to smell the roses, shall I?'

'Well . . . maybe one or two. But that's not the point.'

'And what is?'

'That even if everything you say is true, you're still in Morocco rather than grey, damp London. You're living in one of the most amazing cities in the world. Writing about one of the most extraordinary women in the world. You're standing under blue skies in a rose garden with a man who's just about to buy you the best coffee in town. Life can't be all bad, can it?'

In that moment, Freya realised she was in trouble. They were words she had longed to hear from Paul; an affirmation that their impulsive decision to move to Marrakech had been the right one, that its rewards far outweighed the problems they were facing. She understood, suddenly, that the previous night's intimacy had been provoked by the feeling of a shared goal. For those few hours up on the roof terrace, poring over her laptop, trying to formulate a plan of action, they had both wanted exactly the same thing. It was an increasingly rare experience.

Paul glanced around the gallery and rehearsed the phrase in his mind once again. It wasn't fair to finish things with Racine in such a public place, but at least she wouldn't be able to react. There would be no possibility of her persuading him out of the decision. He had to do it. Last night had reminded him of what he had with Freya: something *real*, built on a decade of shared experiences and knowledge. He couldn't believe he had even thought of throwing it all away – and for what ? Everyone knew a relationship built on sex, however mind-blowing, wouldn't last, and he and Racine had little else in common. It was a moment of madness, a brief period in his life when he had somehow forgotten quite who he was, and the man he wanted to be. But it was over, now. He had seen sense, just in time.

'Paul.' He turned to see Dame Edith, swathed in a floor-length orange kaftan, her neck thick with a dozen chains of beads. 'I'm surprised to see you here.'

'Dame Edith.' He forced a smile. 'Why surprised?'

'With all this business at the Farzi houses, I would have

expected you to be there. Quite a business, what they found in that trench.'

'You've heard?'

'Of course I've heard.' She shook her head in exasperation. 'I am Hamad's eyes and ears when it comes to that project. When a wall comes down, I know about it. When a workman takes a day off, I know about it. And when the remains of a man are discovered, I certainly know about it. So how I know isn't the point. The question is, what are you going to do about it?'

'I've got the situation in hand, thank you. And Hamad is up to speed on developments.'

'I'm glad to hear it. And you're still planning to go to Fez? With . . . ?'

Paul looked away from the elderly woman, distracted by the sight of Freya walking into the gallery, Tim close behind, both of them laughing. He thought of the text she had sent earlier: *Running late, sorry. Meet you at the gallery.*

'Good evening *grandmère*.' Tim extended his hand. 'Paul. Good to see you.'

'Late as usual, Timothy.' Her face softened as she spoke. 'What's the excuse this time?'

'A real one, actually. Taxi broke down. Freya and I were coming back from La Vie en Rose and it turns out the idiot teenager behind the wheel had forgotten to put any petrol in.'

'La Vie en Rose?' Paul tried to keep his voice warm. 'What's that?'

'An old rose farm,' said Freya. 'It's a few miles outside the city, a really beautiful place. I thought we were just going for a coffee in the medina, but Tim unexpectedly whisked me off.' She glanced down at her trousers, brushed off a patch of dust. 'Not really dressed for such a glam event, I'm afraid – but if I'd gone home and come out again, I'd have missed the whole thing.'

'Well, well. Isn't this quite the gathering?' Tim stepped back to allow Racine to enter the group. Paul pressed his lips together; she looked – he tried to think of the word – glorious. Her hair was glossy, tumbling down her back, her shoulders bare save for two slim straps in midnight blue that ran down to a silk top that just met the waistband of her wide, white trousers.

'Ah, *la femme du vin*.' Edith wrapped her fingers around Racine's arm. 'How are you, my dear? Taking time off from waiting tables, are we? Does this mean the Palais du Jardin's esteemed clientele are having to pour their own wine this evening?'

There was a pause. Racine let her eyes drift over the kaftan, the heavy strings of beads, the strands of white hair that had escaped from the clips. 'Dame Edith. Such élan. Such panache. You could almost be French, *n'est-ce pas*?' Before the older woman could answer she turned away, the crowd parting as she drifted through it, stopping to talk to a woman with a sharp white bob. Paul watched her move, his body alight with desire. He recognised the woman, and the sharply dressed, silver-haired man standing next to her. Sabine and Jean-Charles. A memory surfaced from the evening at Villa Merteuil: the man's hand in the small of his wife's back. He looked over to where Freya was chatting with Tim.

'That *woman*.' Dame Edith waved her empty glass in Tim's direction. 'Get me another, would you, Timothy? I need something to lower my blood pressure.'

Paul watched him take the glass and move towards the bar. 'I didn't know you two were so chummy,' he said, raising his eyebrows at Freya. 'Why didn't you tell me you were meeting him for a coffee?'

'It wasn't a big thing. I just thought we were going to meet somewhere in the medina. You don't mind, do you?'

'Of course not. It's just—'

'There's someone I want you to meet.' Edith broke across the conversation. 'An archaeologist friend of mine – he's been working on a dig down at Volubilis for the past couple of months, but he's here in the city at the moment. I called him earlier, told him about your unexpected discovery at the Farzi houses, and invited him along.' She turned slowly, waved across the room. 'Wonderful. There he is.'

'Great,' said Paul, trying not to sound unenthusiastic. 'An archaeologist?'

'With a working knowledge of osteology, which makes him the perfect man for the job. Osteology? Study of bones?'

'I'm aware of what osteology is.'

Freya stepped back as a slim, grey-haired man leant in front of her to pass Edith a glass of champagne. 'Paul, allow me to introduce Wilhelm Björnsson. Will, this is Paul, the architect on the Farzi houses. He'd be very grateful for your help.'

'Good to meet you.' The man's hand felt damp and slightly limp. 'Can I also introduce my wife, Freya.' He glanced across, waiting for her to speak.

'Wilhelm Björnsson. A pleasure to meet you, Freya. But, forgive me, haven't we met before?'

CHAPTER 17

It wasn't often that Edith admitted to herself she had a made a mistake. Such a thing involved looking back, re-evaluating; usually she had no time for either. But introducing Wilhelm to Paul had definitely been a miscalculation. In the taxi from the gallery, he had recounted the incident with Freya and Tim on the terrace at Larousse with such glee, it left her in no doubt he would tell the same tale to Paul. It made her nervous. In twenty-four hours, she would have executed her plan; Wilhelm could wreak whatever damage he liked. For now, the status quo had to remain as it was.

Freya's arrival at the gallery with Tim had only served to confirm her suspicion that something was developing between them. The thought pleased her; Freya was going to need support in the coming days. Tim could prove a useful distraction. She fought back a wave of guilt. Collateral damage was inevitable in situations like this, but it was unfortunate that Freya was going to get caught in the crossfire. She had always felt oddly protective of her, ever since that first lunch in Antica Bella. She made a mental note to call Mustapha.

'Good afternoon, Granny.' She glanced up to see Tim smiling down at her. 'You're a vision, as usual.'

'And you're late, as usual.' She liked the feel of his face against her cheek; he reminded her of Robert. 'And please drop the "Granny". Edith is what it's always been, and that will do just fine.'

'Sorry.' He settled into the chair opposite her. 'So how are you? Recovered from last night's little soirée?'

'I have.' She peered at him over her glasses. 'You made quite the arrival, turning up with Freya. Not the first time you two have had a secret liaison, or so I understand?'

'I don't know what you're talking about.'

Edith shook her head. 'You never could tell fibs, even as a small boy. The dinner at Larousse? Hamad told me you left soon after I did – something about a deadline for a piece? But we both know that's not true, don't we? You did not go home to your laptop. Instead you went to the upstairs bar with Freya.' She raised her hand. 'No, don't apologise. I'm actually rather pleased you two have become friends.'

Before Tim could speak, Edith nodded at the waiter lurking nervously beneath the nearby palm tree. 'My usual,' she said. 'Timothy?'

'Beer, please.'

'I'm sorry to have to change our day this week,' she said, as if the previous conversation hadn't happened. 'But I have plans for tomorrow.'

'Doing something nice?'

'I wouldn't call it nice. Necessary, perhaps. A situation that needs . . . resolving.'

'How very enigmatic.' Tim raised an eyebrow. 'A dangerous thing to be around a journalist. It might make me think you were up to something.'

'Don't be ridiculous. At my age? I can barely get out of this chair.' She glanced up as the waiter laid the drinks on the table. 'Ah, excellent. Lunch has arrived.'

Tim watched as a platter of French cheeses, baskets of bread and a whole, dressed crab were laid on the table. 'A feast, Granny. Feels like we're celebrating.'

'Indeed we are. We're celebrating justice. Something all too rare in life, I find.' She scooped up a spoonful of crab, smearing it onto a piece of bread. 'But I want to hear about you. Are you still going to Imlil? I do hope you're not planning some exposé on Hamad. He is family, whatever you feel about him.'

'I know it's difficult for you. But it's my job. It's not personal. If Hamad was anyone else but your grandson, there'd have been far more coverage about Hassan Azoulay's death. I don't know how many favours you called in.'

'If the man chose to take his own life, I fail to see how Hamad can be held responsible.'

'Really? Because I don't . . .' Edith's knife slipped from her fingers and clattered onto the table. He took a breath. 'Look, shall we agree to disagree?'

'No. Let's not.' Edith blotted her lips with her napkin and leant forward. 'For a journalist, you can be very blinkered, can't you? Your envy, or distrust, or whatever it is you feel towards Hamad, is blinding you to who is the real cause of all these problems.'

'Enlighten me.'

'Racine. That woman is at the root of everything. If it weren't for her frankly inexplicable decision to move to Marrakech, none of this would have happened. The Farzis would still own the houses, Hassan Azoulay would still be alive, and that dreadful, duplicitous man would still be in London. Now there *is* someone to despise.'

'I'm sorry, you've really lost me now.'

'I'm talking about Paul.'

'Paul? What's he done to offend you? I'm not his biggest fan – I've no idea what Freya sees in him. But I'm not sure he quite deserves—'

'Really?' Edith drew her body up in the chair; her face looked pinched, almost hawkish. 'Shall I tell you a story about Paul Hepworth? About how he killed a woman, ten years ago, and has never faced up to what he did? About how he let Hamad take the blame, shoulder all the responsibility for a crime he never even committed? You sit there and you criticise Hamad, yet you know nothing. He's capable of acts of generosity, of loyalty that you cannot even comprehend.'

'Paul killed someone? Granny, are you sure?'

'Of course I'm sure,' she snapped. 'I was there. He called me, like some snivelling child, insisted that I come and help them. They'd been involved in an accident, a few streets from where I lived. Paul was driving – but he'd been drinking. By the time I reached the scene he had already disappeared, leaving Hamad to say it was him who had been behind the wheel.'

'Wow. That's quite a lie.'

'He did it for Freya. She was very vulnerable at the time – her mother had died the previous year and she was still struggling to come to terms with it. She and Paul had plans to go travelling. Hamad knew that if the truth came out, Paul would be arrested. He didn't think she would be able to cope.'

'And the other driver . . . ?'

'Died in hospital, several days later. It was unexpected – although we knew she'd been quite badly injured, the prognosis was fair. The night before they left for Thailand, Hamad told Paul she'd been discharged from hospital, that there was nothing for him to worry about. Freya never even knew there was anyone else involved. The following day we got a call. She'd had a brain haemorrhage. Apparently, it is a risk, with the kind of injuries she'd sustained. But no one had told us it was a possibility.'

She could see Hamad as if it were yesterday, sitting in the armchair in her Cambridge flat, his fingers still wrapped around the phone's receiver. It happened increasingly, memories from years ago crystallising in her mind while she struggled to remember details of the previous day. *She died.* His face had gone pale, frozen in shock. It was one of the only times she and Hamad had ever argued. He had won. There would be no phone call to Thailand, no struggle to find the words to tell Paul what had happened. Hamad would deal with it all.

'And Paul never knew? Hamad never told him?' She tried to remember who she was talking to, the identity of the young man sitting in front of her. 'Incredible. But why bring it all up now? It's an astonishing thing to have done, but if it was ten years ago . . .'

'Tell me about you.' It was a phrase she relied on; a way to manage the sudden, unexpected gaps. She could feel the concern in his glance.

'Oh.' He frowned. 'OK, well, to come back to where we started, yes, I am going to Imlil. The day after tomorrow.'

The mists cleared. 'Really?' She raised her eyebrows. 'And is Freya going with you?'

'I don't think so.'

'Really? Even after your . . . assignation at Larousse?'

'It wasn't an assignation. Freya made that very plain.'

'Don't be coy with me. I may be old but I'm not blind – anyone can see you're infatuated with her.'

'I don't know "infatuated" is the word I'd choose. I just like her. She's intriguing. But she's also married.'

'Intrigue is overrated. There's too much of it in this city, too many spoilt women who mistake self-indulgence for non-conformity. As for being married, I'm not sure that's something you need to take into account.'

Tim raised his eyebrows. 'Granny, your morals—'

'It's not my morals we're talking about here.' Edith snapped her mouth closed; she had already shared too much with Tim. 'Why don't you ask her again? She might have changed her mind. You shouldn't be so defeatist.'

'Why are you so keen, anyway?'

'Because I like Freya,' she said crisply, 'and she deserves more than that ghastly excuse for a husband. She deserves some happiness. And I fear in the days to come, Marrakech is the last place she's going to find it.'

*

'Is this some sort of a joke?' Wilhelm turned, a long piece of bone between his fingers. He waggled it at Paul, frowning. 'You ask me here for this?'

Paul peered into the trench. The finger bones lay untouched, splayed neatly to form a skeletal hand. 'What do you mean?'

The Swede picked up one of the longer bones and pretended to nibble along it. 'Yum yum. Spare ribs. Delicious.'

He climbed out of the trench, dusting off his creased khaki trousers. 'I'm happy to tell you that you do not have the body of a man down there, rather the bones of a pig. And two, perhaps three, chickens.'

'What?'

'I think you've been victim to a . . . what's the word? Prankster? A very thorough one. the bones are well arranged – and pig ribs are very similar in size and shape to humans'.'

'Why would someone do that? You don't bury animals in the foundations of a house. Christ, what else could be down there?'

'These weren't buried in the foundations. I'll be surprised if they've been there longer than a couple of days.'

Paul frowned. 'But the foreman said . . .'

Wilhelm passed the bone across; it felt smooth and cold against his fingers. 'Sniff it. You can still smell the flesh. These ribs were walking around last week.'

'But that's not possible. He said they'd gone through tiles and cement to dig that trench.'

'And you believed him?' Wilhelm shook his head. 'Come along, my friend. How long have you been in this city? They lie, all of them – say whatever they like, as long as it gets them what they want. Perhaps they did drill through cement. Perhaps not. Perhaps they wanted a few days off. Paid, of course.'

'I don't think so.' Paul thought of the horrified expression on the foreman's face. 'They were as surprised as we were.'

'Well then, you have someone else who wants to make a point.

Someone who, perhaps, isn't entirely happy with what is being done to these houses? Or who now owns them?'

'That would be quite a long list.' He looked down at the bone in his hand and shuddered. 'I'm so sorry to have wasted your time. I'm beyond embarrassed. Let me at least make you a coffee.'

Wilhelm put up his hand and smiled. 'That would be great. And don't worry about asking – I'm pleased you did. This city is littered with all sorts of treasures, and people just plough across them, or ignore them, or – worse – dig them out themselves and all but destroy them. It's quite rare to find someone who's actually put something *into* the earth, rather than taken it out.'

'I suspect I know who it was.' Paul gestured towards the courtyard and followed Wilhelm out into the alley. 'These houses have a guardian. Yusuf. Yusuf believes, very strongly, in jinns. These houses are riddled with them, apparently. His full-time job seems to be catering to, or appeasing, the jinns – he's always leaving food out, opening the windows, telling me I can't take down this wall, or dig in that room, because the jinns will be angry. I suspect this is just another attempt to cater to their whimsical needs.'

'I don't envy you. In the older generation these beliefs are very powerful. You would do well to try and accommodate some of what he suggests. Or you may find episodes like this will not be irregular.'

'So I've been told.' Paul unlocked the door and stepped into the lobby. The sound of sweeping filtered through the gloom. 'That's him. Hear it? He's always sweeping.' He sighed. 'Between a client who wants to open a wine bar in a Muslim medina, a guardian who communicates with the dead, and a bureaucratic system that has more rules than anywhere I've ever worked, I'm starting to think I'm doomed.'

'All the more reason to find some . . . pleasurable diversions, don't you think? I hear you had an evening at Jean-Charles's and

Sabine's a couple of weeks ago. I hope you and your wife enjoyed yourselves?'

Paul felt a wave of discomfort. 'Er . . . well, it was interesting, I guess.'

'Interesting. Yes. Evenings at Villa Merteuil are always interesting.' The smile became a little more knowing. 'You will soon learn, Paul, if you haven't already, that although huge numbers of Europeans call this city home, very few of them are interesting. They are – how can I put this? – dull ex-teachers and small-town solicitors who believe they have done something adventurous, something dangerous, by moving to such a place to live. *We have thrown everything we know aside*, they think, and then they come here and live in entirely the same manner they would at home. Those who actually choose to live differently – there are few. And Jean-Charles and Sabine are two of them.'

Paul saw Jean-Charles suddenly: the sharp jaw, blue eyes framed by black-rimmed glasses, the expensively cut grey hair. He had never met anyone so unassailably confident. 'Amazing house they've got,' he said, passing Wilhelm a mug of coffee. 'A really beautiful place.'

'And their style of entertaining?'

He began to wish they were outside; the kitchen felt too small. He had a sudden sense of the other man's body next to him.

'Not my thing. Each to their own, of course, but . . .'

'Of course,' Wilhelm said, placing his coffee back on the side. He let his hand slide onto the counter and then let it drift across to where Paul was leaning. 'Perhaps a different sort of evening? Same freedoms, different –' his fingers brushed gently along Paul's thumb – 'players?'

Paul's arm rocketed backwards; the palm of his hand grazed against the sharp corner of the worktop. A sliver of skin ripped apart.

'Or perhaps not?' The older man's tone was soft, disquieting. 'Oh dear. You're bleeding.'

'It's fine.' Paul lifted his hand to his mouth and licked the snagged skin. His tongue felt hot and wet. Wilhelm's faded silver eyes looked on, a hint of amusement resting above the pink rims.

'My apologies. I hope I haven't offended you.'

Paul glanced at his palm. He felt queasy. 'Forget it. I'm aware all sorts of things go on in this town. They're just not for me.'

'So it seems. It's just . . . Of course, it's none of my business.'

'What's none of your business?'

'Just that those who go to Villa Merteuil are usually of a more broad-minded persuasion. And your wife is clearly more . . .'

'Clearly more what?'

'Now, this is awkward.' Paul got the impression Wilhelm wasn't finding it awkward at all. 'I just assumed . . . you know. When I – quite literally – bumped into her and Edith's grandson the other night, they were so – how can I put it? – *engaged* with each other that I naturally assumed you would enjoy the same freedoms.'

'Freya and Hamad? Sorry to disappoint you, but they're just very old, very good friends. Anything you think you saw—'

'But I'm not talking about Hamad. I mean her other grandson – what's his name? Tim? Up on the terrace at Larousse. When would it have been? Sunday? Quite late. I fear I spoilt a rather . . . intimate moment between them.'

Paul felt the muscles in his neck tighten. 'I'm afraid you're mistaken. My wife and I were both at Larousse on Sunday evening, having dinner with friends. Including Edith and both her grandsons.' He picked up the mugs and put them in the sink. 'Don't let me keep you any longer. I'm sure you have things to do.'

'I've offended you, haven't I?' Wilhelm raised his eyebrows in mock apology. 'I've obviously got it wrong. It's just such a confusing place, Marrakech, isn't it?' He pulled out his wallet and handed a fifty-euro note to Paul. 'But I do insist you give your wife this. My friend spilled wine on her dress. So careless. I insisted I would cover the cost of the dry-cleaning, and a gentleman never leaves a bill unpaid.'

'I don't think Freya will want your money.'

Wilhelm shrugged. 'Whatever you say.'

Paul felt his phone vibrate. 'I have to take this.'

The older man nodded and picked up his keys. 'Of course. And please forgive my clumsy comments about your wife. I do so hate to offend.'

It was dark by the time Paul turned into the alley that led to Dar Simone. He'd put off returning, trying to regain his composure after the insidious conversation with Wilhelm. His face still burned at the memory of it: the man's hand on his, the insinuations about Freya. Normally he would have dismissed them without a moment's consideration, but coming on top of Hamad's comment about Tim's attraction to Freya, and her unexpected arrival with him at the gallery the previous evening, it was hard to entirely discount his words. He thought back to the dinner at Larousse, to Freya's unexpected text, Tim's early departure from the meal. It would be entirely out of character for her to have lied and sneaked upstairs while he sat at dinner below. Yet he had a strong sense that was exactly what had happened.

The irony was that he had genuinely meant to finish things with Racine the previous evening. Only circumstance had prevented him from having the conversation, but the events of the morning had made him reconsider it as a course of action. If something was going on between Freya and Tim, why should he give up something so extraordinary? The thought of the trip to Taroudant made him shudder with anticipation. He slipped his key into the lock, and stepped into the hallway. He would say nothing, for now at least.

'Paul? Is that you?'

He hadn't seen her, curled up on the sofa in the corner, a glass of wine on the table beside her. As he moved into the light she looked up; her face was unexpectedly tense.

'How did it go?'

He came to sit beside her. 'OK. Bit weird. Turns out they're pig and chicken bones. Someone did it for a joke, a bit of a stunt.'

'A joke?' She raised her eyebrows. 'That's a bit sick.'

'Yep.' He let his hands rest against the cotton on the sofa. 'He was a bit of an odd bloke. Bit sleazy.'

'I know.' She pulled her hair off her face and held it in a ponytail; he recognised the gesture as something she did when she felt awkward. 'I meant to say, actually. I met him before. He probably didn't remember – he was pretty drunk. Threw a glass of wine all over me.'

'He mentioned something about it.' Paul tried to keep his tone steady. 'It was all a bit vague, really.'

'Oh, right. OK.' She paused for a moment; he had the sense there was more to come. 'Look, I need to ask you something. Don't get angry I just . . . It's something I need to say.'

'All right . . .'

She straightened her back, pressed her palms against her legs. 'Are you having an affair?'

He felt his insides lurch. 'What? That's quite a question.'

'Well, are you?'

'Are you?'

'Don't be ridiculous.'

'I'm not being ridiculous. You're right, Wilhelm did mention you. And he wasn't vague at all, he remembered the whole incident very clearly. Larousse, wasn't it? The night of the dinner? You and Tim were very – how did he put it? – engaged with each other. Seemed to think we might be up for another swingers' party, based on your behaviour.' He ran his fingers through his hair. 'For God's sake, Freya, you told me you'd gone home. What were you doing, sneaking upstairs like that?'

'I don't know what I was doing.' She stood up unexpectedly and hurled the wine glass to the floor. The noise stunned him; it split like rain across the terrace, fragments glinting on the tiles. 'I don't know anything right now. But not because I'm having some illicit affair . . . because *you* are. Don't look so shocked. I've known about you and that French bitch for weeks.'

He couldn't catch his breath. 'You know . . .'

'About you and Jacqueline? Jesus, couldn't you have gone for someone a little less desperate?'

'Jacqueline?' He almost laughed. 'I'm not having an affair with bloody Jacqueline. What do you take me for?'

'I heard you. In the garden at Villa Merteuil. I heard you tell her it was over, that it wasn't going to happen again.'

'Well, then you must have misheard.' He tried to think back. 'I never said such a thing. Why would I? There's nothing to *be* over. And frankly, I'm surprised you had the time to hear anything I was saying. You couldn't leave the table with Jean-Charles quickly enough.'

'Yes, and now you know why. Or are you going to accuse me of having an affair with him, too? For God's sake, Paul, when have I ever given you any reason to think I'd cheat on you? You just want to believe I'm shagging someone else so you can feel better about your own sordid little adventure.'

'So you're telling me nothing's happened between you and Tim?'

Freya stared at him for a moment, then bent down to retrieve her bag from under the table. She pulled out her phone, typed a message and turned the screen towards Paul. *Hi. Would love to come to Imlil. Call me to make a plan. F x.* 'I'd said no. You're right, I am attracted to him. That happens, doesn't it? It's inevitable in a marriage. You meet someone, there's a connection, you step back. That's what I've done. I know things aren't great between us, but I hadn't give up, in spite of the fact you're shagging that bloody Frenchwoman.'

'I am *not* sleeping with Jacqueline. And I thought things were better . . . the other night—'

'The other night I was *drunk*.' She glared at him. 'Look, I know something's going on. Why won't you just admit it?'

'Because there's nothing to admit.' He wished, desperately, it was the truth. 'Freya, I'm sorry. If I've got it wrong . . .'

'Oh, you've got it so wrong.'

'Let's have a drink. Talk properly . . .' He reached towards her; she snatched her arm away.

'What, so you can throw more ridiculous accusations at me?' She began to walk across the courtyard, then turned briefly. 'I'll sleep in the spare room tonight. Don't bother to wake me before you go to Fez.'

CHAPTER 18

The car jolted suddenly; Edith felt her eyelids stagger upwards. Her knees ached from sitting still too long, and the air conditioning had made her mouth dry and sore. She was exhausted, and the main business of the day hadn't even begun. She thought back to the previous day's lunch with Tim; she had eaten too much rich food, the champagne had been a mistake. She should have spent the time quietly, preparing for today. But she hadn't wanted to cancel; had found herself unwilling to pass up any chance to spend time with her newly acquired grandson. She was painfully aware the number of meetings they had left was dwindling fast.

Outside, the road blurred past. Where was she going? She peered at the dark-haired man in the driver's seat. Madani. All these young men, so like their fathers, their grandfathers before them. Sometimes her life felt almost dreamlike; yesterday, for one joyous moment, she had actually believed it was Robert, bending to kiss her. The problem was, these days, the young didn't seem to know how to organise their own lives – Hamad was making bad decision after bad decision, Tim was still drifting after the divorce. She thought of Freya. Perhaps she should have told her what she had discovered on the night of the dinner party. It hadn't been easy, listening to her misplaced fears about Jacqueline. But there was no telling what she would have done; the risk to her own plans was too great.

'Dame Edith? We're in Taroudant. What was the name of the riad?'

She looked out of the window. 'We can't be. We've only just left Marrakech.'

'The joy of the motorway,' said Madani. 'So much quicker than the old road. Perhaps you dozed a little too.'

'I don't doze. I was thinking.'

'Of course. But can you tell me the name of the hotel?'

Edith peered into her handbag and retrieved a folded piece of paper. She was still rather proud of the technical ability she had displayed on her visit to the Farzi houses. Paul's absence had made the whole thing much easier, and once she had sent Laila out for chocolate, it had been remarkably simple to find the link to his inbox and scan the emails for something that proved her suspicions. She'd seen it almost immediately: a confirmation email for two nights at the Riad la Belle Étoile in Taroudant, on exactly the dates he was supposed to be in Fez. She'd just managed to print it out and close down the inbox before Paul had stepped through the door.

'Here it is.' She passed the paper to Madani, who took it slightly impatiently. She suspected he wasn't entirely pleased at spending his Sunday driving to Taroudant and back. It was Mustapha who had insisted he act as chauffeur, clearly discomforted by the fact she refused to share her plans. She had wanted to tell him – he had always been her confessional, a moral touchstone against which she judged her own, more fluid, beliefs. But he would have tried to persuade her out of it; worse, she would have disappointed him. That would have been almost impossible to bear.

Moments later, the car slowed to a halt. She levered herself upwards, leaning gratefully on Madani's arm. The street swung a little as she stood, the air thick with the scent of horse-dung and diesel and the sour tang of *kif*. A *calèche* rattled by, the horses' hooves sharp against the tarmac, two families piled onto the battered leather seats. Behind the car, a row of trestle tables was covered with mounds of strawberries and bundles of tarragon and mint. A plump woman was shouting at the man serving; he was ignoring her, scooping the fruit into faded plastic bags with grubby, mud-stained hands.

'Riad la Belle Étoile is just there.' Madani pointed at a wide, polished-wood door flanked by two olive trees. 'I'll walk you.'

'Thank you, Mustie. That's kind.'

'Dame Edith? It's Madani.'

She peered at him. 'What? Who's Madani?'

'Me. I'm Madani. Mustapha's son. Remember? Mustapha's at home. In Marrakech.'

She closed her eyes for a moment and tried to think. Every day it was getting worse. She was beginning to dread waking up in the mornings, knowing that there would come a time in the not-too-distant future when she wouldn't recognise anyone at all.

'Of course. Stupid of me.'

They moved forward slowly, stepping over the broken paving slabs and oily puddles of water that had gathered on the uneven surfaces. By the time she reached the door she had forgotten the long, uncomfortable journey, aware of nothing but the sheaf of papers in her handbag and the retribution she had come to deliver. The wide brass knocker was cool against her palm, a trickle of adrenalin beginning to feed into her veins. As the door creaked open she remembered the woman she had once been: powerful and fearless, afraid of no one.

'Hello. Can I help you?' The German accent wrong-footed her; she had been expecting to need French, possibly Arabic.

'Yes.' She smiled at the younger woman. 'I'm here to see one of your guests. Racine Delacroix.'

'Of course.' The woman drew back and Edith stepped into the dimly lit lobby. 'Is she expecting you?'

'Not exactly. But we're very good friends. I know she'll be delighted to see me.'

*

It was two hours since Freya had settled into the lounger on the rooftop, and still there was no sign of Jacqueline on the opposite terrace. She could just walk through the gate and ask one of the houseboys to find her, but that would mean the possibility of hearing the answer she feared most: *She's not here, madame. She is in Fez.* And then what? It was all very well for Edith to talk of proof, but once Paul's infidelity was a fact, everything would change. This odd no-man's-land of suspicion might be uncomfortable, but at least it avoided the necessity of change. She was slightly ashamed of how daunting she found the prospect.

She wished Paul hadn't tried to talk to her before he left. Sleep had done little to lessen her anger; his apologies had just fuelled her resentment, the sense of a spectacular injustice. Every thought and fear she'd had since she'd walked into the empty suite in Doha came boiling to the surface; she'd found herself shouting, throwing accusations. He'd hurled them back: Jean-Charles, the rooftop at Larousse, even the suggestion that her guilt was fuelling the lunatic theory about Jacqueline.

The text from Tim had arrived just minutes after Paul had slammed the front door, her phone vibrating through the silence. There'd been others since: arrangements, pick-up times, an assurance that there would be two rooms rather than one. She was glad he hadn't called. There was something illicit in the anonymity, a feeling that she was doing something outside her own skin.

The flat tones of the door bell interrupted her thoughts; she padded across the rooftop and peered down into the street. To her surprise, Mustapha stood in the gloom of the alley, head bowed beneath the sharp lines of the *kufi*.

'Mustapha?' He glanced up and waved. 'I'll come down.'

Her footsteps echoed on the stairs. She caught her toe in the strap of Paul's satchel lying in the hallway, and almost tripped, steadying herself against the wall. 'Oh, just fuck off!' She didn't want to be reminded of him, or the row, didn't want to be the betrayed wife. Not in front of Mustapha.

'Freya.' The kindness in his face made her throat tighten. 'How are you? I was out walking and I remembered your husband is away in Fez. I thought you might like some company.'

'That's kind.' She swallowed hard. 'But I'm not feeling very well, to be honest.'

'Perhaps a walk will help.' She could feel his gaze taking in the raised pink skin around her eyes. 'It is the best time of day – the low sun, the cooler air . . . How do you say in English? – to blow away the cobwebs?'

'Perhaps.' She glanced down at the faded leggings and T-shirt she had pulled on in the aftermath of the row. 'I should change . . .'

'Nonsense.' He held out his hand. 'Come. Be spontaneous.'

Almost before she realised what had happened, the door to Dar Simone had closed behind her and they were walking up the alley in companionable silence, broken only by the slap of the elderly man's *babouches* on the dusty street. As they weaved towards the square, she began to feel she was seeing an entirely different medina. Mustapha didn't point out the mosques and the hamams, or tell stories about the houses that lay hidden behind featureless doors. Instead he talked of the people who nodded their heads in greeting as they passed: Abuddin the tailor, who had once made dresses for Elizabeth Taylor; Salma, who came out of the spice shop to kiss his hand and pass over bags of *ras el hanout* and saffron; Ismail, smoothing out Berber rugs for a group of tourists.

'It's all nonsense,' Mustapha said, shaking his head. 'Those carpets don't come from his family's farm. He's from Casablanca, a city boy like me.'

She was about to reply, when an elderly man in a hooded *djellaba* stopped to press his hands around Mustapha's. She waited while they spoke; a nub of intimacy among the swarm of tourists. The stillness in both men was almost hypnotic.

'Wafiyah is a good friend of mine,' said Mustapha when they began to walk again. 'Brother to Hassan Azoulay.'

'I'm so sorry. I still feel so terrible. To lose your brother – I can't imagine how hard that must be.'

'Harder because he cannot grieve as one would normally do. Instead he is angry. Ashamed. Suicide . . . It is an offence to God. What Hassan did has brought terrible shame on his family.'

'On top of losing their land . . .'

'Indeed. The Azoulays have suffered much in these last months.' He gestured to a cluster of café tables further along the pavement, filled with men drinking coffee and smoking. To one side, a garage spilled scooter engines and tyres onto the kerb; on the other an African hawker had spread tribal masks on a block-printed sheet. 'It doesn't look much, but they serve the best coffee and *chebakia* in the city. Shall we?'

'So, how are you really?' Mustapha lifted his cup and smiled at her. 'It's been quite a week, I think, with all this nonsense at the Farzi houses.'

'It's been quite a month,' said Freya wearily. 'I do love this city, Mustapha, I really do. But it's hard to get your bearings. Things are different to how I thought they would be. People are different.'

'People?'

'Paul. And Hamad. Edith, maybe. Sometimes I feel, I don't know . . . like everyone has become a different version of themselves since we moved here. Or maybe I'm just seeing the reality. I still think of Hamad as the same man I knew at university, but coming here has made me realise that most people see a very different man to the one I know. Tim always says he just swans in and throws his money around to get what he wants. And then Paul . . . I feel constantly wrong-footed by him, as if I can't ever quite predict what he's going to do or say next. It's like with Edith – he's so odd around her. They obviously dislike each other, but I've no idea why. Do you know?'

Mustapha picked up a *chebakia* and bit into it, showering sesame seeds across the table. 'Delicious,' he said, smiling. 'But a little messy. Like life, I think.'

'Seriously, Mustapha, I need to know. Does Edith know something about Paul?'

The old man leant back in his chair and spread his palms towards the sky. 'I suspect Edith knows something about all of us. She is a keeper of many secrets, Freya, as I'm sure you have discovered. This is one of the reasons why I wanted to see you. Do you know where she is today?'

Freya shook her head.

'She has left the city – the first time she has travelled outside Marrakech in over a year. I asked where she was going, but she refused to tell me. I am a little worried. Edith has very few reserves – even something like last Sunday's dinner takes her a day or two to recover from.'

'You love her very much, don't you? And yet you never married?'

Mustapha burst out laughing. 'Marry? Ours is not that kind of love affair. It is ironic, no? Our feelings have withstood months, even years, of separation, and yet if we had lived each day together, side by side, I think the love we felt for each other would have withered within a week. Routine, monotony – these things are anathema to Edith. If I'd tried to bring them into her life, it would have destroyed everything she felt for me.'

'But she was married once?'

Mustapha sipped his coffee. 'Yes. To Farouk. Has she told you much about that period of her life?'

'Some. To be honest, it's a little confusing.'

'She gets confused, too. I know. This is why I worry.' He sat up straighter suddenly, as if deciding something. 'Freya, this is difficult, but I would like you to consider not publishing the book.'

'Really? But she's had such an extraordinary life, it would be a tragedy if it wasn't remembered in some way.'

'An extraordinary life.' Mustapha stroked his beard with his thumb and forefinger. 'Yes, she has certainly had that. But such lives, by their very nature, do not always embrace the norms that most of us live by. There may be . . . transgressions. Incidents. Things that some people would find hard to understand.'

'But she doesn't have to tell me everything. And what would I tell Hamad? It's important to him, he wants to do this for his grandmother.'

'Freya.' He leant forward and took one of her hands in his. 'Edith is not Hamad's grandmother.'

'Of course she's his grandmother. He adores her.'

'And she adores him. I think, for Edith, Hamad is a chance to atone for the problems that beset Abdullah, his father. But there is no blood link between them.'

'So Hamad's father wasn't Edith's child? Did she adopt him?'

'I wish that were the case. But, Freya, I know Edith has talked about her love affair with Robert Jenner. That she got pregnant and had to give the baby away. What she probably hasn't admitted is that by the time she got back to Cairo, she was suffering very bad post-natal depression. It wasn't called that then, of course, wasn't understood in any way. She turned to Farouk, one of the few friends who had known about Robert, and – as you know – they began their own liaison. It caused a terrible rift with her parents, but being with Farouk did help. She began to get better. And then one night – at a party of all places – she bumped into Robert with his wife and the baby. *Her* baby. It was a terrible shock; she'd understood the baby would be brought up in England, that she would never have to see her. Seeing the three of them together, a happy family unit, was more than she could bear. She decided to drive herself home, even though she was in a terrible state.'

'How do you know all this?'

'I knew Farouk, when we were both in Algiers. They were divorced by then, although still close. Farouk needed to be free, he was that sort of man, but he wouldn't abandon Edith until he knew she would be taken care of. I was the one to do that. But to do it properly I had to know everything. And that meant the truth about Abdullah – Hamad's father.'

'Which is . . . ?'

'Edith should never have been driving that night. By the time Farouk caught up with her it was too late. She'd swerved into the path of another car, which had run off the road and overturned in a ditch. The driver pulled himself free and disappeared into the darkness. The woman in the passenger seat was dead. In the back of the car there was a young child, miraculously unhurt. By the time Farouk arrived, Edith was sitting at the side of the road, with the boy in her arms. He took them both back to his house in Cairo and tried to make her understand she had to take the child to the police. But Edith begged him not to say anything, told him that the boy was sent to her from God, that his mother was dead and his father such a coward that he had run away, rather than try to save him.'

'Did no one look for the baby?'

'The chauffeur was picked up soon afterwards. It was assumed he'd abducted the child and possibly sold it. He always protested his innocence, but he died in custody, before there was even a trial. Not that Farouk or Edith knew any of this at the time. Whenever he tried to persuade her to hand the child over, she became hysterical, begged him to take them both away from the city. In the end, he gave in and took them back to Arabia as his wife and son. He had been in Egypt for almost three years, and the boy couldn't have been much more than two. Farouk was important enough in his tribe for no one to question it.'

'And you seriously think that someone reading the book now – over sixty years later – would remember that? Would put it all together?'

'Perhaps I am being paranoid,' he said wearily. 'But one is never too old for one's sins to come calling. It was quite the society story for a while. The car had been traced to Edith, and there were questions raised over whether she knew what had happened to the child, particularly as she disappeared so soon afterwards. It's a long time ago, of course, but it was a terrible thing to do. And someone, somewhere, will remember.'

'I don't know what to say. I can't . . .' She thought of Hamad. 'He can't find out. Hamad, I mean. It would break his heart.'

'I know.' Mustapha ran his thumb and forefinger over his beard. 'It's the worst of ironies, isn't it? Hamad is the one who has pushed Edith to write her autobiography. And yet this is a story that he really shouldn't hear.'

CHAPTER 19

'Life,' said Dame Edith, sipping her tea, 'is full of people. Isn't it? They come and go, friends and lovers, colleagues, acquaintances. They mean everything to us for a period of time and then – *pouf!*' She touched her fingers to her lips and blew them open. 'They disappear. Gone.'

'I suppose so.' Racine's tone was thinly polite. Edith had to hand it to her; after the first moment of surprise – shock, even – she had completely recovered her composure. 'Do you have friends in Taroudant? Is that why you're here?'

'Here?' She shook her head. 'No, I don't know a soul in this city. Now, where was I? Oh, yes, Jacques Richaud. You're probably thinking: *Who is Jacques Richaud?* A fair question. A long-forgotten friend of mine, a comrade from a different age. It shames me to admit it, but I'd almost forgotten I ever knew him. And then suddenly, out of nowhere, he reappears in my life.'

'In Marrakech?'

'Hardly. Jacques Richaud is dead. He was quite celebrated in his day – worked for *Le Monde* for decades, their North Africa Bureau Chief. What he didn't know about the Algerian uprising wasn't worth knowing.'

'And you're telling me this because?'

Edith glanced around the courtyard; she had no intention of being rushed. Paul had picked well; there was an elegance to the place – huge urns spilling jasmine and bougainvillea onto the mosaic floor, banana palms shading saucer-shaped basket chairs and low, copper tables. 'Because it turns out that my old friend Jacques was an acquaintance of your grandfather. Rémy, wasn't it? Rémy Delacroix, vintner extraordinaire. His wines, Château Beauvarin, were some of the most sought after in the world when I was a girl.'

'My grandfather is dead.'

'Yes. There's no justice, is there?'

'What?'

'Justice. For a man like your grandfather, to live quietly into old age surrounded by family.' She leant forward. 'Only he wasn't surrounded by family, was he? His only son, his two young granddaughters . . . How often did you see Rémy when you were growing up?'

'I don't mean to be rude, Dame Edith, but I'm not sure my family arrangements are any of your business.'

Edith's face tightened. 'You don't mean to be rude? You really are . . . Now, what is it Timothy says? That's right. A piece of work. You really are a piece of work. How does a woman get to be like you, Racine?'

'The same way she gets to be like you,' said Racine smoothly. 'Just lucky, I guess.'

'Of course. Fortune plays such a role in life, doesn't it? Everything just an accident of birth. Wealth or poverty, health or frailty, pride . . .' She paused. 'Or shame.'

Racine pushed her chair back and stood up. 'I'm sorry, Dame Edith, it's been delightful to see you but I really must—'

'*Sit* down. Unless you want the hotel staff to hear what I have to say.' She didn't bother to look up. That was the thing about power: when you had it, when you *really* had it, you didn't need to try to intimidate anyone. It could simply be felt. She heard the scrape of the chair, the clatter of Racine's bag on the floor.

'Good. Now, where were we? Yes, of course, your grandfather. Now, you're obviously a bright girl. Didn't you ever wonder why your father turned his back on the hugely successful wine house Rémy had created? Why he moved to Paris? Almost as if the Beauvarin name was something to be, well, ashamed of, rather than proud?'

'I assume he simply wanted to be independent. He carved out a different life, established himself in his own right. I respect that.'

'And yet, after Rémy died, he moved back to Burgundy, took over the land and suddenly became a wine producer. What was that, do you think? A mid-life crisis? A sudden change of heart?'

'I've no idea. I was a child at the time.'

'So the same land but a different name. So strange. Why not maintain a brand that was as profitable and well-regarded as Beauvarin? Unless, of course, the business was tarnished. Unless the man behind it was a monster, a traitor of the worst kind. A man responsible for the deaths of innocent men, women and children.'

'What are you talking about?'

Dame Edith reached into her bag and placed a brown paper folder on the table. 'I'm talking about betrayal on an unimaginable scale, of illicit, immoral deals between your grandfather and the men who came to destroy his country. You want to know why your father disowned the Beauvarin name? Because it was a Nazi favourite, because your grandfather grew fat and rich on German reichsmarks at a time when others in his country were giving their lives in the fight against them.'

'This is obscene. How dare you accuse my grandfather?'

'Accuse him? What is it you think I accuse him of?' Edith's eyes were locked onto Racine's face. 'Selling wine to the Nazis? No, no, my dear – that's just a taste of his treachery. Your grandfather sold people. Jews.'

'What? Why would you say that?'

'Why? Because I *know*. I know what you are and I know what he was. There are tunnels beneath the vineyards where your family lived, Racine, tunnels where thousands of bottles of wine are stored and kept from sight. In the war they were used to hide something entirely different – a sanctuary for those whose only other destination was the death camps. Entire Jewish families hid in those tunnels, their existence kept secret by brave men and women who fought for France, fought for humanity. But there were others, men who craved power and status, who shared those secrets and muted their consciences with the money such betrayals provided.'

Racine moved the tea glass back onto the tray. Edith noticed a slight tremor in her fingers. 'I don't understand why you're telling me this.'

Edith's hand smacked against the table; a spoon fell from the sugar bowl, clattering onto the floor below. 'Because you have the blood of your grandfather coursing through your veins. You are also a betrayer. A liar. You think I don't know why you're here? You think I don't know about your sordid little sessions at the Farzi houses? Well, I do. I know it all. And what I know most strongly is that you are a self-satisfied, spoilt, moneyed little bitch who's never been good enough for my grandson. I knew it before I found out about you and Paul, before the ghost of Jacques Richaud appeared in my life with stories of the horrors your grandfather inflicted on numerous Jewish families.'

'How dare you . . .' Before she could finish her sentence, Dame Edith pushed the folder across the table.

'Take a look. It's all there. Witness statements, photocopied ledgers, tax records. Proof that your grandfather didn't just supply wine to the Nazis, he also supplied *Jews*.'

Racine stared at the file. 'How can you say such things? If this were true, I would know, my family would know. My grandfather would have been prosecuted.'

'Your grandfather stockpiled so much filthy Nazi money that by the time the war was over, he could buy off anyone – including the editor of *Le Monde*. People knew Rémy Delacroix did business with the Nazis, but few were aware of the darkest side of his dealings. It was a time when people didn't want to know – they wanted to move on, forget. Jacques would have found this story hard to sell, but now . . .' She watched as Racine opened the envelope, pulled out the sheaf of documents. 'And what exactly makes you think your father doesn't know?'

'He doesn't . . . he couldn't . . .'

'Why else would a man turn his back on such a profitable business? Imagine the horror of such a legacy, how terrified you must be of exposure. What a shame it would be for him – and your mother – if all this were to come out, so many years later.'

Racine looked up from the papers, her scarlet lips garish against skin the colour of milk. 'Exactly. *So many years later.* No one will care, no one will—'

'You must think me very naive. You think because I am old, I'm unaware of who you are? Of the fact your sister's wedding featured in the pages of *Le Monde*? I've seen the magazine spreads of your parents' palatial homes in Lyon and . . . where was it? Mustique? There's nothing people love more than the downfall of the rich and famous. And what a fall from grace it will be. Michel Delacroix, son of a Nazi collaborator. Suddenly his wine will not taste so good.'

Racine said nothing. Edith felt a thrill of triumph. She took a biscuit from the plate and crunched it noisily, the almond paste sweet against her teeth.

'What is it that you want from me?'

Edith ate the other half of the biscuit and raised a napkin to her lips. 'I want you out of my grandson's life. For good.' She pulled an envelope from her bag. 'This is a plane ticket from Agadir for tomorrow afternoon. You're leaving Marrakech, Racine. Leaving your job. And, I hope it goes without saying, leaving Paul.'

'You're crazy. I can't just disappear.'

'I think you'll find you can. Or the current editor of *Le Monde* – who I am assured is much less corruptible than his predecessors – will find these papers on his desk on Tuesday morning.'

'This is ludicrous. What will I tell Hamad?'

'That is the other condition. You will have no contact with Hamad from this point onward. Or anyone else in Marrakech. No phone calls, texts or emails. And if I hear – or even suspect – you've been in contact with anyone, this package goes straight to the papers. In fact –' she leant across the table – 'I think I'll take your phone. Just to remove the temptation.'

Racine stared at her. 'This is insane. Why can't I call anyone? What will that achieve? You seriously think if Hamad can't get hold of me, if he can't find me in Marrakech, he won't just come to France? He won't let me disappear. What you're asking makes no sense. The first thing he'll do is get on a plane to Lyon.'

'Not if he is told the house is empty, that your parents are away. A cruise, perhaps? He may come eventually. If he does, you will simply tell him your relationship is over. Make him believe it. Because I mean what I say, Racine. You will tell no one about this conversation. You can have a final night with your –' her lips pressed together – 'paramour, but there will be no contact with anyone else. That includes Jacqueline. Disobey me and your family will be ruined.'

'You really are a malevolent witch.' Edith felt a throb of triumph. 'What I don't understand is why you want to hurt Hamad, too. Why not let me tell him to his face? End it gently?'

'And let Paul get away with the betrayal of my grandson? You think this is about punishing you, don't you? Everything must always be about you. But all you have to do is leave. It is Paul I want to suffer. That insipid excuse for a man – he thinks he can betray Hamad without paying a price? How many months has he been hiding this secret? How many times has he looked him in the eye and lied? After everything my grandson has done for him! Well, now he'll have to lie again, but this time beneath the lie will be fear – panic. What has happened to you, where have you gone? Everyone will be wondering. And he will have been the last person to see you – a fact he will be unable to share with anyone. That will be the secret he has to carry, and it will weigh heavily. I want him to know anxiety and confusion and bewilderment. I want him to fear that everything he has built is about to fall apart. I want him to *suffer*.'

'And Hamad? He'll suffer, too. Is that what you want?'

'Sometimes a painful surgery is necessary to cut out the cancer,' said Edith stiffly. 'And that is what you are. A cancer in my grandson's life. Well, not any more. Now, shall I leave you to look through those papers? Or have you seen enough?'

CHAPTER 20

Paul glanced across the table at Racine and felt his heart sink. She was doing it again: the odd, middle-distance staring, eyes locked on some indiscernible point on the other side of the restaurant. He'd never seen her look so pale – dark smudges beneath her eyes, hair pulled back in a messy ponytail. The concern he'd felt the previous evening, when he'd arrived on the roof terrace at Riad la Belle Étoile to find her curled up on a lounger, limp and monosyllabic, was hardening into frustration, almost disbelief. He'd tried to keep his patience through an excruciatingly silent dinner, had swallowed his disappointment when she had slipped into the king-size bed and turned out the light without even really acknowledging he was there. He had told himself that in the morning there would be an explanation, an apology. Then their time together would really begin.

'*Salade maison?*' He watched her nod blankly at the waiter.

'*Merci bien.*'

The man laid a bowl in front of Racine, and picked up the wine bottle from the cooler. Liquid gurgled into the glasses. Paul felt his fingers knot together in his lap.

'Racine, you need to tell me what's wrong. Something has obviously happened, I've never seen you like this.' He reached across to cover her hand with his. 'I want to help, but if you won't tell me, then I don't know what to do.'

'I can't tell you. I'm sorry.'

'You keep saying that. But if this is how you were going to be, what on earth was the point of coming? I've lied to Freya, lied to Laila, I've got a foreman who's jumping up and down at being left with a trench full of animal bones . . . I thought you wanted us to have some time together, so that we could talk.'

'*You* wanted us to come here. And just like every other time, you got what you wanted.'

'What does that mean? I don't understand, Racine, what is it I'm supposed to have done?'

'How can you even ask that?' She lifted her wine glass, drank hungrily. 'I told you, right from the start, that you and Freya coming to Marrakech was a disastrous idea. You must have known it couldn't end well. Did you ever think what it might mean for me? That it could jeopardise everything?'

'But we talked about this at the time. You know it was almost impossible for me to say no – Hamad and Freya both wanted it so much, and the houses were an incredible opportunity.'

'Those bloody houses. I wish Hamad had never bought them.'

'Believe me, so do I. Look, I really don't want us to argue. We are where we are, there's no point looking back.'

'Tell that to Edith.' She downed the contents of her glass. '*Salope.*'

'I'm sorry?'

'I said –' she laid down her fork and met his gaze – 'she is a bitch.'

'Oh.' He felt slightly taken aback at the fury in her tone. 'Well, yes. She can be tricky. But I don't want to talk about Edith, or the houses. We came here to talk about us, didn't we? What we're going to do?'

'Do?'

'About this. Us.'

'Paul, there is no *us*. Why can't you understand what I'm telling you? This is *over.* Go back to Marrakech. Go back to your wife. You can't seriously think I'd ever have left Hamad—'

'For what? For me?'

'That wasn't what I was going to say.'

'Wasn't it?' Humiliation burned through him; he could see, suddenly, how ridiculous he must seem to her. 'Do you know, I've got absolutely no bloody idea what you're doing here. More to the point, I've no idea what I'm doing here.' He pushed back his chair and strode across the restaurant, slamming his palm into the glass door that led out onto the restaurant's driveway.

'Taxi?' The doorman raised an eyebrow.

He nodded, too angry to speak.

'OK. *Deux minutes.*' He started to move away, to where the gravel drive met the main road.

'*Monsieur?*' Paul caught at his sleeve. '*Une cigarette?*' He waved a ten-dirham note; the doorman pulled a softpack and lighter from his breast pocket and wrapped his fingers around the cash.

It was years since he had smoked. The nicotine felt dirty against his gums, his brain spun in his skull. He took another drag; his pulse was racing now, the sun hot against his skin. How had he got everything so wrong? Had she brought him here just to humiliate him, some twisted display of power to somehow compensate for the lack of control she felt around Hamad? It was as if she had no conception of what he'd risked for her, what he had been prepared to sacrifice. Instead of being grateful, she'd simply been contemptuous. Anger spiked, he took another pull on the cigarette; behind him, he heard the sound of a door opening, the rhythmic click of heels on concrete.

'Paul? I'm sorry . . .'

'Just leave me alone.' He flung his arm out. It connected with something solid; an odd, surprised cry broke across the stagnant air. He spun round to see Racine sprawling on the ground, her head against the kerb. For a moment he wasn't sure if she was conscious.

'Oh my God.' He crouched down beside her. 'I'm so sorry. Christ, I didn't know you were behind me. Are you OK? Are you bleeding?'

'You hit me.' Her eyes were wide with disbelief. 'You *hit* me.'

'*Mademoiselle, est-ce que vous allez bien?*' The doorman bent towards Racine and slipped an arm under her elbow. '*Avez-vous besoin de la police? L'hôpital?*'

'It was an accident, I didn't mean . . .'

'*Mademoiselle? La police?*'

'*Un taxi, s'il vous plaît.*'

'Racine, please.'

A taxi appeared at the bottom of the drive, rolling slowly towards them; the doorman steered her towards the car, holding the door open as she slipped into the back seat.

'*Racine!*' He could see her through the window, her palm flat against the side of her face where she had fallen. The car began to pull away. 'Please don't go. I'm so sorry.'

'Another whisky, monsieur?'

Paul pushed the glass forward. He had expected the first one to burn off the shock, but instead it just intensified the shame. Nothing about the past twenty-four hours seemed real; it was as if Racine had become a different person, entirely absorbed by something she either couldn't or wouldn't share. The truth was, he wasn't sure who either of them had become – he could still feel the shock of her cheek against his hand. His phone lay silent beside the refilled glass. He wondered if it was too soon to text her again.

The alcohol seared his throat and he lit another cigarette. It was self-pity, he knew, but it was hard to avoid feeling that somehow this was what he deserved; that this was what happened to men like him. For the first time he could actually imagine how it would be if the truth ever came out: the slow grind of the divorce process, the gradual disappearance of their mutual friends. His sisters would despise him; he could picture the disappointment on his parents' faces. He would never be able to make them understand what Racine had brought to his life: an unlooked-for, alchemical transformation that rendered him almost unrecognisable, even to himself. That a woman like her would even *want* him had seemed extraordinary.

He looked at his watch. How much time before she began to recover from what he had done? Days, probably weeks. He didn't have that luxury; he needed to apologise now, to see her just once more, before Marrakech swallowed them up, and everything that had happened became some vague, unreal memory. He threw a pile of dirhams onto the counter and walked out into the dusk.

The night air was thick with the scent of jasmine and the rasp of cicadas. A taxi slowed and he climbed in, watching the dry scrubland glimmer in the half-light, the curry-coloured ramparts loom towards him. He missed England suddenly: the soft rise of the Downs as the train pulled southwards from London, the slow drift of Sunday mornings, punctuated by warm croissants and the rustle of the papers. Nothing was familiar here. Nothing made sense.

'*Bienvenue, monsieur.*' The houseboy nodded as he stepped into the courtyard.

'*La femme. Mademoiselle Delacroix. Elle est ici?*' Paul felt like a fool, scrabbling for his schoolboy French.

The boy shrugged.

He nodded and walked across the courtyard, his feet slippery on the stairs. 'Racine?' The room was in darkness; he let the door close behind him and felt for the light switch. His stomach lurched. The maid had been in; Racine's slip was folded on the pillow, her toiletries neatened on the dressing table. He stretched out his arm to open the wardrobe; her dresses hung in the darkness, her leather overnight bag beneath them, stored beside his. He sank back onto the bed and pulled out his phone.

Racine, I'm at the hotel. Where are you? If you've gone back to Marrakech, that's fine, I understand but . . . I'm just so sorry for what happened. Please let me know you're OK. x.

The call to prayer echoed suddenly through the silence. Paul put his head in his hands; he hated the sound at the best of times. Tonight it felt like castigation, recrimination for his sins. For a moment he thought about pulling the clothes from the hangers, throwing the bags into the boot of the car. He could be back in Marrakech within hours, the whole episode an unpleasant memory. He sighed. There was no way he could leave before the morning. If she came back to find him gone, he would look a coward as well as a bully.

An image of Freya appeared in his mind: packing a case, selecting clothes for the trip to Imlil with a man who wasn't him. He thought of their flat in Battersea, the comfortable monotony of Friday night takeaways and weekday mornings, snippets of conversations exchanged between showers and toast. They'd had routines, patterns; reassuring ways of being together that he had dismissed so carelessly as dull and predictable. Now they could barely be in the same room without accusations being thrown. He didn't want her to go to Imlil thinking so badly of him. It made him fearful of where her resentment could lead.

He picked up his phone and pressed her number; listened to the flat tone of her voicemail. 'Frey, I . . .' He realised he had no idea what to say. 'I just rang to say goodnight. I'm so sorry for what happened yesterday. I hope you're OK. I do love you. Sleep well.'

Silence swept in. Paul let his body fall back onto the bed and stared up at the ceiling. The sound of horses' hooves rose up from the street; he pictured the *calèche* jolting past the ramparts and out into the empty land beyond the city. Nobody knew he was in Taroudant. To Freya, he was in Fez with Laila. To Laila, he was in London with his wife. The lies seemed ridiculous suddenly, the frisson of danger, of liberation, entirely quashed by the events of the afternoon. Now, in the quiet of an empty hotel room, in an unfamiliar city, he just felt horribly, shockingly alone.

*

Freya listened to the message twice. She looked at the bag on the bed, half filled with the socks and jumper Tim had told her she would need up in the mountains. On the table, her laptop was still open from the slightly tense conversation with her sister. She'd wanted reassurance that she was right to go to Imlil; that Paul's behaviour entitled her to behave as she liked, however impulsive it seemed. Instead, Ali had tried to persuade her to come back to England, albeit temporarily. But Freya didn't want to go home. It felt like a defeat.

It had been an act of bravado, that first text to Tim: a show of defiance to Paul, sent in the heat of the moment. As soon as he had replied, it had become something different: a slowly building anticipation with every detail shared. The few hours with Mustapha had been an unexpected distraction, her mind turning over the revelation about Hamad and Edith as she fell asleep. But from the first seconds of wakefulness, she had been able to think of nothing but the trip to Imlil and where it would lead.

Sorry to miss your call. She considered ringing Paul back, but something hard and unexpected told her not to risk it. If something was wrong, she would know. If he sounded vulnerable, she would find herself texting Tim, apologising for changing her mind. *Been on Skype with Ali. Tired now. Let's speak tomorrow. Hope all going well in Fez. x.*

Freya turned her phone to mute and looked around the room. Sleep was an impossibility. Instead she went into the bathroom and pulled her sponge bag out of the cupboard, filling it with miniature bottles of shampoo and conditioner. She kept her eyes focused downwards, away from the mirror that hung above the washbasin. She couldn't bring herself to look into it. She wasn't entirely sure she'd recognise the woman looking back.

CHAPTER 21

It felt good to be escaping the city. Freya wound down the window and leant her head on her arm; beyond the windscreen, the road was lined with eucalyptus trees, empty save for a distant truck, gradually increasing in size as it rumbled towards them. On either side, fields rose up to faded hills, softened by small clouds of silvery blossom, billowing up between the houses.

'Almond season,' said Tim, following her gaze. 'Perfect time to come.' It made her jump slightly to see a different face in the car alongside her. Nothing had been familiar since the moment he had appeared out of the mêlée at Bab Agnaou, clutching a paper bag stained with sugar and two cardboard cups.

'*Sfenj*,' he'd said, nodding at her to open the bag. 'Moroccan doughnuts. Perfect fuel for a road trip.' They'd driven out of the city, her lips flecked with cinnamon and sugar, the car filled with the scent of strong, bitter coffee.

'I can't believe we're only an hour from Marrakech.' She thought back to the bedroom at Dar Simone, her phone glinting accusingly in the half-light. *Coming back from Fez early. Have you left yet? If not, maybe don't? We could talk. Properly, I mean. I love you. x*. It had unsettled her, like the voicemail the night before.

Sorry to miss you, already en route. Talk later. F x. There had been no reply.

The yellow truck roared past them, breaking across her thoughts. She wanted to leave it all behind: the row with Paul, Mustapha's unexpected revelation about Hamad and Edith, the low hum of guilt about Hassan Azoulay's death. It was as if her life had come to resemble the souk – a mass of tangled half-truths and unnavigable relationships that she found increasingly bewildering. She glanced at Tim and wondered – not for the first time – if he was the only person keeping her sane, or whether he posed the greatest threat of all.

'You're not falling out of love with our crazy city, are you?'

'It's not that. It just gets a bit intense sometimes – kind of hard to navigate. Like I was saying when we were at Larousse . . .' She felt herself blush.

'Come on, Mrs Hepworth.' Tim looked across and grinned. 'I thought we'd put that to bed. As it were. A moment of madness. You're married. I do respect that.'

'You never married?'

'I did. I just wasn't very good at it. I'm a terrible cliché, I'm afraid: married to the job. I didn't realise how useless I'd be at commitment until I actually made one. Bit of a wandering soul.'

'That's Edith coming out in you.'

'I know. Weird, isn't it?'

'Does it bother you? Finding out . . .'

'Quite the opposite. When we were kids I desperately wanted her to be my grandmother, too. I told her once, when we were staying at her house in Amman. She'd bought baklava, but Mum insisted I could only have one piece. I can hear Edith now, scolding her for being parsimonious. I didn't even know what the word meant. When she came to say goodnight, she'd smuggled up three extra pieces in a napkin. I told her then that I wished she was my grandmother.'

'And what did she say?'

'She said that if that was really what I wished, then it should be so. She said – and I remember this particularly – that we shouldn't allow others to dictate the roles we have in people's lives. I didn't understand what she meant then, but now . . .'

'You think she meant about not being allowed to keep her baby? Your mother?'

Tim nodded.

'And your mum still doesn't know?'

'She's not well.'

She waited for him to say more. Silence rose.

'So tell me why we're going to see the Nanda?' she said brightly. 'What's Hamad doing that you're so unhappy about?'

'I don't actually know if he's done anything yet,' said Tim, turning onto a smaller, dusty road. 'But when luxury hotels get built in places as unspoilt as Imlil, it always makes me nervous. These top-end resorts are all the same – they say they'll build new infrastructure for the villagers, offer employment. But it's all bullshit. Very few people who live in Imlil have more than a few words of English. They might employ one or two as gardeners or kitchen porters, but most of the staff will have to be bilingual. You can't charge six hundred quid a night and have waiters who don't understand the difference between poached and scrambled eggs.'

'But it must bring some money into the area?'

'Hardly anything. It's always the same. Hotel companies go on about *renewal* and *respecting the earth's energies*, and then they bring in trucks and diggers, lower the water tables or cut down rainforest. And when it's finally built, gaggles of braying millionaires arrive in helicopters, demanding Krug-fuelled picnics served by picturesque poor people. It's colonialism by wealth. Soon all the most beautiful, unspoilt places on this planet will only be accessible to the rich.'

'Ooh, you are cross.'

He grinned at her. 'I am. But I will save my wrath for Hamad.'

Freya looked out of the window: a battered sign read *Kurmeyez 38 kms*; beyond it a line of shacks and workshops sat beneath the trees. In the rutted earth that separated the buildings from the road, children in faded T-shirts and with grubby knees scrambled over ripped-up tyres, banging sticks against old scooter engines and a pile of rusty sinks. A thin boy in ripped shorts waved from the doorway of a workshop. She lifted her hand, letting her fingers ripple in the breeze. He let out a whoop of delight, began to run towards the car.

'He just wants money.'

His small face hardened with disappointment as they glided past. 'I could have given him a few dirhams.'

'Yes. But it doesn't help.'

'It would have helped him.'

'Perhaps. Money doesn't solve everything.'

'Hamad's a good man, you know? It's easy to misjudge him.'

'Perhaps. I know he's a good friend to you. I like him for that.' He pointed to the glove compartment. 'Why don't you put some music on? I've got a bit of a treat in store – today's a public holiday and there's a festival on the Kurmeyez *wadi*. I thought we'd stop, take a look. Don't go expecting Glastonbury or anything. But it's definitely something to see.'

After the quiet roads of the countryside, it felt almost surreal to be surrounded by so much life. Cars were parked haphazardly, families lifting rugs and carrier bags and bewildered-looking children from back seats. Beyond the road, a dry river bed stretched into the distance, scattered with brightly coloured tents, twists of smoke eddying up from dozens of small fires. Camels stood in disgruntled clusters; a muffled sound of drumming rolled out beneath the chatter.

'You're very at home here,' she said as he threw his arm around the back of her seat and reversed into a tiny parking space.

'It is my home.' He let the engine die and pulled a packet of cigarettes out of the glove compartment. 'I was born here, lived here till I was seven. Dad was a diplomat – nothing particularly high-ranking, but enough to give me a pretty exotic childhood. Mum hated it though. When my sister got to school age she put her foot down and said she was taking us back to England. So Dad got a job in Westminster, although I'm not sure he ever quite forgave her for it.'

Freya opened the car door; the air was hung about with the scent of *kif* and roasting meat. 'Interesting, though. Your mum married someone who wanted to live abroad, you live abroad . . .'

'I know. Edith again. This part of the world – North Africa, the Middle East – it's in our blood, ever since Grandad was in Cairo.' He smiled at her. 'But of course you know all this, don't you? Probably in more detail than me.'

'She's certainly had an extraordinary life.' Freya linked her arm through his as they began to weave through the cars. 'I don't know whether the book's going to work out, though.'

'Why? Edith's always telling me how much she enjoys talking to you, how much she's remembering.'

'It's not that I don't want to finish it. It's just . . . It's something Mustapha said.' She wished she hadn't spoken. 'Aren't you going to show me this festival?'

He looked at her for a moment, then smiled. 'I certainly am, Mrs Hepworth. If you're ready for a bit of a scramble?'

She took his hand and let him guide her down the steep slope towards the *wadi*, grateful that he didn't press her more about Edith's book. It was one of the things she found so easy about him: he never pushed for answers, allowing her to give away only as much as felt comfortable. It was part of what made her feel new around him; with Paul and Hamad – and Ali – everything she said was overlaid with decades of knowledge, shared experiences, her thoughts seen through a prism of who she'd once been, rather than who she was now.

As they strolled towards the crowds, she realised his fingers were still wrapped around hers. She had no desire to pull away; there was something liberating in the sense of being free of everything that usually defined her. Here, among the storytellers and the drummers, she was just part of an anonymous couple; to those who passed, they could be married, children at home, a lifetime of experiences stored together. The speed at which her old life could disappear was dizzying.

'Tell me why you love it so much,' she said as they walked past a fire, crackling and spitting around a white-veined slab of meat. 'Morocco, I mean.'

'I like the way their society is. They've kept so much of what we've lost – the importance of family, of friendships. It's a far more cooperative world. If a friend asks for help, you help them – not out of duty, but because you should want to. You can meet a man in the street and by the end of the conversation you'll be invited into his home to share a meal, even if there's barely enough to go round.' He stopped walking; a small girl in a bright-pink dress whirled past, pointing at the camels. 'It's far from perfect. Nothing ever happens on time, no one can ever lose face, truth can be something of an elastic concept. To most outsiders, Moroccan society looks beyond chaotic. But once you see behind that . . .'

'I envy you. I don't know how to access that world. Sometimes when I'm with Madani, or Mustapha, it's like being given a glimpse of something, but then the door closes. I don't want to be on this side – with Jacqueline and Racine and those awful people from Villa Merteuil. I suppose I'm just not sure where I belong.'

'According to who?' He stopped beside a rock and hoisted himself onto it, pulling her up alongside. 'No one sits around defining what's the real Marrakech, and what isn't. You need to stop searching for this mythical version of Moroccan society, and just find your own way. You told me that you came here because you wanted to live differently – so do that. Live how *you* want to. The Arabs have a saying: "Every age has its book." Maybe Mustapha's right – maybe it's time to stop focusing on the book of Edith's life, and concentrate more on your own.'

'You look comfortable.' Freya opened her eyes to see Tim peering down at her. 'Have you forgiven me yet?'

She shifted slightly on the lounger, tweaked the cushion behind her head and gazed out over the patchwork of rooftops to the woods that separated the upper village from the lower. Below, the spiny minaret of the village mosque gleamed white against the slate-faced slopes of Mount Toubkal. The sun was drifting downwards, softening the alleyways beneath the terrace with rounded, inky shadows.

'I'm not sure I've ever been more comfortable,' she said, smiling. 'And yes, of course I've forgiven you. I wasn't being cross, just thoughtful. If you're going to offer a sermon on how to live my life, what do you expect?'

'It wasn't a sermon . . .'

'I'm teasing.' She winked at him. 'How was the hotel?'

'Interesting. Better than I expected, I have to admit.' He picked up the water bottle from the table and swigged the contents. 'I'll tell you over dinner. Right now what I really need is a shower. Give me ten minutes?'

'Take as long as you need. This is just glorious. I can't believe how different it is from down there.' She pointed to the lower village, thinking of the winding road edged with dusty-windowed cafés offering *briouates* and free Wi-Fi, gaggles of backpackers sitting on the crumbling walls, poring over maps. She'd been disappointed, even saddened by the finger-smeared fridges stacked with Coke and Fanta, the racks of cheap sleeping bags and second-hand walking boots, copies of yesterday's *Daily Mail*. Tim had said nothing, just kept on driving until the road fell silent, rising to a second clutch of houses on the hillside above.

'The curse of tourism.'

'Go and have a shower.' She kicked his shin. 'Don't spoil my peace with another rant.'

He grinned and moved away. She watched him go, his long legs spanning the terrace in wide, measured strides. It was drawing closer: the moment when she was going to have to decide. To her surprise, having separate rooms made little difference; the possibility was still there, glowing in the distance, slowly crystallising in her mind. It didn't help that she had never been anywhere quite like Imlil. As the road had pulled away from the lower village, she'd realised that she was entirely in Tim's hands, that nothing about the next twelve hours was going to be familiar. They'd changed into walking boots at the roadside, scrambling down the gravelly path towards a tall, bald-headed man, cloaked in a faded *djellaba*. He had led them through a tangle of hot, silent alleyways to an old Berber house filled with scarlet rugs and unlit lanterns dotted up a weathered central staircase.

A metallic chime broke across her thoughts. She knew, without looking, who it would be. He'd texted as they were leaving Kurmeyez; her phone had buzzed again just as they were checking in. *I really need to speak to you. Please call me. Px.* She sighed and pressed his name.

'Frey?' It hadn't even rung once. 'You're OK?'

'Hello. Of course I'm OK. Why did you think I wouldn't be?'

'Because you didn't text me back? I thought you'd been in an accident or something.' He sounded tense, almost breathless.

'Are you all right?'

'Yes. I'm fine. Bit tired.'

'What happened, then?'

'What do you mean?'

'You came back from Fez early.'

'Right. Yes.' She waited. 'Well . . . nothing happened. We'd just seen everyone we needed to see.'

'OK. Look, was there something particular you wanted?'

'I didn't realise I needed a reason to call you. Am I interrupting something?'

'Well, yes, actually. My time away. My chance to see something of the country. I don't see why it's any less valid than yours. I didn't keep pestering you when you were in Fez.'

'I didn't mean . . . I'm sorry you see it as pestering. It's just . . . we left things in a bad way, didn't we? Both said things we didn't mean. You were right, you've never looked at another bloke all the time we've been together. I had no right to accuse you. I just wanted you to know that I love you, that's all. And I miss you.'

Something stirred in her. How did he do that? Move her in the way he always did, make her want to soothe whatever was wrong. 'I'll be back tomorrow. Are you sure you're OK?'

There was a pause. 'I'm fine. It's just this bloody town, it's all so bonkers.'

'I know. It's nice to be away.'

'With him?'

'For God's sake, I am not having that conversation right now. We can talk when I get back tomorrow night.'

'Freya . . .'

'I'll see you tomorrow.' She ended the call and held her finger on the button until the screen went dark, throwing the phone back into her bag. Glancing up, she realised a web of cloud had begun to knot its way around the sun, blurring the sunset into a hazy mauve-grey. She lay back and closed her eyes. Bloody Paul. Bloody, *bloody* Paul.

Paul stepped out of the shower and reached for the tumbler of whisky, balanced on the rim of the washbasin. He tried not to notice that there was room for the glass because Freya's electric toothbrush was missing. The tube of hand cream had gone too, along with the bottle of perfume. Small things. Clarins hand cream, red lettering on a white background. Coco Chanel, the black label mirroring the shape of the heavy glass stopper. It wasn't that he'd tried to memorise the name of the perfume or the brand of hand cream. They were just there, every morning; tiny snippets of her, individual parts of her daily routine.

He glanced at his phone. Tipped back the whisky. The towel felt rough around his waist. His phone vibrated on the bed, Hamad. *Again.* He had to get out of the room.

Up on the roof, he felt less claustrophobic. At least the day was drawing to a close, although that meant twelve hours had passed since he had woken in the empty bed in Taroudant, surrounded by Racine's uncollected possessions. At first, he'd seriously considered leaving them in the room; packing her clothes and toiletries felt like an act of uncomfortable finality. In the end he'd bundled everything into the leather holdall and thrown it into the boot of the car, trying to forget it was there.

'*Bonsoir, chéri.* Did you find her? Was she at the Palais?'

He turned to see Jacqueline slipping through the gate. 'No.'

The word stuck in his throat. All the way up the motorway he had played out the scene that would unfold when he arrived at the Palais du Jardin: the call from reception to the restaurant, Racine crossing the lobby, glacially elegant, her face miraculously unbruised. 'The receptionist rang her villa but there was no answer. He said he hadn't seen her, that she's on leave until Thursday.'

'Well, there you are. She's probably sunning herself in Agadir. Or even popped home to Lyon.'

'Have you heard from her?'

She sat down on the neighbouring lounger. 'I've sent another text. But she's not always the quickest to respond.'

'Well, she's definitely ignoring me.'

'Are you surprised? You said you'd had a row. This is what we do when we want to punish men. It is ironic, no? You say we talk too much, we chatter, we gossip. Yet when we go silent? This is what makes you really uncomfortable.'

Paul took a long sip of the whisky and watched the woman on the roof opposite unpeg her washing. He wondered if she was the one who had made Freya the *djellaba.* He didn't even know her name. 'Why do we always want more?' he said, almost to himself. 'Why do we always think there's something better?'

'*Vive la différence,*' said Jacqueline, leaning across to take a cigarette. 'It is not more. It is not even better. We crave the different.'

'I understand that Racine's angry with me. I get that. But even before we argued she was so . . . odd. Something had definitely happened. And then she just said that it was over. Like it was nothing.'

She shrugged. 'It was always going to end sometime, you must have known that. And it is better, yes? Before anyone is truly hurt? If this liaison can pass without your wife or Hamad finding out, you must view yourself as very fortunate. Such adventures, the risk they involve, the dangers . . . Sometimes one pays a very high price.'

'God knows what you must think of me.' Paul shook his head. 'I do know how appalling it all is. I do love Freya, you know?'

'I know.' Jacqueline laid a hand on his arm. 'The stories we're told as children, to love one person only, to mate for life, fairy tales, *n'est-ce pas*? We are built to love many people, in different ways, at different times.'

Before he could answer, a soft peal of chimes twisted up from her bag. She scooped out her phone and glanced at it before turning the screen towards Paul.

'Don't answer.'

'I have to.' She pressed the speakerphone icon. '*Âllo?*'

'Madame Delon? This is Karim. I am calling to see if Racine is with you?'

Jacqueline raised her eyebrows at Paul. '*Bonsoir*, Karim. No, she's away for a couple of days. A wine course in Paris.'

'Yes, that is the information I had. But she is not here.'

'You're in Paris? Is Hamad with you?'

'*Sayyid* Hamad and I flew in this afternoon. It was intended to be a surprise. But they have no record of her registering for this course.' There was a pause. 'I have spoken to the Palais du Jardin. They say she is on leave. I believe *Sayyid* Hamad has called Mr and Mrs Hepworth, but hasn't been able to raise either of them. Are you aware of their whereabouts?'

'I'm afraid not,' she said, keeping her eyes on Paul's face. 'Do tell him not to worry, Karim. She's probably just having a night out somewhere in the city. I'm sure she'll call as soon as she picks up the messages.'

'I'm sure she will. But I'd be grateful if perhaps you could try calling her? And if you speak to her, would you please inform me. We stay in Paris tonight, but *Sayyid* Hamad will fly on to Marrakech tomorrow morning if she hasn't been in touch.'

'Of course. Have you arranged accommodation? Would he like to stay here?'

Paul was rigid in his seat. 'No,' he mouthed, cutting through the air with his hand.

'Thank you, but I have reserved a suite at Mamounia.'

'Well, please tell him to call me if there's anything I can do.' Jacqueline shook her head at Paul. 'She's due in at work on Thursday, so I'm sure she'll be back tomorrow.'

'*Inshallah.*' The line went dead.

'He's coming here?' Paul's voice tight. 'What on earth am I going to say to him?'

Jacqueline looked at him; her face was serious. 'Paul, I'm starting to get a little concerned. That she doesn't answer your texts – I am not surprised. Mine, also perhaps not so unusual. But to not call Hamad . . . I cannot find an explanation for this. Did something else happen when you two were in Taroudant?'

'What do you mean?'

'I don't know. But you said the row was a bad one. I wonder now what you meant.'

'It got . . .' Paul closed his eyes. 'Things got a bit out of hand.'

'By out of hand you mean . . .'

'I don't know,' he snapped. 'She was really odd, from the moment I got there – barely spoke to me for the first evening. And the way she ended it, I just felt dismissed. Humiliated. I was so furious I stormed out of the restaurant – she came after me, started to apologise . . .' He tailed off. 'I didn't realise she was standing behind me. I didn't mean to . . .'

'Didn't mean to what?'

'I just threw my arm out. I didn't even see her.'

'You hit her?'

'It was an accident, Jacqueline, you have to believe that. And she was fine, she got in a taxi.'

'No woman is fine if a man hits her.' Jacqueline spat the words out. 'Did she fall? Hit her head?'

'She was all right, I promise you. She got up, the concierge put her in a taxi and that was the last time I saw her. I went back to the hotel, waited for her all night, but she never came back.'

'She never came back. And now no one has heard from her in two days?' Her eyes drilled into his face. 'Is this true, what you're telling me?'

'Of course it is. You think I'd make something like that up? You think I'm proud of myself? It's driving me crazy. I just want to know where she is, and if she's OK.'

'Well, you were the last person with her,' said Jacqueline quietly. 'So I'd say you're best placed to answer that question. Wouldn't you?'

CHAPTER 22

Freya woke suddenly. She lay still for a moment, trying to remember where she was. The air was thick with the scent of woodsmoke and mint; her feet felt cold beneath the scratchy woollen blanket. A low rasp of breathing fell from the other side of the bed. She turned slightly in the darkness. Beyond the shrouded curve of the unfamiliar body, a light flashed on the table, illuminating the room. On the screen, in black letters, she could make out the word 'Hospital'.

'Tim.' The screen faded; the room retreated into darkness. She pressed her fingers against his arm. The skin felt warm and slightly sweaty. 'Tim. Can you wake up?'

'Huh?' He rolled towards her and she felt relieved that she couldn't see his face. 'What is it? You OK?'

'Your phone. I woke up . . . Someone was calling. It said . . . on the screen, it said *Hospital*. I thought maybe . . .'

'Shit.' He sat up and flicked on the light; awkwardness rippled through her at the sight of his unfamiliar body. '*Shit*.' He snatched the phone from the table. Freya drew her knees into her chest. 'Oh, God. It's not Mum. It's Edith.'

'How do you know?'

'I've got a missed call from La Mamounia. At one in the morning, last night.'

She waited as he listened to the message; wanted to touch him, didn't know how. Memories of the previous night flickered into her mind; her face felt hot. She suspected neither of them had expected the evening to end the way it had.

'We have to get back to Marrakech.' He turned to look at her. 'I'm sorry. We need to go now. Edith's had a stroke.'

'Is she OK?'

'It doesn't sound good. She had a couple of mini-strokes a few months ago. The doctor warned me then there was a risk of something more serious. A room-service boy found her collapsed on the floor of her bedroom. He must have been taking up her whisky – she always has one before bed.' He pushed back the duvet, pulled his jeans from the chair. 'They rang hours ago. God knows how she is by now.'

She wrapped her hands around his; they felt cold, unfamiliar. 'She'll pull through, Edith's such a fighter. Look, you go and check out and I'll sort out the room. I'll be down in a minute.'

He nodded and opened the door; a blast of thin, night air blew in. Freya shivered and pulled on her clothes, looking around the small, scarlet-walled space. How long had they sat up last night, the fire crackling in the corner, the thick shawl wrapped around her shoulders? Her head nagged; she remembered the brandy, sloshed out of Tim's hip flask into the lacquered glasses, the unexpected direction the conversation had taken. Perhaps it was better they hadn't woke up in their own time. She had no idea what she would have said.

By the time she reached the salon, the night porter was already struggling with the rusted lock in the door that led onto the street. Outside, the alley was silent and dark. Without asking, Tim took her hand and they moved fast through the village, their footsteps breaking up the silence.

'She'll be OK,' she said, as Tim threw the bags into the car and leant across to unlock the passenger door.

'She's eighty-five.'

Beyond the peak of Mount Toubkal, the sky was beginning to soften. The lower village looked less tatty without the racks of newspapers and sleeping-bag stands, and the empty café tables stacked neatly against the wall. She remembered, suddenly, that she had switched her phone off after the irritating conversation with Paul. The screen shimmered back into life: half a dozen missed calls, one voicemail, two texts. Hamad's name was listed five times.

'You're not the only one they've contacted. I've got loads of missed calls from Hamad, and two texts asking me to ring him.'

Tim shook his head. 'What's the point of ringing him when he's in bloody Doha? They know I'm the first point of contact in emergencies.'

'Well, he's heard somehow. I'd better call him.' She pressed Hamad's name on the screen.

'Now?'

'He's three hours ahead out there. He's always up early, anyway.'

'Freya. At last.' Hamad's voice was thin and tense. 'Where on earth have you been?'

'In . . .' She glanced at Tim. 'It doesn't matter. Sorry, I've had my phone turned off. Are you OK?' A loud roaring echoed down the phone. 'Where are you?'

'Charles de Gaulle.' His voice was barely audible above the engine noise. 'Literally just getting on a flight. Look, Racine's missing. I came to Paris. She was supposed to be on a wine course. They didn't have any record of her. Do you know where she is ? Have you heard from her?'

'He's lost Racine,' she mouthed at Tim, covering up her phone. 'I don't think he knows about Edith.'

'Wait till we know more,' Tim mouthed back. 'He can't do anything where he is.'

'Freya? Have you spoken to her? When was the last time you saw her?'

'I haven't seen her since the dinner party. Is she not answering her phone? Have you rung the hotel?'

She heard him sigh heavily. 'Karim's rung everyone. I've tried her parents, but they're away, apparently. No one knows where she is. Look, I've got to go. Flight gets in at midday, can you meet me? Karim's flying back to Doha from Marrakech, his father's seriously ill. I've got someone flying out this evening to cover, but he won't be in Marrakech until tonight.'

'Of course. Did you speak to Paul?'

There was a pause. 'I left a message. He hasn't called me back.'

Freya felt a stab of anger. 'I'll try him. Listen, honey, she'll be fine, she'll just have taken off for a few days' holiday somewhere. I'll talk to Paul and see who else we can get in touch with. And I'll see you at Arrivals. OK?'

'Thank you.' The line went dead. She looked at Tim.

'Racine running rings round him, is she?'

'It looks that way. Odd, though. He went to Paris to meet her. She was supposed to be on some wine course. I remember her mentioning it at that bloody dinner. But she wasn't there – wasn't even registered for the course. Obviously a complete lie. But why?'

'Playing away,' said Tim briefly. 'What other reason?'

'Why would she cheat on Hamad? He's got to be the dream partner for someone like her. Rich, powerful, loyal . . .'

'Maybe.' He pressed his foot harder on the accelerator. 'What time did he say his flight lands in Marrakech?'

'Not till midday.'

'Good. That means I can see the doctors and get things straight before he arrives.' He shook his head. 'The last thing I need right now is Hamad.'

'Oh, Tim. She looks so old.'

'She is old.' He sounded tired. 'We all forget that sometimes. She's so indomitable. Frailer than she would ever admit. I should have taken better care of her.' He took off his glasses and rubbed his fingers across his eyes; Freya slipped an arm through his. She looked through the window into the sterile, square room. Only Edith's head was visible, her white hair streaming across the pillow, the rest of her body tucked neatly beneath the sheet. Her mouth was covered with a plastic ventilator, giving her an odd, almost elephantine look. Freya wasn't sure if it was just because she was tired, but there was something nightmarish about the inert body surrounded by tubes and lines and machines that stood guard, beeping and humming to themselves.

'Mr Matheson?' They turned to see a short, balding man in a white coat, holding a clipboard. 'I'm Dr Achaari.'

Tim held out his hand. 'Doctor. How is she?'

He gestured down the corridor. 'Perhaps we could talk in my office?'

'I'll go and call Paul,' said Freya.

'Outside, please,' said Dr Achaari firmly.

'Of course. I'll come back once I've spoken to him.'

Tim nodded; she watched him walk away, his tall body a little stooped beside the stout figure of the doctor. Weariness flooded over her. The last hour of the drive had been tense – Tim flinging the car around the mountain roads, her fingers clenching the door handle, willing herself not to flinch, or ask him to slow down. The river bed at Kurmeyez had lain silent and empty, the only signs of the festival the burnt-out fires and scattered piles of rubbish. She hadn't been able to think, her mind fogged with shock and an odd sense of dislocation.

Even getting back to Marrakech hadn't helped her focus. It wasn't until she stood in the Polyclinic, looking at Edith through the glass, that she began to realise what it would mean: to Hamad, to Mustapha, to *her*. She was stable, the nurse had said when they first arrived, but it had been a serious stroke. She had smiled as she told them, a rueful, sad little smile that gave Freya a far clearer prognosis than her words.

Outside, the day was already growing warm. Men in short-sleeved shirts were hurrying along the street to take up their positions behind concierge desks and bank counters. The day she had watched rise in the mountains was moving forward, the convoluted machinery of the city's millions of entwined lives cranking to life. She retrieved her phone from her bag and thought of Dame Edith in the small, white-walled room; hers was an opposite trajectory, drifting mutely away from the light.

'Freya?' Paul's voice sounded unfamiliar; it felt like months since she had seen him, a different time. 'Where are you? Are you on your way home?'

Something in the way he said the word made her throat catch. 'I'm back already. In Marrakech. Edith's had a stroke. I think it's serious. We came straight to the hospital.'

'Oh, no. I'm so sorry. I'll come, shall I? Just tell me where you are.'

'That's kind of you.' When did things get so formal between them? 'But there's not really any point. She's unconscious. Tim's with her and I'm going to get Hamad from the airport in a bit. Have you heard from him? He's in a terrible state. Went to Paris to meet Racine – she was supposed to be on some wine course, but she never turned up. Hadn't even registered. And now she's not answering her phone. You haven't seen her, have you?'

'Me? No, why would I have seen her?'

'Because you're working on her houses?'

'Well, no. No, I haven't.'

Freya waited for him to say something more; to offer to pick up Hamad or ask how he was. When it became clear that nothing more was forthcoming, she coughed, awkwardly, simply to fill the gap.

'Right, well . . . I guess I'll see you tonight then.'

'Yes. Look, text me when you're leaving the hospital. I'll make some dinner, have a bath waiting. You're going to be exhausted.'

'Thanks. I'm not sure how long I'll be with Hamad, but I'll text you. Have a good—'

'Freya?'

'Yes?'

'It's so good to have you back.'

She slipped the phone back into her pocket and stood for a moment, unsettled by the tense, almost anxious, tone in his voice. Something had clearly happened in Fez. She took a breath and began to walk back towards the clinic. Paul would have to wait.

Inside, the artificially cooled air felt harsh against her skin. She could see Tim through the glass, a chair pulled up beside the bed, his body upright and stiff. He turned at her footsteps, mouthed, 'I'll come out.' The door creaked irritably; his face was bloodless, dark shadows beneath his eyes.

'They want me to sign a Do Not Resuscitate order,' he said, the words rushing out as if he needed to be rid of them. 'Apparently a coma, after a stroke . . . with her health the way it is, it's unlikely . . .'

'I'm so sorry.'

'Did you talk to Paul? Everything OK?'

'It's fine.' She took his hand. 'Will you wait? To make the decision about the DNR? I think Hamad . . .'

'Of course. It's not a decision I want to make alone anyway.'

'Are they really saying its hopeless?'

'They're not saying anything definite, you know what doctors are like. It depends on when – if – she regains consciousness. The longer she doesn't . . .' He closed his eyes. 'I get the impression they think it's unlikely she'll wake up.'

'God, we must ring Mustapha. He's going to be heartbroken.'

'He won't be the only one,' said Tim, glancing back through the window. 'There'll never be anyone like her, Freya. She's a one-off.'

*

Paul sat back in his chair and stared at the phone. Almost forty-eight hours had passed since the lunch in Taroudant and it was becoming increasingly clear Racine wasn't going to call. He plunged his head into his hands and tried to beat back the anxiety; she hadn't hit her head when she'd fallen; he had watched her stand up, speak to the doorman. She was fine. Just teaching him a lesson. By the time Hamad landed, there'd be a message on his phone and the whole mess would just disappear.

'*Âllo?*' The front door groaned shut; he glanced through the office window.

'Laila? What are you doing here?'

She appeared in the doorway; he thought how young she looked. 'What are *you* doing here? I thought you were away with Freya.'

'You're supposed to be in Fez.'

'I was in Fez.' She tweaked the scarlet scarf around her neck. 'Best silk in Morocco. Don't worry, I didn't spend all my time shopping. But I managed to see everyone we needed to yesterday, so I got an early flight back. Thought I'd come in and catch up on some work. What happened to your trip?'

'Um . . .' Paul couldn't even remember where he'd said they were going. 'We came back early too.'

'From London?'

Shit. 'Yes.'

'But I thought your mum was ill? Is she better? It sounded so serious when you said you couldn't come to Fez.'

'She's a bit of a hypochondriac,' he said vaguely. 'Look why don't you take the day off? Fez was work, really, so you're due a bit of time in lieu.' He needed time; Hamad would be in the city soon; he had to have an explanation for why he'd been ignoring his calls. Worse than that, he had to be able to shrug his shoulders about Racine, to feign polite interest.

The faint sound of scratching in the courtyard outside broke into his thoughts. 'Is that Yusuf?' Laila glanced out at the hooded figure sweeping the floor in slow, circular motions.

'Yes.'

'Good. Get him in here. I still haven't spoken to him about those bloody bones.'

'I'm not sure . . .'

'Just get him.' He felt a need to take control of something, to combat the feeling that his entire life was in freefall.

'*Salaam alaikum.*' Yusuf appeared in the doorway, his head shrouded by the hood of his *djellaba*.

'*Alaikum salaam*, Yusuf.' The elderly man moved slowly forward; the cloak gave the impression that he was gliding rather than walking. He stopped directly in front of the desk, his head slightly to one side, like a bird considering its prey.

Paul glanced at Laila. 'Please could you ask Yusuf what he thought he was doing –' he pulled open the drawer and retrieved two of the bones that were found in the trench – 'with these? Does he understand a stunt like that could have closed us down for weeks? Was it some sort of joke? Or was it to appease the bloody jinns, who I am *so* tired of hearing about?'

Laila's eyebrows shot up; the skin around her mouth tightened. He knew she was offended, but he was past caring; he'd had enough of tolerating the old man's ludicrous behaviour, enough of being toyed with by Racine. Yusuf's voice rose as he spoke, the guttural Darija echoing off the office walls.

'He says he knows nothing about these bones,' she said, raising her palms. 'He asks why you would think this of him?'

Yusuf muttered something, cutting a diagonal swipe through the air with his right hand.

'He asks for your respect. For both himself and the houses.'

Paul took a breath. 'Please tell Yusuf that I have shown him respect.

That I have allowed him to continue to live here, to live in the way he always has. I have tolerated his behaviour and accepted the many different manifestations of his faith. But he must also respect me, and the job I am trying to do. I would be grateful if he stopped putting hindrances in my way. And please ask him to stop sweeping all the time. I can't think.'

Before Laila could speak, Yusuf stepped forward, laying his palms flat on the desk. He glared at Paul, his small eyes glowing beneath the hoods of wrinkled skin that sagged from his bushy eyebrows.

'You do not respect this house,' he said quietly.

Paul was astounded; he had never heard Yusuf speak a word of English. The old man raised the index finger of his right hand.

'You –' he paused – 'do not respect –' another pause – 'this house.'

He turned, and shuffled slowly out of the office, mumbling to himself. Paul stared at Laila.

'Did you know he spoke English?'

She shook her head. 'We always speak in Darija. I'm as surprised as you.'

'Do you think it was him?'

'Probably. If he feels you have disrespected this place . . .'

'How can you disrespect a building? For God's sake, it's like trying to live in the bloody Middle Ages.'

'Paul? Is everything OK?'

He stared at her. In an hour Hamad was going to be in Marrakech, demanding answers to the same questions that were dominating his thoughts. Racine's disappearance would become the only topic of conversation, one in which he could say nothing of what he knew. Freya was clearly still angry with him, and he had no idea what had or hadn't happened between her and Tim in Imlil.

'Yes.'

'Can we talk about Fez? I've got some figures.'

'Not now.'

'But we really need to—'

'You know what, Laila, we really don't.' The anxiety swung in again; what if Racine really was missing? 'Look, I have to go.'

'But the figures—'

'Forget the bloody figures,' he snapped. 'They don't matter, none of it matters. Racine is missing, she's disappeared, no one's heard from her for two days. Hamad's worried sick, he's coming to Marrakech to look for her. And if she doesn't turn up, if something's happened . . . then this is over. Do you understand? These houses, everything. It's all just over.'

CHAPTER 23

It felt odd, being alone. Several times during the flight from Paris, Hamad had turned to say something to Karim, only to see the profile of an unfamiliar face in the adjacent seat. He felt unsteady, needing the quietly spoken reassurance that Racine would be fine, that there would be an explanation. It had taken some time to convince Karim to fly home, to persuade him that his family's need was greater, gathered around his father's bedside in Doha's gleaming hospital.

He thought of Edith; the muscles in his stomach tightened. She had always been his ally: an example of how to live a different kind of life. It was her persistence that had got him to Cambridge, she who had brokered the deal with the sharp-featured Director of Endowments, who had wrapped his hands around his father's money and welcomed Hamad to the university with a sincerity that was entirely transparent. She had made it happen, but it was Paul and Freya who had helped him build a life, encouraged him to see beyond the rarefied world he grew up in. They had saved him in a way, just as he had saved Paul. He had always found the reciprocity pleasing.

His phone buzzed; he smiled at Freya's text. The queue moved slowly in front of him, but finally he stepped up to the window and slipped his passport out of its cover. A photograph fell onto the counter: Racine, standing on the terrace of his penthouse in Doha, her face shaded by a wide-brimmed hat. He remembered taking the picture, the night she arrived from Lyon. It had felt momentous: the beginning of a chapter in his life that he would finally share with someone other than Karim. He thought of the neat box tucked into the corner of his case, the glittering diamond inside. The man behind the counter slipped his passport under the glass.

'Ham.'

She saw him first, waving from the other side of the barrier in the Arrivals hall. He thought how tired she looked.

'Freya.' Her body felt small against his, unusually tense. 'It's so good to see you. Thank you for coming.'

'Of course. I'm just so sorry about Edith.'

'How is she?'

'Comfortable. But still not conscious. I don't really know . . . Tim's been talking to the doctors.'

'I'll bet he has.'

Freya glanced up at him as they walked out into the sunshine. 'Look, you two fighting isn't going to help anyone. You need to pull together on this.'

'You're right.' He put an arm around her shoulders and drew her into him. 'And how are you? Are things with Paul any better?'

'We're OK. But what about Racine? Still no word?'

Hamad shook his head as he held the taxi door open for her. 'Nothing. It's so odd. She definitely said she was doing a wine course, didn't she? She said it at that dinner, at Larousse.'

'I thought so, but I wasn't really listening.'

'Well, I was. I've been over and over it. She's lied to me, clearly.' He turned to face her. 'Why, though? And where is she?'

'I have no idea. But there'll be an explanation, I promise. She'll have lost her phone or something. We all expect everyone to be connected twenty-four hours a day, but sometimes that's just not possible. Have you rung her parents?'

'I have. Got the housekeeper. They're on a cruise somewhere, apparently. I didn't want to say too much, didn't want them to think . . .' He tailed off. The phone call had been excruciating; a forced admission he had found entirely humiliating. 'Anyway, Racine will have to wait. Right now, the only person that matters is Edith.'

The Polyclinique du Maroc was cold and stark. The cotton shirt he'd thought to be light enough for the Moroccan heat was scant protection against the sharp blast of the air-conditioning system. Hamad made a note to speak to the doctor; surely Edith's room should be warmer? The sheets looked thin and worn against her skin; her neck seemed uncomfortably tilted on the pillows. He'd send Karim up to the Ville Nouvelle to buy new bedding, some cashmere wraps, a reading lamp. Edith would scold him once she regained consciousness, but he could deal with that. It was only when he pulled out his phone that he remembered Karim wouldn't answer. He would be halfway back to Doha by now.

'Please wake up, *jaddah*.' He leant forward, wrapped his fingers around hers. 'I need you.' Edith's face remained immobile; the machine beside her bed kept up a short, high beep. 'I won't sign that form. He doesn't know you like I do, not really. You'll fight back. You always do.'

The door clicked open and he turned to see Mustapha, Freya behind him. Beneath the *kufi*, the old man's face was grey and drawn. Hamad moved out of the chair and gestured to Mustapha to take his place.

'Well, well, *habibi*.' He sat heavily, leaning in to smooth the hair away from Edith's forehead. 'What trouble have you got yourself into now?'

Hamad raised his eyebrows at Freya. 'Where's Tim?'

'He had to take a phone call. He'll only be a minute.'

'I can't bear to see her like this.' Mustapha turned; his eyes were pink and glassy. 'Do they have any idea what caused the stroke?'

'Dr Achaari said that, with her history, it was always a possibility.'

Hamad leant back against the glass wall of the room. 'I should have made her come to Doha. I could have looked after her there; she could have had everything she needed.'

'No one could ever make Edie do anything she didn't want to,' said Mustapha. 'But I should have tried harder to stop her. I don't think it's a coincidence . . .' He leant in towards Edith. 'I'm sorry. I shouldn't have let you go.'

'Go where?'

'Taroudant.'

'Taroudant?' Hamad stared at Mustapha. 'When did she go to Taroudant?'

'On Sunday. I tried to ask why she was going but . . . well, you know your grandmother.' He glanced at the bed. 'You didn't want to tell me, did you? She said it was better I didn't know.'

'Well, you should have found out,' said Hamad exasperatedly. 'How far is it – three hours' drive? She's in no fit state to travel that kind of distance. You shouldn't have let her go.'

'And how, exactly, would I have done that? We have just agreed that no one can stop Edith when she has decided on a course of action. Should I have locked her in her suite?'

'If that's what it took. You're supposed to be her friend.'

'I am her friend.'

'What's going on here?' The two men turned to see Madani standing in the doorway. '*Baba*, are you OK?'

Mustapha raised his hand. 'I'm fine, son. Hamad is just upset about Edith making the trip to Taroudant. Understandably so. Particularly in the light of . . .'

'Didn't you know about it?' Madani frowned at Hamad.

'No. Why would I?'

'I thought she would have mentioned it.'

'I haven't spoken to Edith since the dinner party.'

'I didn't mean Dame Edith. I meant Racine.'

Hamad raised his fingers to his forehead and screwed up his eyes. 'Racine? What are you talking about?'

'I thought she'd have told you. I don't know why Dame Edith decided to go all that way when she could have seen her in Marrakech. But the person she met in Taroudant was Racine.'

Freya pushed the door closed behind her and let her head rest on the wooden frame. Her head was tight; her skin felt clammy, covered with a film of pink-grey dust. She longed for a shower, to let the water strip the metallic smell of the hospital from her skin. It felt like a month since the she had woken in Imlil, the light from Tim's phone breaking through the darkness. She had been someone different there, a bolder version of herself that had sustained her through the long hours at the hospital.

No one could have foreseen how the day would end. After the argument between Hamad and Tim, she had sat with Mustapha while he spun stories of a younger Edith, a time when newspapers ran articles about her extraordinary adventures, and she gave sold-out talks at Carnegie Hall. She'd watched Tim, on the other side of the bed, his fingers wrapped around Edith's white, liver-spotted hand and felt bewildered at how someone so vital, so *alive*, could be so utterly, completely reduced. And then, suddenly, Edith had opened her eyes.

'Freya?' Paul's voice floated down from the upstairs balcony. 'Is that you?'

'Yes.'

'I thought you were going to text.' He appeared suddenly out of the stairwell in the corner of the courtyard. 'I haven't started cooking yet. Would you like a drink?'

'Love one.' She followed him into the kitchen. 'It's been quite a day. Edith woke up.'

Paul poured white wine into glasses and handed one to Freya. She noticed how tired he looked; white flecks in the shadows beneath his eyes. 'That's fantastic news. I thought you said . . .'

'I know. Tim and Hamad spent most of the day arguing about a Do Not Resuscitate order – which they never signed, thank goodness. And then this afternoon she just opened her eyes. She still hasn't said anything, but she's definitely conscious.'

'And how's Hamad? Has he heard from Racine?'

'Nothing yet. He's going out of his mind. What with that and Edith, I think he doesn't know which to worry about first.' She sipped her wine. 'I keep telling him she'll just have gone off somewhere for a few days, although it is rather high-handed, even for her.'

'Nothing's too high-handed for her,' said Paul angrily. 'She's a bloody nightmare, that woman. Where's Hamad now?'

'He'll be at the hospital for a while, I expect, but he's staying at Mamounia. Why don't you go and see him for a drink later? I invited him for dinner, but he said he had work to do. I'm sure he'd love to see you.'

'Maybe later. I want to see you. Talk to you.'

'We are talking.'

'Not about this. About us.' He took the glass out of her hand and laid it on the side, pulling her towards him.

Freya closed her eyes. 'Paul, I can't do this now. I know we have to talk, but I'm beyond exhausted. Hospitals are so draining, and I had to spend half the day refereeing between Hamad and Tim. And then there was this whole scene with Mustapha about Edith going to Taroudant . . .'

'Taroudant?' Paul stepped back. 'What on earth was she doing in Taroudant?'

'This is the weird thing. Madani is convinced that she went there to see Racine, of all people. He drove her to some hotel or other, left her there for an hour and then drove her back to Marrakech. But why go all that way when she could have just got in a cab to the

Palais? And why did she want to see her anyway? Edith can't stand her. It's beyond odd. Hamad's said that if Edith has a good night and Racine doesn't show up for work tomorrow, he's going to go down to Taroudant, and go to the gendarmerie. I don't know whether he's overreacting or not.'

'Hamad's going to Taroudant?' He drained his wine glass, then poured some more.

'Are you OK?'

'No, I'm not. I don't want to talk about Edith and Hamad and *bloody* Racine. What matters is us, what's happening to us. The last time we saw each other, we both said things we shouldn't. Stupid accusations. I should never have gone to Fez, with that hanging over us. And when I got back and I knew you were in Imlil with him, it just felt horrible. I couldn't stop thinking about . . .'

'Nothing happened,' she said quietly. 'Nothing like you mean, anyway.'

'Really?' His face rippled with relief. 'God, Freya . . . it's so good to hear that. And you're wrong, too, about Jacqueline, you really are. I do know, though, that I've not been great to be around recently. It's been such an odd time, hasn't it? I think I got a bit lost, somewhere, with the move, and everything being so different. But I'm going to try harder. We can still make this what we wanted it to be.'

'Paul.' The kitchen felt cramped, suddenly, the wine sour on her tongue. 'I'm sorry, I know you want to talk right now, but I'm just beyond it.'

'OK. Look, why don't you go and have a shower or a long bath . . . whatever you want. Whatever you need.' He slipped an arm around her shoulders; she felt claustrophobic beneath the unexpected weight. 'And then let's eat pizza and watch a DVD, and try and forget about Edith and Racine and those bloody houses. Let's make tonight just about us.'

CHAPTER 24

Freya stepped off the bus into a wall of heat, and thought how strange it was that the sombre rooms of the Polyclinique du Maroc were where she felt most comfortable right now. The previous evening had been excruciating: the pizza tasted sharp and wet; the film, *Butch Cassidy and the Sundance Kid*, was one she had seen far too many times. Paul had tucked the duvet around them, pulled her body towards his, insisted on reminiscing about the first time they had seen it together. She had nodded and smiled, but when she had thought back to that rainy Sunday afternoon – the two of them cocooned on beanbags in Paul's messy bedroom in Davison Road – it seemed impossible they were the same people.

She pushed open the glass door of the hospital; here she understood how to be – to soothe Hamad, to comfort Mustapha. She wasn't sure exactly what her role was with Tim. He was the less emotional of the three, although she knew he felt everything just as keenly. When he had hugged her goodbye the previous night, his face ablaze with the relief of Edith's unexpected resurgence, it had taken all her strength to pull away. She felt her cheeks colour at the memory of how the night in Imlil had ended; she hadn't exactly covered herself in glory, but he had been so kind. It had been a while since she had been on the receiving end of such gentleness. It made the backs of her eyes sting.

The woman on reception smiled as she crossed the foyer. She was about to turn into the corridor that led to Edith's room when she recognised the dark-haired woman walking towards her.

'Laila. Hello.'

'Freya. I almost didn't recognise you.' She pointed at the *djellaba*. 'You're visiting someone?'

'Dame Edith. Paul didn't tell you? She's had a stroke.'

'Oh, no. I'm so sorry to hear that. Is it serious?'

Freya smiled. 'You know Dame Edith. Yesterday the prognosis wasn't good, but then she regained consciousness last evening. I haven't seen her yet today, but we're all hopeful.'

'That's good. It must be the last thing you need, coming on top of Paul's mother.'

'Paul's mother? What about her?'

Confusion flashed across Laila's features. 'I thought . . . I mean, Paul said that you . . .' She stopped and shook her head. 'Perhaps I misunderstood. Sometimes my English . . . I speak it better than I understand it.'

'What did Paul say?'

'Just . . . I just thought he said . . . she wasn't very well. But I obviously got it wrong.'

'When was this – when you two were in Fez?'

'In Fez?' Her eyebrows shot up. 'Freya, I'm really sorry but my aunt's expecting me. I really want to see how she is.'

'Of course. I'm sorry. I hope it's nothing . . .' But Laila was already moving away, her footsteps echoing down the white-tiled floor. Freya felt chilled; it was obvious the girl wasn't telling the truth. She slid her hands down the sides of her *djellaba* and straightened her shoulders, moving slowly along the corridor. She wasn't the same woman who had sat, humiliated, at Villa Merteuil, who had made such a fool of herself with Jean-Charles. As she opened the door to Edith's room, she could see Mustapha bent over the bed. Tim and Hamad were squeezed in next to each other, on the opposite side.

'Don't worry about this now, Edie. Try to sleep.' The door closed behind her; Mustapha glanced up, his face taut with anxiety.

'But the child . . .' Edith's voice was barely more than a whisper. 'There was no one, you see . . . Who would leave a child like that? He was my son. *My son.* And I wasn't drunk, whatever they said later. *Paul* was drunk. And then he ran away. But he didn't take the baby. The baby was mine.'

'Shhh, *habibi.* Shhh.' Mustapha bent in to kiss her forehead. 'No more talking, now. Sleep a little.'

Freya raised her eyebrows at Tim. 'Is she all right?' He nodded towards the corridor and she stepped back out of the room.

'She's very confused,' he said quietly. 'She's been like it since I got here. We've asked the doctor to give her something to help her sleep, but they're not keen to at the moment.'

'What was that she was talking about? What baby? And what did it have to do with Paul?'

'She doesn't know what she's saying, Freya. Earlier she kept calling Racine a Nazi, saying she'd done terrible things during the war. Dr Achaari said it's not uncommon for someone to be confused after a stroke. Mustapha's the best at keeping her calm; Hamad just seems to agitate her. I think she thinks he's Abdullah.'

The door clicked open behind them; Hamad nodded at Freya. 'Thanks for coming. How are you?'

'I'm fine.' She hugged him; he felt tense and cold. 'Are you OK, sweetheart? Any word from Racine?'

'I'll go back in,' said Tim quickly.

Hamad waited until it was just the two of them. 'I'm sorry. I just find it very difficult to talk about this in front of him. I can't . . .'

'I know.' Freya was aware of the anguish he would be feeling. Pride defined him; *It's an Arab thing*, he'd say vaguely, whenever she tried to suggest that it was OK to admit things weren't perfect, that a deal hadn't been quite as successful as he had hoped. 'But it's just me now. Still no word from her? Nothing at all?'

Hamad shook his head. 'She was supposed to start work at nine. Achaari says Edith's in a stable condition, so I'm going to go to Taroudant this morning. Aziz flew in last night – he's in the car outside. Madani gave me the name of the hotel she visited, so I'll go there, see if they can tell me anything. I have to do something. I can't just sit here and wait. It's driving me crazy.'

'Do you want me to come with you?'

'That's kind. But it's a long journey and I can work in the car.'

'Always work.' Freya smiled.

'Well, at least it's one thing I'm good at.' He looked at his hands. 'Although maybe that's not really true, not in this country.'

She knew what he was thinking. 'Hamad, it wasn't your fault.'

'Whose else was it? Hassan Azoulay's death will always be on my conscience, Freya. It's something I have to live with. It's just ironic . . .' He tailed off. 'Look, I have to go. Call me if there's any change with Edith.'

He kissed her, moving away without looking back. Freya stood for a minute, trying to define how she felt. Laila, Tim, now Hamad. She wasn't imagining it. None of them were telling her the truth.

'You look tired, *chérie*.' Freya opened her eyes to see Jacqueline standing on the other side of the gate. She sat up slowly; the sun had still been high when she had curled up on the lounger; now the western half of the city was cloaked in shade. '*Ah, je suis désolée*. You were sleeping. I didn't see.'

'It's fine.' She smoothed back her hair and gestured to the Frenchwoman to come through onto the terrace. 'Hospitals are exhausting, aren't they? I don't know why, you just sit around all day.'

'How is she?'

'Hard to say. We all thought it was such good news when she regained consciousness, but she's very confused. It's been quite distressing for Mustapha – she's been saying very odd things. I'm quite glad Hamad hasn't been there since this morning.'

'He went to Taroudant?'

'Yes. He rang a while ago . . .' She glanced at her watch. 'I don't know what he's found out, but he didn't sound good.'

Jacqueline nodded. 'I am sorry for Hamad. He doesn't deserve any of this.'

'It's nice to hear you say that. Not everyone is so sympathetic.'

'People are always jealous of money,' she said dismissively. 'Few see beyond it. They never stop to wonder whether it has made the person happy, whether they are content. This is why you are so important to him, Freya. It is an irony, no? In all this, the true love affair is you and Hamad.'

Freya stared at her. 'What on earth do you mean? You can't think there's anything going on between us? Does Paul think that? Has he said something to you?'

'You misunderstand me. I do not think you and Hamad are lovers in the way you mean, but there is a connection between you, an intimacy. Such things are precious. It is what he wants with Racine, but no amount of houses or jobs or private jets can buy what you two have. Chemistry, *n'est-ce pas*? Something unseen, beyond understanding. Sometimes a bond such as that forms a marriage, sometimes a passionate affair. With the two of you it has created a friendship.'

Freya pulled her knees up to her chin. 'Do you think she's left him?'

'She already did, didn't she? Coming to Marrakech? Only a man like Hamad wouldn't have understood what that meant. And so the houses. How could she possibly end it after that?'

'Do you think that's what she wants? To finish things? I would have thought Hamad was the perfect man for someone like Racine.'

'A woman like Racine doesn't want perfect. She wants . . . excitement, unpredictability, a little danger perhaps. When you grow up as she did, surrounded by money, given everything you want, then it is what you cannot have that proves the most . . . alluring. Hamad would have seemed like something very different, a challenge. But I think perhaps the reality of being with him was not what she was expecting.'

'I thought she was a friend of yours. You don't sound as if you like her very much.'

Jacqueline smiled. 'I like her well enough. But I'm not sure friendship is something she is particularly concerned with. Racine is very single-minded. Things either matter very deeply to her – her family, for example, her father's wine – or not at all.'

'Do you think something's happened to her?'

'I doubt it. If she has disappeared, I suspect it's because she wants to. The only question is why.'

'Perhaps she's run off with another man.'

'No. It's not that.'

'How can you be so sure?'

'I just am.'

Freya's phone vibrated. She glanced down. 'Hamad. He wants me to meet him at Mamounia.

'You see?' Jacqueline stood up. 'It is you that he needs, that he relies on.'

'It's mutual. He's always been there for me.'

'I'm glad to hear it.' She laid a hand on Freya's arm. 'You are a good woman, Freya. You and Hamad have something unique, I think. Don't let anything – or anyone – spoil it.'

Freya stepped into the Jemaa el Fna just as the evening call to prayer began to wind across the rooftops. The first food stalls were opening, the twirling notes of the snake charmers' *ghayta* lilting above the rumble of the drummers and the rush-hour traffic, roaring in the distance on the Boulevard Mohammed V. It felt good to be alone, surrounded by a whirl of noise and figures who wanted nothing from her, enmeshed in their own lives, unaware she was even among them. She needed a distraction from the thoughts that were plaguing her; the worries about Racine and Edith, the unnerving sense that both projects – the book and the houses – were on the brink of falling apart. As the flame-hued walls of La Mamounia came into view, a wave of anxiety rolled in. She didn't want to go back to England, to reassemble the lives they had left. She wasn't even sure she could.

She saw Hamad as soon as she stepped into the garden, sitting alone in a corner of the terrace, a tall man beside him. The table in front of them was littered with papers, phones and coffee cups. She felt relieved; whatever he had found out, it couldn't be too serious if he was continuing to work.

'Freya.' One glance told her the reverse was true. His face was haggard, skin chalky against the black hair of his beard. 'Thank you for coming.'

'Of course.' She moved to hug him, but he gave a minute shake of his head.

'Have you met Aziz?' The man looked up from tidying the papers; a wide, thick-featured face that showed little emotion. 'Aziz, this is my very good friend, Mrs Hepworth.'

'A pleasure to meet you.' His hand was moist and fleshy. 'Shall I . . . ?'

'Yes, yes.' She could hear the impatience. 'Just send those emails and then the evening is yours. But send a waiter with a bottle of Bombay Sapphire, would you?'

Freya tried not to react as Aziz slid the folders into a leather satchel and moved away across the grass. He seemed oversized compared to Karim, who wove around Hamad like a featherweight boxer, always in position, always one step ahead. Aziz walked heavily, his wide shoulders slightly hunched, as if something had made him cross.

'He's no Karim.'

'No.' She laid her hand on his arm. 'Are you all right?'

Hamad shook his head, pulled a cigarette from the packet on the table. The snap of light from the match glowed briefly in the gloom; a waiter appeared, unloaded glasses, an ice-bucket, bottles of tonic and gin.

'Thank you. We'll pour our own.' He signed the chit without looking up.

'Ham, what are you doing? You don't drink.'

'I do today.' He poured a slug of gin, threw in ice cubes, knocked it back. 'When you find out the woman you . . . you were about to propose to – is sleeping with another man . . . I think that's an appropriate time to start drinking, don't you?'

'Oh my God. Are you sure? Who told you?'

He poured more gin. 'The boy at the hotel. Where she stayed . . . where *they* stayed. He was most informative. I've seen the suite, the roof terrace where they had breakfast, even the hotel register. "Mr and Mrs Delacroix". Two nights in the Alilah Suite. Best room in the hotel, apparently. Always the best for Racine.'

'Ham, I'm *so* sorry. I don't know what to say. Why would she . . . I mean . . . Do you know who he was? Don't all hotels have to take photocopies of passports?'

He shook his head. 'Whoever he is, he's not stupid. Racine's was there, but "Mr Delacroix" somehow got away without giving his passport in. All the boy could tell me was that he was American. Which is even more bizarre – she hates Americans. She's always saying how uncultured they are, that they don't know a Riesling from a Rioja.'

He fell silent; Freya pictured her suddenly: tall, willowy Racine. For the first time she seriously considered whether something bad had happened to her.

'But that still doesn't explain why she hasn't been in contact with anyone – or why she hasn't been back to work. Even if what you say is right, even if there is someone else, surely she'd come back to Marrakech, if only to pack her things.'

'You think I should care about that? After what she's done?'

'I know it looks bad. But I don't think you've got the full story. Where are we today . . . Thursday? And no one's heard from her since Sunday – that's a long time. Did you go to the police?'

Hamad drained his glass. 'I did.'

'And what did they say?'

He shrugged. 'That they would make enquiries. But it was obvious what they thought. I've never felt so humiliated. It was unbearable.'

'Oh, Ham. I'm so sorry. You don't deserve this, after everything you've done, everything you've given her.'

'I really thought she was different, you know? This time, finally . . . I know you don't really like her, you and Paul. But there was something in her that I could never quite capture – an independence, something mysterious. When you can have anything, buy anything . . . when you meet someone who never quite reveals themselves, there's something so original in that, so *new* . . .'

'I know you love her.'

'I did.' He straightened his back. 'But that's over. I can't allow myself to think of her in that way after this. Instead, she will be a footnote, an error of judgement that I rectified as soon as I had time to consider the situation properly. My focus has been elsewhere – building relationships in the UK, in Rabat. The Farzi houses were simply a way to keep Racine quiet, to stop her demanding attention that I didn't have time to bestow. And now I have had time to think, I have left her. This is how it will be.'

'Not with me, Hamad. Or with Paul.'

He sighed. 'I can't face telling him. Will you?'

'Of course. What will you do now?'

'I'll stay until the matter is resolved. I need to be here anyway, for

Edith. I will find out who she was with, though – and what happened down there. And when I find him . . .'

'Hamad . . .'

'Freya, she lied to me. She's taken everything I gave her and smashed it up, rendered it worthless. She'll pay for this, I'm telling you. They both will. No one does this to Hamad Al-Bouskri. Neither of them will go unpunished.'

CHAPTER 25

'Good morning, *chéri*. How are you? Any news?'

Paul squinted up through the sunlight and felt his heart sink at the sight of Jacqueline standing at the counter behind him. In the days since Hamad had arrived in Marrakech, he had tried desperately to avoid her. She was the only one who knew the truth – *his* truth. It threatened the artifice he had managed to create.

'She's not making a lot of sense, I'm afraid.' He nodded unwillingly as she collected her coffee and gestured towards the seat opposite his. 'Sleeping most of the time. It's hard to tell how full her recovery will be.'

'I didn't mean Edith.' She stared at him unsmilingly. 'I meant Racine. Don't bother with Hamad's version. We both know he has no idea where she is.'

Paul said nothing. He still struggled to understand why the fates had dealt him such good fortune. God knows, he didn't deserve it. When Freya had told him that Racine had been in Taroudant with a mystery American, he'd retreated to the bathroom, locked the door, and sunk down onto the tiles, gasping with relief. Hamad's lie – that he had finished things with Racine, that she had gone back to France – made it easier still.

'Still no news, I'm afraid.' He glanced across to the other side of the square. 'I'm just waiting for him, actually. He's coming to have breakfast with us.'

'Such a supportive friend.' The sarcasm was palpable.

'I know you won't believe me, but I do really care about Hamad.' The irony was that the last few days had made him remember exactly how much. Unable to talk about Racine, and with the Farzi houses somehow off limits, they had reverted to their younger selves, playing long games of tennis on the palm-lined courts at La Mamounia, reminiscing about seminars and lectures and afternoons spent punting on the still waters of the Cam. With every day that passed, Paul became increasingly bewildered at how he could have betrayed his friend so badly. Below everything, an unspoken sense of waiting hummed like a wasp.

'So it seems.' Jacqueline sipped her coffee. 'I have been watching you with him, these last few days. And I ask myself – if a man can cover his betrayal so completely, what else is he capable of?'

'You're really asking me that? You, of all people?' He shook his head. 'Come on, Jacqueline. I've seen you playing the happily married couple with your husband.'

She laughed. 'You think because I have the occasional liaison, I am not happily married? Honestly, Paul, I would have expected more sophisticated thinking, from you of all people.'

'I love Freya.'

'I'm sure you do. But you're a fool if you think this situation is resolved. If Racine doesn't turn up soon, the police will ask more questions. Talk to different people. It would perhaps be wise to tell the truth now, voluntarily. Before it is forced . . .'

'She'll turn up.' He wished it sounded more convincing. 'She will.'

'And if she does? You think things can go back to how they were before? It's over, between her and Hamad, wherever she is. That changes everything.'

'I'm well aware of that.' Although he had said nothing to Freya, in the quiet hours of the night, when sleep refused to come, he had already begun to plan their return to England. If he could just get her home, away from Tim, away from everything that threatened them, there might still be a chance. 'Look, Jacqueline, I don't want you to think that I'm finding any of this easy. If you don't think that I feel a complete and utter bastard, the whole time—'

'There's Hamad.' She pointed across the street. 'But think about what I said, Paul. If something has happened to Racine, and the police find out you haven't admitted to being in Taroudant with her . . . Well, it will not look good. To anyone.'

'I have to go.' He didn't want to think about what she was saying. He moved through the tables, trying to repress the sense of panic that was beginning to rise. As he drew nearer, Hamad raised his hand, then said something to Aziz, standing by the car. A wave of guilt rolled in.

'Morning.' Hamad clapped his hand on Paul's shoulder, his face bruised with tiredness. 'Was that Jacqueline? Has she heard anything?'

''Fraid not. She was just asking after Edith, really.'

'I've just come from the hospital. They said she had a good night.'

'I'm pleased.' They fell into step, heading towards the archway that led into the medina. An elderly woman, hunched up on a crate, held out her hand as they passed. Hamad pulled a handful of dirhams from his pocket and dropped them into her palm.

'*Sayyid* Hamad.' Paul turned to see Aziz running towards them, waving a phone. '*Sayyid* Hamad, it is the police.' There was a gleam in his eye; it almost looked like excitement. It was the most emotion he had ever seen on the man's face.

Hamad took the phone and moved away. '*Oui?*' There was a pause. 'OK.' He slipped it back into his pocket.

'What did they say? Is there news?'

'Yes.' He turned slowly. When his eyes connected with Paul's, they were glassy with shock. 'They've found a body.'

Paul couldn't feel his feet. He knew they must be there because he was moving – the souk swaying past him, the bag seller and the chicken vendor and the old woman sitting in her cardboard box. But any sense of physicality was gone; it was as if he were floating, adrenalin and fear flooding his brain like some internal tidal surge. Somehow he'd managed to respond to Hamad, attempted to reassure him that it wouldn't be Racine. There'd been no response – he had already moved away, Aziz following, leaving Paul grappling with panic. By the time he was in the alley that led to Dar Simone, every myth he had constructed – that Racine was on a beach in Agadir, at her parents' house in France, that she would call at any moment – had crumbled.

The wooden door loomed up at him; he slipped the key into the lock and heard the latch click back. 'They found a body,' he whispered, feeling the consonants kick against his teeth. 'But it won't be her.' The conversation with Jacqueline surfaced in his mind; maybe he should confess now, before the truth came out another way. He tried to imagine Freya's face as he said the words. It hurt just to think about it.

'Paul?' She appeared out of the kitchen, wiping her hands on a tea towel. 'Where's Hamad?'

'He . . .' His mind froze for a moment; he couldn't think. 'He's gone to Taroudant. The police called.' He sucked in a breath. 'They've found a body.'

'What?' She moved towards him, her face etched with concern. 'And they think it's Racine?'

'They don't know. I mean . . . it won't be her, though. But I suppose they have to do these things, it's procedure, isn't it? . . . Although really tough for Hamad. I should have offered to go with him, I don't know why . . .'

'Paul?' The weight of her hand on his arm pulled him back. 'Are you OK? You seem . . .'

'I'm not. Not really.' He had no idea what to say; there was nothing adequate, no words to encompass all that he was feeling. What if she *was* dead, lying on some sterile metal tray in an airless drawer, everything that had made her so astonishingly, uniquely alive drained from her body? He felt himself choke; something blocked his throat. He had to sit down, had to breathe. 'Sorry.' He kept his eyes on the floor. 'It's just quite shocking.'

'God, I hope it isn't her. What an awful thing. And, well, if it is, Hamad will be just devastated. I mean, it's hard enough to learn that the person you love has left you for someone else—'

'She didn't leave him.'

'Well, she's disappeared with another man – what would you call it? She lied, she deceived him . . .' Freya's voice was harsh. 'Or perhaps that doesn't seem so shocking to you.'

'Don't. Please. I can't have another argument. Not now.'

'I don't want an argument, I just want you to tell me the truth. You've been dodging the conversation for days, but I want to know what happened in Fez. Laila may be many things, but she's a terrible liar. Why did she think your mother was so ill, Paul? Why did you come back from Fez early?'

'I don't . . . Look I just can't do this now.'

'Well, when, then? Or shall I go and ask Laila? Ever since Fez—'

'I wasn't in *bloody Fez*.'

'What?'

He couldn't speak. The pressure of spending time with Hamad, the weeks of lying, the conversation with Jacqueline – it was all coalescing in his mind, forcing words he hadn't meant to say. He felt overwhelmed suddenly, images of Racine flooding his mind, at the Farzi houses, in her villa, in the candlelit suite in Lyon.

'What do you mean, you weren't in Fez. *Paul.* Where the hell were you if you weren't in Fez?'

Every bone in his frame felt locked.

'Paul.'

'Taroudant.'

'What were you doing in Taroudant? Did you see Racine?' She stared at him. 'Oh my God. You can't mean . . .'

'I'm sorry, Frey. I'm so, so sorry.'

'But he was American. The boy said . . . the boy at the hotel . . .'

'No.' He raised his glance; her eyes were beginning to fill, the lower lids softened by a gleaming, wet ridge. Such a strange thing, the spontaneity of tears. Something bit, hard inside him. He'd always hated seeing her cry.

'You . . . ?' The dam had broken, her face was wet. 'You . . . were in Taroudant?'

'I'm so sorry, Frey. You can't . . . I never meant to hurt you.'

'You were in Taroudant.' She stared at him. 'With . . . Racine?'

'Yes.'

'But I thought . . . I heard you tell Jacqueline it was . . . Jesus!' She stood up suddenly, backed away from him. Her face was so tense he could see the outline of her cheekbones beneath the skin. 'Do you know where she is?'

'No. I wish I did.' He wished she would stop staring at him. 'I do know how appalling this is. There's nothing I can say.'

'Don't.' She pushed her thumb and index finger against her eyes. 'Don't do that. There's a million things you can say . . . When it started, why you did it, why *her*. What happened in Taroudant. What you're going to do when Hamad finds out. Because he will, and when he does . . .'

'Don't.'

'I can't believe it. I can't believe you'd do this. How *could* you?' She closed her eyes. 'How long?'

'Does it matter?'

'Of course it matters.' Freya lurched for the coffee cup on the table and hurled it onto the terrace. 'Of course it matters. It all matters. Every last detail. Why her? When? Where? How often? How long, Paul? How *FUCKING LONG?*'

'Since . . . I don't know. A while.'

'We've barely been here six weeks.'

Paul said nothing.

'Oh, no. You can't be serious. This was going on *before* we came here? You moved our whole existence to Marrakech just so you could be nearer to her?'

'Don't be ridiculous. I moved to Marrakech for you. I slept with her once. Just once. It didn't mean anything.'

'When?'

'That first business trip to Lyon. I'd emailed her – just to ask for tips on where to stay, what to do. She said they did tours at her father's vineyard, so when one of my meetings was cancelled I went along. I had no idea she'd be there – honestly. I was stunned when she turned out to be leading the tour. She had some time between leaving her job in Doha and starting in Marrakech, so she was staying with her parents for a week or two.'

'And so what, you just decided to sleep with your best friend's girlfriend? Of all people, Paul. How could you do that – not just to me, but him, too? Look at everything he's done for you.'

'Don't you think I know that? I'm not a monster, Freya, I was eaten up with guilt. Afterwards there was no contact, I didn't email her or anything, I just wanted to pretend it had never happened. I thought she and Hamad would split up once she'd moved to Marrakech, that none of us would ever see her again. I never dreamt she'd be in Doha. When I found out she was, we agreed that it had been mistake, that we would take it to our graves.'

'You saw her in Doha?' She thought of the empty suite. 'That's where you were, that first afternoon? You lying bastard. You told me you were in the gym.'

'I know. And I'm sorry.'

'You seriously expect me to believe that's all you were doing? Having a conversation?'

'It's true.'

'Well, you clearly didn't keep to it, did you?'

'I did try. We both did. It just . . . happened. I know that's what people always say . . . but it was like being crazy or something. Nothing seemed real. Our life . . . when you and I were together, it was like it wasn't happening, I just boxed it away.'

'And when you were with her, you boxed *me* away?'

'I'm sorry.'

'Where is she, Paul? You must know. If this is some twisted plan so you can run off with her, just tell me.'

'Of course it isn't. I've no idea where she is.' He could hear the panic in his voice. 'I wish I did. When I met her in Taroudant, something had clearly happened to upset her, but she wouldn't tell me what it was. We were there for a night. The next afternoon we had a big row and she stormed off. I thought she'd come back to the hotel eventually, but she didn't. The next morning, when I got back to Marrakech, I went to the Palais du Jardin, I asked Jacqueline . . . Nothing. I've still got her bag, she left it in the room. But she had money and she must have had her passport with her because it's not in the bag. I checked.'

'And how come Hamad didn't find out you were the man staying with her?'

'I gave them a false name. Never handed in my passport. Paid in cash.'

'Mr and Mrs bloody Smith,' she said slowly. 'What a cliché you are. What a cliché we are.'

'I know. But what if something *has* happened to her? The last time I saw her, she was getting in a taxi. No one's heard from her since. What if . . . it *is* her?'

'It won't be. She'll have gone home to Mummy and Daddy. She's just having a tantrum, making you suffer a bit.'

'They're not there. They're on some cruise. The staff at the house haven't seen her. No one's seen her.'

'Well, she's somewhere. Playing some ridiculous game, pleasing herself. God, you two deserve each other.'

Paul shook his head. 'But even if she wanted to freak me out, to make me angry, she's got no reason to want to do that to Hamad. Look at him, he's out of his mind.'

'Like you care.'

'I know you won't believe this, but I do. I can't believe . . .'

'Oh just *shut up*. I can't listen to you a moment longer.' He caught her arm as she began to walk away.

'Don't go. We need to talk about this. Hamad's going to . . .'

'I don't think you're going to want me here when Hamad gets back, are you?' She pulled her arm out of his grasp. 'Who knows what I might say?'

'You need to be here. She could be dead.'

'As if.'

'Freya. Don't go. Please. I love you.'

She'd struck him before he even saw her hand. He staggered backwards, pain shooting through his jaw. 'Don't ever say that to me again.'

Out in the street, the heat was vicious. It smacked into Freya the second she closed the door; even in the shade of the alley she could feel the sweat begin to settle on her skin. She leant her head against the wall; closed her eyes. Her hand stung from where it had connected with Paul's face. She couldn't take it in. Her husband and Racine. The betrayal was on a scale she simply couldn't grasp.

'Freya? You OK?' She looked up to see Fatma, peering down from the roof.

'Fine.' She pushed her lips upwards, hoping it would pass for a smile. 'Got to go, sorry.'

She began to walk, anger powering her forward. The street was busy, but the vendors and the tourists and the old men in grubby *djellabas* stepped aside to let her pass. There was a force in the way she moved, an unconscious assertion of power. When she reached the Jemaa el Fna, she remembered the sound of the explosion at the Limonia, the fear that had spiralled, the unanswered calls and angry texts. Had he been with Racine then? It was Tim who had looked after her, Tim who had made her feel safe. She pulled out her phone: *Are you home? I need to see you.* Within seconds it vibrated in her hand; *Yep. You OK? Remember how to get here? Second left after Larousse. Says Dar Tchika on wall outside. Wine?*

Freya didn't text back. She had to move before she could think, before the voice that was telling her she was about to do something stupid managed to assert itself over the adrenalin-fuelled recklessness that was currently in charge of her mind. She plunged into the souks, swept past the sign for Larousse, cringing at the memory of the dinner party, at how wrong she had been about Jacqueline. The alley was empty, the sound of her fist against the door of Dar Tchika shattering the silence.

'All right, all right.' Tim's voice echoed through the woodwork. The door swung back. Suddenly he was there, barefoot, his long body encased in faded blue shorts and a greying T-shirt. She didn't speak; stepped into the hall, heard her bag drop to the floor, and then they were kissing, her lips hard against his. For a moment she knew it was her, just her, and then there was heat and skin all around her, her feet left the floor, her legs connecting with his hips. He pushed her against the wall, his hands pulling at her shirt, sliding across her sticky, heat-soaked skin.

'I thought we weren't going to do this. In Imlil you said . . .'

'Forget what I said.' She felt drunk suddenly, pleasingly out of control. 'It doesn't matter. Nothing matters but this.'

CHAPTER 26

Hamad stepped out of the car and gestured to Aziz to stay where he was. A wave of dusty heat swept towards him. Beads of sweat popped on his forehead; the skin at the nape of his neck was already damp. The plaque on the wall gleamed in the sunlight: *Riad la Belle Étoile, Taroudant*. He wrapped his fingers around the heavy brass ring, trying not to picture Racine standing in exactly the same spot. Within seconds, the iron latch creaked against the wood; the face of the young porter appeared, the boy who had told him so carelessly of Racine's betrayal on his previous visit. Irritation swelled at the sight of his flat, clumsy features.

'*Bonjour. Je cherche le directeur?*'

To his relief, the boy gestured to him to enter. He stepped through the doorway into the candlelit lobby, remembering the high, carved ceiling, the L-shaped reception desk, sunshine flowing in from the central courtyard.

'*Attendez, s'il vous plaît.*' The boy ducked through the gap under the reception desk and Hamad walked out into the light. The garden had been recently watered; the *zellij* floor glistened, four square flowerbeds were brimming with shrubs and tangles of creamy-white jasmine. Beyond it, a long pool shimmered a deep, iridescent turquoise; he thought of Racine gliding up and down in the water, her long legs draped over one of the sunloungers, head tilted back in the sunshine. A thought hit him unexpectedly, a sudden realisation of what he might have to witness at the morgue. He sank back onto a chair, almost tipping it over.

'Hello? May I help you?' Hamad turned to see a middle-aged woman smiling at him. Her English was accented but it came easily. She extended her hand. 'I'm the manager. Helena Schiff.'

'Ms Schiff. Hello. Did your porter tell you why I am here?'

'He said that you're looking for someone?'

'Racine Delacroix. She is . . .' He swallowed, trying to forget the photograph in his wallet. 'She stayed with you last Sunday and Monday, and I haven't been able to contact her since. I'm very concerned. I'm trying to find out what happened to her while she was in Taroudant, and I wondered if you might remember anything? She's French, very striking; tall, very slim. Long dark hair.'

She nodded. 'I do remember her, yes. But I have already talked to the police about this. Forgive me, but isn't it better to leave it to them? I'm sure you understand that hotels operate on a policy of discretion. I cannot talk about my guests with just anyone.'

Hamad fought down a wave of irritation. 'I do understand that, of course. Such discretion is admirable. But Mademoiselle Delacroix and I . . . we're getting married. I am in contact with the police of course, but I feel that perhaps it is . . . advisable to also make my own enquiries.'

She looked at him for a moment, and then gave a small nod of understanding. 'I suppose I can tell you what I told them, although I don't have much to share. I checked Ms Delacroix in – she said her husband would be coming later. An elderly woman visited her about an hour after she arrived. I presumed she was a relative, although when I called the room, she seemed astonished anyone would know she was in Taroudant. It was clearly an unexpected call.'

Hamad thought of Edith lying in the hospital. 'Do you have any idea what passed between them?'

'I'm afraid not. I went home at five and didn't see either of them again. In the morning there was a note on the register that her husband had arrived, although he hadn't formally checked in and we needed his passport.'

'Which you were never going to get.'

'So it would seem.' There was a pause. 'I'm sorry, I'm really not sure what else I can tell you.'

'I've come to identify a body,' Hamad said brusquely. 'The police telephoned me this morning. They think it may be her. Whatever happens this afternoon, I need to know . . . I need to find out what happened to her here. Are you sure there's nothing more? Please think, Ms Schiff. Something that may seem trivial to you might have a different meaning to me.'

'I suppose . . .' She straightened up suddenly as if making a decision. 'I'm not sure if it's relevant, but they had a disagreement. My office is on the roof and the window opens onto the terrace. Usually I have it closed to assist with the air conditioning, but I wanted a cigarette and didn't feel I could go outside as they were there. I opened the slats and I could hear them talking. It seemed a tense, uncomfortable conversation. He was talking about risk, about what he had risked to be here. I must admit, I did wonder when I heard them if they were genuinely married.'

Hamad balled his fingers into fists. 'And you can't tell me anything about the man she was with? The American?'

Helena frowned. 'I'm sorry? He wasn't American.'

'But the houseboy said . . .'

'Ahmal? I'm so sorry, I didn't realise he'd told you that. Ahmal's only experience of life outside Taroudant is watching endless US TV shows. They subtitle them here, so he thinks everyone who speaks English is American. But the man with your . . . with Ms Delacroix was definitely British.'

Hamad let his chin slump onto his chest. What did it matter, anyway? British, American – all that mattered was that she had been with someone else. He stood up suddenly; he needed to go, couldn't stay in this place that held knowledge of his grandmother and his lover and some unknown British stranger, who took Racine to bed as his own. He reached into his wallet and pulled out a business card.

'If you think of anything else . . .' She glanced down at the card; her eyes widened.

'Well, now that is strange. Your name's Hamad?'

'It is.'

'Well, that's one thing I did hear him say. She said something about him not being the only one taking a risk, and then he said – quite loudly – that it wasn't the same for her. *He's the best friend I've got*, he said. And then he said it again more slowly: *Hamad is the best friend I've ever had.*'

Hamad stood blindly on the pavement. Paul and Racine. The betrayal was almost beyond comprehension. He relived the moment over and over again: his finger on the screen of his phone, flicking through images until he came to a photo of him and Paul at the Farzi houses, Laila laughing in the background, Freya hidden behind the lens.

'That's him,' Helena Schiff had said, pointing at Paul.

'You're sure?'

'Absolutely.'

He had just about managed to mutter a thank you before the door closed behind him. It wasn't until he felt Aziz at his arm that he realised he was standing motionless, entirely unable to process what he had just been told. Paul had been a friend since he was little more than a boy; why would he commit such an unforgivable betrayal? Hadn't he done all he could for him? Brought them to Marrakech, found him a project . . . and all on top of the secret he carried for him, a secret that continued to haunt him, ten years later?

'*Sayyid* Hamad?' Aziz turned in his seat. He was surprised to see concern in the man's face. 'Are you all right? We go back to the gendarmerie?'

'I'm fine, thank you, Aziz. And yes, the gendarmerie.'

As the car moved away, he felt the first wave of anger. How many lies had they told him? Had they laughed at his ignorance – taken his money, the opportunities he offered, and mocked his largesse? He thought of Freya suddenly; how dismissive he had been of her suspicions. Humiliation ripped through him at the memory of the effort it had taken to buy the Farzi houses, attempting to build a life with a woman who had chosen to betray him so appallingly.

As the faded walls of the gendarmerie swung into view, Hamad realised his fatalism had deserted him entirely. He wanted it to be her on the slab; she deserved whatever had happened to her. Over the time they had been together he had grown used to the interest she drew from other men, the way guests at the Palais du Jardin called her to their table just to let their eyes rest on the curves of her body. She could have had anyone. She didn't have to choose his oldest friend.

Inside, the office was damp and cold. A lank-haired man behind the desk pushed forward a dog-eared book with a pencil attached on a dirty piece of string, watching mutely as Hamad scribbled his name.

'Are you ready, monsieur?'

Hamad glanced down at the book; the signature was unrecognisable. His fingers had locked around the pen, the final *i* had turned into an elongated *r* as the weight of his hand dragged the nib across the page. 'I need a moment.'

'*Bien sûr.*'

His phone vibrated. He glanced down to see Freya's name. She'd known about Paul. The wrong woman, but she'd known all the same. He hadn't listened; had told her Paul would never betray her, that he loved her, had always loved her. Hamad closed his eyes. He had been wrong about that. Wrong about so many things. He ended the call and slipped the phone into his pocket. He didn't have the words. Not yet.

'Shall we proceed?'

Hamad nodded. His gums were coated with a thin, sour liquid, his palms slid greasily against the weave of his jeans. The man gestured towards the dingy, strip-lit corridor, following closely behind. His shoes clicked on the grubby linoleum.

'*Ici.*' He slipped a key into a metal door, heaved it open with a grunt. Thin, refrigerated air rushed at them. Hamad shivered. 'Through here.'

The room smelt of cleaning fluid and something odd, like old, stale tea. An older man was leaning against a desk; sallow-skinned with thinning hair. The gendarme muttered something in Darija, pointed to the large steel cabinet that took up most of the far wall. Hamad had seen enough films to know what it was. Six compartments. Six bodies. Even in his state of shock he could feel the grotesqueness of the situation. He had always been unusually squeamish.

The balding man pulled down the handle on one of the panels, slotting his fingertips underneath to lever out the drawer. The runners squealed. Lying on the shelf was something wrapped in what looked like white plastic.

'Are you ready?'

'I am.'

Hamad smoothed his beard with his thumb and forefinger. The plastic sheet crackled as it was peeled away. He glanced down; the body was discoloured, mustard and purple bruises spreading like faded ink beneath the skin. Her hair was smoothed back from her forehead, lashes long against her cheeks. The room swung gently. He reached out his hand to steady himself on the corner of the gurney.

'Monsieur. Is this . . . ?'

Hamad closed his eyes for a moment; he felt disorientated, unable to process what he was seeing. A word rose in his throat; he swallowed hard.

'I understand this is difficult.' The man's voice was surprisingly gentle. 'But can you . . . ?'

'Yes.'

'Monsieur Al-Bouskri? My apologies, but I must be clear. You are saying this is . . .'

'Yes.' His fingernails bit into the skin on his palms. He looked up into the man's blank face. 'This is the body of Racine Delacroix.'

It wasn't until they were halfway back to Marrakech that Hamad spoke again. He had nodded at the paperwork – the death certificate, the pamphlet for Rapatriement International. The grey-haired man had tapped his finger on the pamphlet; '*Très utile.*' Hamad suspected he was on some sort of commission; a fat wedge of dirhams for each body loaded into one of their gleaming hearses. He hadn't responded to the words of sympathy, of farewell. The shock of what had just happened left him physically unable to speak.

He had underestimated Aziz. Once his mind had begun to clear, he had fired instructions at him, each sounding more outlandish than the last. But there had been no reaction to what Hamad was asking, beyond slight nods of the head. The faintest hint of a smile had lightened his features when the extra money had been mentioned, but he hadn't asked how much, or when it would be paid. He had simply nodded his thanks and increased the speed slightly, the engine note rising as the barren mountains blurred past. Once the conversation was complete, silence settled back in, merging with the air conditioning.

Night had fallen by the time they arrived back in the city. Hamad felt relieved; sunlight made him feel exposed, the intricacies of what was coming laid bare. This was why he had to tell Edith. She would understand. She always did. Now that a corner had been turned, it was time to begin planning her relocation to Doha. It would be something for Karim to do. He didn't want him to feel usurped by Aziz.

'*Sayyid* Hamad? We are at the Polyclinic.' He realised the car had stopped, the white-panelled walls of the hospital looming out of the darkness. 'You will go in?'

'Yes. You will make all the arrangements?'

'Of course. Everything will be booked for you. I'll ensure there is a car waiting at Lyon tomorrow.'

'Excellent.' His phone vibrated: Freya. He closed the call. Almost immediately a text message flashed up. *Are you OK? Let me know what happened in Taroudant. Starting to worry, F x.*

He sighed. *Can't talk now, sorry. Am OK though. x.* She didn't deserve what was going to happen, and yet he could see no other way. Paul had to pay for what he had done; it was a matter of honour. He would explain everything, in time. But not here. Not yet.

He didn't watch Aziz drive away. Moving through the doors of the Polyclinic, he forced himself to smile for the girl at reception. She blushed as he leant on the counter, laying his wallet on the polished marble.

'You are here to see Dame Edith?'

'Yes. Is anyone with her at the moment?'

'No.'

'Good.' He pulled a wedge of dirhams from his wallet and pushed them towards the girl, glancing at her name-badge. 'Noura, I would like some time alone with my grandmother. If anyone else comes to see her, could you say that she mustn't be disturbed? And I would be grateful if you didn't mention I was with her.'

The girl's fingers closed around the money. 'Of course. You will find more improvement today, I think. She was sitting up earlier. She even had a little to eat.'

'That's wonderful. No doubt because of the care she is receiving.'

He walked away before she could answer, noticing the peeling paint on the wall and the fingermarked banister. If Edith was improving, it was down to her sheer force of will rather than anything being done in such a grime-ridden clinic. He made a note to talk to Achaari, ask when she would be fit enough to fly. He had a sudden sense of satisfaction at ends being tied off, a gradual unravelling of the chaos.

He peered through the window; Edith was asleep. The door glided open noiselessly and he lowered himself into the chair. Noura was right; she did look better, her cheeks less ashen, a fresh nightgown on her skeletal body. Gently he lifted his hands to wrap around her cold fingers, and swallowed hard against the emotion rising from his lungs.

'You're looking better, *jaddah*. It does my heart good to see.'

Her eyelids flickered for a moment; unexpectedly she looked directly at him, her eyes sharp and focused. 'Hamad.' The voice was barely more than a whisper. 'You look dreadful.'

He allowed himself a smile. 'Much has happened, these past few days. You have been missed. It is so good to see you back with us.'

'God will have to wait for my soul for a little longer yet. Perhaps he will get bored and look to someone else.'

'*Inshallah.*'

'You have something to tell me?' Edith turned her head slightly on the pillow. 'Don't lie, Hamad. Your face always told a story.'

'I've no intention of lying.' He tightened his fingers around hers. 'And you are right, as always. I do have something to tell you. I have come here to confess.'

CHAPTER 27

The call to prayer woke her. There was something different about it, the long syllables of '*Allahu Akhbar*' more gentle than the chant that spun from the minaret opposite Dar Simone. Freya lay still for a moment; the cotton of the pillowcase felt rough and unscented against her face. On the far wall, the last of the afternoon light was flowing through a gap in the curtains, picking out a low, curved archway; beyond it she could see a washbasin and a white slipper bath. She twisted her body slightly; the head beside her was dark, shoulders slimmer, wisps of grey among the hair on his chest.

'Hello.' He was looking at her; unfamiliar without his glasses. 'Are you OK?'

'I think so.' She wondered if he would kiss her. 'I'm . . . well. I guess you must think I'm a bit mad. After what I said in Imlil. Then to turn up and—'

'Ruthlessly use me for sex?' He grinned; the awkwardness lifted slightly. 'There are worse things that can happen to a man. But I am a bit surprised. In Imlil you seemed so . . . sad about how things were with Paul. I got the sense you really wanted—'

'He's been having an affair with Racine.' The humiliation was overwhelming. 'Sleeping with her. It was him. In Taroudant.'

'Jesus.' Tim pulled himself up and picked up his glasses from the side table. 'Are you sure?'

'He told me himself.'

'Oh.'

'Yes. Oh.'

'God, I'm so sorry.'

'Me too.'

'And Hamad? Does he know? Haven't you guys been friends, like forever?'

'Yes. So it's not just me he's done this to. And if Hamad finds out, God knows what he'll do. I genuinely don't think he'll be able to cope with it. Being betrayed by Racine was bad enough, but with Paul . . .' She closed her eyes. 'I still can't believe it. It's like, I just don't *know* him. How did I not see? How could he let any of this – the move, the houses, Edith's book – happen? It was always going to end in disaster. How could he be so stupid?'

'I've no idea.' He shook his head. 'You don't deserve this, Frey. He's an idiot.'

'He's a fucking bastard.'

'I thought she was supposed to be with some American?'

'That's what the boy at the hotel said. I don't know why. But I suspect Hamad may have found out the truth by now – he went back to Taroudant this morning. The gendarmerie rang to ask him to go and identify a body.'

Tim's eyes widened behind the frame of his glasses. 'And they think it's her?'

Freya shrugged. 'They must think it's possible. I don't understand why Hamad hasn't called – he must have been there by now. I rang him while you were asleep, but I just got his voicemail. He sent a text saying he was OK, but that doesn't tell me much. It may mean he's been to the morgue and it wasn't her . . . or it could mean it *was* her, and he's just not ready to talk about it. I've no idea which. Not that that should be surprising. I think recent events have proved I'm the least perceptive person on the planet.'

'Don't do that.' He kissed her again. 'Don't let your husband's appalling behaviour make you start questioning yourself. You're beautiful. Funny. Clever. He's just a walking cliché who's tried to overcome the inadequacy Hamad makes him feel by shagging his girlfriend.'

'Is that what you think? That it's about getting at Hamad?'

'I don't know. Maybe. Men are pretty stupid creatures at times. But it takes two, don't forget. I don't expect Racine is blameless in all this.'

'Do you think something's happened to her?'

He shook his head. 'I've never met a woman so well-equipped to take care of herself. She'll turn up when she's good and ready.'

'I hope you're right. Because if that is her, if Hamad . . . if . . .' She couldn't form the words. 'Well, that's going to make me wonder if Paul knows something about what happened.'

'Freya, stop. Don't start spinning fears and anxieties that are impossible to answer right now. Let's get up. Do you want to eat something? Shall I walk you home?'

'God, no. I don't want to go home. Unless . . . I mean, if you have stuff to do.'

'The only thing I was going to do was pop in and see Edith. I try and visit every evening, make sure she's settled for the night.'

'Well, I could come with you. If that's OK?'

'Of course.' He pushed the duvet away and stood up; she tried not to blush at his nakedness. 'Let's go and see my redoubtable grandmother, and then I'll take you somewhere for a large, anaesthetising drink. Does that sound like a plan?'

It was dark by the time they left Dar Tchika. The alleyway was silent and gloomy, the red walls scarred with graffiti, broken up by thick wooden doors that gave away nothing of what lay behind. A man appeared out of a side passage and pushed past her, his face covered by the hood of his *djellaba*. Freya felt the same sense of disorientation she had experienced in Tim's bedroom. She had grown used to the residential feel of the kasbah; the rumble of the luggage trolleys, the shrieks from the boys playing football. This silence was something different.

She was glad when they found themselves among the hubbub of the Jemaa el Fna. She needed life to be where she could see it, to evade the increasing sense that the whole city was keeping secrets from her, that the reality she saw and experienced was just a contrivance. Simply walking beside Tim felt different; the length of his body, the speed at which he moved – so much quicker than Paul's loping pace. Even though it was just hours since she had felt his skin against hers, it already felt unreal. She had committed adultery; an unfaithful wife to a cheating husband.

'Isn't that Hamad?' Tim pointed across the street to the Polyclinic. 'Talking to Dr Achaari?'

The lights changed as he spoke; the trucks and cars parted to allow the waiting families and tourists to move across the street. It *was* Hamad, talking animatedly, his right hand slicing through the air. As she drew closer, it became clear a disagreement was taking place. The doctor's face was creased into a frown, his arms forming triangles to his body, hands tight on his hips.

'Ham? *Ham?*' He turned, his face dark with annoyance. 'Are you all right? Dr Achaari, I'm sorry to interrupt your conversation . . .'

'It is finished, anyway.' The doctor's voice was thin. 'I have made my position clear, Monsieur Al-Bouskri. Dame Edith is not to be moved.' He nodded at Freya and moved away.

'What happened?' She laid a hand on Hamad's arm. 'Ham? What happened in Taroudant?'

'I can't talk now. Aziz is waiting.' He gestured to the Mercedes.

'I'll go and see how Edith is.' Tim raised his eyebrows at Freya. 'See you in there. Good to see you, Hamad. I hope everything's OK.'

Freya watched him walk away. 'Now will you tell me?'

Hamad ran his hand across his mouth and shook his head.

'Oh, no. It was Racine, wasn't it?' She pulled him towards her; the hug felt unwilling, somehow disconnected. 'I'm so sorry, Ham. Why didn't you call me?'

'How do you say something like that on the phone?' He drew back and straightened his shirt. 'And I don't even know how to feel. She slept with someone else, Freya. Why should I care what happened to her?'

'Don't say that. I know you care. Do you know how . . . ? I mean . . .'

'Cause of death is yet to be established.' He sounded as if he were reciting a statement. 'But they think . . . someone killed her. Strangled, most likely.'

'Jesus.'

He looked at her, eyes sharp on her face. 'You know, don't you?'

'Know what?'

'Who she was sleeping with.'

'Yes. Yes I do. Do you?'

'I do now. That he wasn't an American . . .'

'It was Paul.' One of them had to say it.

'Yes.'

'Do you think he killed her?'

To her shock, Hamad shrugged. She had expected her to tell him not to be so ridiculous, to ask how she could think such a thing. 'Of course, it was always you who was really my friend. Not him.'

'Of course.' She had to let Hamad tell any version of the truth he needed to.

'And you?' He peered at her; she got the impression it was the first moment he had really seen her. 'Don't think I don't understand how awful this is for you. You knew, didn't you? You just got the wrong woman. And I didn't listen, didn't believe you.'

'That doesn't matter now. I'm just worried about you . . . about how you are.'

'I'm fine. Really. Look, I have to go. I have a flight to catch.' He took her hands suddenly, squeezed them between his. 'Come with me. You don't have to stay and deal with all this.'

'You're leaving now? But what about . . . I mean, won't the police have more questions? There'll be an investigation, surely . . .'

'There will be questions.' His tone was oddly calm. 'But they have everything they need from me. Aziz will return to Taroudant tomorrow morning to deal with the outstanding administrative matters. I'm going to Paris tonight, then Lyon in the morning, to see Racine's parents.'

'I thought they were in Alaska?'

'I doubt that. I suspect they just didn't want to speak to me. But whatever their behaviour, this is not the kind of news that can be shared by phone or email. But you could fly straight to Doha, I could have Karim meet you there.'

'Hamad, that's really kind of you, but I can't just leave. Edith is so sick, I want to be here for Tim –' she saw his eyebrows shoot up – 'and Mustapha. And I need to work out what to do about . . . about Paul.'

'You've got to leave him, Frey. You can't stay with him after this.'

'I know.' It was a shock to hear herself say it. 'I'm just so sorry for what he's done to you.'

He tightened his fingers around her hands. 'I don't ever want to hear you apologise for him. None of this is down to you. But, look, if you really don't feel you can come now . . .' He pulled her gently towards the waiting Mercedes. 'Aziz? Do you have the ticket for Mrs Hepworth?'

'Of course.' He reached back into the car and handed a white envelope to Hamad.

'I understand why you don't feel you can leave.' He wrapped Freya's fingers around the paper. 'But there may come a time when you do want to be somewhere else. This is an open ticket to Doha. Any flight, at any time. I have to go, Frey, but that doesn't mean I'm deserting you, or Edith. The moment you want to come, just text me. Everything's in place.'

'Hamad, you're worrying me.'

'I'm sorry.' He kissed her suddenly, his beard rough against her cheek. 'I love you, you know that. And you'll get through this. We all will.'

'She's dead?' Tim's eyes widened. Freya felt an inexplicable desire to laugh. 'Christ. No wonder he looked so ashen. Where's he gone now?'

'He's flying to France tonight. Going to tell her parents.'

'I don't envy him that job.' He slipped an arm around her shoulders. 'Are you OK? It's a huge shock. I just . . . I'm absolutely stunned.'

Freya looked beyond Tim to the inert figure on the other side of the glass. 'How is she?'

'Asleep. She looks comfortable. Achaari said that she's stable, although he's pretty up in arms at Hamad's suggestion that she's well enough to be flown to Doha. And offended by the insinuation that the standard of care would be better there.' He shrugged resignedly. 'Hamad's probably right about them, but it won't be what Edith wants, even if she does recover enough to make the journey. Her life's here.'

It was over, she realised suddenly, with such clarity that she couldn't believe she hadn't thought it before. There would be no job for Paul any more. Hamad was planning to move Edith to Doha. Everything they had come for had been destroyed.

'You OK?' He tipped her chin up towards his face. She wanted to cry. 'Shall we get you that drink?'

'Don't you want to stay with Edith for a bit?'

'I'll just pop in to say goodnight.'

It took her a minute to realise that he hadn't come straight out; that instead he was leaning over over the bed. It was clear some sort of conversation was taking place. As she stood uncertainly in the corridor, Tim turned and beckoned to her to come into the room.

'She wanted to say hello.' He leant back towards the bed. 'Edith. Freya's here.'

The older woman said nothing for a moment, her eyes moving slowly between the two of them. Freya felt herself being examined afresh, Edith's blue-eyed gaze undimmed by the stroke and the extended periods of unconsciousness.

'Hello, Dame Edith.' Freya tried to move her mind away from Racine, from Racine and Paul, from the sense that her life was tipping over into an abyss. 'It's wonderful to see you looking so much better.'

'Hamad,' she muttered, the name almost lost between short, wispy breaths. 'He told me. Racine.'

'Oh.' Freya looked across at Tim.

He shook his head and mouthed, 'I can't believe him.'

'Try not to concern yourself with that now. The police are dealing with it. Nothing for you to worry about.'

'He won't . . .' The breathing was getting more laboured. 'He won't save him this time.'

'Save who?'

'Paul.' She swallowed.

'Granny, you're tired.' Tim leant over the bed. 'Don't try to talk. I'll come back tomorrow. You'll feel better then.'

'I'm not . . . dead . . . yet.' She lifted her hand limply; Freya felt the fingers clench around her wrist. 'He has to be punished this time. You still don't know . . . do you? He killed her, you see. Even though he was far, far away.'

'What do you mean? Killed who? Paul's never . . . he wouldn't . . .' She looked at Tim, who shook his head and glanced down at the bed. Edith's breathing had already changed.

'She's asleep.'

'What does she mean?'

'Come outside.' He steered her out into the corridor. Freya snatched her arm out of his hand.

'What was all that about? Is she saying that Paul killed Racine? Is that what Hamad thinks?'

'Freya, you need to calm down. Just breathe a little. Edith's very confused right now, you know that. None of what she was saying made any sense.'

'Don't patronise me. It all makes sense. Hamad's just come from Taroudant, he's told Edith . . . the police must know about Paul, they must have some evidence it was him.'

'There's no evidence, Freya. You can't seriously believe your husband killed Racine?'

'I wouldn't have believed he was capable of sleeping with her until this morning.'

'That's a different thing.'

'She meant it, Tim. "*He killed her, you see.*" She was talking about Paul. And she wasn't confused, she knew exactly what she was saying.'

'Let me take you for that drink . . .'

'I don't want a bloody drink. I want to know if my husband has killed someone.'

Tim sighed. 'You'd better sit down.'

'Oh my God.' Freya clapped her hand to her mouth. 'It's true, isn't it?'

'Not Racine. But there was . . . something else. An accident. A long time ago.'

'What are you talking about?'

'Something Edith told me. It was when you were all in Cambridge, a car crash, late one night. A woman died, Freya. And Paul was driving.'

CHAPTER 28

'Sorry. Can I just . . . ? Sorry. Um . . . would you mind . . . ?'

Freya became aware that the clipped English consonants were directed at her. She glanced up to see a young man attempting to squeeze past her table, hampered by a bulging rucksack. 'Sorry.' She pulled her chair in; the table leg scraped against her ankle. 'Ow.'

'Did I get you?' His pink-tinged features pulled together in an apologetic frown.

'No.' She watched as he let the straps slither off his shoulders and wedged the bag against the wall.

'I've just arrived,' he said, grinning. 'My mate's flying out tomorrow. Looks like a crazy city, huh?'

'Yes.' Freya signalled for the bill. 'It's certainly crazy.'

'You're going?' He looked disappointed. 'I was hoping you might be able to give me some tips. Know any cheap places to stay?'

Freya pulled out her purse and tipped the coins into the palm of her hand, counting out the price of the espresso she hadn't touched. 'I'm sorry.' She passed them to the waiter and stood up. 'I don't know anything about Marrakech.'

She looked back at him from the door of the café; he was already talking to the couple sitting at the table behind hers. She envied him his excitement, the belief he had come to an unknown world that he would slowly unravel. There had been a time when she had felt similarly, when the chaos that defined Marrakech had seemed navigable, an unfamiliar rhythm she would eventually master. Instead it continually confounded her; throwing up half-truths and revelations that rendered everything questionable and unclear. But nothing had prepared her for the story Tim had told: the accident in Cambridge, an unknown woman dead at Paul's hands.

The worst of it was that she had always known there was more to the crash than they had admitted. She had remembered the evening instantly; lying in the darkness in Paul's messy bedroom in Davison Road, watching the figures on the bedside clock clicking forward. By the time she finally heard the key in the door, her fingers were locked into tight, balled fists, her breathing hard against the pillow. He hadn't come to bed immediately; there'd been the sound of the shower, the chink of a glass in the kitchen. She'd accused him: *You've been with bloody Sophie Clarke!* The sentence was barely out of her mouth before she saw the bruising on his face.

He'd played it down – they both had – a minor accident, no one hurt. She'd wanted it to be true; so much so that when Hamad admitted the car was a write-off, she still hadn't asked for details. All that had seemed important was to reassure him – accidents happened, Paul wasn't seriously hurt. It could have happened to anyone. Her face burned when she remembered how kind she thought she was being; condescending words of comfort to the man who hadn't even been behind the wheel.

It occurred to her, as she crossed the Jemaa el Fna, that she had absolutely no idea what to do with the information Tim had shared. The vengeful part of her knew the distress it would cause Paul, yet even after everything he had done, she still couldn't bring herself to wilfully hurt him. It was enough to walk into Dar Simone, having come from another man's bed. She remembered suddenly that she didn't have to lie about it or try to dissemble. She could be as brazen as she wished. Nothing she could ever say, or do, would equal his betrayal.

'Paul. Jacqueline. Good morning.' They hadn't heard her cross the roof terrace. Paul's face was white and tense, his skin flecked with short spikes of stubble, shadows under his eyes. He looked appalling. For a moment she felt guilty that her staying out all night had caused him such distress. And then she realised. It wasn't anxiety she could see in his face. It was grief.

'Freya. You're here.'

'Yes.' She sat awkwardly, then looked across at Jacqueline. Her face was pink, eyes slightly swollen. 'How are you? This is a terrible shock. I know you were friends.'

'I can't believe it,' she said slowly. '*C'est une tragédie.*'

Paul reached for the pack of cigarettes on the table. 'How was Hamad? When did you see him?'

'Like you care.'

'Don't be like that.'

'If you'll excuse me,' said Jacqueline, rising from her chair. 'Can I have breakfast brought up to you?'

'Actually, that would be wonderful.' Freya realised she couldn't remember the last time she had eaten; the thought of slicing bread or boiling eggs seemed unthinkable.

'Freya, I'm so sorry.' Paul reached for her hand; she snatched it away.

'Don't bother. I'm not interested in your apologies.'

'Please. You have to understand . . . I didn't mean to . . .'

'I don't have to understand anything. And it hardly matters now anyway. Your sordid little affair, it's a sideshow, isn't it? Because she's dead. Lying on a slab in Taroudant. They're treating it as murder – did I tell you that?'

'What?'

Freya was disturbed to find she was almost enjoying herself. 'Hamad told me.'

'I didn't have anything to do with it, I swear to God. The last time I saw her she was getting into a taxi.'

'Keep your voice down.' She nodded towards the couples eating breakfast on the far side of the terrace.

'That's easy for you to say. I'm the prime suspect – they'll throw the bloody book at me once they've found out I was in Taroudant with her. You know how it works in countries like this. They don't care who's actually guilty, they just want to bang up whoever they can get . . .'

'Why on earth did you come to Marrakech, Paul? You obviously hate everything about it.' She shook her head. 'Oh, silly me. Of course. We both know why you came.'

'It wasn't like that.'

'I think it was *exactly* like that.'

'Freya, I can't do this now. I can't . . .' He pushed back his chair; the metal legs shrieked against the floor tiles.

'Where are you going?'

'To the houses.'

'Now?' She stared at him. 'You really think that project is going to move forward after all of this? It's over, Paul. Everything. All of it.'

'I know. Do you think I'm stupid? But the crew will have turned up for work . . . I need to tell them. Tell the foreman. He's going to have to lay them all off.' He ran his fingers through his hair. 'Christ, what a mess. Will you be here when I get back?'

'Maybe.'

'I really am sorry, Freya. I do love you. Whatever else you believe, believe that.'

She looked at him. For a moment she could see the boy he had been when they first met; the shy, long-legged teenager who had appeared in the darkness outside Antica Bella and charmed her with his blushing, stumbling speech. She said nothing; then picked up her sunglasses from the table and slipped them on before the first tears began to fall. He wasn't going to see her cry. She wouldn't allow it.

'*Chérie*? Paul has gone?' She glanced across the terrace to see Jacqueline, carrying a jug of orange juice and plate of *msemen*.

'Yes. You'll join me?' She didn't want to be alone.

'*Bien sûr.*'

Freya took one of the pancakes; the crispy dough was hot against her fingers. 'I remember the first time you gave us these. Feels like another life.'

'It's all so shocking,' said Jacqueline, settling into the chair opposite and pouring coffee. 'I know you weren't close to Racine, but . . .'

'It was Paul that was close to Racine.'

'Well, the house was a big project . . .'

'It wasn't the house. You know that, Jacqueline. Don't treat me like an idiot.'

'Yes.' She smiled ruefully at Freya. 'I am so sorry.'

'Why are you sorry?'

'Because . . .' She spread her hands apart. 'This is . . . very hard. Will you tell Hamad?'

'He knows.' She thought of him standing outside the Polyclinic the previous night, his face haggard, shoulders stooped. 'I'm not supposed to tell anyone, you know what he's like. But he was devastated. How could Paul do it, Jacqueline? Not just to me, but to Hamad as well? After everything he'd done for him?'

'I'm not trying to excuse him,' she said slowly. 'But in my experience these things are rarely deliberate. Sometimes they just happen.'

'Bollocks,' said Freya, luxuriating in the ugliness of the word. 'That's what people always say, but nothing just *happens*. And even if I did believe that, it's not like it was a one-off, is it?' She locked her eyes onto the Frenchwoman's face. 'How long have you known? The truth, please. There's been enough lies.'

Jacqueline looked down at her hands. 'Since before you came. Racine told me about the night in Lyon. It was so ironic that it was Hamad who first threw them together.'

'Hamad?'

'Yes.' She lit a cigarette. 'The first time they met was at Hamad's suggestion. Racine was in London for some wine course or other. She didn't know anyone, and so he suggested you and Paul took her to dinner. You didn't know?'

'Yes. I knew.' She saw Ali suddenly; dizzy and weak. 'I was supposed to be there. But my sister was ill. Please tell me they didn't sleep together then?'

'No.' Jacqueline looked uncomfortable. 'But I think there was an attraction.'

'So the first time was in Lyon?'

'Yes.'

'And then here.'

'I told her it was a crazy idea, that she must persuade Paul to turn down Hamad's offer. It was only ever going to end in disaster.'

'I thought it was you, you know? That Paul was having the affair with.'

'Me?' Her eyebrows shot up. 'Freya, why would you think such a thing? You were my friend . . .'

'I heard you. At Villa Merteuil. Whispering together in the garden. Hardly the behaviour of a friend. For weeks I believed it was you.'

'I'm sorry.' She shook her head. 'It was very difficult for me. When you first came, I didn't really know you. It was Racine who was my friend, I saw only her side. But over the weeks . . .'

'Does everyone know? Am I the only person who didn't see it?' She thought of the odd conversation about Paul's mother at the hospital. 'Laila knows.'

'Perhaps.'

'Was it obvious? Would you have seen it if Racine hadn't told you?'

'Honestly? It's possible. In this job I am often witness to such intimacies.'

'How?'

Jacqueline sipped her coffee. 'Because people forget I'm here. It's always that way with staff. Say the four of you are having drinks – Paul announces he has left his wallet in his room, Racine says she must go to the bathroom. You don't question it – why would you? But I – sitting unnoticed in my office or lighting the fire in the lounge – I see the kiss, hear four footsteps walking into a bedroom rather than two. Up on the roof, talking to Hamad, you don't even notice the minutes pass. But when time is stolen, even the deepest intimacies can be accessed in a matter of seconds.'

'*Madame Jacqueline?*' Freya glanced over at the houseboy who had appeared at the top of the stairs. '*Les gendarmes . . . ils cherchent Monsieur Hepworth.*' He looked at Freya. Something fluttered in her stomach.

'*Monsieur Hepworth n'est pas lá,*' said Jacqueline smoothly. '*Peut-être . . .*'

'I'll talk to them,' said Freya suddenly. Anything was better than sitting on the roof, listening to Jacqueline explain the intricacies of her husband's affair. She followed her downstairs. In the courtyard, two blue-shirted gendarmes stood awkwardly, staring at the bright orange sculptures and the angular, high-backed chairs.

'Mrs Hepworth?'

'*Oui.*' Freya looked into his face; it was expressionless, his eyes dark and clear. '*Mais, je regrette mon mari n'est pas ici en ce moment.*'

He cleared his throat. 'I think perhaps English is easier for you? Can you tell me when your husband will be back?'

'Can I ask what this is concerning?'

The men exchanged looks. 'Do you know a woman called Racine Delacroix?'

'I do. She's . . .' Her chest tightened. The room started to sway.

'Would you like to sit down?'

Freya nodded, gulping air as the older man pulled a chair towards her. 'It's just so horrible. We were all friends.'

'I'm very sorry,' said the man, more gently. 'I understand you must be upset. But . . . can you tell me what your husband was doing in Taroudant with Ms Delacroix? I understand the houses he was designing – they were hers?'

'Yes.'

'Did they often travel together?'

'No. I don't think so. This is the first time my husband has been away since we moved to Marrakech.'

'And how long ago was that?'

Freya realised she was answering the man's questions without any emotional engagement. Her voice felt disconnected from her body; it felt unreal to be discussing whether she had spoken to her husband when he was in Taroudant, or whether she had been there when he got back. Had she noticed anything strange? She hadn't noticed anything; not in all the time he had been sleeping with their best friend's fiancée.

'Monsieur, you can see Mrs Hepworth is upset.' Jacqueline laid a hand on her shoulder. 'Surely you should be asking her husband these questions?'

'Very well.' The older man stood, his face unmoving. 'Thank you, then, for your time. But in case we don't find him at the Farzi houses, please do mention our visit. It's important that we talk to him, Mrs Hepworth. Very important indeed.'

Freya watched Jacqueline follow them to the door. The panic began to rise again; it was as if her life were rolling away in a direction over which she had no control. Her phone vibrated in her pocket. *Tim.* She ignored it. She wasn't ready to talk to him, not yet. Seconds later a text appeared. *I need to speak to you. Not about last night. Please call. T x.*

Anxiety rippled through her. She pressed his name; he spoke before she'd even heard him pick up. 'Freya. I need to see you. I found something.'

'What you do mean? Found what?'

'I'm in Edith's suite. Came to get a few things . . . Look, I can't really explain on the phone. Can you come here? To La Mamounia?'

'Now?'

'Yes. Now. The thing is, what I found . . . I think I know what happened to Racine.'

CHAPTER 29

It felt odd, walking into La Mamounia again. Freya stood for a moment in the lobby, watching the familiar swirl of figures; the waiters and the bellboys and the beautiful couples. The memory of Hassan Azoulay, barrelling across the space towards Hamad, came into her mind.

'May I help you?' The concierge's features lightened as he recognised her. 'Ah, Madame Hepworth. How good to see you again. I just saw Monsieur Matheson. He brought good news of Dame Edith. We all miss her here at Mamounia. I hope she will be back with us soon.'

'I hope so too. It's actually him I came to see – I believe he is in her suite?'

'I've just seen him walking towards Bar Menzeh – should I escort you?'

'I'll be fine, thank you.'

'Of course.' He stepped back to let her pass, a slight hint of obsequiousness in the tilt of his head. She realised suddenly what a rarefied position her association with Edith had gifted her, how quickly it would slip through her fingers.

Outside, the sunlight was blinding, the palm trees throwing long shadows across the lawns. She saw him immediately, face half hidden behind a beige paper folder, a pile of letters and forms wedged under a whisky tumbler. It seemed impossible he was the same man she had woken beside hours earlier, his arm around her body, chest warm against her back. She attempted to push the image from her mind.

'Morning.' She gestured to the glass. 'Isn't it a bit early, even for you?'

'Hi.' He stood up to kiss her; his hand was warm on her waist. She wanted him to leave it there. 'Thanks for coming. How are you?'

'Better for a shower and clean clothes,' she said, trying to sound bright. She glanced at the waiter, who had appeared silently behind Tim. 'Just a mint tea. And maybe some *macarons*, in honour of Edith. You've seen her this morning?'

'I had to do something after waking up to find I'd been abandoned.' He winked at her.

'I'm sorry. I know it was rude to just disappear.' She tried to smile. 'I just . . . didn't know how to be. It would have been awkward.'

'How were things when you got home?'

'I've had easier mornings. Paul's a mess. He looked like he hadn't slept.'

'Not entirely surprising.'

'No.' She felt unsure what to say next, watching as the waiter placed the *macarons* on the table and poured the mint tea. It reminded her of the first meeting with Edith, her unexplained hostility towards Paul. She had known nothing, then. She felt a sudden longing for her unrealised state of ignorance.

'What *is* all this?' She pointed to the sheaf of papers and pile of notebooks, covered in messy French handwriting. Below the notebooks she could see what looked like invoices, delivery receipts with an image of a chateau in the top right-hand corner, the words *Maison Beauvarin* picked out in red below. Something caught her eye. She pulled out a letter with a swastika printed at the top.

'Grim.' Tim took the paper out of her hands. 'Grim is what this is. I don't know who put all this together, but basically they're someone's notes – a journalist, presumably, who was investigating the wartime dealings of a wine producer called Rémy Delacroix. It doesn't make pretty reading, I can tell you.'

'I've seen these papers before.' Freya thought back to the conversation with Edith, the odd sense of triumph she had exuded. 'Edith was reading them when I visited a couple of days after the dinner party at Larousse. She was quite odd, actually, talking about some journalist she'd known, decades ago, in Algeria. Jacques Richaud, I think it was. But she wouldn't tell me what was in them. Presumably Rémy Delacroix is something to do with Racine?'

'Her grandfather.' Tim reached for the whisky glass. 'He was also a wine producer; best known for a wine called Beauvarin. It was the Château Lafite of its day. Racine was telling me all about it at that dinner party – how she was going to bring the label back, how she didn't really understand why her father had changed the name. I've been googling Michel Delacroix. Turns out he was a banker for years before he went into the wine business. They lived in Paris when Racine and her sister were small, didn't move back to Bordeaux until both his grandparents were dead. And this –' he tapped on the papers – 'makes it clear why. And why he didn't want to use the Beauvarin name. Racine's grandfather was a Nazi collaborator. It's all here: wine deals, shipments . . . and more. From Richaud's notes it looks as if he colluded in giving away the whereabouts of Jewish families hiding in the wine cellars.'

'Are you serious? That's horrendous.' She felt cold suddenly. 'Do you think Racine had any idea?'

'I doubt it. I always got the impression she adored her father.'

'She did. It was one of the only times I ever felt any real warmth from her, when she talked about her family.' Freya closed her eyes. 'She knew, didn't she? Edith, I mean. She knew about Paul and Racine. That's what she meant.'

'Meant about what?'

'When I saw her that day, with these papers . . . she said something about Jacques Richaud. That he'd come back into her life with a solution to a problem she had no idea how to solve. What if that problem was Racine? This must be why she went to Taroudant. She'd found out about the two of them, and wanted to punish her.'

Tim nodded. 'I'd had the same thought.'

'But that's a really awful thing to do. I can't bear Racine, but still – to find out something like this about your family . . . Do you really think Edith would have told her?'

'I'm afraid I do.' Tim ran his fingers through his hair. 'I love my grandmother, but I'm under no illusions as to what she's capable of. Some of the stories she's told me over the years . . . She plays to quite different rules to most people. And loyalty is everything to her.'

'But you don't think—'

'That she had her bumped off into the bargain?' He smiled. 'No, I don't think that. But it may have something to do with her disappearance. It would have been such a shock. She may have felt she couldn't tell anyone, even Hamad.'

'So, what are you going to do with all this?'

'Take it to the police. But otherwise, I think we should probably keep it to ourselves, don't you?'

'More secrets. I've never been somewhere where everything is so hidden. Edith warned me when I first came here, but I didn't really understand.' She shook her head. 'God, I was so naive. Right from the start Paul was lying to me, so was Racine – even Jacqueline knew what was going on. Now it turns out that Edith discovered the affair and didn't tell me. It feels like I can't trust anyone.'

He leant forward. 'You can trust me, Freya. I promise.'

'I know. And that's the irony, isn't it? I've known you – what? A few months? But I feel I can trust you more than people I've known for years. I'm just not sure who anyone is any more. I believed Edith when she told me that she didn't know who Paul was having an affair with. You say Paul won't be involved with what happened to Racine, but how can I know what he's capable of after all this? It's obvious he became a completely different person when he was with her. If I never met *that* Paul, how can I know what he might do?'

Tim pushed the glass of whisky towards her. 'People can always surprise us. Edith talked to me once about how she saw life as something made up of infinite versions – of history, of events, of people. Paul is the same man he always was, he's just revealed a slightly different version of himself – albeit not a very nice one. But that doesn't make him a murderer. It just means he's capable of something you didn't expect. We want to believe that we know every facet of the people we love, but it's rarely the case.'

'I thought I knew all of Paul. Does that make me naive?'

'I think it just makes you human.'

'Perhaps. But even if you're right about Paul, to the police he's the obvious suspect. They're probably questioning him as we speak.' She took a sip of whisky, felt the alcohol bite against her throat. 'Do you think they'll arrest him?'

'Honestly?' He reached for a *macaron.* 'I don't know. But if they do, I think you should call Mustapha Chenouf. Call me a xenophobe, but I don't have a huge amount of faith in the Moroccan legal system, and you'll do much better with a local on your team. Paul's right about one thing – they're going to want to find a culprit as soon as possible.'

'Well, maybe these papers will help. And we need to speak to Edith. How was she this morning? Is she well enough to talk about this?'

'I don't know. She seemed quite odd, drifting in and out of sleep. It was like she wasn't quite there. I'll see what Mustapha thinks. But I don't want to worry him. I know he'll feel guilty about sharing this with Edith if it turns out to have had anything to do with Racine's death.'

'I can't bear to think of Mustapha upset.' Freya sighed. 'Could this be any more of a mess?'

'Are you including me in that?' He smiled. 'OK, don't answer that.'

'Look, Tim . . . last night was . . .'

'Memorable? Amazing? A one-off?'

'Definitely the first two,' she said, smiling. 'As for the third . . . right now I . . .' Her phone vibrated against the tabletop. 'It's Paul.'

'Do you want to answer it?'

'No, I don't. In fact I'm going to switch the bloody thing off.' She fiddled with the screen and dropped it into her bag.

'Don't do that on my account.'

'I'm not. After what he's done, he can't expect me to be at his beck and call any more. I'll talk to him when I'm ready.'

Freya slipped the key into the lock at Dar Simone. A sudden twist of breeze slammed the door behind her. She wondered if the police had caught up with Paul, whether they were sitting in the office at the Farzi houses, asking what he was doing in an unfamiliar city with a woman that wasn't his wife. She decided to take a bath, but when she walked into the bedroom something struck her as odd. It took a moment to realise that Paul's clothes had disappeared from the armchair, his shoes gone from under the bed. In the bathroom, one toothbrush sat in the glass; no razor or deodorant or battered leather bag that held the products he used.

'Freya?' She turned to see Jacqueline standing in the doorway. 'I'm so sorry. Paul's gone.'

'What do you mean, gone? Gone where?'

Jacqueline raised her palms. 'The airport. I'm sorry. He said . . . he just said, tell Freya I'm sorry.'

'He said what? "Tell Freya I'm *sorry*"?'

'I was walking back up the alley and saw him coming out of the riad, carrying that leather holdall. I tried to stop him, but he said . . .' She took a breath. 'He told me he had been questioned by the police for two hours. He believes they think he killed Racine.'

'And he didn't think to have this conversation with me?' Freya sank down onto the bed.

'He did say he'd tried to call you. But your phone went to voicemail.'

'So he just decided to flee the country? God, if they didn't think he was guilty before, they will now. What is he thinking?'

'He's not thinking. He's panicking. He said, "If my own wife doesn't believe me, what chance have I got with the police?" He said he wasn't going to end up in a Moroccan prison.'

'But it's OK to leave me here to face everything? For God's sake, just when I think he can't be any more reckless . . . Why didn't you stop him?'

'How was I going to do that? You might catch him, though – he only left about half an hour ago and I don't think there's a flight to London until about six.'

'Why the bloody hell should I?' She pulled her phone from her bag, switched it on and pressed Paul's number, trying not to notice the six missed calls. 'None of this would be happening if he hadn't fallen into bed with that bloody woman.'

'She's dead, *chérie*,' said Jacqueline, slightly primly. 'Don't speak ill of the dead.'

'I'll speak of her how I like . . .' Paul's voicemail broke across her words. '*Paul.* Answer the bloody phone. What the hell do you think you're doing? How is this going to help anything? The only way for you to get out of this mess is to stay here and deal with the questioning. The police didn't even say they suspected you, and if you haven't done anything . . .'

A long beep cut Freya off. She raised her fingers to her forehead and pressed them against her skin, trying to push away the suspicion, the thought she couldn't bear to look at. 'Jacqueline.' She had to say it. 'What if he's run because . . .'

'Don't be ridiculous. That husband of yours may be many things, but he's not capable of murder. How can you not know that?'

'He had an affair with his best friend's girlfriend.'

'You English.' Jacqueline shook her head exasperatedly. 'Why do you confuse sex with life? Sex is just a moment, it can be a meaningless exchange. Why does sleeping with Racine suddenly make Paul capable of killing someone? He's still the same man, he just had sex with someone else. It may not be a comfortable truth, but that's all there is to it. Don't make it something more.'

'Don't make it something *more*? What does that mean? Doesn't fidelity mean anything to you?'

'And you? Do you really think it wasn't obvious this morning that you'd come from another man's bed? Be anything you like, *chérie*, but don't be a hypocrite.'

She glared at Jacqueline. 'That's not really any of your business, is it? Paul may have chosen to enlighten you with the details of his sordid little affair, but my private life is exactly that. I'd be grateful if you gossiped about someone else.'

'I'm sorry.' She shrugged elegantly. 'But this is Marrakech . . .'

'No,' said Freya, picking up her bag. 'This is *your* Marrakech. It has very little to do with mine.'

The taxi jolted suddenly to a halt. Outside the terminal, families were pulling cases towards the yellow *Departures* sign, taxi drivers clutching boards with scribbled names. She pushed a wedge of dirhams at the driver and sprinted into the building. To her relief, the indicator board was showing a delay on the London flight. She knew Paul wouldn't go through passport control until a new departure time was showing; they'd argued about it on countless occasions. She scanned the check-in queue, looking for his familiar sandy head among the squabbling families and sunburnt couples, dashed upstairs to the café, running her gaze over the worn formica tables. And then, walking back down the stairs, she saw him, standing at the back of the long line that stretched from the security gates. For a moment, in spite of everything, she felt the old familiar pull.

'Paul.' She ran towards him. '*Paul.*'

'Freya. You're here. Thank God. Have you got your passport? Are we on the same flight?'

'For God's sake.' Her palms smacked into his chest; he staggered backwards. 'What are you doing? You can't run, you can't just *go*. I've come to bring you back, not go with you.'

'I've got to,' he hissed, pulling her away from the queue. 'They're going to arrest me, I know it. I was the last person to see Racine alive, we had a row in that hotel, people saw us. I . . . I hit her, Freya – it was an accident, she was behind me, I didn't see her. But the doorman, the man who helped her up . . . If they've talked to him, I'm done for. I'm the adulterous lover, the hapless foreigner – they don't have anyone else, they don't *need* anyone else. Racine's not just anybody, once her parents get here – and they will come – the police will be under huge pressure to arrest someone. And it's not going to be me, I'm not—'

'And what about me? Did you even think about me? You disappear back to England and I'm left here to deal with everything?'

'But they can't do anything to you. You're not involved, you weren't even in Taroudant.'

'Don't be so stupid. I'm your wife. They'll think I helped you, or that I was involved in some way. I don't know what the Moroccan equivalent is of aiding and abetting but I bet there is one. Is that what you want? Me to end up in a Moroccan prison so you don't have to?'

'Of course not.' He closed his eyes. 'This whole thing is a nightmare. An absolute bloody nightmare.'

'So you're just going to run away? Leave everyone else to clear up your mess? Well, I suppose I shouldn't be surprised. It's hardly the first time, is it?'

'What do you mean?'

'Don't play the innocent. I know it was you who caused that accident in Cambridge all those years ago – the one we all blamed Hamad for? I know you were drunk, that you left him to sort out everything while you ran home like a child.'

'What? Where on earth has that come from?' He closed his eyes. 'Hamad. Of course. He knows, then.'

'Yes, he knows. He knows you betrayed him in the worst way possible.'

'Stop trying to take the moral high ground.' His face was taut suddenly, his lips thin and red. 'You're hardly beyond reproach yourself, are you? What about Tim?'

'Don't you dare,' she spat. People were looking at them, murmuring to each other. 'I slept with him once. Last night. And you know exactly what pushed me into that decision. All the time you were shagging that bitch, I was trying to save our marriage. Until . . .'

Paul pushed his hand across his face. 'All right, *all right*. You can't make me feel any worse, so don't try. I know I've ruined everything. And if I stay here it's only going to get worse.'

'God, you really are spineless, aren't you? How did I never see it, how did I never see what a coward you are? If only I'd known the truth about that accident . . .'

'Christ, you're talking about something that happened a decade ago. I wasn't drunk. I'd had a couple of drinks. There was a dog, it was raining. No one was seriously hurt.'

'You stupid, ignorant man.' Freya could barely breathe. 'Hamad saved you that night. Saved you for ten years. He would have saved you your whole life if you hadn't slept with Racine.'

'Saved me from what? What are you talking about?'

'Saved you from the knowledge of what you did. The woman in the car? The one you thought wasn't seriously injured? She died, Paul. You killed her.'

CHAPTER 30

'Tim?'

'Freya. It's good to hear from you. I've been worried. Are you OK?'

She thought back to the events of the previous day: the scene at the airport, Paul mute in the back of the taxi, the soft click of the spare room door. He'd shaken his head at her offer of a drink, a sandwich, the chance to talk through what she had told him. She could see the horror in his face, the shock at having committed an act of such finality, without ever having known it had occurred. In that moment, Racine had been forgotten.

'Not really.' She wanted to see him. 'Paul tried to fly home yesterday. Back to the UK.'

'What?'

'I know. Can you believe it? Jacqueline told me he'd gone when I got back from seeing you. I had to go after him, persuade him not be so bloody stupid. He'd been questioned for two hours by the police. I know that he's panicking, that he's scared . . . but I was so angry. Things got a bit out of hand. I ended up telling him what you told me . . . about the accident in Cambridge. About the woman that died.'

'Christ. How did he take that news?'

'Pretty much as you'd expect. Came home without a fight. He's barely spoken since. I feel guilty for telling him like that – it's a terrible thing to find out. I can't believe I just threw it at him in the middle of an airport.'

'Don't waste your time feeling guilty. He clearly isn't giving you any thought at all.'

'Maybe. I've emailed Hamad to try and talk to him about it, but he's gone completely quiet. I don't even know whether he's in Lyon or back in Doha. I hate not being in touch – he must be going through hell, and I'm the only person that can really understand. But it's like he's keeping me at arm's length. I'm starting to worry that he blames me in some way.'

'I wouldn't try and imagine what's going on in Hamad's mind right now. Anyway, it's you I'm worried about. Do you want to . . .'

The creak of a door on the floor below cut across his words. Something like despair washed over her; there had been a few minutes earlier, with the call to prayer echoing across the rooftops and the jumble of walls glowing in the morning sunshine, when she had actually felt peaceful. She'd even managed to exchange a few words with Fatma. It was a trick the city played sometimes; unexpected moments of tranquillity among the chaos. 'Paul's up. I need to go.'

'OK. Call me later?'

'OK.' She hung up, pictured Tim's lean, angular face. It was as if some unspoken transposition had occurred, a shift of allegiances. He was her supporter now, the man on whom she relied. Paul was a problem that needed to be managed.

She heard his footsteps on the stairs; smoothed her hair back, pulled her chair out of the sun. When he appeared on the terrace, it was clear he had made an effort; freshly showered, a clean T-shirt and wet hair.

'Did you sleep?' She needed to keep the conversation brisk; emotion was dangerous.

'A bit.' He sat down. 'I'm so sorry, Frey. Sorry for everything I've put you through. But it ends now.'

'What does that mean?'

'Don't worry. I'm not talking about doing anything stupid. Well, anything more stupid. They're going to arrest me. We both know that. And when they do, I'm not going to fight it or rant and rail or make life difficult for you. I'll go with them. I'll plead guilty, if that'll make things easier.'

'Paul,' her heart was thudding against her rib cage. 'You can't mean . . .'

He shook his head. 'I'm telling you the truth about Racine, although there's no reason why you should believe me. But I am guilty. I am . . .' To her horror, she realised he was going to cry. His he bought his hands up to mask the emotion; she moved closer, put her arms around him.

'It was an accident, honey. An accident a long time ago.'

'It was my fault.' The words were muffled. 'I'd been drinking.'

'Were you drunk?'

He drew back. 'I wasn't drunk . . . but I shouldn't have been driving. A couple of bottles of beer before dinner, two glasses of wine with the meal . . . I wasn't staggering around or slurring, but still . . . there's no getting away from it. I went over and over it after it happened; would I have been able to react more quickly when the dog ran into the road, would I have been able to swerve the car if I'd been sober. I'll never know. When I thought the woman – the driver – had recovered, I guess I just felt like I could mark it up to experience. I've never had a drink and got behind the wheel again.'

Freya shook her head. 'I never knew why you were always so strict about that.'

'Well now you do. But do you know the biggest irony of all? I told Hamad he couldn't drive home that night because he wasn't insured on my car. I didn't want to break the law. How's that for a joke?' He dragged his fingers through his hair. 'Of course, he'd have had to deal with all that too. He probably lost his licence for driving uninsured. I still can't believe he would take the blame for me like that. It's extraordinary.'

'He thought you were his friend. That *we* were his friends. I guess when he volunteered to say he'd been driving, he couldn't have known what was going to happen.'

'He told me she was OK. Honestly, Frey, the day after we left Cambridge, he rang and said he'd been to the hospital and they were just keeping her in for observation. Then he called the night before we flew to Thailand and said she'd been discharged. The relief, I can't tell you. And look at how I've repaid him. Whatever's coming I deserve it. And more.'

'Why did you do it? Sleep with Racine, I mean? Of all the women you could have chosen . . .'

'I didn't choose her. It just happened. I didn't want to have an affair, Freya, I loved you – I still love you. But it was just . . . I don't know, things between us weren't good, were they ? I felt like everything I did irritated you, it was almost as if you didn't *like* me any more. And then to spend an evening with someone who . . . I don't know, thought I was funny, who seemed interested in what I had to say . . . it felt like I was someone different. A better version of myself.'

'And you couldn't be that version of yourself with me?'

'I don't think so. We'd kind of lost each other, hadn't we? You were so focused on your sister . . .' he raised his hand, 'don't . . . because I know that you had to be, I do understand that. But it felt like I couldn't do anything right. Work was going badly, I didn't seem able to help you, and then Hamad started telling me that I had to look after you more . . .'

'What?'

'That night, in October, when he came for dinner. I don't know where you were – in the kitchen, I think. He meant well, but it came out badly. It kind of crystallised something I'd always felt; that he thought I wasn't good enough for you. I was so angry that I emailed

Racine the next day, asking her for recommendations in Lyon. I didn't mean to meet up with her, it wasn't about that. Hamad just made me feel so inadequate – you two have such a bloody *thing*. Sometimes I used to think that when we were old, you'd tell me Hamad was the love of your life, not me.'

'Oh, Paul. I never loved Hamad in that way. You must know that. It was always you.'

'It wasn't, though, was it?' He smiled sadly. 'Come on, Frey. We might as well be honest with each other. Can you seriously tell me that when you first met Hamad you didn't hope . . . You know.'

Edith's words came back to her: *He was never going to jump into bed with you.* The words had stung; to know that their incompatibility had been so obvious from the start. 'I think,' she said slowly, 'that it's simpler than that. I just wanted you both. And you were generous enough to allow that, to allow another man in my life who spoke to something different in me. I was always grateful.'

Paul nodded. 'But what you had with Hamad, all those years . . . I never had it. I know you talked to him in a way you didn't talk to me. Shared things. I know he made you feel different . . .'

'He didn't make me feel betrayed.' Freya could feel the anger bubbling inside her. How dare he make this her fault? 'He didn't humiliate me, lie to me, destroy everything I spent twenty years building for a quick shag and a cheap thrill.'

'It wasn't like that.'

'I don't care what it was like. You sit there trying to tell me that because I've had Hamad in my life all these years, that gives you a right to sleep with someone else? And not just anyone, but Hamad's girlfriend?' She sat back in the chair. 'D'you know what? I think you *did* choose her. I think it answered something in you, it squared things off. You're pathetic.'

'Don't, Freya, please. I'm not trying to justify what I did, I'm just trying to explain. To tell you how I felt. I was lonely. You're not supposed to be that in a marriage, are you? I just . . . felt lonely.'

Freya said nothing. She felt bereft, suddenly. How had it come to this, after everything they had shared? Two people sitting on a rooftop in an unfamiliar city, hundreds of miles from the life they had built together. 'We never had a hope, coming here, did we? How could you let me upend my life, change everything, when you already knew we were doomed?'

'It wasn't a case of letting you.' He smiled sadly. 'You wanted to come so much. After everything you'd been through, how could I say no to you – or Hamad? But don't think I came for Racine. I came for you, for us. It was an such an extraordinary opportunity. I just didn't want to disappoint you.'

Freya laughed hollowly. 'Now that *is* ironic.'

'I know. But if Hamad wants me to pay for what I've done, he's going to get his wish, isn't he? I'll get years for this. For Racine.'

'You can't be serious.' Freya closed her eyes. 'For God's sake, Paul, do you really feel that martyring yourself for a crime you didn't commit is somehow going to atone for what happened ten years ago? How is rotting away in a Moroccan prison going to help anything? It might soothe your conscience, but how does that help me – or Hamad?'

'I don't know.' He put his head in his hands. 'I'm just trying to think what's best. I don't . . .'

A loud knock at the front door made both of them freeze. Freya stood unsteadily and peered over the wall. In the shade of the alley she could make out the neat blue uniforms of the gendarmes.

'Is it them?'

'Yes. I think we'll have to let them in.'

'I know.' He stood up and took her hands in his. 'Freya, I want you to understand me. I don't want you to try and help with this. I've put you through enough. Whatever is coming, I'll deal with it.

I don't know what you'll want to do now, if you want to stay here, or go back to England for a bit, but—'

'Don't be so bloody dramatic. I'm not going anywhere. You might be happy to indulge in some orgy of self-pity, but I'm not. What happened with Racine is nothing to do with you, and we'll prove that. I won't see you go to prison for something you didn't do.'

His fingers tightened around hers. 'God, you're amazing. When did I stop seeing that?'

'I'm not amazing. But you did stop seeing me.'

'I'm so sorry, Freya. I do love you. I'll always love you.'

'I know.' She could feel the tears building.

'But I've ruined it, haven't I? Ruined us?'

She nodded, her throat so tight she could barely speak. 'Yes. I rather think you have.'

Hamad closed the phone and tried to think how to feel. So Paul had finally been arrested. He'd hoped to feel a hit of triumph, but instead there was only a sick sense of guilt. At least it was a brief distraction from the seemingly endless frustrations of the day: stuck at Charles de Gaulle for hours, now forced to wait at the car hire desk in Lyon airport while the inept girl behind the desk poked and prodded the grubby keyboard. He missed Karim; tried to fill the hours in the airport lounge with business calls and emails to the contractors on the Nanda property in Imlil. But each time he paused, the shame rolled in again: that they had *both* betrayed him, that those he had believed loved him – those he loved – had been revealed as liars, careless of everything he had given them.

His phone buzzed. He scanned the email from Freya. She deserved an explanation, an apology for his complete withdrawal at a time when he knew she needed him. Neither was possible. Not yet.

'Your keys.' The woman behind the counter gestured to the man who had appeared beside him. 'Alain will take you to your car.'

Outside, the drizzle chilled his skin. His jeans felt damp against his legs as he touched the ignition button; it was months, possibly years, since he had driven a car. The bored voice of the sat nav guided him onto the *autoroute*, fat drops of rain bursting against the windscreen as the toll booth loomed out of the gloom. He had been here before and yet he recognised nothing. Memories flooded back: the sun bright against the car windows, Racine beside him on the back seat, Karim's reassuring presence behind the wheel. He felt alone suddenly; alone and angry.

It had been impossible to prepare for what was to come. He had tried to run through various scenarios, but events had moved so far beyond his control that he found it impossible to predict what might come next. He had honed his thoughts far enough to believe that everything that had happened – that was *going* to happen – was justice, not revenge. Outside, the rain kept falling; buildings morphed into trees that meshed together above the road to form a dense, dripping tunnel. A figure appeared from between them, hood up against the rain, a shaggy-haired dog running behind. He veered sharply, looked in his rear-view mirror; then something lurched violently inside him. So he had been right. Right to come. Right about everything.

He recognised the house instantly. He let the car glide past the ornate gates and glanced at the neat rose beds, visible through the railings. How horrified they had been that first time, Michel and Valérie, a veneer of politeness overlaying their discomfort at his ethnicity. He let the engine die and picked up the copy of *Le Monde* from the passenger seat.

Before he had finished reading the front page, the gates began to grind open. A silver sports car nosed out, a middle-aged man and woman behind the glass. Hamad smiled to himself. This was better than he could have hoped for. As the car pulled away, he stepped out into the rain, moving swiftly to slip through the dwindling gap between the slowly closing gates. His timing had been perfect. As he pressed the cream button on the left side of the door, he imagined the drive back to the airport, the flight to Paris, the long wait for the final journey back to Doha. Perhaps he would finally feel some peace.

The door clicked open and a tired, hollow-eyed woman with hair pulled back into a ponytail opened the door. Her skin was still damp from the rain.

'Hallo, Racine.' His voice was steady. She froze. 'Aren't you going to invite me in?'

CHAPTER 31

Paul looked down at his watch. Twenty-three hours. One thousand, three hundred and eighty minutes. He felt as if he had counted each one as it passed: sixty long seconds, panic inching steadily towards him like an encroaching tide. Yesterday had been bearable; the grubby room, the endless questioning, the sweet mint tea. The gendarmes had been patient at first, even polite, but as the minutes had stretched into hours he had realised, once the door had slammed shut and low voices spun Darija in the corridor, that he would not be going home any time soon.

It hadn't taken long to realise everything he had said to Freya was nonsense. There had to be another way to atone for the terrible outcome of the accident he had caused. One night in a police cell and already he was beginning to feel oddly disassociated from himself. An extended stay was unthinkable. He prayed inwardly that Freya had done as she promised: found a lawyer, talked to Mustapha, to Madani, to anyone who might be able to help. He may not deserve her support, but he didn't deserve this, either, however many sins he had committed.

He glanced at the sheet of paper on the bench next to him; he'd known enough not to sign it, however much the gendarmes insisted that the *procès-verbal* was just a formality. It might be exactly that: just an agreement of what had transpired during the questioning, a signature that would see him back in Dar Simone before the day had ended. But something told him it was considerably more. When the gendarme had realised his refusal to sign was unshakeable, he had grown angry – spat on the floor, leant on the table and whispered threats that smelt of tobacco and stale coffee.

The sound of footsteps broke across his thoughts. A key rattled in the lock, the door swung open. Paul found himself looking at a tall, silver-haired man in a pale brown suit that had seen better days. The guard barked something at him in Darija and withdrew, clearly unhappy.

'Mr Hepworth?'

'Yes.'

'I am Racha Kantari. Your lawyer.' He picked up the sheet of paper. 'You didn't sign this?'

'No. My lawyer?'

'Yes. You have friends in high places, it seems. A lawyer is not usually allowed to see his client before the first court appearance.'

'Who appointed you?'

'Your wife. She was recommended to me by a mutual friend, Tim Matheson.'

Paul pressed his lips together. 'Oh. I thought perhaps you knew Mustapha.'

'Mustapha who?'

'Er . . .' He tried to think. 'Chenouf, I think.'

Racha whistled. 'You know Mustapha Chenouf? No wonder I am allowed to see you. To have him on your side may be helpful. This will be quite the case, Mr Hepworth. Racine Delacroix was quite a high-profile person, as I understand it? Involved with Hamad Al-Bouskri?'

'That's right.' The lawyer shook his head. 'Is that a problem?'

'It may be. Al-Bouskri moves in some pretty elevated circles. Governmental circles, I mean. He has influence. There will need to be a quick result in this case, and a desire for the culprit to be non-Moroccan.'

'Your English is impressive.' He couldn't bear to focus on what Racha was actually saying.

'I was in America for three years. Seattle. It always rained.'

'Can you get me out, Monsieur Kantari?'

'That is my intention. But I have to be honest, the odds are against us. After the hearing today, it may go to court as early as next week. And don't expect a jury. You will be up in front of three judges.'

'But that's no time to get evidence. You need to get to Taroudant, talk to people. I didn't *do* anything, I swear to you. The last time I saw Racine Delacroix she was getting into a taxi.'

'Good.' He nodded. 'So, if that is the last time you saw her, perhaps we should start with the first? I need to know everything if we are to have any chance of getting you out of this situation. But talk fast, Mr Hepworth. We do not have much time.'

Freya had never been more grateful for the soft folds of the *djellaba*. Her face hidden inside the hood, she was just another dark-haired woman slipping through the souk. No one would know they were passing the wife of a man arrested on suspicion of murder, that the figure beneath the cloak had stood in the courtyard of her own home little more than twenty-four hours ago and watched as the gendarmes led her husband away. She could barely believe it herself. It was the last moment she could remember clearly; the rest of the day had been a blur of phone calls, questions, Mustapha's quiet reassurance, Jacqueline's face thin with suspicion.

Tim had arrived barely an hour after the gendarmes had taken Paul, bringing with him a thin, hollow-eyed man in a brown suit who talked about things she didn't understand – the *procès-verbal,* the *tribunal de première instance*. Nothing he said gave her any cause for hope. The only chink of light was a call from Mustapha, who talked vaguely of old friends and favours, and said that the lawyer would be able to have ten minutes with Paul the following day. It felt strangely reassuring, as if the other Marrakech, the city she could never quite reach, had been corralled into the cause.

As she pulled the door to Dar Simone closed, her phone vibrated against her hip. Hamad. At last. *How are you? Sorry to have been out of touch. I really need to see you. It's important. Can't talk on the phone or email. Can you come to Doha? You have the ticket. Just let me know when. Karim will collect you. H x.*

She reread the message three times, slipped the phone back into her bag, and began to walk. It was an astonishing text, even by Hamad's standards. She was fairly certain that he would know about the arrest; asking her to fly to Doha felt wholly unfair, as if she were being forced to make a choice. Part of her suspected that he saw it as a way to torment Paul with the knowledge that while he languished in prison, she had chosen to be thousands of miles away.

I can't just bloody come to Doha. And I can't talk about this on email. Ring me? She wasn't inclined to sign off with a kiss.

She swept across the Jemaa el Fna and ducked into the metalwork souk. A moped hooted; she stepped to the side, realised she was just one street away from the Farzi houses. They had been together there, hadn't they? Her husband and Hamad's lover. Where else had they met? Racine's villa? Dar Simone? She wondered suddenly how long Hamad had really known about the affair, whether Dame Edith had shared what she had discovered. It still stung, that she had kept it a secret, lied to her face. She had always thought the older woman to be on her side.

'Freya.' She looked up to see Madani and Mustapha sitting on the low wall in front of the Polyclinic, cigarette smoke twisting between them. 'What are you doing here?'

She moved towards Mustapha, felt the warmth of his skin against hers. 'I had to get out of the house. I can't just sit . . . Tim's coming with the lawyer again later so I thought . . . How is Dame Edith? Improving, I hope?'

'It's hard to tell. She drifts in and out of consciousness. She is quite confused, today.'

'I wanted to thank you again for getting Monsieur Kantari in to see Paul this morning. I hope it will give him a lift, help him realise that we're doing everything we can.'

Mustapha raised his hands. 'I wish I could do more. Your husband is innocent, Freya, I have no doubt of that.' He glanced at Madani. 'Why don't you sit with Edith for a while? I'm sure she's tired of looking at my grizzled old features. Perhaps Freya and I could take some lunch together?'

'That would be lovely. Are you sure?'

'Please, Freya.' Madani smiled at her. 'I have been trying to get him to go home for hours. He has been here all night.'

'All night?'

Mustapha nodded. 'She was uncomfortable. And I know the *directeur*. He allows me certain freedoms.'

Freya glanced at the elderly man; it occurred to her that his relationship with Edith was more one of equals than she had ever realised. She might have had the glamour, the exotic sense of celebrity, but he was the one who granted her access to the unseen, parallel Marrakech, who crossed easily from one world to the other. She understood suddenly that the quiet power that lay behind the faded *djellaba* and the neat, white *kufi* came from a surfeit of knowledge. Mustapha wasn't just the keeper of Edith's stories and secrets; he held the keys to the entire city.

'Good to be out of the madness, eh?' Mustapha smiled. 'You've been here before? It was once the city's post office. Now . . .' He gestured around the high-ceilinged room, edged with green velvet banquettes and potted palms. '*Très chic*, as the French would say.' He glanced up as a waiter appeared. '*Deux omelettes aux fines herbes. Deux verres de Chablis. Merci beaucoup.*'

Freya raised her eyebrows.

'I'm sorry,' he said. 'I wasn't thinking. I always order the same thing when I come with Edith. It's a tradition of ours. Would you like something else?'

'That sounds perfect. Do you and Edith come here a lot?'

'Every Thursday lunchtime for the past five years. She used to call it her *bulletin hebdo.* Weekly bulletin. Edith loved to know the gossip.'

'When I first met her, she told me this was a city that runs on gossip. She said that all that mattered was what you can prove.'

'In this, as in all things, she is right. Which is why we must prove that your husband is innocent.'

'You do believe that?'

Mustapha ran his thumb and forefinger over his beard. 'Freya, I know your husband has behaved appallingly, but whatever happened to Racine, I am sure he had no hand in it. To kill a man – or a woman – takes a certain state of mind.'

'You mean deliberately.'

He looked at her closely. 'Freya?'

'You know, don't you. About the accident? In Cambridge?'

'I do. But I didn't think . . .'

'Tim told me. Only a few days ago. And I . . . Well, Paul knows now, too. It's been quite a shock.' She reached for her wine glass. 'Have you always known?'

'Yes. I visited Edith in Cambridge not long after it happened. It had been a very difficult time. She'd had to call in a lot of favours to avoid Hamad having to go to court. The police decided it was a no-fault accident, but he was driving uninsured. I believe he lost his licence for a few years. But I'd forgotten about it entirely until you both arrived in Marrakech. Edith was very angry with Hamad for giving Paul the job on the Farzi houses. She'd never forgiven him for what happened.'

'So when I asked you that time, that Sunday evening when Paul was in Fez . . . you knew what Edith had against Paul.'

'Yes.' He smiled sheepishly. 'But it was not my secret to tell. And I hoped that it was long buried. I thought Edith was wrong to make her feelings so plain, but once she has formed an opinion . . . And of course, when she found out about Paul and Racine, it simply reinforced everything she had always believed.'

'Do you know why she went to Taroudant?' Her fingers tightened around the stem of the glass; it suddenly seemed immensely important that he didn't lie to her again.

'Yes.' He shook his head slowly. 'I'm afraid I do. And the truth is that if Edith is involved in any way in what happened to Racine, then so am I. There was a friend of ours, a journalist. When he died, he left me all his files. Like many in his trade, he knew many stories that he never told. And one of them – very, very dark – was about Racine's family.'

'I know.' She couldn't add another untruth to the seemingly infinite deceptions that swirled around her. 'Tim found the papers in Edith's suite.'

'Then you'll know what a shocking story it was – one that I should never have shared with anyone. But when I did, I was unaware of Racine's liaison . . . of Edith's fury.' He closed his eyes for a moment. 'I am a foolish old man, Freya. I should have known that she wouldn't have been able to do nothing with the information, once she was aware of it. All that would have mattered to her was getting Racine out of Hamad's life.'

'It would be helpful to know,' said Freya carefully, 'what went on between them. What was said? Maybe after lunch I could ask her a few questions? Just very gently.'

Mustapha sipped his wine. 'I'm afraid the time for that has passed.'

'I thought she was making progress?'

'So the doctors say. But I know Edith better than anyone. She is slipping away from us, a little more each day. She knows it. As do I.' His blue eyes grew wet.

'Oh, Mustapha. I'm so sorry. But then you shouldn't be here. Wouldn't you rather be with her?'

'I cannot sit and watch her leave me,' he said, so quietly she almost couldn't catch the words. 'We have said our goodbyes, Freya. Now all there is is time. I must fill it somehow. It is a Thursday, so I am here, eating omelette and drinking Chablis. She would like that.'

Freya sat back to allow the waiter to lay the plate in front of her. 'I'm not going to write the book.'

'Really? But all your work . . .'

'It doesn't matter. Not in the scheme of things. I know you didn't want me to publish it, and you and Madani have done so much for me. How can I repay you by going against your wishes? And it's about Hamad, too – he's lost so much, I can't risk him finding out Edith isn't his grandmother. When you first told me, I didn't really understand. It had all happened so long ago that I couldn't see how there would be any risk in the present. But this thing with Paul and Hamad, and now all this with Racine . . . The past is never truly buried, is it?'

The question hung in the air for a moment. Mustapha cut into his omelette and lifted a forkful to his mouth. 'Tarragon,' he said, peering at the triangle of egg. 'Edith's favourite herb. What a trivial thing to know about someone, eh? I can't even remember why I know it. But those kind of things . . . they are who a person is.' He laid down his fork and smiled at her. 'You're right, Freya. We are all bound by our pasts, however much we may wish it not to be so. And none more so than Racine.'

A metallic chime broke across their conversation; Freya reached down into her bag. 'I'm so sorry.' She glanced at the screen: *Just come, Freya, please. I'll explain everything once you're here.*

Without speaking, she passed the phone to Mustapha, who reached into the pocket of his *djellaba* for his glasses and scanned the lines of text.

'You should do as he asks.'

'I can't just fly off to Doha. Now? With Paul where he is? I need to be here.'

'To do what. Help prove his innocence?' He pointed at the phone. 'You think this isn't about what's happening with Paul? What's happened to Racine?'

Freya felt a chill settle on her skin. 'You don't think Hamad had anything to do with Racine's death?'

'I suspect no one,' said Mustapha gravely. 'As Edith told us both, only believe what you can prove. But perhaps that is what Hamad is offering you? Are you sure you shouldn't do as he asks?'

'How is he?' Even as Freya spoke the words, she felt a wave of hypocrisy. It seemed wrong to be sitting alongside Tim in Dar Simone, playing the role of concerned wife, after the conversation she had had with Mustapha as they walked back to the Polyclinic. He'd shown no surprise at her faltering admission that her marriage was over, just nodded quietly, and tucked her arm through his. There had been relief in saying it – a sense of lightness had carried her back through the alleyways – until the sight of the door to Dar Simone had brought reality crashing in.

Racha nodded without smiling. 'Your husband is as well as can be expected. It will have been a traumatic day for him. I'm afraid I have to tell you that he was formally charged in court this afternoon with Racine's murder.'

'Oh my God.' She couldn't catch her breath. 'Were you there?'

'Unfortunately no. This is how the Moroccan system works. A lawyer is usually taken on after the official charge has been made. My meeting with your husband this morning was exceptional.'

'Can you get him bail?'

'I'm afraid not. It's rarely given for foreign prisoners as they're considered a flight risk. But justice moves very fast here. We could have a trial date as early as next week. I have to be honest, however – the odds are not good.'

'But he hasn't done anything,' said Freya. 'Tim, we must be able to do something? This is insane.'

'Racha, perhaps you can just tell us what you know? This is a big shock for Freya.'

He sipped his coffee. 'The good news is that although we still have the death penalty, it's rarely, if ever, used.' Freya felt the breath whistle into her body. 'Still, he may be looking at twenty years or longer. There's no option for parole. The best possibility is that after half the term, foreign prisoners can be transferred to a jail in their home country.'

'Why are you telling me all this?' Freya's voice was tight. 'You're supposed to be defending him. It sounds as if you've already decided he's guilty. If that's the case, then please, let's not waste any more of each other's time.'

Racha held up his hand. 'Mrs Hepworth, please. I'm sorry if you feel I'm being negative. All I can do is lay out the facts. The good news is that the evidence against your husband is all circumstantial. The fact that he was . . .' He pressed his lips together. 'Forgive me . . . that he was having an affair with this woman, doesn't prove anything. But I have been able to find out that the police have talked to the concierge at the restaurant where they had lunch on the day she disappeared. It seems there was an . . . altercation.'

Freya felt her face redden. 'Yes. An accident.'

'Indeed. But it is . . . unhelpful. The concierge remembered the incident very clearly. However, he has also confirmed what your husband said – that she seemed unhurt and was driven away in a taxi. The problem is that no one has been able to find the driver.

Neither the concierge nor your husband can remember the licence plate. That makes them the last two people to see Racine before she disappeared.'

'But there must be a way to find the taxi. There can't be that many in Taroudant, surely?'

'The police insist they've tried to find the vehicle, but I am afraid what's important for them in a case like this is to charge someone without delay, ideally a non-national.' Racha raised his eyebrows at Tim. 'Moroccan justice is not always . . . Well, let's just say that there are occasions where a result is considered more important than the process by which it is obtained. I fear this might be the case with your husband.'

Before Freya could reply, a burst of Arabic pop music broke into the air. Tim pulled his phone from his pocket, glancing at the screen. 'I need to take this, it's the clinic.' He moved away across the courtyard, leaving her alone with the lawyer.

'Can I see him? Paul, I mean.'

'I'm sorry.' Racha shook his head. 'They're refusing a visiting order, I don't know why. But there is an hour each evening, between seven and eight, when a telephone is made available. I've ensured he has a phone card. He'll try to call tonight.'

'OK.'

'There are two people I would like to speak to,' he said, shuffling his papers on the table. 'The first is Hamad Al-Bouskri. I understand he's flown back to Doha? Mr Matheson gave me a contact email for him, but he hasn't responded. Are you able to reach him?'

'I can try.' For some reason she didn't feel comfortable telling him about Hamad's email, his strange demand that she fly to Doha.

'Well of course in light of the . . . situation, he may not want to help.' He smiled politely. 'The other person that's key in all of this is Dame Edith Simpson. I understand she was in Taroudant the day before Racine disappeared? She may well have information that could be useful. But she's in hospital, I understand? Do you know if anyone's been able to question her yet?'

Freya shook her head. 'She's had a stroke. I was talking to a friend of hers today and he thinks she may know something . . . but she's very weak. He didn't want her bothered.'

'We may need to bother her,' said Racha firmly. 'Tim has mentioned to me that Edith knew something about Racine's family. I'd like to ask her about that.'

'I'm afraid that's not going to be possible.' Tim sat down heavily in the seat opposite Freya, his face pale. 'That was Mustapha. Dame Edith died twenty minutes ago.'

CHAPTER 32

Freya gazed out of the window as the tips of the West Bay skyline became visible through the haze. It felt wrong, being so far away, as if she had been airlifted out of a crisis zone, leaving other people on the ground to manage their grief and panic without her. She thought of Paul, spending his second night in prison; Mustapha, grieving for Edith. Tim's angular face appeared in her mind; the skin on her cheeks begin to flame. She could no longer dismiss what had happened between them as a one-night stand. The events of the previous day had left them both exhausted; one drink had led to another, then another, until they had simply fallen into each other.

They'd barely slept. Now, thousands of miles away, she struggled to reconcile the uninhibited woman in the darkened bedroom at Dar Simone with the feelings of bewilderment and betrayal that threatened to subsume her by day. Something in Tim, in the very newness of him, obliterated everything else. She wondered painfully if it had been that way for Paul, if Racine had simply made him forget the man he had always believed himself to be.

The plane banked sharply; the city roared upwards, surreal against the vast expanse of desert. It was the first time she had flown to Doha alone. She thought of their previous visit, leaving behind the last desolate days of December. They'd been unhappy. She could see it now, looking in on them like a couple of strangers, knitted together in mute acceptance of a status quo neither knew how to change.

'We'll be landing in thirty minutes.' The stewardess removed the uneaten croissants, the porcelain dish that held half a dozen identically sized strawberries. The pastries looked as if they had come from a French patisserie, the fruit tasted of sugar and warm summer days. She thought about the people sitting at the back of the plane, squeezed in together, eating coagulated beans and hard omelette. God knows what Hamad was going to tell her. Money made anything possible, good and bad.

When she finally stepped off the plane it was a relief to see Karim standing on the tarmac. The heat swung in, the light almost blinding after the semi-darkness of the cabin. He moved forward to take her bag, gesturing to the familiar black Mercedes parked a few feet away.

'Mrs Hepworth. A pleasure to see you again. How was your flight?'

'Long. An hour on the tarmac at Charles de Gaulle. But I'm here now. How are you? How's your father?'

His face brightened beneath the black coil of the *ghutra*. 'Much improved, *maşallah*. How kind of you to remember.' He gestured towards the car. 'Please. Escape our terrible heat while I attend to immigration. You have a suite waiting at the Nanda. Hamad will meet you for lunch at two.'

'And how is he, Karim? How has he been?'

'I would say . . . distracted. It has been a terrible time – the business about Ms Delacroix, obviously, but now the news about his grandmother . . .'

'I know. It's so terribly sad. I suppose it's inevitable that he would be . . . somewhat reduced at the moment.' She waited for him to agree. 'Karim? Is there something I should know?'

'I am not sure.'

'Karim, please. You know we have been friends for many years.'

'I do know that, Mrs Hepworth, and I am very grateful you're here. "Reduced" is a good word. But there is something else. Not just grief. Something more has happened, that he cannot or will not share with me.'

Freya felt a stab of anxiety. 'Well, perhaps he will share it with me.'

'I do not think there is a "perhaps". I think this is why you are here.'

It was the necklace that undid her. As she stood in the front of the mirror in the vast hotel suite, struggling with the clasp, she remembered opening the box that held it; in bed with Paul in Venice on their third wedding anniversary. The linen sheets were soft against her skin, the shouts of the gondoliers rose up from the canal below their window. They'd been so happy, rambling from bar to bar, drinking Valpolicella and nibbling on *cicchetti* and swaying back to the hotel to strip off each other's clothes and tell each other things would always be this blissful, that nothing would ever, could ever, spoil it.

Instantly a different image replaced it: Paul's lips against Racine's skin, her varnished nails raking up his back. Freya felt as if she had been punched. The loss suddenly seemed overwhelming; of him, their life, of moving from a time when such a thing would never have seemed possible, to now, when she found herself dumbfounded by the scale of his betrayal. For the first time she allowed the full force of the blow to hit her. She sank onto the sofa, doubled up with shock and grief.

I've always loved you. It had been the last thing Paul had said when they had spoken the previous evening: the one moment of vulnerability in a conversation that felt surreally normal. She'd been aware of the effort he was making to sound calm, to save her from any more distress. Ironically, it had just made the conversation harder. She didn't want him to behave well. She didn't want to be reminded that she'd always loved him too.

A knock on the door broke across her thoughts. She picked up her bag, expecting Karim.

'Hello, Freya.'

'Ham.'

'It's so good to see you.' Before she could speak, he pulled her towards him. The hug felt unfamiliar; the stiff folds of the *thobe*, his beard bristly and unkempt, the scent of something sour on his breath. 'I thought I'd come to your suite. Thought we might need some privacy.'

He moved aside to allow Karim to wheel in a trolley, stacked with bottles and glasses, small plates of *meze*, a basket of flatbreads. 'I didn't know what you'd like . . .'

'It looks wonderful.'

'Don't worry, Karim. We'll help ourselves.'

She waited until he closed the door. 'I thought coming to my suite would be . . . I don't know, inappropriate.'

He shrugged; sloshed wine into two glasses, passed her one. 'People can think what they like. I just wanted us to be able to talk. Really talk. It's so good that you came, Freya. There are things I need to tell you.'

'OK.' She felt oddly nervous; there was something different about Hamad, something brittle and unfamiliar. 'I'm so sorry about Edith. She was . . . an extraordinary woman.'

'She was.' He sighed. 'It's a great loss, if not a great surprise. I suspected the last time I saw her would be . . . well, exactly that. I asked Karim to arrange a suite for her at the Doha Clinic. I'd hoped when she was better . . . but on some level I knew she would never make the journey.'

'She loved you very much.'

'And I her.' He closed his eyes. 'I told her, you know? About Paul and Racine, about . . . what I want to tell you. It was a terribly selfish thing to do. She didn't need to hear all that. She was so ill.'

'She would have wanted to know what was going on with you. Edith was Edith, right up to the end. And you'd just had such shocking news, Ham. You needed to talk to someone.'

'Such shocking news. Your husband and my girlfriend, you mean?'

'I'm so sorry, honey. I could kill Paul. I don't know how he could have done it to you – to both of us. I know how much you loved Racine.'

'Paul knew that too, though, didn't he?' He picked up his glass and raised it towards her. 'To my good friend, Paul Hepworth. Remember when I said that, up on the terrace, the night I told you about buying the Farzi houses? I believed it, you know? That you were my friends, that somehow the differences in our cultures, how we lived, none of that mattered. I thought knowing you two gave me some, I don't know . . . insight into the West. That I understood it. And then Paul does this. You know, whenever I'm in Europe, I have to put up with snide comments about my people, my religion, bloody Arabs, how we choose to live and behave. I get it all the time. But we don't behave like this. We don't repay those who love us like this.'

'It's an appalling betrayal, I know.' She leant towards him, laid her hand on his arm. 'Particularly after everything you've done for us. Not just recently, with the Farzi houses . . . I know about the accident, too – all those years ago in Cambridge. I know it wasn't you who was driving, that the woman in the other car . . . that she died. I still can't believe you took the blame, Ham. I can't begin to imagine how that must have felt.'

'I did it for you, not Paul,' he said quickly. 'You were so fragile, Freya. I knew how much that trip meant to you, that going travelling was your way of coping with the end of uni, with what happened with your mum. I couldn't let him take that away from you, I couldn't let him destroy it. You deserved some happiness.'

'And I was happy – that trip, it really helped me draw a line. Find some peace. You gave me that. And I never thanked you or said anything, because I didn't know.' She could feel tears rising. 'You've always been the most amazing friend to me. I feel so awful about what Paul did to you.'

'It's not your fault.' She realised Hamad was struggling too. 'What he's done to you is worse. Your marriage, all the years you have been together . . .'

'Don't. I feel like everything we had, everything we built over twelve years was just . . . pointless.' She took a gulp of wine. 'They've arrested him, did you know that? Charged him with Racine's murder.'

Hamad nodded. 'I asked the police in Taroudant to keep me informed.'

'It's an absolute nightmare – the only evidence they have is circumstantial, but even our lawyer thinks it doesn't look good.' She glanced across at Hamad; he looked away. 'You don't think he did this, do you? I mean, you know Paul's not capable of something like this?'

Hamad flexed his fingers and took a deep breath. 'I don't think he was involved in what happened to Racine. But that doesn't mean I don't want him to suffer. Don't you?'

'I want him to feel guilty. To understand the pain he's caused you – and me. But I don't want him to go to prison. Particularly for something he hasn't done.'

'But what about the things he *has* done? Doesn't he deserve to be punished for what he's done to you? If not that, then for what happened all those years ago? Death by dangerous driving. That's what I was nearly charged with. Shouldn't he pay for those crimes?'

'Maybe.' Freya was beginning to feel uncomfortable. 'But not like this. Not least because someone did murder Racine and if Paul gets put away for it – God, I can't even believe I'm saying the words – then whoever did it goes free. If we know it wasn't Paul, we have to prove it, in spite of what happened with Racine. You see that, surely?'

Hamad put his glass on the table and plunged his head into his hands. Freya pressed her lips together; she knew better than to pressure him to speak before he was ready.

'No one murdered Racine.' His voice was barely audible.

'What?'

He sat up, his face haggard behind the dark beard. 'I said, no one murdered her. She's . . . she's in Lyon, with her parents. Racine's alive.'

Even under the thick white parasol it was unbearably hot. Freya stared out across the beach to the curved building at the end of the jetty; she remembered the excitement she'd felt, listening to Racine talk about Marrakech, to Hamad's anecdotes about buying the Farzi houses. She had truly believed he was offering the chance to step away from the lives that were stifling them, and create something new.

'Freya?' She turned to see Hamad, his *thobe* blazing in the sunlight.

'Ham. I said I needed a bit of time.'

'I know.' He sat on the sunlounger beside her. 'But I can't bear it if you're upset with me. You have to understand, I didn't intend to do it. I was in shock, I couldn't believe what I'd just heard. And I thought – I genuinely believed – that it was going to be her lying in that morgue. When it wasn't, when they pulled back the sheet and I realised it was a different woman, I just couldn't take it in.'

'But you told me it was Racine. You stood in the car park at the Polyclinic and you told me she was dead. How could you do that? How could you lie to my face?'

'I'm sorry. I just . . . It all got out of hand so quickly. In the car on the way to the morgue, when I genuinely thought that it would be her, I knew they'd probably arrest Paul. And I wanted that – just for a day or two, until they found the real culprit. I wanted him to suffer, can't you see that? A couple of days in a Moroccan prison wouldn't make up for what he'd done, but God, I just wanted him to know what it felt like to lose everything. So I said . . . I said it was her.'

'And did you even stop to think about who was really lying on that slab? She'd have had family, kids maybe . . .'

'Do you think I don't know that?' He leant forward and dug his fingers into the sand. 'Her name was Amira Kettani. They think she'd been murdered by her boyfriend. She has two sisters, both parents still alive. I've seen to it that they won't want for anything in future.'

'That doesn't make it all right. You have to undo this, Hamad, you have to talk to Racine.'

'I said everything I needed to say to Racine when I saw her in Lyon.'

'You *saw* her?' Freya pictured her standing on the tarmac the first morning they arrived in Marrakech: the dark sunglasses, the flame-coloured dress. 'Did you know where she was all the time? Was any of it true?'

'I had no idea whether she'd be there or not. But I knew her parents would know where she was. All that rubbish about an Alaskan cruise – I never believed that. They just didn't want to talk to me.' He paused for a moment, as if deciding whether to say something. 'I saw her, you know? Before I got to the house. She was out in the rain, walking the dog. She looked so *small*. The relief of seeing her, Frey – even after everything she'd done. I thought I'd be angry, but it was just . . . awful.'

'Hamad, I know it's hard, but you can't just blame Paul. She's equally responsible for what happened.'

'I know. But she was so . . . odd. Different. I don't think she was surprised to see me – she seemed pleased, on some level. But she wouldn't explain why she'd disappeared, or why she hadn't returned anyone's calls. Said she just needed to be alone, that it was best for everyone. Best for me. I asked her and asked her, said surely I deserved an explanation, at the very least. And then . . . she started to cry.' He looked down at his hands, twisting together against his *thobe*.

'Hamad, you can't feel sorry for her.'

'But you can pity Paul? She was distraught, Freya. Something had changed in her. Something had happened.'

'Did she say what Edith was doing in Taroudant?'

He ran his fingers over his beard. 'Not really. Something about visiting a friend. That she'd just happened to stop in at the hotel for a drink. I knew it wasn't the truth, but there wasn't any point in pressuring her.'

Freya thought of the pile of documents she had looked through with Tim, the story they told about Racine's grandfather. There was no doubt that Edith had used them in some way, blackmailed the Frenchwoman into leaving Morocco, leaving Hamad. For a fleeting moment she felt grateful to Racine, that she had chosen not to share with Hamad what Edith had done.

'And so you just left? With no real explanation for why she did what she did?'

'I'm not a bully,' he said quietly. 'And I do still have some pride. She told me she loved me, that she hadn't meant to hurt me, all the standard things. In the end, she simply said I was better off not knowing. And I believed her.'

'Aren't you curious?'

He raised his palms. 'It sounds odd, but I think she was trying to protect me. I don't know from what. But . . . it's enough. Losing Racine. Losing Edith. If there's more to bear, I don't need to know it right now.'

'You'll have to tell her. The truth, I mean. We have to get Paul out.'

'I don't have to tell anyone anything.'

'Ham, please don't be this person.' She shook her head. 'You said you wanted him to suffer for a couple of days – you've had that. Believe me, he's in seven shades of hell right now. We have to get him out. You can't have him put away for a crime that he didn't commit.'

He stood suddenly, moved towards the window. 'I know.' The

words were barely a whisper. 'I know you're right. But then . . . what? They just both get away with it? You can forgive her, forgive Paul?'

'Don't think that. I want Paul out of prison because it's wrong that he's there – morally wrong. But when he does get out – and I will get him out – I'm filing for divorce. Our marriage is over. I think, actually, it's been over for quite a long time. Perhaps I should thank Racine for bringing things to a head.'

'At least you have something to thank her for.' He looked so desolate that Freya slipped an arm around his shoulders and pulled her towards him.

'She didn't deserve you,' she said softly. 'Seriously, Hamad. I know you won't believe me, but she isn't worth all this.'

He looked at her for a moment and pulled out his wallet, slipping a business card across the table. 'That's her parents' number.' He closed his eyes. 'She'll think badly of me.'

'Yes.'

'And you?'

'I don't know what to think. I'm not sure you're the man I always thought you were.'

'I'm not sure I am either.' Hamad sighed and looked out towards the jetty. 'But then perhaps I never really was.'

CHAPTER 33

Paul picked up the phone, his heart beating wildly. The skin on his hand stuck to the receiver; he couldn't remember the last time he'd washed. It seemed pointless. Everything seemed pointless.

'Paul? This is Racha.'

His brain was so fogged through lack of sleep and fear that for a moment he couldn't think who the name belonged to. 'You're the lawyer?'

'That's right. I have news. Incredible news. Racine Delacroix is alive.'

'What?' Paul felt his eyes widen in their sockets. 'What are you talking about?'

'The woman Hamad Al-Bouskri identified: it wasn't her.'

'But he went to Taroudant. Saw her in the morgue.'

'He was lying. Listen to what I'm telling you, Paul. Racine is alive. I have just put down the phone from speaking to her.'

'But she vanished. Where is she? Is she all right?'

'She's very shocked by what happened . . . but she was extremely helpful. I think this can all be resolved quite easily. It's a simple case of proving her identification to the French police, and they will then liaise with the gendarmes in Taroudant and Marrakech. Once they have those documents, they'll have to release you. If Racine Delacroix isn't dead, there's no charge for you to answer.'

'Oh my God.' The ramifications of what Racha was telling him started to filter through Paul's exhausted mind. 'How do you know? I mean . . .'

'I believe your wife found out what had happened. She is in Doha, correct? I presume that Al-Bouskri confessed to her, and she then made contact with Ms Delacroix. It's an astonishing thing for him to have done. I'm sure you can bring charges if you wish.'

'No.' Paul thought of Hamad – saw them suddenly, sitting on the sofa in Davison Road. 'I just want all this to be over. Are you seriously saying I'll be released?'

'I can see no reason why you shouldn't be out before the end of the day.'

'I don't know what to say. Thank you, Racha.'

'Just doing my job. And anyway, I think it's your wife who really deserves your thanks.'

The line went dead. He looked at the guard who had walked him from the stinking, dark cell. For a moment he couldn't move. That Racine was alive, that everything had been a lie . . . it was too much to take in. Relief flooded his system like adrenalin. It had to mean something, that Freya had gone to so much trouble to prove his innocence. He stood unsteadily. Perhaps this wasn't the end, after all. They'd have to go back to London now; once they were home, away from Racine – away from Hamad – he would repay Freya a million times over, be the husband he always should have been. Paul breathed out as the cell door closed behind him. It was as if they had been granted a second chance.

Freya was lost. Somehow she'd taken the wrong turn out of Souq Waqif, and found herself sucked into a lattice of alleyways littered with fraying cardboard boxes and odd snippets of material, glittering in the gutter like discarded paper notes. She peered more closely; they *were* notes – Qatari riyals; the alleyway was covered in them. Two women in burkhas whisked by; a boy on a brightly coloured bicycle wobbled out of a side street. Why was no one stopping to pick the money up? She walked on, past shop windows stacked with trays of *kunafa* and *basboussa*, the sticky, syrup-drenched pastries Hamad loved to eat, past scarlet oil cans piled high with scarlet chillies, neat heaps of star anise, mounds of saffron, glowing in the sunshine.

Around the corner, the alley opened out into a street she recognised. An elderly man in a *djellaba* appeared. He looked like Yusuf; gestured towards a door she recognised as the entrance to Dar Simone. It opened without him touching it. Inside, she could see the courtyard of the first Farzi house, filled with furniture from their flat in Battersea. She glanced up. Paul was on the roof terrace of Riad des Arts, calling something to her that she couldn't understand. Suddenly the call to prayer broke out from the mosque behind her: a strange, mechanical chant that wasn't coming from the minaret, but somewhere else.

Freya opened her eyes. The phone beside her bed vibrated angrily on the bedside table; she stretched out an arm, switched off the alarm and lay for a moment in the darkness. Snippets of the previous day came back to her: Hamad's astonishing confession, the brief, awkward conversation with Racine. She'd refused to believe her at first, accused her of concocting such a ludicrous story as some form of revenge for the affair with Paul. It was only the mention of Rémy Delacroix that seemed to change her mind. Once she realised Freya knew her grandfather's secret, her tone had changed to one of almost passive acceptance.

The phone buzzed again. She brought the screen up to her face.

'Morning, Tim.'

'Hey there. How are you?'

'Apart from very odd dreams, OK I guess. You?'

'I didn't get much sleep. I still can't get my head round what Hamad did. I can't stop wondering what would have happened if you hadn't gone out there. Do you think he'd have just left Paul in prison?'

'No.' Freya pulled herself up in bed and pushed her hair out of her face. 'He knows what he did was wrong. But Hamad doesn't function well by himself. If he'd had Karim with him when he went to Taroudant, I doubt any of this would have happened. Or if, when he told Edith, she'd reacted like I did, it would have stopped then.'

'I can't believe she knew and didn't say anything.'

'I suspect she thought that Racine and Paul both deserved what was coming. She'd never forgiven him for the car crash. It probably seemed like justice, to her.'

'And what about you? Are you OK?'

'Not really. Things were left oddly with Hamad yesterday. I'd like to see him before I fly, but I feel . . . I don't know, like I let him down in some way. Didn't support him.'

'You did exactly the right thing.'

'I know. But he's so hurt. He doesn't deserve any of what's happened. What he tried to do for us was so amazing. And now everything's in ruins, thanks to bloody Paul and Racine. I suppose they'll have released him by the time I get back?'

'I think so. I just spoke to Racha – he says they'll just want to make the whole mess go away as quickly as possible. Paul owes you a serious debt of gratitude, Freya. You've gone to a lot of trouble for him.' There was a note in his voice; Freya recognised it. They all thought the same thing – Mustapha, Tim, probably even Paul. But she wouldn't change her mind.

'What else could I have done? Once he's released and I'm back in Marrakech, then . . .' She couldn't bring herself to finish the sentence, even though she had spent most of the evening playing out scenarios of a life without Paul. They would have failed at being married. She couldn't imagine how it would feel to be divorced; it still felt like a term that applied to other couples. It wouldn't matter that it was

Paul's infidelity that had destroyed everything. On some level, she too had been at fault.

'What will you do? Will you stay on in Marrakech?'

'I don't know. Paul will be on the first plane home, I'm sure. And now I don't have the book . . .' She tailed off. The future looked bleak suddenly: a humiliating return to London, weeks of bitter negotiations with Paul, the gradual dismantling of a life.

'Look, don't worry now. Just concentrate on getting yourself home – let me know when your flight gets in and I'll pick you up.'

'OK.' A knock at the door broke into Freya's thoughts. 'There's someone at the door so I'd better go. But thank you. Yet again.'

'No need.' She could hear he was smiling. 'See you tonight.'

She got out of bed and pulled on a robe, trying to ignore the sense that Marrakech was unlikely to be her home for much longer, whatever Tim said. Her limbs grumbled as she padded across the carpet. She felt as though she could sleep for a week.

'Good morning, Mrs Hepworth.'

'Karim.' His embarrassment at the dressing gown was palpable. 'I didn't realise it would be you. Give me one second . . .'

He smiled politely. 'No need. I just came to ask if you would join *Sayyid* Hamad for breakfast before your flight? When you are ready, of course?'

'I'd love to. I just need to dress and collect my things. Half an hour?'

'That would be perfect. I know he'll be delighted to see you.'

Freya glanced in the mirror and tried to smile at the worried-looking woman staring back. She cleared the small amount of cosmetics she had left in the bathroom, rolled up her dress from the previous night and slipped her feet into the jewelled flip-flops that were the only footwear she had brought. She thought of Paul suddenly; the relief he must be feeling. Even now, after everything he had done, she still couldn't bring herself to want unhappiness for him.

It felt good to leave the suite behind, to close the door on the explosion of grief, the conversation with Racine, the odd broken night's sleep fractured by unsettling dreams. As the lift doors opened, she straightened her body, forcing her shoulders to drop from their hunched position. She hoped Hamad wasn't going to be angry or resentful of what she had done. She didn't want to think badly of him, too.

She saw him immediately, sitting at a corner table in the restaurant, scanning his phone. He stood as she approached, awkwardly formal, an uncertain smile on his face.

'Hamad.' He kissed her on both cheeks. 'I didn't know if I would see you again.'

'I didn't know either,' he said truthfully. 'But I woke up this morning and I felt so wretched. I didn't want to leave things as they were.'

A waiter pulled out the chair opposite Hamad. She sank into it. 'I spoke to Racine. She knows.'

His expression didn't change. 'And Paul?'

'The lawyer's been in touch with him. He'll be released by the end of the day.'

'You are an extraordinary woman, Freya. You deserve much better than either of us has given you over this last year.'

'I certainly do.' She smiled. 'But what you did . . . That was Paul's fault too, really. It was an insane thing to do, but . . .'

'There are no buts.' Hamad shook his head. 'I could make all sorts of excuses – Paul's behaviour, Racine's, the fact that Morocco makes me feel . . . I don't know, out of control in some way. I don't understand how things work there. But none of that takes away from the fact that I've behaved appallingly to you. Instead of supporting you, I've just added to your distress. In my anger with Paul, I allowed myself to forget how my behaviour would impact on you. You've always been the most amazing friend, I have been blessed to have you in my life. Platonic friendships of the sort we have – they don't happen in my culture.'

Freya blushed a little. 'Anything I've given to you, you've given me much more in return. But please don't talk about us in the past tense. I don't want what happened with Paul and Racine to affect our friendship. If I'm going to become a single woman again, frankly I'm going to need all the friends I've got.'

'You still plan to leave him?'

'I should have done it some time ago, or he should have left me. But we were both too scared, too comforted by the status quo. We'll be happier without each other, I think.'

'Well, I don't care about him,' said Hamad briskly, 'but if that's true for you, then I'm glad. You deserve happiness, Freya, you deserve all good things. And so, well . . .' He pushed a slim white envelope across the table towards her.

'What's this?'

'Something that no longer has any worth for me, but which may for you. If you mean what you say about Paul, your life is going to change massively. Good to have something to help with that change, I think.'

Her fingers shook slightly as she opened the envelope. The previous day's revelations had left her unsure as to exactly what Hamad was capable of. She pulled out four neatly folded sheets of A4, stapled in the left-hand corner, her eyes widening as she scanned the pages. On the final piece of paper there was space for two signatures. Hamad had already signed. Below, she read her own name.

'Hamad? These are the deeds to the Farzi houses.'

He nodded. 'Your houses.'

She laid the papers on the table. 'Don't be ridiculous. You can't sign those houses over to me. They're worth hundreds of thousands of pounds . . .'

'They're worth nothing, Freya. All they do is remind me of a hope

I once had. A humiliation. I bought these houses for a woman. I just didn't know that woman was you.'

'I don't know what to say. It's an incredibly kind thought, so generous . . . but you must know I can't possibly accept. They're your houses, Ham. Make something good from them. Open the museum, or a school, or some sort of foundation.'

'I want to give them to you,' he said, and there was a touch of frustration in his voice. 'You're the good that will come out of them. I haven't forgotten, all those months ago in your flat in London. You asked for my help. What I did, that wasn't about helping you. It was all about me, fitting you into some plan to impress Racine. That wasn't what you needed. But perhaps now . . . this is.'

She sipped her coffee and tried to think how best to manage the situation. 'How about this. Why don't you let Laila carry on working on the houses? She's more than capable – maybe she could just focus on the museum for now. I could work with her – source exhibits, talk to Omar Farzi about what he would like. I'm sure Madani would come as my interpreter. And maybe we could have a space dedicated to Dame Edith?'

His face brightened. 'That's a wonderful idea. See, Frey, they're yours already. Sign the papers.'

'Really, Hamad, I can't. But what I will accept is the chance to finish the job I came to Marrakech to do, to help preserve Dame Edith's legacy. I think an exhibition on her life and travels would be much better than a book.'

'You don't want to finish it?'

She thought of Mustapha, the secrets he held. 'It's not that I don't want to,' she said carefully. 'But some of what Edith told me . . . it wasn't always easy to tell what had really happened and what was perhaps a slightly fictionalised version. I think it would be a legal nightmare to actually publish. But an exhibition? All of Edith's artefacts, her wonderful clothes – maybe we could take over the whole of the second house – perhaps a café, a library too.'

'Yes.' He banged the table happily. 'This is what they should become – not some ludicrous wine bar. And you'll stay on in Dar Simone. *Yes.*' He held up his hand. 'This is work. Edith's legacy. I will provide you with a house and a salary. Please. Just accept.'

She laughed. Somehow Hamad always got what he wanted. 'OK. More than OK. Amazing. Thank you, thank you so much. And you'll come? To see the progress? You'll keep in touch?'

'Of course. But I can't come there,' he said quietly. 'Not to that city.'

'Not even for Edith's funeral?'

'Karim will represent me,' he said slowly. 'Your ways in these things are not mine. In truth, it would mean little to me. And I want to remember her as she was, a life force, an extraordinary woman. But if you do what you say, if you create a celebration of her life at the Farzi houses, I will come. I'll come for that.'

Something tightened in Freya's throat. The woman he adored as his grandmother had lied to him her whole life, set in motion the events that had caused such terrible pain. Even after all their conversations, she had come to realise that she had no idea who Edith really was. To Hamad she was a doting grandmother, to Mustapha a lover, a great and brilliant mind. To Racine she was vengeance. She pictured her, sitting on the terrace at Bar Menzeh, talking of truth and how it left no room for manoeuvre. Freya suspected Edith had spent the greater part of her life manoeuvring.

'Mrs Hepworth?' She looked up to see Karim. 'Are you ready to leave for the airport?'

She looked at Hamad. 'I think so.'

He smiled. 'I wish you didn't have to go. And I'm so sorry for everything. For your marriage. In some way I feel responsible. If it wasn't for Racine . . .'

'If it wasn't Racine, it would have been someone else,' she said, moving towards him. 'But I don't want the last thing we say to each other to be about her. I want us to survive this, Hamad. Our friendship. Think of Edith and Mustapha. They were in each other's lives for over fifty years. Wouldn't it be lovely if that was one of her legacies to you – a friendship that enduring?'

He bent to kiss her. 'She'd like that. Edith did always love to be right.'

EPILOGUE

One week later

'You look lovely.' Paul came to stand beside her. She looked at their reflection in the mirror. He'd lost weight, but the haggard expression had started to fade. 'Well, perhaps "lovely" is the wrong word. Elegant. Edith would approve, I think.'

Freya glanced over the wide black trousers and sleeveless top, brightened by a fuchsia-pink sequinned scarf. 'Had to throw in something a bit OTT,' she said, remembering Edith's extraordinary outfits. 'She never really did understated, did she? Mustapha's asked everyone to wear something bright in her memory. Hopefully the church will be a riot of colour.'

'How is he?'

'Broken.' She thought of their lunch yesterday: omelette and Chablis at the Grand Café de la Poste. She understood, without it being articulated, that she would be there every Thursday. 'I've never seen anyone so bereft.'

'Perhaps the funeral will help. Are you sure you don't want me to come?'

'That's kind, but it's fine. Anyway, don't you have to be at the airport by two?'

He looked away. Freya felt a pulse of guilt. 'Yes. Yes, I do. Well, I'd better finish packing.'

He turned and moved out into the corridor; she followed him into the spare room. A half-filled suitcase lay open on the bed.

'I'm sorry. I know this is hard. But we agreed.'

He turned to look at her; the sorrow in his face made her catch her breath. 'Yes. I know, after what I did, that you've got every right to throw me out.'

'I'm not throwing you out. That's not fair. You *want* to go home. I don't. We want different things, Paul, surely you must be able to see that?'

'I want you.'

'It's too late. Please let's not have this conversation again.'

'What happened with Racine – I never stopped loving you.'

'This isn't really about Racine,' she said slowly. 'If it wasn't her, it would have been someone else. We just . . . lost it. Somewhere. In amongst work and the miscarriage and Ali being ill. We didn't take enough care. I'm as guilty of that as you are. Racine's just a symptom.'

'I'll start talking to estate agents as soon as I've sorted myself out.'

'I've said there's no rush. I'll come back in a few weeks and we can talk again – work out how we're going to do this. But be gentle with yourself. I think you're going to need some time to get over what's happened.'

'Maybe you're right.' He slumped onto the bed, put his head in his hands.

She could feel herself weakening. The guilt was going to weigh heavy, not just for Racine, for bringing about the end of their marriage, but for the memory of a rain-soaked night, over a decade ago. She could lift that a little, make both their lives easier by giving in to what he wanted. He'd tried to persuade her to consider it a trial separation – time apart, with her in Marrakech and him in London. She couldn't make him understand she was different now; that she had grown apart, not just from him, but from the woman he had married.

'Frey . . .'

'I have to go.'

'Of course. Well . . .'

She hadn't expected it to hurt this much. How could she walk away from the man who had been at her side since she was a grief-stricken teenager? Where would it all go – the memories, the time they had shared, the lives they had built? It wasn't supposed to be this way, they were supposed to go on, to grow old, to weave their stories together as the decades rolled past.

'Have a good flight.' Before she could move, he had wrapped his arms around her body. For a moment she let herself be swallowed up; the familiar scent, the curve of his chest, the sense of being home, being safe. She began to cry.

'I love you, Freya.'

The words hung in the air as she drew back. He was crying, too, his face pink and wet. 'I'll see you in London.' She couldn't say goodbye. It was the most extraordinarily painful moment of her life.

Freya wept all the way through the funeral. Each time she raised a tissue to her eyes, she would remember Paul sitting on the bed, wonder what he was doing; the last clothes folded into a suitcase, his coffee mug on the side in the kitchen, every last vestige of him slowly stripped from Dar Simone. Tim's hand around hers felt like an intrusion, but she didn't have the strength to move away. Instead she sat, motionless, while he read an extract from one of Edith's books and Mustapha gave the eulogy in a cracked, stumbling voice. The church was full – elderly expats, young Moroccans, three rows of staff from La Mamounia – the pews scattered with blues and yellows and scarlets, like a giant flowerbed, filled with blooms.

'She would have approved, I think,' said Tim as they filed out of the church.

'It was a wonderful service.' Freya was finding comfort in clichés. They allowed her to speak without having to think.

'Isn't that Karim?' He was impossible to miss, the white *thobe* like a beacon in amongst the dark-hued *djellabas*.

'It is. Will you give me a moment?' Freya walked towards him, forcing her face into a smile. 'Karim. How lovely that you came.'

'Mrs Hepworth. A pleasure to see you. A wonderful service, I think. *Sayyid* Hamad will be pleased.'

'How is he?'

'Better, I would say. Not entirely as he was, but business is going well and he was very heartened by your conversation before you left.'

'As was I.' She laid her hand on his sleeve. 'Look after him for me, won't you?'

He nodded. 'You do not have to ask.'

'Freya?' She turned to see Mustapha standing behind her, stooped with grief. Karim smiled and moved away; she slipped her hand through the elderly man's arm and felt him lean slightly towards her.

'How are you? What you said about Edith was so beautiful.'

'The last thing I could do for her. I wanted to do it well.'

'You did. It made me cry, it was so lovely.'

'I do not think you were crying just for her.' He raised his eyebrows. 'Paul's gone?'

She nodded, unable to speak.

'I'm sorry, *habibi*. I know how hard it must be. Endings, of whatever nature, always bring great sorrow.'

'I don't know, Mustapha. If it's the right thing, why is it so incredibly painful?'

He smiled. 'Because a story is over – long before you thought it would be. But there will be another. There always is. Just make sure it's yours this time. Don't rush to be a part of someone else's.' She followed his gaze to where Tim was talking to Jacqueline. 'You're stronger than you realise – you know that? Take some time, Freya. Take some time.'

She looked at him for a moment and then slipped her arm from his. 'Do you mind if I come along to Mamounia a bit later? There's somewhere I need to go. Just for a few minutes.'

'Of course. Do whatever you need to do.'

She kissed him, and moved through the crowd towards the pavement, dodging the traffic hurtling along Boulevard Mohammed V. The medina was quiet; shops locked up, stalls padlocked, the vendors and street traders at Friday prayers or home with their families. Even the metalwork souk was silent. She stopped at the top of the alley that led to the Farzi houses and waited for the memories to fade. They weren't Racine's houses any more.

She pulled the key from her bag and slipped it into the lock. She'd visited once since she got back from Doha; a long meeting with Laila, explaining the changes that were to take place, the gallery space for Edith, the fact that she was caretaking the houses for Hamad for a while. What had begun as an embarrassing explanation had ended as an impromptu planning meeting, with ideas flowing between them.

Today, the houses were empty. She picked her way across the rubble and pulled a chair up to the *sahridj* in the middle of the first courtyard. Above her, the sky was a flawless blue; two chiffchaffs called to each other from the branches of the citrus trees. She tilted her head back and closed her eyes; something about the houses soothed her, helped her to feel calm.

'*Salaam alaikum*, Mrs Freya.'

She jumped; opened her eyes to see Yusuf standing in front of her. There had been no sound of footsteps, no crunch of rubble beneath his shoes. 'Yusuf. *Alaikum salaam.*'

His face creased into a smile. 'You are well?'

She was stunned to hear the English fall from his lips. 'Yes, Yusuf, *shukran*. I am well. And you?'

He nodded briefly.

'No work today? No sweeping?' She pointed towards the broom, leaning against the far wall of the courtyard.

'Sweeping finished.' He lowered himself into the chair opposite, then lifted his hand towards his ear, slowly rotating his fingers. 'Listen. What do you hear?'

She paused for a moment. Every other time she had visited, there had been the noise of the workmen talking, drills whirring, tinny Arabic pop pouring out of the radio. And underneath it all, the slow rhythmic sound of Yusuf, sweeping. Suddenly, even the chiffchaffs had gone quiet. The silence was almost overwhelming.

'Nothing. Nothing at all.'

'Then all is well.' He glanced around slowly and tipped back the hood of his *djellaba*. 'The jinns are satisfied. The houses are at peace.'

ACKNOWLEDGEMENTS

I'd been warned about the 'difficult second novel' but – like most writers, I suspect – I blithely assumed it wouldn't happen to me. How little I knew; writing *What Lies Within* has been more challenging than I could ever have imagined, and without my endlessly supportive friends and family, I'm not sure I would have stayed the course. Huge thanks to my wonderful UKC girls, who were always on hand with vats of wine, boxes of tissues and brisk talking-to's – whether in the UK or Norway – and particularly to Sara, who has read more versions of this book than anyone else (including me).

Huge thanks too, to Midge, for coming up with the title and breaking his usual I-don't-read-books rule. To Caroline, for early reads and absorbing a considerable amount of my frustrations and anxieties, to Penny and Debs for their unstinting support and wise words, and to my fabulous nephews and nieces, for being such a source of joy in my life. To Roy and Alan for never taking me seriously, and Sue and Fleur for never taking *them* seriously, and to my co-Brymore writers, Jon and Marky B, who deserve all this just as much as I do. Thanks also to my ever-patient, always-supportive agent, Laura Longrigg at MBA, and to the team at Quercus.

But the biggest thanks of all belong to Mark, who climbed unwittingly onto the rollercoaster, some years ago (with his mad, adorable cat), and never lets go of my hand. Thank you, thank you, thank you, my love. The next one will be easier, I promise.